Mike Edwards is a senior news reporter with Scottish Television and has covered every major story to have broken in Scotland for more than 20 years. He has worked on the Piper Alpha, Lockerbie and Dunblane tragedies, as well as the creation of the Scottish Parliament and the G8 summit. He also followed Scottish soldiers into action, reporting from the battlefields of Bosnia and Kosovo. A Major in the Territorial Army, he was called up for the war in Iraq, and also served in Afghanistan, where "Friendly Fire" is set.

FRIENDLY FIRE

Mike Edwards

Friendly Fire

With very best wishes,

Mike Edwards

August '06

Pegasus

PEGASUS PAPERBACK

A CIP catalogue record for this title is available from the British Library

ISBN 1 903490 19 7

Pegasus is an imprint of
Pegasus Elliot MacKenzie Publishers Ltd.
www.pegasuspublishers.com

First Published in 2006

Pegasus
Sheraton House Castle Park
Cambridge England

Printed & Bound in Great Britain

Dedication

This book is dedicated to the memory of my father, Able Seaman Donald Edwards. He served aboard the V&W Class Destroyer HMS Wivern on the Atlantic convoys and in the Mediterranean and Pacific theatres of World War Two. When my call to arms came, I went for six months. When his came, he went for six years.

Acknowledgements:

I would like to thank the following people for their invaluable help and support;

All at Pegasus;

My dearest friends Ron and Debbie MacKenna and their sons Calum and Luca;

My colleagues Alex Burton, Robin Gray, John MacKay and Alan Saunby;

The Gallagher family;

My mother, for so many things - among them buying a typewriter the day she heard her 12 year-old son say he wanted to be a writer;

And Theresa, the wind beneath my wings, without whom nothing in my life is possible.

I owe a special debt of thanks to the secret men of the SAS,
in Kabul and elsewhere, for their anonymous help.

This is a work of fiction aimed at anyone who enjoys a good yarn. I have tried to be as accurate as possible in every area, but I have deliberately watered down some of the military procedures so as not to confuse the reader. This is a story based around events which have actually happened. All the characters are my own, except those who have their place in history. Any likeness with any person, living or dead, is purely coincidental. It is not my intention to besmirch the reputation of anyone, especially the finest fighting man on earth - the Scottish soldier.

Mike Edwards
Kabul, Afghanistan

GLOSSARY OF MILITARY TERMS

A-DAY – The start of the air war.

Abrams – The M1A1 Abrams, main battle tank of the US Army.

Adjutant – CO's right hand man or woman with special responsibilities for administration.

AK-47 – Russian assault rifle produced in tens of millions by Andrei Kalashnikov in 1947.

ALS – Army Legal Service. Branch dealing with all legal matters relating to the service.

Apache – US Attack helicopter.

APC – Armoured Personnel carrier.

APOD – Air Port of Disembarkation (airport).

Ariana – Afghan airline.

ASU – Active Service Unit.

AWACS – Airborne Warning and Control System. Boeing 707 fuselage with a radar dish on top.

Badged – To become a soldier in the SAS and literally wear the winged dagger badge.

BAOR – British Army of the Rhine.

Basha – Shelter fashioned from a large, waterproof poncho, attached to trees, vehicles etc, by bungees, tent pegs and paracord

Battalion – Grouping of around 600 soldiers from one cap-badge.

Battlegroup – Modern army formation comprising the assets needed to win the battle – ie infantry, armour, engineers.

BATUS – British Army Training Unit Suffield. Training area in Canada used for major armoured exercises.

Beasting – Nickname for an unpleasant physical regime imposed on soldiers by instructors and seniors, often as a punishment.

Bergen – Standard British Army rucksack.

Berm – Arab word for sand barrier.

Bluey – Airmail letter, coloured blue.

BMP – Soviet APC (wheeled)

Bouncing Betty – Bounding munition, jump mine. Leaps to varying heights before detonating.

Bradley – US equivalent of Warrior.

Brigade – Large formation usually comprising three battalions/battlegroups.

BTR – Soviet APC (tracked)

BV – Boiling Vessel. Electric cooker inside a Warrior used for cooking food, heating water.

CASEVAC – Casualty evacuation

Cav - Cavalry

Cavalry – Once mounted troops, who now operate in tanks.

Chaingun – Electrically powered machine gun, usually in vehicles or aircraft.

Challenger – Main battle tank of the British Army.

Chinook – Large twin rotor heavy-lift helicopter.

Chobham – Ceramic armour of a secret design for tanks and APCs.

Coaxial – Gun rotating around central axis.

Colours – Regimental flags. Of great historical importance to a unit.

Colour Sergeant – Rank immediately above Sergeant in an infantry battalion. Responsible for supply and replen.

Combats – Camo patterned clothing.

Convoy Cock – Masturbatory practice carried out by soldiers while driving to relieve the boredom on long convoy moves.

CQMS – Company Quartermaster Sergeant – supply sergeant.

CR – Confidential Report.

Crown – Rank badge of a Major.

Cuidich N Righ – Gaelic motto of Queen's Own Highlanders meaning "Protect the King."

Daysack – Small rucksack.

Division – Large formation usually comprising three Brigades.

DLB – Nickname for UK commander in Gulf War One, General Sir Peter de la Billiere.

Donkey wallopers – Slang term for the cavalry.

Double – March very quickly.

Drone – Pilotless aircraft used for reconnaissance.

Dropshorts – Derogatory nickname for the artillery, focussing on their alleged lack of accuracy.

DS – Directing Staff.

ENDEX – Literally 'end of exercise' but used as a term for anything finishing.

ETA – Estimated time of arrival.

Families' Officer – Officer who stays behind to look after welfare when unit deploys.

FCO – Foreign and Commonwealth Office.

Feldgrau – Field grey, colour of German uniforms.

Ferry – Housing estate in Inverness.

Field dressing – Gauze bandage issued to soldiers.

Figure 11 targets – Man-sized rifle range targets with facial features of Russian solider.

Fireteam – Four man infantry half section.

Four Tonner – Ubiquitous British Army lorry.

G-DAY – The day the ground campaign starts.

Gazelle – Small, fast manoeuvrable British reconnaissance and casevac helicopter.

GCHQ – General Communications Headquarters. Cheltenham-based UK listening station.

Gone firm – When soldiers occupy an area with intent to hold it, they "go firm."

Gong – Medal.

GPS – Global Positioning System. Satellite navigation aid the size of a mobile telephone. Accurate to a few feet.

Green Slime – Intelligence Corps, so-called because of the Cypress Green colour of their berets.

Gun camera – Camera in belly of aircraft which runs when weapons fire.

Gunners – Artillery soldiers.

H Hour – Time on G-Day/A-Day when operations begin.

Headshed – Any command element.

Hesco Bastion – Heavy wire and canvas, rubble-filled, cylindrical emplacements used for building defences. Designed by former UK miner who started the company in the 1980s with his redundancy payment. It is now worth millions.

Hexamine – Solid alcohol fuel.

H Hour – Time on G-Day/A-Day when operations begin.

HK – Heckler and Koch. German arms manufacturer.

Hooch – Unofficial office or hangout.

Hood – Nickname for an SAS soldier.

HUMVEE – High Mobility, Multi Purpose, Wheeled Vehicle. Rugged US equivalent of a Land Rover.

Hull down – Buried up to the turret.

HUMINT – Human Intelligence. The information provided by people on the ground, usually civilian.

IED – Improvised Explosive Device, Home made bomb.

Infil – Infiltrate.

Int – Intelligence.

IRA – Irish Republican Army.

ISO – International Standards Organisation. Generic term for large containers hauled by lorries, carried by ships etc.

Jap-slapping – Slang term for judo or karate.

Jock-bopping – Slang term for Highland dancing.

Jocks – Slang term for Scottish soldiers.

Kepi – Hat worn by French police and service personnel.

Kevlar – Bulletproof material.

Laagered up – Laager, German for camp. Camped up.

Lines – Accommodation in army barracks or camp.

LO – Liaison officer.

LP – Long playing record, predecessor of CD.

Madrasses – Fundamentalist Islamic schools, usually in Pakistan.

Manoeuvrist doctrine – Modern military tactical thinking espousing movement and power as opposed to attritional warfare.

MILAN – Anti-tank missile.

Miniflares – Small coloured flares fired from pen-sized launcher.

MLRS – Multiple Launch Rocket System. Modern, mobile artillery piece firing rockets.

MPs – Military Police.

MSR – Main Supply Route, main road.

MT – Motor Transport.

MUFTI – Hindi term for disguise.

NAAFI – Navy, Army, Air Force Institute. Shop, café etc.

NBC – Nuclear Biological and Chemical.

NCO – Non-commissioned officer.

Ned – Glasgow term for young delinquent.

Nussgipfel – German nut-filled croissant.

NVGs – Night Vision Goggles.

OC – Officer Commanding

O Group – Orders Group. Meeting where orders are issued.

OHMS – On Her Majesty's Service. Stamp on envelopes bearing military correspondence.

OP – Observation Post. Concealed hides used to monitor enemy activity.

Orbat – Order of Battle. List of units involved in an operation or exercise.

OS – Ordnance Survey. UK Map manufacturers.

Paracord – Thin yet very strong nylon cord, used for parachute rigging and much else.

Patriot – American radar guided anti-missile missile.

PCBC – Platoon Commanders' Battle Course.

Pinked – When an officer is selected for promotion from Major to Lieutenant Colonel, he is placed on the pink list, so-called because it is printed on pink paper.

PMC – President of the Mess Committee.

Point element – The lead soldiers in an advancing unit.

Poncho – Article of clothing made from green waterproof nylon also used to build shelters.

Pressel – Transmit switch on a radio.

PSP – Prefabricated Steel Planking, used for building roads, runways etc, on sand.

QOH – Queen's Own Highlanders. Scottish regiment, amalgamated in 1994 with the Gordons to form the Highlanders.

QM – Quartermaster. Usually a major who is commissioned after around 22 years in the ranks. Specialist who deals with millions of pounds worth of clothing and equipment.

Quarter – Soldiers' homes.

RAMC – Royal Army Medical Corps.

Rarden – 30mm cannon on a Warrior.

Recce – Reconnaissance. Specially trained soldiers who go ahead of a formation to monitor enemy movements.

Redcaps – Headgear-based slang term for RMP.

REME – Royal Electrical and Mechanical Engineers. Specialists who repair and maintain equipment ranging from Land rovers to helicopters.

Reorg – Reorganisation.

Replen – Replenishment.

RMP – Royal Military Police.

Roulement – The rotation of units through a posting, usually every six months.

Royal Engineers – Specialist soldiers who build bridges, clear obstacles etc.

RPG 7 – Former Eastern Bloc Rocket Propelled Grenade.

RRF – Royal Regiment of Fusiliers.

RSO – Regimental Signals Officer. Commands the signals and communications of a unit.

RSM – Regimental Sergeant Major. The senior soldier in the regiment. The CO's right hand man when dealing with the men.

RTU – Return to Unit.

Rupert – Soldiers' nickname for officers.

RV – Rendezvous.

Sabre Squadron – SAS equivalent of a rifle company.

Saltire – Scottish flag, the cross of St Andrew.

SAM – Surface to Air Missile.

Sangar – Usually concrete and sandbag defensive emplacement.

Sappers – Nickname for Royal Engineers.

SAS – Special Air Service. Elite UK special forces unit.

Scoff – Slang for food.

SCUD – Medium range Soviet designed ballistic missile with NBC capability, fired at Saudi Arabia and Israel during the Gulf War carrying conventional high explosive warheads.

Sea King – Multi-purpose helicopter.

SEALS – US Navy special forces. (SeAirLand)

Selection – Term for process of joining the SAS.

Septics – Rhyming slang. Septic tanks, yanks. Americans.

SF – Special Forces.

SF Herc – Special variant of the C-130 Hercules fitted out for SF operations.

Shamagh – Arab head scarf.

SIB – Special Investigations Branch of the RMP. Military equivalent of CID.

Sickener – Element of SAS selection designed to test character. Very often make a candidate walk back the way he came for 20 miles or more.

SIGINT – Signals intelligence.

SITREP – Situation report.

Slot – To shoot. To kill.

SOPs – Standard Operating Procedures.

Space blanket – Tinfoil sheet to keep heat in the wearer.

Sports pages – Pornographic letters.

Staff College – Year-long course to train officers in staff and admin duties.

Stag – Sentry duty.

Stag-on - General term for carrying on doing something boring.

Steamies – Glasgow back-green laundries.

Stinger – US heat seeking SAM.

SUSAT – Sight Unit Small Arms Trilux. Telescopic sight on SA-80 rifle.

Syrette – Small syringe for administering Morphine.

T-55, T-62, T-72 etc – Soviet tanks.

TA – Territorial Army, reserve soldiers.

TAB – Tactical Advance to Battle. Walk a long way carrying unfeasible weights.

TAM O SHANTER – Scottish soldiers' headgear.

TOGS – Thermal Optical Gunsight, fitted to Challenger tank.

Toms – Nickname for English soldiers, after Tommy Atkins – generic name for a trooper in Wellington's army.

Trabant – Former Eastern bloc car.

Tracer – Illumination round which allows the firer to see the fall of shot.

UOTC – University Officer Training Corps.

USMC – United States Marine Corps.

Victory Roll – Manoeuvre performed by a pilot after a successful sortie.

Warrior – UK APC. Tracked vehicle with a turret and a crew compartment beneath.

Webbing – Belt and braces supporting pouches containing personal equipment.

WMD – Weapons of mass destruction.

Zastava - Former Eastern bloc car.

Zero Alpha – CO's radio callsign.

432 – Squat, tracked, UK APC. In service for nearly 50 years.

When you're wounded and left on Afghanistan's plains
And the women come out to cut up what remains,
Just roll to your rifle and blow out your brains
And go to your God like a soldier.

Rudyard Kipling

PARIS
July 30th 1983.

The girl who never swore, swore aloud.

And in a cemetery too.

For the record, the words were, "you useless bastard."

But even if the ears didn't recognise the language, they knew the tone.

Amid much tutting, and "ooh la-la-ing" from passers-by, she stormed off towards the Metro.

How was he to know you could buy a map? For a cemetery? Who would have thought it?

He didn't find out until it was too late, way too late. By then her bad mood was in full swing and a blazing row was in the post.

But there they were, on sale on a trolley at the gate, resplendent in red, white and blue covers. The uniformed tourist board official selling them must have been away for his lunch when he and Kirsty had walked in earlier. The maps were only five Francs each; peanuts, and well worth the investment to ward off one of her moods.

But after three-and-a-half sweaty, unguided hours looking for the grave of Jim Morrison, that mood was a tremor measuring seven on the Richter Scale and he was at the epicentre. If previous scenes were anything to go by, this one would terminate within the hour in a huge row.

They had left their hotel that morning hand in hand, one of a million courting couples holidaying in the most romantic city in the world. They'd walked along the Rue de Dunkerque towards the Gare du Nord, oblivious to the bustle of the commuters, the constant noise of the traffic or the smell of breakfast coffee. Their senses were full of each other.

Her tiny, manicured hand was wrapped in his dark, strong paw. Then, a few blocks later, she was precisely where he liked her - tucked neatly into his armpit with his tanned arm draped over her shoulder. There she was safe and comfortable and he was marking his territory.

At the start of the day, at least, she had been in good humour. But by four that scorching July afternoon, the tactile affection had dripped away onto the dusty paths of the Père Lechaise cemetery with every bead of sweat.

The postman was about to deliver.

It had all been his idea. He had insisted on going to the cemetery during their romantic week in the city of light, sold her the idea, assured her she would enjoy it. And she had agreed, albeit reluctantly.

Who would ever have thought of going to visit a cemetery while on holiday?

But to be fair she had played the game until they kept getting lost.

Her temper began to fray when he persisted in singing Doors songs for a full hour after she'd asked, who the hell was Jim Morrison anyway? It all went downhill from there. Far from lighting her fire, it was nearly the end.

He'd tried to sweeten the pill by telling her that Oscar Wilde and Edith Piaf were also buried in Père Lechaise and that the cemetery was one of Paris's most popular tourist attractions. She'd appeared to be interested by this and it pleased him, and if he was being honest, fuelled the part of him that liked to show off to her.

But after the hours of wandering, or following crowds on the off chance that they might know the way, they got nowhere. He'd asked for directions in good French and had been given them. But come what may, the shrine to the enigma who was Jim Morrison, remained an enigma to them.

When you're 18 and like Fraser MacLean had devoted every breath, every thought, every second to only one girl, these scenes spelled disaster. A sharp word here, a hard stare there, a silence somewhere else – each was a knife thrust deep into his heart.

He knew that trotting after her like a pet poodle towards the Metro along the Boulevard Menilmontant debased him, but he did it. Each pace she took was another knife in his heart and each pace he took in pursuit was a twist of the blade. And although he did not like to dwell on it, he knew these moods were getting more and more frequent and more and more fierce.

Better do it tonight then, he told himself, *do it tonight and she'll be fine.*

They were back at the Gare du Nord before they spoke again; six stops on the Metro and nearly an hour after she flounced off at the cemetery. And the ice was only broken because she was swept away in the crowds towards the wrong escalator.

"Kirsty. This way darling," was all he said, clutching her tiny wrist and hauling her away from the briefcases and evening papers bound for the Banlieue trains. But he said it in a soft tone, a tone you might use with a child, a tone which said, *'I know you're angry and you're not speaking to me, but don't make this any worse by getting lost'*. It worked to an extent. He didn't let go of her hand until they were back at their hotel. She didn't object, and she didn't let go - but neither did she speak.

The hotel had been another source of tension. He had chosen a small family-run affair near the Gare du Nord. The Magenta was on the apex of one of seven streets which met at a bustling junction.

"It's romantic and full of character" he'd told her.

But she just said it was seedy.

He had to admit the interior fabric and fixtures were old and a bit grimy, but it *did* have plenty of character and at least the bed was clean.

The bed.

Kirsty Buchanan was a virgin and was intent on remaining so until her wedding night. She too was 18 and Fraser had been the only boy with whom she had had any kind of relationship. She loved him, so she said, but she obviously did not love him enough to give him her body. Down the years their relationship had become more and more physical, but no matter what he tried or said, she refused point blank to let him make love to her. Whenever he suggested they take things a stage further, she would curl into a ball and say no.

Fraser blamed her father. He was a widower and she was an only child and naturally they were especially close. Since her mother's death in 1975, she'd become a devout Christian. Fraser had no problem with this, in fact he positively encouraged it. A girl with strong morals would be highly unlikely to stray. But it was the words she used to reject his advances which killed him a thousand times.

"It's for my husband," she would say, as he lay frustrated and panting on the bed beside her. Then she would turn out the light and go to sleep. It was all old man Buchanan's fault, the leading Glasgow lawyer, puritan - and millionaire.

Over the three-and-a-half years since they'd been seeing each other, if that's what you could call a few stolen hours after school in the evenings and weekends, he had managed to entice her into bed on many occasions. He had even got all her clothes off, in stages, and they had lain in the dark and touched each other. But that was as far as it ever went.

She was beautiful, totally and utterly beautiful. She'd stolen his heart from the moment they'd met as awkward teenage pupils at the local secondary school. They'd been together since.

He was first to admit his looks were average. He would wonder why a girl so lovely would want to have anything to do with him. She was easily the most beautiful girl in the school and all the boys lusted after her. They were also hugely envious of him.

And while he was flattered by this, he was terrified of losing her and was insanely jealous of any boy who looked at Kirsty, far less spoke to her. He hated it when other boys made crude comments about her, but in truth he was too timid to do anything about it. He tortured himself with the image of her with an older boy, someone more worldly, more sophisticated than him.

While he was still a boy at 18, she was all woman. Her hair was strawberry blonde and no matter what style the cut, it framed an elfin-faced beauty. She had clear pale green eyes, a skijump nose, which appeared both cute and sexy at the same time, and a small mouth with lips permanently poised, it seemed, to smile or kiss.

Her breasts were full, her waist slim and her legs perfect. She was sweet and good-natured and loved children and animals. She was everyone's friend and she didn't have a malicious bone in her body. She was perfect. He loved her. He adored her. He would do anything for her. He wanted no other and he told her so repeatedly.

And to be fair to her she had returned this unfettered affection. They would spend hours on end planning their future. They would be married in the Parish Church at the cross on Ayr Road in Glasgow, and honeymoon on the Orient Express. Her father would give her away and his friend William would be the best man. He would be a French teacher and she would be a GP. They would live in Glasgow and have two children - a boy and a girl named Andrew and Ellie. They would live happily ever after.

But lately these conversations were fewer and farther between.

The Paris trip had been his idea. Where better than the city of light, the most romantic place on earth, to do what he had to do. And he would do it tonight. It was obvious that her moods, her reluctance to talk about their plans any more and her flat refusal to have sex, were down to him and his tardiness in producing the ring.

He'd read somewhere and had heard older boys talking about it – it was all down to the ring. It was what all girls wanted. When a boy produced a ring, a girl would do anything. Once he'd done that and she'd said yes, then she'd change her mind and agree to his promptings and let him make love to her on the bed in the grimy hotel, which was full of character.

Until then the extent of their sex life had been a series of mutual fumblings. It was enjoyable, but not as enjoyable as he knew full sex would be. But that wasn't on the menu. So he had to satisfy himself with the touching.

But lately, instead of lying back afterwards, and holding each other as they had once done, she would immediately shower and dress. He hated that, it was clinical, as if what they'd done was dirty, shameful.

Shortly before they left Scotland, she'd rationed even further those few moments of physical pleasure they'd enjoyed. Then suddenly she said it must stop.

"God doesn't like it," she'd said.

But the veil had slipped on their first night in Paris and they shared the most erotic moment of their young lives. The sightseeing had been long and hot that day and the journey back to the hotel difficult. But there had been no mood and no scene and they flopped onto the bed like ragdolls. He had instinctively put his arm over her shoulder and she had replied by burying herself into his armpit. It was the first time there had been a response like that for ages.

Seconds later they were all arms and legs and clothes and deep, wet kisses. He just lay back and watched her climb naked on top of him and rub herself on his tumescence. Her face was contorted, her cheeks flushed red and the girl who never swore, moaned the foulest obscenities he'd ever heard.

To his astonishment she then flipped herself around and squatted over his face in what he'd heard and read about as the 69 position. His already raging erection became almost unbearable when she took him in her mouth - as he'd been begging her to do for ages.

Then he could take it no longer. The years of dreaming about this moment, the pent up emotions and hormones and desires and fantasies were made one by her tongue and he exploded into her mouth. He had often wondered how she would react to this moment if and when they ever got round to doing it. She had always refused because she said it was a sin against God's teachings, and anyway girlfriends had told her that a man's taste was foul. But when it happened, she swallowed every drop.

Afterwards he lay back and dozed, bathed in sweat. He had never felt better than he did that afternoon, completely, utterly and hopelessly in love. He wanted her to lie beside him so they could share the peace, the gradually fading warmth of the Paris summer afternoon, the sunset, the acceptance that they would soon be together forever. It wouldn't be long now; first the ring and then the body.

But Kirsty Buchanan was ashamed of what she'd done and had showered long and hot afterwards. Then she got dressed and sat at the tiny desk in the room with her back to him and wrote her postcards in stony silence.

The incident went unmentioned afterwards. Perhaps, he thought, she was too embarrassed to admit that she'd enjoyed it, that it was the way ahead and full sex wasn't far off.

In truth Kirsty was ashamed with herself for giving in, for letting her morals slip. Her shame was evident the next evening when they returned to the hotel at around the same time after another hard day's sightseeing. He had gone to her and made a crude grasp at her, groping her breast through the cotton of her t-shirt.

"Don't think we're going to make a habit of that," she snapped, brushing away his hand.

And it was his turn to feel the shame.

So it would be tonight. Once the anger and the mood from the cemetery had subsided and she'd calmed down, he would pop the question. A lovely meal in a romantic restaurant then a walk along the Seine. It would be perfect. She couldn't say no.

He had cashed in every Premium Bond and Post Office Savings Certificate he owned, he'd scrimped and saved and worked odd jobs here and there on top of his regular schoolboy job in the local supermarket to raise cash for the holiday – and the ring. The bundle of ten £50 notes was secreted in the cloth lining at the bottom of his suitcase. They would spend the rest of the holiday wandering around jewellery shops choosing the ring.

And the French culture? The museums? The galleries? All the treats he'd promised he'd show her in Paris? Well they could all go to hell in a handcart.

In his soapbag, hidden in a box which once held a tube of toothpaste, were the six condoms he'd bought the week before. He knew she didn't take the contraceptive pill, although he wished she did. Not only would it make spontaneous sex a possibility, he'd read somewhere that it calmed down a woman's hormones and ended the moods and the PMT. Anyway, if he had protection at hand in the heat of a moment then it might be the one thing which persuaded her it was right. It was all part of the plan.

And if things went to that plan, they would be back here an hour or so after he proposed, making love on the clean bed in the grimy hotel, which was full of character.

"What are you going to wear tonight?" she asked, after an hour of silence. She was breaking the ice here. He knew this tactic – he had seen it so many times before. He could be difficult with her, cold, and condescending, or he could play along as if nothing had happened.

"What would you like me to wear?" he said, putting down his French novel. He would play along. Of course he would. He would do anything to please her. He hated the moods, the silences. He just wanted them to be a couple, boyfriend and girlfriend, fiancé and fiancée, man and wife. Lovers.

"I like that blue top, the one Tess and Graham gave you for your birthday. And your chinos. Are they clean? Let me see." She busied herself with his outfit in the drawers and wardrobe while he lay back on the bed.

She looked out the shirt and trousers, hung them on the chair then sat down beside him on the bed. She laid a hand on his chest, her fingers toying with the thick fuzz of black hair that covered his upper body. After a moment or two of silence, she spoke again.

"Fraz, I'm sorry about earlier. I really am."

Sometimes she called him 'Fraz'. She used to say that the electricity between them frazzled her. Used to.

He could see tears welling in her eyes. He wanted to hear the words of apology more than any others, but now she was on the verge of crying and instead of being the injured party he found himself desperately trying to console her.

"It's ok Princess," Fraser heard himself say slowly and repetitively as they hugged. She was quiet now, though he felt the wetness of her tears on the nape of his neck. But when the embrace ended, the tears continued.

"I don't know what's the matter with me. I've been a complete bitch to you all week," she sobbed. "All you've wanted to do is please me and this is how I've repaid you. I hate myself."

The sight of Kirsty crying, the dishevelled hair, the running mascara, destroyed him. He remembered her tears on the day they met, how she'd been hurt and how he'd gone to her rescue. The thought of her in pain was a notion which still ate him up. He could take her moods, he could take her rationing her sexual favours, but he couldn't take her in pain.

"It's ok. It's ok. I love you, whatever."

It was the voice he used at times like this, a resigned voice, a soft voice – a doormat's voice. "I just want us to have fun. I want us to be together, forever."

This was her cue to say, *"and I want us to be together forever too"*, but lately she'd been missing her cues and there was no prompt in the wings to help her with her lines.

"It's my hormones. They've been haywire over the past few days. It was due this week but…" her voice trailed away. She often blamed the biology, he was used to that excuse. *Well it better not come tonight*, he thought grimly. *I have plans for that neck of the woods*.

It was enough. They had made up. The air was cleared and the holiday was back on. And it was just as well because that night would be the biggest of their lives to date – the proposal, the acceptance and the act.

He was certain she was keeping her body for that promise, the promise which came with the ring. He'd heard of lots of girls who'd held out until they got the ring. Yes, she would say it was a sin before God, but surely it was less of a sin if they were to be married a year hence?

To please her, he did wear the outfit she suggested. But before putting it on he had a long shower and a slow shave. He wanted to be at his best this night.

They left the hotel as they had done that morning, hand in hand, drinking in the sights and sounds of the Paris evening. The Metro was quiet, and the journey to the Champs Élysées brief. They walked, arm in arm this time, down Paris's most famous street until they came to the Coq d'Or a small restaurant which, because it was still early, wasn't busy and had several vacant tables on the pavement.

Fraser thanked the waiter as he sat down. *Good*, he thought, surveying the scene, *and not far from the Seine where he would take her later, go down on one knee and propose. Pont Neuf? Somewhere on the Ile de la Cite? We'll see.*

They started with mussels, steamed in white wine and Rosemary, then she had Chicken Chasseur and he had Rack of Lamb. But he immediately regretted it when he tasted the garlic. He loved garlic but Kirsty didn't like it on his breath. It might throw a spanner in the works of his plan. He wished he'd ordered the steak instead.

The mood was good and the laughter flowed. The earlier exchange, the apology, the tears, had cleared the air. Fraser had been torn to see her cry at the time, but now in a way, he was glad it had happened. They held hands across the table and spoke of the things farthest from their minds. It was like old times again.

"Pardon me for interrupting," the voice came from nowhere, the accent was American. "But are you Scottish or Irish?"

Fraser was so wrapped up in Kirsty Buchanan and his plan to propose to her and make love to her, that he thought they were the only people in the restaurant. He turned to face the voice.

"I'm sorry?" he said.

"Your accent," said the American, "is it Scottish or Irish? I'm afraid I can't tell the difference."

"We're Scottish," said Fraser. "We're both from Glasgow. Do you know it?"

The man at the next table was young, about their own age - possibly a shade older. His hair was blond, closely-cropped at the sides but slightly longer on top. He was good looking too in a movie star kind of way. He was tanned with gleaming white teeth, a dimple in his chin and his eyes were a bright piercing blue."

"Well, no I don't. But I'd sure like to. It's near England right? I know they're not the same country."

"You have a nice accent too," said Kirsty. "Where are you from?"

"Los Angeles. Do *you* know it?"

"No I'm afraid I don't," she said, then after a second's pause, "but I'd like to."

Fraser was surprised. His girl had never expressed a desire to go anywhere other than Paris. And nobody knew his girl better than he did. Anyway, forget LA, tonight *was* Paris and in a few moments they would have dessert, then they'd go for their walk.

"It must be fabulous, the city of the angels. Hollywood, Beverly Hills," said Kirsty again, a dreamy look on her face.

"Forget Hollywood," said the American bluntly, "it's a shit hole. But the Hills are nice. My folks live in Beverly Glen. What do you guys do?"

"Oh we've just left school. Fraser wants to be a French teacher. He's taken me here to show off his French." There was a hint of a sneer in her voice. That hurt. His French was good it was true, but that was down to sheer hard work. And anyway Mr

Bridges his French teacher had told him he had an ear for languages. He'd taken Kirsty to Paris to please her.

"We're both going to university in October," said Kirsty coming out of her shell. "What do you do…"

"I'm sorry, forgive me." The American thrust out his hand. "Eric Decker, Lieutenant, United States Marine Corps."

Fraser couldn't believe it, he even said it the way they did in the films *"lootenant"*. He was a budding linguist and he loathed the way Americans treated the English language. This guy seemed nice enough but he was wasting valuable time. The plan was still on, but the clock was ticking. The waiter came past and Fraser ordered dessert - crème caramel for him and sorbet for her. *Of course, her figure.*

But it was another 15 minutes before the order went to the kitchen for the chefs to prepare. In that time the conversation was becoming more and more monopolised by the American.

"Gosh, look at your muscles. You must work out an awful lot." Said Kirsty, enthusiastically.

"Yes I do," replied the American, looking down at his chest. "I first got fit on Parris Island and have been getting fitter ever since."

"Parris Island? Where is that? Is it here? In the city?"

"No, Miss, not Paris, France," he laughed. "But it's a sweet notion. Parris Island, South Carolina, the home of the Corps. Semper Fei, do or die."

The American launched into his speech. It was well-practised - the rigours of basic training, the brotherhood of the Marines and the history. Fraser came from a military family - his father had been in the Army and his brother was going to join up too - but the whole thing bored him rigid. However Kirsty was enthralled and hung on the American's every word. Fraser checked his watch repeatedly. It was 10.30 pm. Time to go.

"Garcon, l'addition, s'il vous plait," he said when the waiter was next in earshot.

"He *can* talk the talk," said Decker. Then he leant over to Kirsty and winked. "But can he walk the walk?"

"Not really," she said and giggled mischievously.

Another knife thrust into Fraser's chest and he turned to survey the American. He was tanned, broad and the sleeves of his t-shirt stretched over biceps which were obviously the result of a great deal of exercise.

"How long have you been together?"

Kirsty told him and he feigned surprise. "And this is your first trip abroad together? That's nice. That's romantic. In this city of all places."

"Do you have a girlfriend Eric? You must do. I'll bet you look really cool in your uniform." Kirsty was gushing again.

"It is a bit of a babe magnet, I'll admit."

Fraser was incensed now, but he tried not to show it. His girl was flirting with a total stranger. He tried to talk about things exclusive to them, but failed. Kirsty was more interested in the American than the visit they were planning the next day to the Louvre.

"Hey, let me buy you guys a drink. I know a place, near the embassy. It's nice. It's really French. Did I tell you I'm guarding the embassy here?"

"Well that's really kind of you, but…" Fraser checked his watch. It was nearly 11 now and it was time to go.

"Oh don't be so silly Fraz," said Kirsty. "That would be lovely. We haven't spoken to another soul since we came to Paris. We even spent today in a cemetery." The sneer was back.

Fraser stood up and lifted the bill from the table. The meal would be on him tonight. He could hardly ask his girlfriend to go Dutch on the night he proposed to her.

"Back in a tic," he said and disappeared inside.

He paid the bill and gave the waiter a healthy tip to thank him for his attention. Fraser considered the French to be great romantics, so he told the waiter of his plan to propose. The waiter wished him luck. Then he went to the toilet because it would be the last chance for a while. The walk would be long – to the end of the Champs Élysées, across the Place de la Concorde then down to the Seine and along the Quai Des Tuileries. The excitement was growing. Tonight was the night.

As he stood at the urinal he thought about the American. *God love them.* He had met few Americans but he knew they were obsessed with history and he guessed it was because they had so little of their own. At least this guy hadn't done what the others had and told him that they were, in fact, also Scottish and distantly related to Flora MacDonald.

And this pub near the embassy was really French was it? What? In Paris? A pub that was really French in Paris? Fuck me, thought Fraser, *and it's pronounced left-enant you cretin.* He smiled as he washed his hands.

But the smile disappeared when he went outside again to find Kirsty and the American had gone.

2

The panic didn't rise in him for 20 minutes. He trotted up the road towards the Charles de Gaulle Metro station, but when he couldn't find them he ran back to the Coq d'Or. Then he doubled back the other way for a few hundred yards without success. He crossed the busy Champs Élysées and ran up and down the other side of the wide avenue looking for them there. By the time he returned to the restaurant he was sweating and gasping for breath. Fear and anger were bubbling under the surface.

Their table was already occupied by another young couple. Fraser found the waiter who had served them and interrupted him as he brought the newcomers their starters.

"Est-ce-que vous avez vue ma copine et L'Americain?" he asked between sobbing breaths. But no, the waiter hadn't seen his girlfriend nor the American. In truth there were so many comings and goings in a place like that that he barely even remembered Fraser. He thought for a moment and then it clicked into place.

Le pourboire, the big tip, the proposal. Ah yes, I remember. She was a beauty. And the American was big and strong. You've got a fight on your hands there mate.

But he said nothing and shook his head and shrugged his shoulders in the silent Gallic sign of indifference.

The embassy! They've gone to that pub near the embassy. But where was the fucking embassy? He didn't know, but a taxi driver would. Fraser stepped out into the thronging traffic of the Champs Élysées and flagged down a blue and white Citroen cab. He leapt into the back and ordered rather than requested the driver to find it and take him there. The traffic was busier now and the journey back along the Champs Élysées to the embassy on the Avenue Gabriel took 20 minutes.

He asked the driver if he knew the pub where the embassy staff hung out, but he didn't. *Were there any popular places round here then?* But the driver knew of none. He took 30 of Fraser's Francs and left him panting outside the embassy's high and firmly locked gates.

Inside the courtyard, up a short gravelled drive and beyond a long red and white barrier, was a small booth. Fraser gesticulated to the portly middle-aged man sitting inside. He wasn't a policeman, thought Fraser, more likely to be a security guard. Whatever he was, he saw Fraser but ignored him.

"Je suis Americain," he screamed from the street. "On a volé mon passeport."

The guard straightened up. He knew that a stolen American passport was bad news and could cause ructions. He swore silently and left the comfortable seat in the booth, donning his hat as did so.

Fraser was thinking on his feet here. His panic was alive and kicking, each kick was landing low and hard into his abdomen.

How could Kirsty do this? Had she run off? With a stranger? No she'd never do something like that. Never. They'd just missed each other in the crowds. The Champs Élysée was very busy at night after all. The American would be looking after her, protecting her until he could get to her.

"Je cherche le café ou les Marines boivent," Fraser said to the security guard, who had at last ambled to the gate. But the guard was more interested in a stolen passport than the café where the Marines drank. He thought they were arrogant shits and they could all fuck off as far as he was concerned.

"Et votre Passeport?" he asked scathingly, ignoring Fraser's pleas about the pub where the Marines drank.

"S'il vous plait Monsieur, mais c'est grave." The Frenchman stopped. There was something about Fraser's plea, the pain in his voice, the stark panic on his face, that made him think again. And the boy was foreign, not American, but his French was perfect.

"Trois cent metres, Rue D'Anjou." he said and gestured with his head into the darkness. Fraser sprinted off, but he was unfit. The pains in his chest and legs were shrieking at him.

The street had three cafes and Fraser scanned the terraces outside then ran inside and checked the booths of each. Nothing. He described Kirsty and the American to the waiters, but none had seen them. Now Fraser was in agony.

He walked the streets around the embassy checking for other restaurants and cafes. He found one but it was closing and the staff couldn't help him. He checked his watch. It was one am. He was drained, exhausted and on the verge of tears. He wanted to go home but he wanted to go home with Kirsty, hear her voice, smell her perfume and feel her touch.

He trotted to Madeleine, the nearest Metro station and caught the last train of the night back towards the Gare du Nord. But when he changed lines at Pigalle there were no more trains because it was so late and he had to run back to the Magenta.

It was after two in the morning and he was panting and sweating when he reached the hotel. It too was closed, but the night porter was sitting behind the desk watching a portable TV. Fraser rang the doorbell impatiently. The man was in no hurry to leave his programme and let him in. By the time he did, Fraser was in a frenzy and burst through the door and into the lobby.

"Ma copine. Elle est ici? Elle est dans notre chambre? Chambre 86?"

The porter nodded his head.

Yes his girlfriend was inside. Who could forget her? The young redhead with the tits? Yes she was in.

Fraser almost collapsed with relief. Kirsty had made it home by herself.

Thank Christ for that. Oh thank you God. Thank you for getting her back safe and sound.

He bounded for the lift.

He wouldn't be angry, he said to himself in the tiny damp claustrophobia of the compartment. He couldn't be angry. The relief far outweighed the anger. He'd given his word to old man Buchanan back in Glasgow, the night before they got on the train to London, that he would look after Kirsty on her first trip abroad with Fraser.

"She's very precious to me," Buchanan had said that night in the front room of his mansion.

"You and me both mate," thought Fraser.

All that panic, all that stress, racing to the embassy, checking all those pubs. And for nothing. You've totally overreacted, you idiot. She's no mug your girl, of course she could get back to the hotel by herself. She could speak French well enough. Your French is better of course, but she had enough to get back. And she knew how the Metro worked. No, you won't be angry.

Fraser smiled to himself as he left the lift and strode towards the door. He had been going to propose to her that night. Had all gone to plan they would have been engaged by this time.

Who would have thought things would have ended up like this – getting separated in a crowd. How silly.

He laughed now at his overreaction. At least she was home safe and sound. Everything was all right.

He had no key. The night porter didn't have one to give him. Kirsty would have taken it upstairs when she got in. Fraser checked his watch and wondered how long she'd been back.

I'll bet she's been really worried about me.

He tapped gently on the door. There was no response so he tapped again, but louder.

A few moments later the door opened and Eric Decker stood there silhouetted in the half light from the bedside lamp, naked as the day he was born.

3

Fraser MacLean had never been in a fight. He'd always managed to avoid the playground scraps at school. He was not a violent person but that night he tried to kill Eric Decker.

He launched himself through the door at the American, in a flurry of fists and feet. He wanted to do the utmost damage, he wanted to hurt, maim, kill. *Yes that's it, kill.*

But Eric Decker was a Marine and knew all about violence. He avoided Fraser's every lunge and kick. He feinted backwards allowing his attacker to come into the bedroom. Decker chose the killing ground. He wanted the space, he wanted the light and he wanted the audience.

Once on his own territory, he ended the scene in an instant. He swung his right arm outwards, and gripped Fraser by the throat with his thumb and forefinger. Then he pushed him back against the wall beside the door.

Fraser couldn't breath. The iron lock of the American's grip crushed his windpipe and he could feel himself becoming faint. There was a roaring in his ears and a flash of blinding coloured lights before his eyes. His head was pinned against the wall and he quickly realised there was nothing beneath his feet as he was being lifted off the floor.

Then he saw her.

Kirsty Buchanan was lying naked on the bed. She had clearly been sleeping but the commotion had wakened her.

Eric Decker extended the four fingers of his left hand and thrust them into Fraser's soft midriff. The wind exploded from his lungs with a whoosh.

He doubled up in agony then collapsed to the floor, unable to breath. His mouth tasted the rancid carpet of the room, but he could not inhale.

He had been winded once before, playing football, when big

boys had made him stand in the defensive wall for a free kick. The striker had seemed to blast the ball not at the goal, but directly at him. He'd coiled himself up in a kind of standing foetal position to protect himself, but the ball had caught him in the stomach. His PT teacher, and his father, had told him he had to toughen up. Only Mr Bridges gave him any sympathy. But this was a thousand times worse than the incident on a Glasgow playing field years before.

He tried to get up, but couldn't. He tried to breath in, but couldn't. He felt a rough hand grab his hair and lift his head.

Then he heard her scream.

"No Eric, leave him. Please leave him."

Fraser sank to the ground again and slowly the wind came back to his lungs in sobs.

"Honey, you were right," said the American walking away from the prostrate figure, "he talks the talk, but he can't walk the walk."

Fraser clutched his adam's apple and watched from the other side of the room as Kirsty and Decker got dressed.

He eyed Decker enviously. He was lean and fit and had a v-shaped torso. His thigh muscles rippled and his calves bulged. Between his legs dangled his manhood. It was thick and veined and nearly reached his knees.

He watched forlornly as she slid on her white cotton pants and hurried into her bra. Then she scrambled around on the floor for her jeans and t-shirt. The agony was complete when he saw that she'd already packed her case.

"Kirsty. Look. We have to talk. You hardly know this guy." Fraser hated himself for the feeble words spoken in the feeble voice, but in pain, shock and grief, it was the best he could muster.

"What did you say?" snapped Decker.

He strode back across the room towards him, but Kirsty interrupted.

"Leave him Eric, leave him."

Dressed now, she walked over to where Fraser lay on the floor.

"God doesn't want us to marry," she said coldly. "It's over. You know it is. It has been for ages. I'm sorry it had to be like this, here of all places. I didn't want to come back here but Eric can't take women into his barracks."

She paused. "It was only a matter of time. It might as well be now."

The voice was cold and devoid of emotion. But there was

something else. What? Fraser didn't understand. It took a moment before he got it. Then it clicked. She spoke as an adult all of a sudden. She'd never spoken like this before, ever. She spoke as a teenage girl before. Now she'd become a woman - more than that, she'd become a woman in control. And when she spoke next it cut him deeper than anything she'd ever said before.

"God has someone beautiful for you," she said.

"It's you," replied Fraser hoarsely.

"No," she said, "it's not me."

Then she and Decker walked from the room in the seedy hotel with lots of character, leaving the door unclosed behind them.

Fraser cried. Huge rasping sobs, aloud. He staggered over to the bed and fell onto it.

He cried a lot more moments later when he saw blood on the sheet.

"And what would your God say about that?" he screamed to the empty room.

4

Sleep was slow coming to Fraser MacLean that night. And when it came it only touched him lightly. He woke in a thousand agonies shortly after nine. The stiff back from sleeping on the floor was nothing compared to the ache around his adam's apple.

But neither came close to the pain from his slowly breaking heart.

He didn't know where to start, how to analyse it all, how to unpack the events and the emotions. Normally at this time of day on his holiday he would wake beside Kirsty and cuddle up to her. He knew that it wouldn't involve sex, but he wanted to be close to her anyway.

But that morning it would be Eric Decker who woke up next to Kirsty Buchanan in a room on a hot Paris morning, and it *would* involve sex. Kirsty was having sex with another man - not him - at that very moment. He was hard and she was soft and he was sliding inside her that very second, feeling her tightness gripping him and milking him before he lost control and his physiology took over and they'd both moan and sweat and lie together before doing it all over again and again and again.

He assumed the American was sexually experienced. He knew Kirsty was not. That morning should have been a new journey of exploration for Fraser and Kirsty. Instead it was a journey she would make with Eric Decker holding her hand and leading the way. She would experience new heights, explore new places and feel new delights – with Decker and not Fraser.

He repeatedly tortured himself with that thought. He imagined it in intimate detail - since the age of 15 he had thought of little else but making love to Kirsty Buchanan.

More than anything else he had wanted to be the first and the only – but more importantly the first. Since they'd met he'd fantasised about the moment when he would slide his manhood through the tiny scrap of flesh, the act which turned her from a girl to a woman, and him from a boy to a man. The moment of dreamt ecstasy was now a living agony.

The agony abated and the tears dried, for the moment. He rose and he showered. It was a beautiful day. He would feel better if he went out. And he was right, but only just and not for long. He didn't want to go anywhere he'd been with Kirsty and neither did he want to go anywhere he'd planned to go with her. In the end he just walked.

He could control the sobbing for around 20 minutes at a time, then he had to let it out. He waited until he was quite alone, or was sure nobody would see or hear him, and let out a howl. This would last just a few seconds and once it was over, he was back to normal again - for the next 20 minutes at least.

It was a hot day and after three hours of walking and sobbing through the anonymous streets, he felt quite drained. He stopped at a café near the Place de la Bastille and tried to think it all through. His nostrils caught a waft of cigarette smoke and found it surprisingly pleasant. He had never smoked in his life because he thought it was a vile habit. But out of curiosity, and a sense of rebellion because Kirsty hated smoking, he bought a packet of Gauloises and lit one. He felt sophisticated and very French with the cigarette between his fingers, but he gagged when he dragged the smoke into his lungs. The world spun and he felt sick, but the nausea soon passed.

The agony in his heart did not though. It hit him with the precision and power of a sniper's bullet every few moments. His mind would wander onto some other random thought and then bang – the awful truth caught him straight through the heart. His Kirsty had left him for another man. His beautiful princess, who could do no wrong and who was a flawless human being, didn't want him, she wanted some American called Eric Decker.

But it was far worse than that. As if the rejection wasn't bad enough there was more, much more. Not only had she left him, not only had she left him for another man, she had lost her virginity to him, apparently without protection.

She lost her virginity, the precious virginity she'd kept from him, to a total stranger. She had unprotected sex with a total stranger and in the bed she and Fraser had shared the night before. Each piece of the jigsaw fell onto the dirty café table before him. Together they meant everything and yet, together they meant nothing.

Why had she done this? Was he really so bad? All he had wanted was to get married to Kirsty and settle down with her and have the babies she'd always said she wanted. What was wrong with that?

And when he stopped thinking about the events and why they had happened, it just hurt. So he started on the Pastis. And after four of the deceptively strong aniseed liqueurs and 10 Gauloises he vomited all over the table and the waiter made him pay the bill and demanded he never come back.

Fraser jumped onto the Metro and headed back to the hotel. But there were splashes of vomit on his shirt and there was much tutting and ooh la la-ing from the fellow rush hour passengers at the appearance and smell of one so young. He was drunk when he left the café, and by the time he got back to the hotel his hangover had started.

He staggered along the corridor reliving how he'd done so the night before and what had happened afterwards. Entering the room was death by a thousand cuts. For a split second he thought he saw Kirsty lying on the bed reading, as if nothing had happened, but it was only an illusion – what his eye wanted to see.

He replayed the incident and the shock of it all came rushing back to him in waves of nausea. He raced for the bathroom and he vomited again. His hangover was now in full swing and he spent the rest of that evening in agony on the bed, weeping and apologising aloud to Kirsty for whatever it was he'd done to upset her and begging her to come back to him. Nothing could console him, but at least the maid had changed the sheets.

In the morning the hangover had subsided, but the broken heart hadn't. He felt the way the bereft do when they wake the day after their loss. The first split second of normality, then the crushing hammer blow of realisation. He lay sobbing for an hour wondering what Kirsty was doing at each moment. But he knew exactly what she was doing and he could bear his self-pity no longer and dragged himself into the shower.

Today was the last full day of his holiday. Tomorrow afternoon he would get the boat train back to Calais, the ferry to Folkestone, another train to London then the last train of the day back to Scotland. But it was a journey he would make alone.

It was another scorching hot day and he wandered the busy, bleached streets of Paris looking for nothing or nobody in particular. He thought about staking out the American embassy again and the cafes nearby in the hope of seeing Kirsty or the American. But the plan didn't last long. His heart was well and truly broken and he knew he couldn't face either of them again.

Fraser punished himself further as he walked. He thought of all the things he had planned to do with Kirsty in Paris after he'd proposed to her, the expensive dinner in Montmartre, the boat trip along the Seine, the meander around Versailles.

The more he punished himself with this vision, the more it hurt, and in the agony and confusion of his state of mind, the more it hurt the more satisfied he felt.

By lunchtime he hated himself for being useless.

That was why she left you, because you are so useless, so arrogant, so feeble, such a nobody. It didn't have to be the muscular, handsome, American Decker, it could have been anyone. Anyone deserved Kirsty more than you. Good luck mate, I don't deserve her. You do. Crack on.

By mid-afternoon Fraser was sobbing every hour or so and all he felt was fatigue. He wanted to go back to the hotel where he could be sure he was quite alone and have a good cry. An hour later he was lying on the bed, howling. This time the sadness was mixed with anger and resignation. He had been a fool but he would never allow it to happen again.

For the third night running he cried himself to sleep.

In the morning he rose after 20 tearful minutes of wakedness, showered and dressed. Then he quickly packed and prepared to leave. He would deposit the red vinyl suitcase in the left luggage office of the Gare du Nord and then kill time by going for another walk. But because he was suspicious of such places, he carefully removed the £500 he'd brought with him for Kirsty's ring from its secret compartment in the base and stuffed the notes into his moneybelt.

Moneybelt.

That's why she dumped you, you prick, because you use things like moneybelts.

He threw it into the bin and put the notes in the front pocket and his passport in the back pocket of his jeans.

As he left the room he turned to look for the last time. She was right. It *was* seedy, but it had loads of character and all the more for what had happened in it that week.

He went downstairs to check out. His throat and stomach were still sore from where Decker had assaulted him. His eyes and nose were raw from crying and he realised, as he asked the man behind the desk for his bill, that since the incident with Kirsty, he hadn't spoken to a living soul, apart from the irate waiter at the café where he'd been sick.

He'd kept aside travellers' cheques to pay for the room. Fraser's face reddened when he realised that the man who took his cheques was the same man who'd been the porter three nights before. He kept his head down as he signed the cheques because he didn't want to acknowledge the Frenchman. He croaked a "merci, au revoir" to the blotter on the reception desk then turned on his heel and left.

Au revoir to you too monsieur, sneered the porter as Fraser disappeared out the door. *You lost her didn't you? I knew you'd lost her when I saw her come home with the Yank that night. You could hear them screwing down here man, they were so loud – her in particular. It was her first time wasn't it? They always scream like that the first time. You poor bastard. It's a shame for you. But your French is good for one so young.*

And then he laughed, shook his head and returned to the sports pages of Le Monde.

Fraser crossed the road to the Gare du Nord but took a different route to the one he'd taken with Kirsty each day. It was longer and he was sweating by the time he'd lugged his case inside the station. After a few moments he checked it in and put the pink ticket from the left luggage office inside his wallet.

He enjoyed a quick sotto voce sob and wailed out an "Oh Kirsty," when he found himself quite alone for a few seconds between two sets of sliding doors near the booking office. He recovered his composure just as quickly when he saw people approaching. It was another scalding hot day when Fraser, unhampered by the weight of his case, emerged outside the station. He had a few hours left in Paris before he faced the agony of the homeward journey and the prospect of telling his parents what had happened.

But as he stepped onto the busy pavement, he suddenly felt very ill. The crushing on his heart, part emotional part physiological, was replaced by a stabbing pain in his stomach. It pulsed waves of agony through him for a few seconds at a time, then subsided to a dull ache which would not go away. He slumped against an advertising hoarding.

Then he realised what was wrong. Since the fateful meal with Kirsty three nights before, he hadn't eaten a thing.

In a café across the road from the station he gorged himself on croissants and coffee. But he was careful to eat the croissants like a Scotsman would. Dipping them in the coffee and eating them soggy like Mr Bridges told him the French did, was the kind of thing that Kirsty must have disliked and caused her to turn away from him.

"I can change. I can really change," he said aloud, "if only you'll come back to me."

He jumped on the Metro and went to La Musee de L'Armee – the Army museum. It would not have been his first choice but he knew Kirsty would not be seen there, even though the American was in the Marines. Fraser's father had been a senior Army officer and Fraser and his elder brother had been brought up on museums like this one. Euan would soon join the Army but Fraser had never considered a military career. He loved the arts and he loved language. No soldier could love either, so he settled on a career in academia, much to his father's chagrin.

His train was at four. He had six hours to kill. The museum took two. As he wandered round the Napoleonic displays, he replayed a fantasy scene over and over in his mind.

Kirsty had come back, tail between her legs. She was sorry, deeply sorry, that she had hurt him. And she was still a virgin. No they hadn't had sex. Of course not. She was a good girl and was keeping that for her husband because that was what God said a good girl should do.

And she hoped he still wanted to be her husband. She wanted that more than anything. And the stains? The blood was hers, yes, but it was the start of her period; a little accident.

Although Fraser would have done anything to change the way the whole thing happened in the first place, now that it *had* happened and he was wounded so deeply, he knew he could never take her back. He knew the blood was hers and that she had been taken by the American, soiled by him and the perfection was ruined. And though he loved her desperately and worshipped her and adored her and cherished her while they were together, he realised that in the unlikely event that she did come back to him, it could never be the same again.

She was dirty now.

He was in the First World War rooms of the museum by this time and the slaughter and privations of the trenches were lost on him. His mind was elsewhere.

Kirsty had gone on and on with this charade for months with only recent, tiny hints that there were problems. Instead of discussing it she'd simply flipped and gone off with a total stranger and had thrown it all away by having sex with him. It got worse.

He'd raced into the bathroom after Kirsty and Decker had left, and checked the toilet and the bin for a condom or wrapper. He searched under the furniture, in the drawers and all over the room but found nothing. The betrayal was complete.

You had unprotected sex with him, in my bed!

This is better, thought Fraser, the pain and sadness of the moment was being replaced with anger. And now he directed that anger away from himself and onto Decker. He already hated the American, with every ounce of energy, emotion and passion he possessed, and now he was starting to hate Kirsty. So perfect, so beautiful - so hateful.

To give it all up like that dismayed him. First and foremost her precious virginity - the body she'd kept from him. Then everything she'd had with him, everything they'd shared together, the years at school, the experiences, the intimacies, the laughs, the secret codes. They had so many experiences in the bank, a deposit on their marriage, and she'd spent the lot, given it all away to a total stranger she'd met only moments earlier and a stranger she'd probably never see again. *What was going through her fucking mind? What was happening?* He should go up there to that embassy and Marine or no, punch his fucking lights out.

Fraser walked from the museum to the Metro station at Les Invalides where he boarded a train back to the Gare du Nord. He was tired now and needed a good cry because he'd thought it through so much that it had finally come to him. The blunt, naked fact that he'd tried to avoid, tried to analyse into oblivion, lay before him like an open manhole.

Kirsty had reached that age. The age when she was no longer a girl but a woman. She knew what she wanted, she didn't *think,* she *knew.*

She wanted to have sex but she had had enough of him and didn't want him to be the one, the first. Eric Decker was a breath of fresh air in her life and he had arrived at exactly the right place at the right time. Her hormones were raging and her libido was screaming. The American was fit and attractive and interesting - everything Fraser MacLean was not.

And she had exercised her right, the right which has baffled men down the ages and which will baffle men forever, the right of a woman to do the unexpected, the bizarre and the hurtful, for no apparent reason whatsoever.

There were four people in the carriage with Fraser, but when they got out at Opéra, he was alone and able to let the tears flow for a few moments before he had to stop because the train was approaching Strasbourg St Denis, where he had to change from Line Eight onto Line Four for the Gare du Nord.

He had three hours to kill before the boat train to Calais and London and he had no idea what to do next. He had had more than enough of Paris and he was desperate to leave, to get on the train home and fall asleep in some anonymous corner.

This city was to have been the start of a new life for him. He smiled wryly, it certainly was the start of a new life but not one he could have foreseen in his wildest nightmares.

He'd thought it through and admitted to himself there was a slim chance that Kirsty would stick to the travel arrangements he had made for them both all those weeks ago and get the same train home. That he could not bear. The prospect of bumping into her and seeing Eric Decker saying farewell with kisses and roses nauseated him.

So with the anger still alive in his breast, he left the station again and walked off. This time he turned left outside and walked along the Rue de Dunkerque towards unexplored areas. It was dull now but still hot and there was surely thunder and lightning in the air. He crossed the road and stopped at a café for a cup of tea and a sob.

Twenty minutes later he headed south with a view to walking to the first Metro station he found before returning to the Gare du Nord. There he would eat a good meal and board the boat train.

"Vous cherchez quelq'un monsieur?"

He didn't notice the girls until he'd walked past half a dozen of them. Had his mind not been full of Kirsty and the American he would surely have spotted them earlier, standing in the doorways of buildings as he passed. Each was young and scantily dressed, most displayed huge cleavages and extravagant make-up. Fraser was halfway down the Rue St Denis before he realised where he was.

How fucking sordid, he thought, and threw a sneer at the girl who spoke. *You're nothing but a fucking slag*, he told her silently. *Giving your body to a total stranger, a man you'll probably never see again. You make me spew.*

Then the thought hit him, first anger, then pain, then another sob. Kirsty was no better than this. She gave herself to a stranger, a man she'll never see again. She's a slut, a slag, a whore. Tears followed the sob because there was a time when he would have wanted to beat the living daylights out of anyone who called her those names. She was better than that wasn't she?

Losing your virginity to a stranger. What an awful, tacky notion. What happened to your religious beliefs? What happened to your God? You just gave it all away didn't you? Gave away the precious gift of your body, the body you kept from me, to the American. That fucking American.

Fraser kept on walking until he reached the end of the Rue St Denis. Then he stopped and turned around. Anyone who saw the youth stride back down the street towards the hookers would remark on the fixed, determined look on his face. But this was the Rue St Denis, where men with needs and desires walked around determinedly all the time and nobody looked at anyone's face.

He was still a virgin, but Kirsty was not. He hadn't thought of it like that until that very moment. She'd had something to lose, the strip of flesh, the maidenhead, the hymen. He didn't have anything physical to lose, just something emotional. And now it struck him that all along, her virginity, had been more important to him than his own.

Fraser continued to torture himself.

Kirsty and the American bastard Decker were having sex all the time, they were exploring new things. Kirsty had never experienced it before and now she was savouring every position, every climax. To the American filth she was just a notch on the headboard. When she went home, either with a disease or a baby or both, he would move onto the next screw. I would have been gentle with her at the all important moment, told her I loved her, held her afterwards. I would have cared for her, cherished her, married her. It's all so wrong.

"Vous cherchez quelqu'un monsieur?" the voice again. She stood in a doorway wearing a black PVC raincoat open to the waist, and very little else. She was black, busty and very beautiful. Fraser looked her up and down for a few seconds. He couldn't do this. It was dirty. It was tawdry. It was wrong.

But the notion would not leave him that this was Kirsty. This girl was Kirsty. He would screw Kirsty, dirty Kirsty, the way the American had screwed her. He would do what the American would do to Kirsty today, screw her then say goodbye and never see her again.

What happens now? What do you do? How do you pay for it? What happens if someone sees me and tells my mother? What do you say? How do you have sex anyway? With Kirsty it would have been different. It would have been a journey of discovery for us both. But Kirsty is no longer a virgin and after this, I won't be either.

"Oui, et maintenant je l'ai trouvé - yes I am looking for someone and now I have found her. How much will this cost?" Fraser heard himself say the words. He found they came naturally, to haggle over a body, a service. Knowing the language helped.

"Tu es tres jeune, mon cher. Quel-age-as-tu?"

She knows I'm young, thought Fraser, *she'll give it to me for nothing. I'm going to lose my virginity to a prostitute, but I won't have to pay. That makes it less tawdry surely.*

He began to feel the thrill of the taboo, the forbidden fruit, from Kirsty's precious bible.

"J'ai dix-huit ans - I am 18 - how much will this cost?" He heard himself whispering.

"Deux cent Francs." Two hundred Francs, twenty quid. *Twenty quid to screw a whore and lose my cherry.* Fraser wanted to say no. It was too vile a thought, too dirty. He would leave and go back to the station. But the deed was already done and he was already in so deep he couldn't get out. And there was a morbid fascination anyway - he would do this. It was a rebellion, against Kirsty, against everyone.

"Suis-moi," she said, follow me, and turned away up the doorway. Praying nobody he knew had seen him, Fraser dashed after her. She was about his height and walked with a sway of the hips that simply said sex. Then they climbed the stairs.

There must have been eight flights and Fraser was flushed and out of breath by the time they got to the girl's room. Only part of this was the climbing. Most of it was excitement and desire. He couldn't take his mind off the girl's breasts. They were bigger than Kirsty's, much bigger, and he wanted to feel them, squeeze them. Then he wanted to do things Kirsty wouldn't let him. But in his mind's eye the girl *was* Kirsty and his heart beat even faster.

On each landing they passed, men hung around outside doors waiting for what Fraser assumed was a special girl. It was dark and the air was heavy with the rancid stench of stale sweat. The girl's room wasn't much better. The area beside the door was cramped and badly lit. An older woman sat there and gestured to Fraser to sit down. This must be the Madame, he thought. His knowledge of such matters was slim – he'd read about it somewhere. The young black girl told him to take off his clothes, which he did. But he was embarrassed to remove his boxer shorts in front of the older woman. She sensed this and stepped into another room, which Fraser assumed to be a bathroom. When she had left, he stripped completely.

The black girl said her name was Monique. She asked Fraser for 100 Francs - half now, half later. He paid her, and still clutching his wallet, he followed her through a curtain into the bedroom. The room was threadbare, filthy and stank of what Fraser would learn later in life was stale sex. There was nothing to cover the wooden floorboards and the wallpaper was ripped and dirty. In the middle of the room was a bed covered with a counterpane which was caked in the grime of a thousand men. Monique gestured to Fraser to sit down.

Making sure he was watching her, she slowly, teasingly, undid the belt of the PVC coat and opened it. Fraser's jaw dropped as he saw her breasts properly for the first time. They were huge - surely they weren't natural.

An 18 year-old male virgin with little sexual experience other than a few darkened fumbles with only one girl has one reaction to this kind of stimulation. The breasts and the tiny black lacy briefs, brought Fraser to tumescence in seconds.

Seeing his erection, Monique smiled. "Tu es massif, mon hero. Tu me plat," she said. Fraser felt neither huge nor a hero, and he didn't think he would please her either, but he was damned sure she would please him. Monique lay down on the filthy bed beside him and started to drag her red fingernails across his scrotum. The agony was ecstasy. Fraser's heart pounded and his face reddened.

He looked closely at her breasts and saw the faint scars of surgery. He'd read about this and knew that some women had silicone implants to improve themselves. It was such a shame, thought Fraser, because she was lovely and surely didn't need to do this to make her more attractive.

"D'ou es-tu?" he asked – where do you come from?

"Le Brésil," she said. Brazil. Fraser nodded. That figured.

He switched his gaze to her face. She was lovely, black and lovely. Her hair was so black it shone blue. Her make up was heavy but not tarty and she had perfect white teeth. But he noticed she had a little facial hair around the mouth. Fraser closed his eyes and ignored it as Monique's hand moved to his manhood and she slowly and expertly began to pull him off. She was much better at it than Kirsty. *The whore Monique was much better at it than the whore Kirsty.*

Sensing he was just about to explode, Monique stopped what she was doing and got off the bed.

"Baissez-moi," she said standing up, "fuck me."

This is it, thought Fraser. This is the moment of rebellion, the moment of sweet revenge.

You're not a virgin any more Kirsty and neither am I. You're a whore Kirsty and I'm with a whore now. You're screwing a client right this minute Kirsty and now I'm the client screwing you.

He sat up on one elbow and watched Monique turn away from him and take off her briefs. She did it slowly, toyingly, sliding them down her legs, then bending to her ankles to remove them. Then she turned to face him and suddenly his moment of rebellion and revenge and lust became a cruel, stabbing pain. The agony was back in an instant and the tears welled up again.

"No! No! No! Kirsty! No! Not again. You can't do it again! No!" He screamed and started to weep.

Facing him, below the perfect breasts, were Monique's penis and testicles.

5

Fraser could taste the bile hot and bitter at the back of his throat. His erection died in a second and he rolled off the bed in agony. He dived through the curtain into the living room and scrambled into his clothes. He was arms and legs and fumbles and the harder and faster he tried to dress, the bigger knots he tied himself in.

His heart was a steam engine pounding in his chest and he heard the roaring of the blood in his ears again. He felt light-headed but knew he had to keep his wits about him. This was obscene. This was danger. This was hideous. This wasn't Kirsty. Kirsty was beautiful, sweet-smelling, and kind. And Kirsty was a virgin.

"Les Flics, les Flics sont ici." It was the older woman, back from the toilet. The cops are here she said. Fraser translated in a split second. *The cops?* The fucking cops were the last thing he needed. An arrest, a conviction, a return home in disgrace? It would kill his family and it would kill him. He threw on his jacket and poured himself into his training shoes. He didn't bother to tie the laces.

"Dépêchez-vous," said the old hag, hurry, the cops are coming up the stairs. We're being raided. It happens from time to time. Hurry! Fraser bounded for the door and ran down the stairs four at a time. Now the landings were empty and he was the only person in this God-forsaken hole.

Where were all the other perverts, dirty, filthy whoremongers, when he needed them for cover, for comfort? Comfort from what? From a monster? What was Monique? A woman? She looked all woman at the start with those tits. But she had a cock and balls too. She was a he. What the fuck was that all about? Could people find that attractive?

As he ran he tried to get his head round it all. He'd read about them somewhere. Ladyboys? Was that what they were called? They came from Brazil, he remembered that much. But how did they get like that? Drugs? Surgery? It was all too gross.

Eventually, after what seemed like an agonising age, he found himself at the passage leading to the street. He slowed down just before the doorway and took a deep breath before ambling outside as if nothing had happened.

But round the corner he started to sprint and he didn't stop until he got to the Metro station at Chateau D'Eau. And it was only when he put his hand in his jeans pocket for a coin to pay for his ticket back to the Gare du Nord, that he realised the bundle of 50 pound notes was missing.

He checked his back pocket for his passport. Gone.

The shock and the pain of the week climaxed as one. He was numbed. The breath was lost from him and his knees buckled under his weight. He needed to sit down. He needed to think. He stumbled over to a bench at the steps which led down to the Metro station and threw himself down on it. The pumping was back in his chest, the colours flashed before his eyes again and the roaring returned to his ears.

He stared at the ground looking for answers. He had to think straight, erase the trauma, find a way through. Some down-and-outs milled around the bench. One had been sick there after downing a bottle of cheap wine. Fraser hadn't noticed the puddle but now he did. The splashes then the stench filled his senses and this, and the emotion of the past few days - especially the past few minutes - caused him to vomit too.

Think, think straight and quick. You have no money except for a few Francs in your wallet. Your life savings have been stolen, and your passport too, and you have a train back home in how long?

He checked his wrist. His watch had gone too. The Gold one, the one his parents had given him for his 18th birthday only three months before. He cursed aloud – it must have cost £500. He'd put it in his shoe for safe keeping before he dived in to Kirsty's room to screw the whore.

She wasn't a whore, she was a thief. And the old hag too – a pair of good thieves and probably part of a bigger team. And saying the cops were coming? That had been part of the scam too, right? The cops were nowhere near the place. That was a tactic to get me out, get me out quickly before I noticed my cash was gone. I am young and inquisitive and naïve, quite well dressed and a safe bet to be carrying a bit of money too. That was an old stunt, had to be. They'd done that before - a hundred times.

And it's not as if I can go to the cops to report the crime because it was me who'd broken the law in the first place. The hag probably thought it was Christmas when she went through my pockets - £500 cash, a full British Passport and a gold watch.

Fraser assumed correctly that the passport and the bundle of notes were long gone. That very moment they were being fenced back up the line through a massive criminal network. The untraceable cash and the passport would service a drug dealer who would use it to get to the UK and set up a complete new identity there. He could apply for a driver's licence, open a bank account and get a credit card. The credit card would then be used to buy airline tickets to take him all over the globe and it would all be done under the name of one Fraser Andrew MacLean.

The gold watch was sold an hour later to a face in the Paris underworld for 2,000 Francs – less than half its value. Monique and the Madame split the cash between them.

So what now? He could go to Calais and try to bluff his way onto the ferry without the passport but then he remembered that inside the document's blue pasteboard cover was folded the return section of his train and ferry ticket. He couldn't even board the train at the Gare du Nord without it.

But he had to try. He couldn't just sit there. A nobody would have just sat there but it was a nobody like that who used to go out with Kirsty Buchanan. Fraser was now someone different. He got up from the bench and walked down into the Metro. He cast an eye back towards the down-and-outs as he did so and smiled wryly.

You guys don't know you're fucking born.

In his wallet he had 150 Francs, roughly £15. He cashed a five Franc note to buy a Metro ticket and as he did so saw the clock on the wall of the ticket office. He had just under an hour before the train, but the rush hour in Paris can be a killer and it was just starting.

It took 30 minutes to get to the Gare du Nord and he raced up the stairs to the main concourse. He looked up to the massive departures board which hung over the platform area and saw that the boat train was on it and scheduled to leave from platform 10.

He ran over to the left luggage office and swore when he saw the length of the queue. He waited impatiently, shaking with shock and checking the station clock every few seconds, behind a dozen people who seemed to take forever to retrieve their luggage. Thanking his lucky stars that he'd put the left luggage ticket in his wallet, he got his red nylon case from the uniformed railway official and after noticing that it bore no slash marks and was unmolested by thieves, sprinted towards the platform.

He prepared himself to bluff his way past the ticket inspector. *What would he say? What story could he concoct in this short time? Or would he just tell the truth?*

"Vos papiers et vos billets, s'il vous plait mesdames et messieurs," shouted the inspector. He was a small man with a thin face and a badly fitting uniform. In his handkerchief pocket were a handful of pens and below that a badge, which told passengers they were dealing with Claude Lambert. There were four minutes.

Appearing harassed and out of breath Fraser tried to run past the ticket collector and the passengers in the queue before him. But Lambert had seen this stunt before and stepped out at the last moment, blocking Fraser's path.

"Un moment jeune homme, votre billet et pass s'il vous plait," he said, looking the youth up and down. He saw the wide-eyed youngster, pallid and sweating. He couldn't fail to see the sweat-stained shirt and he smelt the vomit on the jacket. The suitcase was obviously stolen. He saw a junkie.

What should Fraser do? Sing dumb? The innocent abroad? *No speaky no Frenchy Mon-sewer. No Parlez vous Franglais. Sorry mate. Not a word.*

No, he couldn't do that. It went against the grain. It went against everything he'd learned from Mr Bridges. He *could* speak French and he would try to talk his way out of this, and fuck what Kirsty would have thought about it.

"Excusez-moi Monsieur, mais mes parents ont mon billet," my parents have my ticket, said Fraser, gesticulating towards the train as if to say they were already on board.

"Mais non, jeun homme," came the haughty reply. No they don't. And what's more, no ticket and no passport, no train. He whistled between his teeth and caught the attention of two colleagues. When they came over he nodded towards Fraser, "Encore un junkie," he said. Another junkie.

It's a shame, thought Lambert, as Fraser slunk away, *he was British from his accent and probably from a nice family. He'd seen it before. They come to Paris, enjoy the lifestyle then get hooked on some shit or other and that's it. They often try to get home for free when they've nothing left. A shame. His French was excellent too.*

The ticket collector shook his head as Fraser walked dejectedly into the throng of people on the station concourse.

Then he blew his whistle and the train which carried Kirsty Buchanan home, rolled slowly from the Gare du Nord.

6

It was raining as yet again Fraser trudged away from the station. Heavy drops fell from the leaden sky, at first gently then in torrents. Fraser was soaked through in seconds, but he didn't care. He walked and carried on walking until he reached the Seine.

The tourists had long since disappeared back to their hotels to escape the downpour and the streets were clear. The air was still warm from nearly 10 hours of scalding sunshine and the cool rain caused steam to swirl up from the pavements.

Fraser went to Pont Neuf, where he would have proposed to Kirsty, and leant against a parapet of the bridge. The Seine flowed quickly beneath him and appeared to be a dirtier shade of brown than usual. *It must be the rain,* he told himself. *It's raining in my heart too, like the song, and I bet it looks like that inside.*

He could throw himself in. He could end it all. That was one way. Kirsty would be sorry then. That would really hurt her. But it would hurt his mother too and that he could not do. His father? He couldn't care less what his father thought; nothing he ever did was good enough for that man. Except Kirsty. His father liked Kirsty and he was proud of Fraser for having her as a girlfriend. Now that he had lost her, the recriminations would start.

"And while we're at it, why are you going to be a teacher? Why throw it all away on that? You should be an Army officer, a leader of men. That was all I wanted to do when I was your age. Your brother is going to do it, why don't you? You're throwing away your life." Fraser could hear it already.

Despite his sheer and utter devastation, Fraser knew suicide wasn't an option. He wasn't religious and was even less keen on religion after the events of the past few days. But he had more respect for life and he had far more respect for his mother. And anyway, he was too much of a coward to kill himself.

He had a more pressing problem. What would he do next? He had no money, no passport, nowhere to stay and no means of getting home. As a sideshow, his heart was broken and he was still in deep shock after his encounter with Monique. He stood on the bridge, which had once been integral to the plan to make him the happiest man in the world, and wept openly.

"Mon pauvre! Jeune homme. Tu es mouillant. Suis-moi." The woman's voice was shrill but well meaning. You poor boy, she said. You're soaked through. And she beckoned to Fraser to follow her. She must have been 70 and wore a fawn suit. She cowered under a large umbrella with an older man.

"Non. Merci. Ca va madame," he replied, it's ok. I'm fine, thank you anyway. But he was weary and emotionally drained and followed them on the last few yards of their journey over the bridge. They crossed the narrow road beside the Seine and dived into the doorway of a large department store for shelter.

The shop was called Samaritaine. Inside, Fraser could see expensive jewellery and wealthy customers browsed happily, unaware of the torrential rain outside. Hundreds of others had the same idea as the elderly couple and the doorway was crowded. Fraser found himself pressed against his new companions, rainwater dripping off his hair and clothes.

"Tu es triste mon pauvre garcon, pourquoi? Why are you sad, she asked.

What should he say? Should he tell her the story?

She was a complete stranger. It struck Fraser that he hadn't spoken to anyone about what had happened. He'd borne the grief himself.

And the encounter with the hooker who was actually a man and was also a thief? He'd never tell a living soul about that.

Even if he told her half of it, he doubted she'd believe him. He looked down at her. She seemed like a kind old soul and she reminded him of his mother. He missed his mother. He wanted to go home, to be protected by her. He could feel the tears starting again.

"Ma copine," he said with a trembling voice - my girlfriend, and rolled his eyes heavenwards.

As she clucked over Fraser, the man spoke for the first time. He shrugged off his daughter's arm and leant shakily towards Fraser. He was older, perhaps around 80, and wore a jersey under his jacket despite the summer heat. He'd shaved badly that morning and white stubble sprung out across his face. Fraser noticed a row of medals beneath faded ribbons on his jacket.

"Take my advice," he said, "forget her," his hand waved Kirsty away dismissively.

"And if you can't forget - join the Foreign Legion."

7

Fraser smiled and thanked the man. It had been a good joke, told to make him feel better. But as time passed, the more Fraser thought about it, the more tempting it was. The old man had long gone but he had planted the seed of an idea in the young Scot's mind. For the first time in nearly a week he felt positive about something.

He would run away and join the French Foreign Legion. Yes that's it. He would be someone, do something. He would show them, all of them - Kirsty, the American, his father. He wouldn't go back to Glasgow, he would stay here and start a new life instead.

The rain had stopped and Fraser could see across the city from his seat at the window in Samaritaine's 12th floor restaurant. The setting sun shone through the moisture-laden atmosphere and a complete rainbow appeared away to the east. It was a glorious evening. The scene was perfect.

Fraser finished his dinner of steak and chips and sat back to survey the view. The shock of the day was slowly fading, but the week's events were still raw inside him.

"Oh Kirsty," he sobbed, "I miss you so very much."

The meal in the Samaritaine cost 50 Francs, but he had been starving and he knew he had a long night ahead of him. He had 50 Francs left – around five pounds - not enough for a hotel room. He had made up his mind that he would just wander through the city during the night and try to find the Foreign Legion barracks first thing in the morning. His case was heavy but at least it had wheels.

He went to a supermarket close to the Pompidou Centre and bought some bread and cheese and a bottle of water and locked his supplies inside the case. But he quickly realised he was close to the Boulevard St Denis and hurried away back towards the river. He wondered what he would do if he saw Monique or the old hag. Would he confront them? Attack them? Go to the police?

But within himself he knew he would do nothing, because he didn't have the guts. He walked on.

In darkness Paris came alive with night people. Fraser crossed the Pont St Michel and found himself on thronging streets. They were dressed up to the nines, out to have a good night in the myriad bars and restaurants of the trendy St Michel district. He quickly regretted the decision to come to this part of the city, but if he was being honest he was running out of places to go.

He didn't realise that he stood out like a sore thumb walking through the packed streets dragging his case. But he found out soon enough when he turned a corner and found himself in a cul-de-sac, surrounded by a gang of about half a dozen youths. He could smell that they'd been drinking and now they apparently wanted some sport. Their leader approached Fraser and pulled out a flick knife which clicked open somewhere below waist height. Fraser knew any kind of resistance was futile. He had no strength left anyway, either physical or emotional.

"La valise," said the youth with a sneer. The other boys behind him laughed hysterically. The case. He was about Fraser's age but the scars on his face made him look much older - a life on the streets made you grow up quickly in this city.

A street away from thousands of people enjoying themselves without a care, Fraser was in the half light, facing six youths, probably all armed with knives. Handing over the case meant nothing to him after the losses he'd suffered that day.

"C'est a vous," he said - it's yours.

He dropped it on the pavement and turned to run away. He'd done enough running away that week - he promised himself he wouldn't run away when he was a Legionnaire.

He retraced his steps and found himself back in St Michel. He was sweating and parched and he was now also getting hungry. By now he was resigned to hardships and being mugged meant little to him – except that the case contained his last valuables. The clothes he could care less about, right now he wanted the long loaf of bread, the cheese and more importantly, the bottle of water.

It was half past midnight and fatigue was now gripping him. He was running on empty. He was at his lowest ebb - in the dark, alone, penniless and hungry. He wanted to cry, but managed only a single laugh of disbelief.

He shrugged his shoulders and walked away from St Michel back over the Seine towards more familiar territory. As he crossed the river onto Ile de la Cite something in the water caught his eye, possibly movement, possibly colour. He looked over the side of the bridge to see his red vinyl suitcase float past.

On the other side of the bridge he saw a man lying on the ground, but when he got closer he realised he lay instead on a metal grille. Beneath was some electrical equipment from the Metro and hot air was billowing out into the Paris night.

Good idea mate, thought Fraser, *but you must be fucking desperate.*

Ten minutes later it was Fraser who was desperate. Tiredness, emotion and hunger had dragged him down. He found a similar grille for himself off the Rue de Lutece behind the Palais de Justice. It was as yet unoccupied. Fraser waited for a few minutes and seeing that the street was off the beaten track enough for nobody to go near it, lay down on top of the grille.

The night was not cold but the hot air added a degree of comfort. He quickly fell into a deep sleep but not before he cried. For the first time that week he did not cry for Kirsty Buchanan. After the most traumatic day of his young life, Fraser MacLean cried for himself.

He woke early. The first Metro trains of the day rumbled beneath his metal bed at around five am and stirred him from sleep. He rose stiffly and walked, stretching, along the Seine, planning his campaign for the day.

He had no money, no passport, no watch and no clothing other than what he was standing up in. More pressingly he had no food and no water. The sun was well up by the time he reached the Louvre and today would be another scorcher.

By 10 am he was frantic with thirst and even contemplated stealing water from a supermarket. But he changed his mind when he saw a policeman.

Looking more and more like a down-and-out with every passing minute, Fraser kept on walking across Paris until, on the Rue Reameur, he found what he was looking for.

He walked gingerly to the bar of the police office and nodded to the desk sergeant. He'd already decided to come clean.

"My money, passport, watch and clothes have been stolen," he said, "my girlfriend has run off with a complete stranger. I have no food or water and I'm starving. I don't want to go home because of the embarrassment. I want to join the Foreign Legion. Can you help me?"

The sergeant was about 50. He was a tall, thin man whose job had given his brow many furrows. Fraser's speech added a few more. He looked the young Scot up and down, saw the soiled clothes and unkempt appearance and heard the pained voice.

He worked the desk most weekends and he'd heard the sob stories a million times. He never believed any of them. But this one? The boy didn't look like a junkie and certainly didn't sound like one. He spoke French very well for someone so young, yet he was obviously foreign. The policeman was used to being lied to, he could tell by the eyes. This young man was telling the truth.

"Tu es d'ou jeun homme? Quel age as-tu? – where are you from? Scotland? Yes that figures. And 18? Wait a moment."

He disappeared back into the office and a few moments later re-appeared on Fraser's side of the bar. He beckoned the teenager to follow him and Fraser found himself in what appeared to be the station's messroom. One wall was covered with noticeboards, the other a line of grey steel lockers. In the middle was a long, worn wooden table. Only a well-thumbed pack of cards lay on it. The policeman sat in one of the eight chairs surrounding the table and beckoned Fraser to take another.

Phillipe Ledanseur had no children, but he spoke to Fraser like a father.

"Are you sure you want to do this? Shouldn't you telephone your parents? Don't you want me to call the British Embassy?" he asked.

"Please, Monsieur," said Fraser after a moment, a sob rising in his voice, "can I have something to eat?"

He felt better after he'd bolted down the cold meat sandwich the policeman's wife had prepared for his lunch. His throat returned to a semblance of normality when he'd drank four cups of coffee. The cop sat back and watched.

Then, for what would be the one and only time in his life, Fraser told someone exactly what had happened – the cemetery, Decker, everything - even Monique.

Afterwards the policeman walked over to the window and stood silently for a few moments, gazing out. Then he reached into a cupboard, lifted out a black plastic bag and threw it on the table. He explained that it contained various items of clothing handed in to the station as lost property and told Fraser to take it into the toilets and find something that fitted. Then he took a soapbag from the bottom drawer of the desk, threw it to Fraser, suggesting he wash while he was about it.

At the end of the corridor was the station's locker room fitted out with a shower and a toilet. Fraser went inside and stripped. The bag contained many items of clothing, most of them female. If something should have been a pair, there was only one inside. He raked through half a dozen gloves and shoes before he found the only garment of any use to him – an old red tracksuit, with the white crescent moon and star of the Turkish flag embroidered on the front.

He tried it on and it almost fitted. He stripped again and jumped into the shower. The hot jets brought new life to him and for the first time in what seemed like weeks, he felt clean. The policeman's bag contained a handful of disposable razors and a number of new toothbrushes. He took one of each, shaved, scraped his teeth and combed his hair. Afterwards, dressed in the tracksuit, he felt like a new man. He returned to the messroom and thanked the policeman profusely.

He sat down at the table again and as well as the cards, lying on the scratched wood he saw a 500 Franc note.

"I did my national service in the Army, but I had dealings with the Legion in North Africa. They're hard bastards but good men." He slid the banknote across the table to Fraser.

"I think you should go home to Scotland," he said, "but after what you've told me, I'm not sure I'd have the guts either. Go for the Legion. But if they say no I want you to promise me you'll go back to your parents."

Fraser mumbled his agreement and picked up the banknote. The policeman caught Fraser's arm as he rose to leave.

"That money is a loan," he said. "Pay me back from your first wage as a Legionnaire." They shook hands and the young Scotsman left.

Fraser had memorised Ledanseur's instructions. He took the Metro across to the east of the city to Chateau de Vincennes, the last stop on Line One. The policeman suggested he take a taxi from there but Fraser wanted to save his money and decided instead to walk to the Legion's recruiting office at Fort De Nogent.

Another young man got off the Metro at the terminus at the same time and the pair walked towards the exit together. The other youth was about Fraser's age but his face looked older than his lean and muscular body. He carried his worldly belongings in a small grip bag. He looked over his shoulder as he climbed the steps from the platform and saw Fraser walk along the road behind him.

"La Legion?" he said, scanning him up and down.

"Oui," replied the Scot. "Vous-etes d'ou?" he added, where are you from?

"Hans Jedele. I'm German.

Fraser grew up in Germany. His German was even better than his French.

"What do you want to forget?" he asked Jedele in his own language.

"Five to ten years for armed robbery."

Hans knew the way to Fort De Nogent. He'd done his research. A friend had also fallen foul of the law in Germany, and had only a few hours to leave town before the police caught up with him.

"The Legion will take pretty well anyone. And everyone has something they want to forget," he said with a smile. "It's over there. Come on."

Fraser couldn't tell Hans his own story. While it had been the biggest shock of his life, Fraser didn't think it came close to the German's tale.

Jedele had been desperate for money to pay off a drug debt and had held up the main post office in Neuss, a large town on the Rhine near Dusseldorf. But he bungled it. The teller had hit the silent alarm and within seconds Hans could hear the police cars' sirens. He dropped the replica pistol and ran.

He hid from his dealer and the police for a few hours at his sister's flat, borrowing money from her and clothes from her boyfriend. Sensing, correctly, that the net was closing in, he slid out of the attic window and clambered across the roof to escape. He caught the overnight train to France minutes ahead of the dealer's muscle men and half an hour ahead of the police.

"If I fail this I am dead one way or the other," he said philosophically. "In Germany either the dealers will kill me, or drugs will."

Fraser was appalled by the rest of the German's story. The physical abuse from his parents and then a foster family in Frankfurt, before the expulsion from school for truancy and theft, then his first jail sentence for burglary. In jail he developed a taste for heroin and by the time his sentence was over, aged 17, he was addicted.

"Thankfully I have strength here," he said tapping his temple with a forefinger. "Every now and then I get clean. Then I lapse for a while and I'm back on the smack. I'm clean just now." He stopped walking and turned to Fraser. "I will get through this," he said.

It was a smile which saddened Fraser. It was a knowing smile, a smile that belonged to a well-travelled grandfather, not a 19 year-old who should be playing football and dating girls, instead of running away forever.

But that's what you're doing too isn't it? You're running away. You'd be just as dead as Hans if you bumped into Kirsty on Sauchiehall Street, not physically but emotionally, you'd be dead as a fucking doornail.

They stopped at an anonymous green wooden door set in a long whitewashed wall and Hans rapped it with scarred knuckles. After a few seconds a tiny hatch opened and a man's face appeared.

"Oui?"

Fraser cleared his throat.

"I want to join the French Foreign Legion."

8

Beyond the door was a narrow cobbled lane leading to a courtyard. There were buildings on three sides, which Fraser took to be barracks. On the fourth was a smaller building which appeared to be an office block. Fraser had grown up on British Army camps in Germany and had been unimpressed with the many parade squares he'd seen in his time. But he was impressed with this one.

On the other side of the square was a group of men marching very slowly. They seemed to be chanting at the same time. Fraser couldn't make out the words but he knew they were singing in French.

The man who let them in disappeared into a small hut beside the door and Fraser heard him speak in hushed tones on the telephone. He stuck his head out and told them to wait.

Two minutes later a second man approached, walking smartly across the parade ground. Aged around 30, he was about five feet eight tall, but just as broad. He wore green fatigues so starched and pressed that they were almost white and his boots were spit-polished and gleamed in the sunlight. His head was shaved at the sides but on top he wore the famous white kepi. Over his right breast pocket were pinned silver paratrooper's wings. His face was expressionless but his piercing black eyes were those of a bird of prey.

"I am Sergeant Littbarski," he said weighing up the pair. "Follow me."

Fraser felt himself drifting away. He had found nirvana. This would be the life for him - a uniform, respect, camaraderie, a home, a living. For the first time in days he had a real sense of purpose; he had something to live for. He even began to think that the incident with Kirsty and the American was fate. Maybe it was all meant to happen so that it would force him to make a decision about his life. Perhaps he was destined to join the Legion.

The marching men had come round the square and Fraser was mesmerised by their slow step and their singing. He'd never seen or heard anything like it in his life before. Sure he'd seen soldiers on parade – his father commanded a regiment once and used to drag him to all sorts of military events. But this was unique. He was spellbound.

Inside the office block the Sergeant told Fraser and Hans to wait in the corridor. The German sat down but Fraser was too excited and walked up and down surveying the recruiting posters on the walls showing the life and times of a Legionnaire. He read voraciously.

The French Foreign Legion was formed by King Louis Phillipe on March 10 1831 to support his war in Algeria. It comprises volunteers of all nationalities aged between 18 and 40, most of whom want to escape their past. It had fought with distinction down the years and the battle honours read like an atlas; Mexico, Sudan, Libya and of course two world wars against the Germans.

More recently, in 1954, the Legion had fought to the death against the Viet Minh at Dien Bien Phu in Vietnam. And it had raced from its barracks on Corsica to stop the Katanga Gendarmerie slaughtering thousands of European civilians in the mining town of Kolwezi in Zaire in May 1978.

The most important battle of all had come during the Mexican campaign on April 30th 1863. Unhampered by his wooden hand, Capitaine Jean Danjou led a patrol of three officers and 62 men against three battalions of Mexican infantry and cavalry. The Legionnaires were forced to seek shelter in the hacienda Camaron where, although hugely outnumbered, they held their attackers at bay. With only three men left they were offered a chance to surrender but replied instead with a bayonet charge. So impressed were the Mexicans that they withdrew and allowed the trio to leave with Danjou's body and the Legion standard. The Mexican commander is said to have proclaimed that the Legionnaires weren't men but devils. Consequently Camaron day is the most important in the Legion's calendar.

Fraser liked the sound of this. He would parachute into a besieged position and hold out until the bitter end, or help form a wall of steel between innocent civilians and African rebels. He wanted to be a Danjou, a hero.

Another poster said the Legion took anyone who was good enough and although most people who wanted to join were no angels, no blood criminals would be entertained. Fraser read on, drinking in the information, becoming more excited by the second.

A Legionnaire displayed exceptional qualities – fitness, smartness, loyalty, generosity and above all courage. He would be bound to his brothers by a code of honour like no other. He would follow his officers to hell and back alive, and in death he would never be abandoned by his comrades.

And better still, if Fraser was wounded in action, he could

become a French citizen. There was a convention called "Francais, par le sang verse," which meant French by spilled blood.

The Legionnaire wore the white kepi, officially part of the uniform since July 19th, 1939 when it was first worn in the Legion's spiritual home of North Africa, with a flap of cloth down the back of the neck to protect the wearer from the sun. The insignia was the hollow grenade with seven flames, two of which pointed downwards. The colours of the Legion were green and red – the colours worn by the Swiss Guard who served the French kings. The parade uniform also comprised a blue sash originally worn as a medical aid to protect against intestinal disorders. But the most famous item of uniform was the white kepi. And now Fraser wanted one badly.

"Who speaks French?" The Sergeant's head popped round the door of an office. The German shook his head. Fraser nodded. The Legionnaire beckoned him inside.

He sat down in front of the Sergeant's desk, scanning the regimental pictures on the walls and the Legion's flag standing in the corner. The desk itself was littered with militaria, including a paperweight made out of a hand grenade.

"The first thing you must do upon joining the French Foreign Legion is surrender your Passport," he said holding out his hand.

"That's easy," replied Fraser. "I don't have one. It was stolen along with my money, my watch," he paused, "and my girlfriend."

Fraser thought the Sergeant would smile at this, but his face remained expressionless as he scribbled on a clipboard. He'd heard it all before.

"What is your nationality?"

"Scottish. Well British really."

Where are your possessions?

Fraser lifted a grip containing a soapbag and a change of underwear.

"Is that it?" asked the Legionnaire.

Fraser nodded.

"And what name do you want to take?"

Fraser hesitated. "I'm sorry? What do you mean?"

The Legionnaire looked up.

"You'll notice I didn't ask your name. Your old life is over. Your new one has just begun. Choose a name, any name."

Fraser thought for a moment. He hadn't been expecting this. After a few seconds he remembered the only person to show him any kindness over the past week.

"My name is Philippe Ledanseur, " he said.

Sergeant Littbarski showed Ledanseur and Jedele to the sleeping accommodation, a huge room in one of the barrack blocks on the north side of the parade square. The room had a high ceiling, and bright fluorescent lighting which starkly illuminated hundreds of bunk beds. They picked a pair near the shower block. Ledanseur threw his grip bag onto the top bunk and followed the Legionnaire who gave them a brief tour of the facilities.

"Don't leave that there," snapped Littbarski. "I guarantee it will disappear before you get back. Think about where you are and the people you are among." Ledanseur noticed Jedele clutched his own small grip bag close to his chest. The German shrugged his shoulders and smiled.

Ledanseur looked around the room. There were about 20 young men already there, all stood beside their bunks staring at the newcomers.

Littbarski turned and screamed at the men with a booming parade ground voice. "What are you ladies fucking staring at? Get back to your fucking work or you'll be cleaning the square with a toothbrush."

Some were mopping the floor, or wiping down the tubular frames of the bunkbeds, others were cleaning windows. The room was already spotless and Ledanseur couldn't see how it could be made any cleaner.

Littbarski led them to the next room. It was just as large but was filled with tables and chairs instead of bunk beds. "The meal times are posted on noticeboards all-over this block," said the Sergeant. He pointed to the kitchens beyond the small serving hatch at the far end of the hall. "That's where you'll be working for the three days or so you'll be here. Then you'll go to Aubagne, assuming you pass the medical."

The men returned to the sleeping accommodation. There the Sergeant addressed the whole group.

"Reveille, 0530. First parade, 0600 for breakfast in the cookhouse. Dress, PT kit." He turned to the newcomer, "Ledanseur, you're in charge." Then he turned on his heel and left.

Ledanseur could barely contain his elation. He'd just arrived and already he was in command of a body of men. This would show his father. Half an hour in the door and he was the leader of 20

Legionnaires. This was the business.

He threw his grip on the top bunk and turned to Jedele. He wanted to talk to him, to share the moment with his new friend, but the German was undressing, about to leap under the blankets.

"How does it feel for you," asked Ledanseur, his voice trembling with excitement.

"Tiring," replied the German. "Go to bed. You'll need all your sleep over the next few days, believe me."

Ledanseur paced between the lines of bunk beds. He'd heard his father say often enough that the wellbeing of his soldiers had been the most important part of his job as a commander. He stopped and tried to speak to the other young men in the room, but they all seemed to be suspicious of him and said little. He noticed how young they all were, but how, like Jedele, their faces appeared older than their bodies. Some looked as though they came from Eastern Europe, some from North Africa. Several were oriental, others black. They all looked tough. They too had come here to forget.

The other recruits started to undress where they stood but Ledanseur was too embarrassed to strip off in front of his new comrades. He went into the shower block and undressed there. He waited for a while to ensure everyone else had gone to bed before he returned to the dormitory. He found his own bunk and climbed onto it.

Ledanseur had wanted the top bunk of the pair but he noticed that Jedele had already taken it. He thought about waking the German to tell him that as the leader, he should have the top bunk. But he was scared of causing a fuss and took the bottom one instead.

But he couldn't sleep. The excitement of joining the French Foreign Legion and starting a new life was pulsing through him. It was freedom. It was a fresh start. The slate was wiped clean. Perhaps Kirsty leaving him in the way she did was meant to be. Maybe it was fated, designed to spur him on. Maybe one day, in time, she would come back to him. He knew he couldn't face her right now, not after the awfulness of the past few days, but one day in the future when they'd both grown a little, she would find him attractive again. She was bound to find him attractive now that he'd made the leap and changed his life to start anew in the Foreign Legion. She was bound to find him attractive in a white kepi.

When he eventually did feel tired Ledanseur couldn't sleep. He was kept awake until 2am by the boy in the bed next to him crying for his mother.

9

Legionnaire, you are a volunteer serving France with honour and fidelity. Every legionnaire is your brother-in-arms regardless of his nationality, race, or religion. You will demonstrate this by the strict solidarity that must always unite members of the same family. Respectful of traditions, devoted to your leaders, discipline and comradeship are your strengths, courage and loyalty your virtues. Proud of your status as a legionnaire, you display this in your uniform that is always impeccable, your behaviour always dignified but modest, your living quarters always clean. An elite soldier, you will train rigorously, you will maintain your weapon as your most precious possession, you are constantly concerned with your physical form. A mission is sacred. You will carry it out until the end, at all costs. In combat, you will act without passion and without hate, you will respect the vanquished enemy, you will never abandon your dead or wounded, nor surrender your arms.

Ledanseur sat at the breakfast table in the cookhouse with the card in front of him. He'd long since eaten the bread and single piece of fruit the Legion provided for the breakfast of recruits. He was still hungry and started to memorise the code of honour to take his mind off the ache in the pit of his stomach.

He called the rest of the men together and tried to hold a meeting about the day's activities. But they were reluctant and when he started to hand out jobs they mumbled their dissent and walked away. He was about to chastise them when Littbarski arrived to take them for their medicals.

They walked in a group around the parade square to the admin block and went up to the third floor. There they entered a locker room and were ordered to strip. There were no cubicles and Ledanseur looked around nervously to see where he could undress in private. There was nowhere.

"What are you waiting for madam?" bellowed Littbarski. Ledanseur was taken aback. He was the leader, surely the Sergeant couldn't be shouting at him?

Ledanseur stripped off nervously and loitered at the back of the group of already naked men. He tried not to look at their bodies and he hoped they wouldn't look at his. He tried to cover his midriff with his shirt. One by one the men were taken into an adjoining room.

It seemed like an age before Ledanseur was called in. He stood nervously at a desk behind which sat two thin men in white coats. He still held his shirt over his midriff.

"Name?" asked one, and it started.

They took turns to prod and pinch him. They weighed him, they measured his height and the capacity of his lungs. They tested his eyesight and his hearing. He had to touch his toes and then his nose.

They asked him dozens of questions about his medical history, and that of his parents. Did he know if he had diabetes? Heart disease? Kidney problems? He thought he would die with embarrassment when one doctor examined his scrotum. But it would get much worse.

"Have you ever been with a whore?" asked the other suddenly.

Ledanseur felt his face colour.

"Why do you want to know that?" he snapped.

"We don't want a dose of clap in here," replied the doctor on the right. "Go with whoever you like," he said without emotion, "just be sure to rubber up."

The examination ended and Ledanseur was told to go to a cubicle at the back of the room. He was aware of the next recruit entering the room behind him.

"Piss in this and put your name on the side," said the doctor, offering a plastic beaker. Now I'll just take a little blood."

Ledanseur froze. Nobody had said anything about giving blood.

"No thanks. I'll do it later. I mean, some other time…" he mumbled.

"It's just a scratch. We have to take a few drops to find out your blood group," said the doctor.

"No. No. Please. Later. I'll…I'll do it later," Ledanseur began to tremble. This wasn't part of the script. Nobody said he'd have to have a needle stuck in him. He hated needles. This wasn't part of the deal.

"The sergeant said I'm the leader. I don't have to do it. I'm the leader. Take it from the others, but not me."

"Come on now son," said the doctor sliding a needle onto the end of a syringe, "don't make a fuss."

Suddenly the other doctor appeared in the cubicle and Ledanseur was cornered. Reluctantly he raised his left arm and looked away.

"No. Please. No. I'll do it some other time. Not now. I'm the leader. You can't make me do it..."

Ledanseur woke on a medical couch in a small room heavy with the smell of disinfectant. He was covered with a rough brown blanket. When he realised where he was and what had happened the nausea started and the world started to spin. Seconds later he vomited on the floor.

"If you're going to be a Legionnaire son, you're going to have to put up with a lot more than a small needle."

The voice belonged to a medical orderly. He was black, in his 20s and wore a starched uniform with a red cross armband. "I'm afraid you're already the talk of the town." The man smiled and shook his head as he mopped up the mess on the floor.

Ledanseur had fainted before when Fraser had been faced with needles. The MacLean family had gone on holiday to Greece two years previously and he'd had to get a tetanus jab. He'd passed out in the GP's surgery and his father had gone on about it for weeks afterwards.

He knew it would happen again, but why did it have to happen here?

He felt deep embarrassment, but he was the leader of the squad. His men would respect that. They wouldn't mention it.

By lunchtime he had recovered and felt very hungry. The murmuring from the other men in the dining hall stopped as he sat down at Jedele's table.

"It's only a little prick with a needle," said one.

"Yes I know you are," said another, "but what are you going to do with it?" The room exploded with laughter.

Instead of joining in with the joke, Ledanseur exploded with rage. He leapt to his feet, his chair crashing down behind him.

"Laugh now if you want," he screamed. "But don't forget I'm the leader here and I can make things very unpleasant for you - all of you."

The laughter increased. Ledanseur was hurt all the more when he saw that his friend Jedele was laughing as hard as anyone. He stormed from the dining hall.

Although he hadn't eaten lunch, Ledanseur joined in scrubbing the pots and pans in the cookhouse with the rest of the recruits. He'd tried to get out of it by saying he was the leader and as such he didn't have to join in. He'd started to walk away but two of the other men grabbed him and dragged him back to the sink. There were muttered threats, but Ledanseur, for all his linguistic skills, couldn't recognise the tongue.

Afterwards they were ordered back upstairs to another classroom where they were given the results of their medicals. Two of the men were ordered to leave - one was a diabetic, the other's eyesight was below standard. Both men protested vehemently, but Littbarski remained firm. They left the room to pack and Ledanseur saw the stark terror on their faces. He couldn't begin to think what they were returning to.

Littbarski addressed the remaining 18 men. They sat before him in rapt attention. Each man eyed the immaculate uniform and the para wings. Ledanseur coveted the white kepi more than anything else. The sergeant flicked papers on his clipboard.

"The rest of you are in. Kim, you must stop smoking, or cut down at least. Ledanseur, watch your weight." Then he paused and looked up before speaking in German. "Jedele, I know why you're here. Your sample nearly melted the test tube. If you take any more of whatever drugs you've been on, you'll be out, or dead. Understand?"

Jedele nodded his silent response. He was clean now and would stay that way.

"Right ladies," said Littbarski pacing the floor and speaking in French again, "you'll leave for Aubagne the day after tomorrow. We leave at six to go to the Gare de Lyon for the seven o'clock train to Marseille. At Aubagne you will undergo a series of tests and security checks. You will be there for three weeks." He stopped pacing and studied the men coldly.

"At Aubagne you will be cut off from the outside world. You will telephone nobody. You will write to nobody. I don't care if your entire family dies in a freak go-karting accident, you will not be contactable.

"The other side of the coin is that the testing is rigorous and you will be failed and sent home at the slightest hint of a problem. You will be grilled about your past and your private life. I warn you now that if we find anything that is unsuitable, anything at all, you will be history."

The Sergeant walked around the men and laid a document on the desk in front of each. It was the contract confirming their entry into the Legion for five years. Ledanseur signed without reading it. He was in.

The recruits spent the rest of that day and all of the next cleaning the dining hall and kitchen and then the dormitory. Ledanseur didn't think it could be any cleaner and when he asked Sergeant Littbarski if he could be excused because he was the leader, he was told to get on with it or he'd be removing the Sergeant's boot from his arsehole.

Ledanseur didn't mind this exchange. He knew it was part of the process of becoming a Legionnaire; he knew the Sergeant was treating him like this to prepare him for leadership during the training programme. Ledanseur scrubbed on and that night had his best night's sleep since Kirsty left him.

They travelled to the station in a coach and walked together along the platform where the bright orange TGV was waiting. Ledanseur had read about them but he'd never seen one before. This was an ultra fast Train Grand Vitesse that would whisk him away from Paris to his new life in the French Foreign Legion.

They all wore tracksuits and carried their grip bags jauntily over their shoulders. They walked as though they had no cares in the world. Most of the men were just glad to be getting away from whatever it was they were escaping. Ledanseur was elated to be leaving Paris. The men laughed and joked together and he tried to join in. But Jedele was the only man who would speak to him.

The others jumped aboard the train and found seats at the back of the carriage. But Ledanseur was their leader and he sat down beside Littbarski. The Sergeant looked at him quizzically.

"My father commanded a regiment in the British Army. It is called the Queen's Own Highlanders," said Ledanseur as the train rolled out of the Gare de Lyon. "He would be very proud to see me here."

"I'm sure he would," replied the Legionnaire.

"When do I get a white kepi?" asked Ledanseur, pointing at Littbarski's headgear.

"Oh, soon enough."

"And the para wings?"

"Shortly afterwards."

"How many uniforms will I get?"

"Enough."

"And when do I get my hands on a gun?"

The Sergeant didn't answer. His head snapped round, the hawk's eyes piercing Ledanseur.

"You know about le vieux alliance - the 'old alliance' between Scotland and France? Against the English? No?"

Ledanseur spent the next 10 minutes enlightening the Legionnaire about the intricacies of Franco-Scottish history. But Sergeant Littbarski appeared to lose interest after a while and even began to nod off.

So Legionnaire Ledanseur looked out of the window at the green French countryside and daydreamed. It was a fantasy he'd started in bed the night before and had embellished over breakfast. Now he would finish it.

The French Foreign Legion and the US Marines were in a battle somewhere against a common enemy. He didn't know who and he didn't know where. It didn't matter. They had come up against a sniper who was picking off the Marines and the Legionnaires one by one. Several men lay wounded in no man's land and as their leader, it was Ledanseur's duty to go and rescue them. He stripped off all his equipment and laid down his weapon before crawling through the barbed wire into no man's land. One by one he dragged the wounded men back to the lines before he went out a final time. There he found that the last casualty to be rescued was Eric Decker.

In his fantasy, although he wanted to leave the American to die, he had administered first aid and dragged him back to safety. Somehow Kirsty Buchanan had got to hear of this (Ledanseur hadn't worked out how yet, but the detail would come) and had turned up at the investiture in Paris where he would be awarded the Legion D'Honneur – France's highest award for bravery. It was the first time she had seen either man since that night in the city in 1983. She was still single, and more importantly still a virgin, and after the investiture she left with Ledanseur and not Decker.

The story was slowly coming together (Ledanseur was contemplating suffering a superficial wound during the rescuing process so he could become Francais par le sang verse) when he remembered Kirsty and why he was on the train in the first place.

Even though he now had a focus, the pain was still there. He missed her dreadfully and he felt the sharp stab of lost love. His sobs were less frequent and more private, much more private given his current circumstances, but they were still there. He took stock as the countryside rolled by. Now he was doing something positive, even if it was running away.

Going home would have been unbearable. His parents would not have left him in peace about what had happened in Paris. His overbearing father would continue to pick on him about the way he was leading his life. From an early age Fraser had been guided by his father towards a career in the military. But, under the guidance of Mr Bridges, he had worked towards becoming a modern languages teacher instead. Losing his girlfriend, the only thing about Fraser's life of which his father approved, to another man would be impossible to explain.

But worse than that was the thought of bumping into Kirsty in Glasgow. It was a chance too risky to take – it may have been a huge city but at times it felt like a village. The American wouldn't be on the scene any more, so that wasn't a worry. And while he was heading for the University of Glasgow to study modern languages that October, Kirsty was going to Edinburgh University to do medicine. If he had gone home he knew he would have had to spend a long, sore few years avoiding her at weekends and during holidays while they were both students.

He had thought of nothing else since the event. Now he wanted Kirsty Buchanan to be a non-person, to cease to be, to die even. He would rather she didn't exist than belong to someone else.

At first the natural reaction was that he wanted her back. But now he realised there was no chance of reconciliation. Even if she begged him to get back together, which he knew was unlikely, he knew he couldn't do it.

Not after someone else had been there. Not after she'd given her most precious gift to another man. She had once been perfect, glorious, whole. Now she was spoiled, sullied. He couldn't bear the thought of someone else having been with her before him. He couldn't take the betrayal.

No, he couldn't go home. He had to get away. And the French Foreign Legion? What did he know of it? If truth be told, not much. They were soldiers from all over the world who came to France to join. They said you joined to forget something. Well he had plenty to forget.

The Legion wore kepis, the famous white-crowned, black-brimmed hats. That much he knew and he was already half way to getting one. They were also all heroes.

Heroes. Ledanseur liked that. He'd like to be a hero, a somebody, admired and respected and not cast aside like a piece of shit the way Kirsty and the American had treated him. He could be someone too. *So the American was a Marine? Well I'll be a French Foreign Legionnaire.* The train rolled on.

It was shortly after noon when they reached Marseille. They walked smartly together down the platform with Sergeant Littbarski at the head. Ledanseur trotted to the front of the group of men and walked along a few paces behind the Sergeant. Outside the massive main entrance of the station stood a green coach, its engine running.

The small town of Aubagne is 15 km east of Marseille and is the headquarters of the French Foreign Legion. It is also the main selection centre and recruits come here from all over the world to join. The journey from Marseille took half an hour during which the men stayed silent. They all realised that their dream was a step closer. After the three weeks selection process here, they would move to Castelnaudary, near Toulouse, where their basic training would begin. If successful, they would get the kepi.

On the edge of the pleasant town stands the huge Legion barracks. Ledanseur could see hundreds of young men in blue tracksuits running around the place, sweating in the afternoon heat. On the square was another group, learning the slow, loping march of the Legionnaire. He could hear the deep song the men sung as they marched. The hair on the back of his neck stood to attention.

The atmosphere here was much different. Littbarski was joined by another two NCOs who began screaming at the recruits as soon as they set foot on the ground.

"Get a fucking move on you useless shower of shits," yelled the first.

"You're not at fucking boy scout camp here, double it!" offered the other.

They ran inside to a dormitory where they were ordered to stand to attention beside a cot bed. The first NCO came in after them and walked up and down the beds shaking his head.

"What a fucking sorry lot of pimps and junkies," he sneered. "Who's the syndicate leader here?"

This was it. This was Ledanseur's first chance. Littbarski had made him the leader back at Fort de Nogent in Paris, but hadn't asked him to do anything. Things would change here.

"I am," he said. The NCO stomped over.

"I am, what?" he demanded.

"I am the syndicate leader," replied Ledanseur.

"I am the syndicate leader, *what*?" he screamed, his face inches from Ledanseur's.

"I don't understand," mumbled Ledanseur.

He doubled up in agony as the NCO's extended thumb caught him full in the stomach. It felt as though the digit had been rocket-propelled.

"I am the syndicate leader, CORPORAL!" screamed the NCO. "You will address me as Corporal at all times. Get it?"

"Yes Corporal," wheezed Ledanseur.

"Well let me tell you this fatboy, if this dormitory isn't spotless in 20 minutes, I'll be playing *Boules* with your bollocks."

It took three efforts to get it right. At the end of the evening of scrubbing and polishing, by which time the men's hands were raw, the Corporal was finally satisfied. Then he ordered them to the cookhouse for their evening meal, but not before he walked with muddy boots over the glinting floor of the barrack room.

"It's to teach you discipline," said Jedele over dinner. "It doesn't matter if the floor is perfect or not, it's to see how you react to the orders, see how you respond to pressure. Do you crack, or do you get on with it as a team. Believe me, it's been a picnic until now. This is where the hard bit starts."

"When do we get to march like those guys out there," Ledanseur gestured towards the parade square.

"All the military stuff happens at Castel," said Jedele. "We've got to get there first!"

The next morning the men met the "Deuxieme Bureau", an Army internal intelligence unit nicknamed the Gestapo. Each recruit sat down in an office with three Legionnaires from the Bureau. Ledanseur was warned that everything he said would be recorded and double checked with Interpol. If the slightest fact or figure didn't add up, he'd be thrown out. The grilling, in English, lasted two hours and during that time Ledanseur spoke of Fraser MacLean's 18 years of life until he joined the Legion.

The boy had been born in 1965 in the military hospital at Osnabruck in West Germany, where his father had been serving with the Queen's Own Highlanders. The family moved to Berlin the next year for a two year tour before the battalion returned to

Scotland for a stint at Redford barracks in Edinburgh.

In April 1971 the battalion returned to Osnabruck for another five year tour and Fraser, his parents and older brother moved with it. By now his father was the Commanding Officer and he left the family in Germany that November and took the battalion to Belfast for a six month tour during the troubles there.

Ledanseur described a golden summer when Fraser swum in lakes and climbed trees in Germany. But it ended when the battalion, and his father, were whisked back to Northern Ireland with a week's notice.

In 1973 Fraser's father retired from the Army and the family returned to Scotland. They moved to Glasgow, his parents' home town, where Fraser had gone to secondary school. He told the Legionnaires that his life after that had been a simple one of study, how he had loved languages and how he had planned to go to university to do French and German, but how he'd decided to join the French Foreign Legion instead.

He was asked if he had had any problems with the police; if he drank or took drugs; if he was in debt; had got a girl into trouble; or was a homosexual. Ledanseur felt guilty that Fraser MacLean hadn't been like that and hadn't had an exciting life at all. He thought about telling the real story behind Fraser's application, about Kirsty, Decker and Monique, but he couldn't.

He returned to the dormitory and was pleased to find that the Corporal was bellowing at one of the other recruits and had emptied the boy's grip bag onto the floor for some minor misdemeanour. Ledanseur was happy. The interview with the Gestapo had gone well. Other people had had more colourful lives and wouldn't be so lucky. Once the dormitory had been scrubbed to the Corporal's satisfaction, Ledanseur went to bed. He wanted an early night because the physical tests started the next day.

As the commander of these 20 Legionnaires, Philippe Ledanseur was awake first. He leapt out of bed at quarter to six and woke the other boys. Then he showered and shaved. It was just as well the dress of the day so far had been PT kit - it was all he had. He donned the red tracksuit again and joined the others for breakfast.

He knew it would be a long day so he ate as much as he could of the bread and jam and fruit available and drank three cups of coffee. When they returned to the accommodation block the green coach was waiting outside with the engine running. Sergeant Littbarski and the two NCOs were already on board, sitting at the front behind the driver. Ledanseur took his place immediately behind them.

The journey lasted only 15 minutes and when they arrived at the athletics stadium on the outskirts of Marseille, the sun was well up and the day already warm. Littbarski jumped down the steps and bellowed at the recruits to get out and line up.

"The first test is simple," he said as they walked down the tunnel and onto the running track. "You have eight minutes to do four laps. On your marks…"

The recruits lined up on the start line. Ledanseur couldn't believe it. Eight minutes to do four laps? One lap is 400 metres. Four laps is 1,600 metres - a mile. Eight minutes for a mile? *I can walk quicker than that.*

"Get set."

Ledanseur did a quick calculation. Roger Bannister broke the four minute mile in the 50s. He now had twice as long to do the same distance. That would be easy. *I've played football and rugby before. That's nothing.*

"Go!"

The recruits set off at the sprint. Probably because he was used to running, Jedele took the lead from the start. The rest of the field was strung out in a line.

At the end of that line was their leader, Philippe Ledanseur.

The pain started in his side after only 300 metres. But by then it was already too late. Although he was running as hard and as fast as he could, he was losing ground. He tried to up his pace but the gap between him and the pack was widening by the second.

He'd eaten too much and he could feel his breakfast swirling around in his stomach. Twice the nausea rose and he tasted the sharpness of vomit at the back of his throat. The pain of the stitch in his side was sharper and more persistent now and he found that he couldn't inhale properly.

His father had always told him the only way to get rid of a stitch was to keep running, but with the sun now high in the sky, he had to stop for breath.

By the time he'd done two circuits, he was gasping. He was then lapped by his friend Jedele, who evidently believed he was still being chased by his dealers and the Neuss police because he showed no signs of slackening his pace. Ledanseur stopped for another breather and walked for a few metres. He would make up the time later. He had ages yet. Just because he was last, it didn't mean he had been beaten by the clock.

Ledanseur hadn't checked his watch at the start because he didn't have one. It had been stolen by the old hag and the transsexual whore Monique who he'd gone to screw after the slut Kirsty had run off with the American bastard Decker. He was spurred on by this notion so he lifted his feet and started to run again.

But as he wheezed over the line after he'd completed the third lap, all the others had finished their four laps and Sergeant Littbarski told him to stop.

He must have seen enough. Thought Ledanseur. *He knows I was going to carry on and didn't think I'd need to bother. He can see what I'm made of.*

"The conditions weren't right," he gasped. "It's too hot. My shoes don't fit. I've eaten too much."

The Sergeant beckoned him over to the mouth of the tunnel.

Littbarski could see what Ledanseur was made of all right. He strode up to the sweating young man and told him to get on the bus.

"Am I going back to the camp? To get my kepi?" asked Ledanseur, panting.

I'm being separated from the others because I'm different from them, better calibre than them. OK I've come last in the run, but that was only a run. Being a soldier was all about being a leader. I can do that. And anyway the Sergeant had been chatting away on the train. I got chummy with him, built up a rapport, we'd talked about Scotland, about history. Surely he'd fix it.

"No," said the Sergeant steadily. "The bus will take you to the station. You've failed."

"Failed? How can I have failed?..." asked Ledanseur incredulously. He could feel a sob coming on, a sob he had not had for days now, a sob which belonged to another person.

The Sergeant stepped up to him so that his nose was an inch from the candidate's. The hawk eyes were now slits, his voice a hiss.

"You've failed because your brother Legionnaires are pinned down by a sniper somewhere and you're a mile away with the machine gun. They call you on the radio because they need you. Your brother Legionnaires are being cut to pieces. You can hear their screams on the radio. They're begging for you to come and help them, save them, kill the sniper. So you start to run. But by the time you get there it's too late and they've all been killed because you were too slow. They're all dead and it's your fault. Now get on the fucking bus."

"But, my bag. It's back at camp."

"Your fucking bag's already on the bus. Do you know how many fail at the first attempt? Do you know how many fucking fantasists like you we get every day?"

Ledanseur was in tears now. The white kepi had disappeared. The dream was now a nightmare.

"But you made me the leader. I thought you saw something in me," he was whimpering now.

Littbarski looked at him in disbelief.

"I chose you to be the leader because you spoke the best French."

10

The coach stopped outside Marseille railway station. Philippe Ledanseur stayed on board. He returned to Aubagne, then went on to Castelnaudary to complete his selection and training. He would wear the white kepi.

It was Fraser MacLean who got off the bus and walked, head bowed, towards the booking office. With the last of the money given to him by Philippe Ledanseur the Policeman, he bought a single ticket for the afternoon train to Paris.

The sadness had gone now. There were no tears left. He was dry. There was no pity, no weeping, no sobbing. He was emotionally wrung out. He was empty.

By the time the train reached Paris that evening the only sensation he felt was determination. He vowed to himself that whatever he did in life, wherever he went, whoever he became, he would never be a failure again.

He took the Metro along Line One from the Gare de Lyon to Concorde and walked up to Rue du Faubourg Saint-Honoré where he knew he'd find the British Embassy. He told the French security guard on the gate there that his passport and money had been stolen and he needed to speak to someone inside.

"We've been expecting you," said the girl at the reception desk smugly.

"Your mother hasn't stopped phoning for a week. You've been officially listed as missing. She thinks you've gone off to join the Foreign Legion."

Fraser ignored her jibe and told her part of his story, how he'd been robbed at knifepoint of his money, passport and clothes and had been forced to sleep rough for a while.

Then came the final ignominy.

While they were issuing him with a new passport, the embassy staff allowed him to use the telephone to make an emergency call. The most humbling part was asking his father to cable him enough money to get home.

Twenty-four hours later he was back in Glasgow.

GLASGOW

He did not succeed in joining the French Foreign Legion, but Fraser MacLean became a new man just as surely as had he won the kepi.

The day after he returned home, he took a black bin liner and filled it with every photograph, every letter, every present - every trace - of Kirsty Buchanan. Then he jumped on the bus into town and threw the bag into the River Clyde from the Jamaica Street bridge. He didn't wait to watch it sink.

Then he walked to a cycling shop in Cowcaddens where he negotiated with the manager over a hire purchase agreement for a second-hand 12-speed racing bike. He put £10 deposit down and arranged to pay the rest off over the next six months. He pedalled to his building society on St Vincent Street and withdrew the remainder of his life savings, £50 he'd kept in the account for a rainy day. Then he went to the bureau de change at the bank opposite and exchanged the £50 for a crisp, new 500 Franc note.

Afterwards he cycled to the post office on Kilmarnock Road where he bought a thank you card, put the banknote inside and sent it to Sergeant Phillipe Ledanseur of the Paris Police.

Then he rode to a dirty sidestreet in the rough Gallowgate area where he took care to secure his bike to a lamppost outside an open fronted garage strewn with cars in various states of disrepair. He'd heard about the place from a friend. He trotted up the stairs to a grimy but spacious gym kitted out with a ring, weights and punchbags of varying sizes. After chatting at length to a small but very tough looking man in a dirty vest, he enrolled in the beginners' boxing class.

The next day he returned to his old job stacking shelves in a supermarket in the nearby suburb of Giffnock. He worked there every day until October, doing as much overtime as he could. Each lunchtime, while his colleagues ate in the small staff canteen, Fraser would fill a rucksack with bricks and go running for an hour. Every week he added another brick and ran a little further.

In early October he left the job to enrol, as planned, in the Modern Languages faculty at the University of Glasgow. On his first day, as he would every day for the next five years, he cycled the six miles to the university, and padlocked his racer in the bike shed.

After he enrolled and attended the introductory briefs for his course, he headed straight to the Fresher's Fair at the university's

Bute Hall. He ignored the chess club, the debating society and the geography field society and made a beeline for the desk of the University Officer Training Corps instead. He signed on the dotted line there and then. The entrance standards would be less rigorous than those for the French Foreign Legion, but that didn't matter to Fraser. He had no intention of failing.

He got chatting to one of the young men behind the desk, a second year maths student who had been in the UOTC since the start of his academic career. They spoke for an hour and agreed to meet up that night for a beer at the Fresher's Ball in the student union. Fraser wasn't much of a socialiser, and that night he wanted to get started on some German poetry from the 17th Century, but he forced himself to go. He wanted to learn as much about the UOTC as he could before he joined.

He waited for 20 minutes in the union but the other student didn't show. Fraser was relieved in a way because the music was too loud and he wanted to go home to start on his poems. But as he turned to leave, he bumped into a small blonde girl with sharp features he'd seen at the matriculation desk in the Modern Languages faculty that morning.

They chatted, nervously at first, of the course, their hopes and plans. When she asked what he'd done during the summer, he quickly changed the subject.

She came from Stornoway and the course took her to Glasgow for the first time. They had a few drinks as they talked and even though he hated dancing, she managed to drag him, protesting, onto the floor. By the time the bar closed that night Fraser MacLean and Eilidh Campbell were the best of friends and during the last slow dance, they kissed long and deep and wet.

They went home to her flat on Elie Street near the university and as they undressed she admitted nervously that she was a virgin. Fraser kept his secret to himself. In the darkness his old touch returned and he quickly found the strip of flesh upon which he'd once pinned so much.

Afterwards, as he lay holding Eilidh Campbell in the darkness of the small hours, Fraser wondered what all the fuss was about.

2

The weekdays were lectures and tutorials, Thursday night was boxing, every other weekend belonged to the UOTC but most evenings were spent with Eilidh.

Fraser's tutors found he did indeed have an ear for languages and he quickly impressed them with his existing knowledge and hunger to learn more French and German.

The regular Army instructors of Glasgow UOTC were struck by the 18 year-old student who displayed a remarkable appetite for the drills and skills of soldiering. They were impressed too by his determination and quickly realised that despite the screaming and petty punishments they meted out during training, whatever they threw at him, he would do well and come back and ask for more. They noted a person who was driven to succeed and marked him down for the future as an excellent soldier and a natural leader.

And Jimmy Mulherron, in all his days of training boxers - including two British and one Commonwealth champion - had never seen a boy as committed and fearless as Fraser MacLean. He would skip longer and harder than anyone else, press and jerk heavier weights than anyone else, and spar with anyone - regardless of height, weight or reach.

Eilidh Campbell found herself the subject of regular and vigorous lovemaking by Fraser MacLean. He would drop by her flat most evenings, padlock his bike to the railings outside and make love to her in the living room, kitchen, hallway, stairs and sometimes even the bedroom. She could not know that in the first few weeks of their relationship, years of sexual frustration were being vented on her and that when Fraser MacLean looked down on her during the ecstasy of union, he saw only the face of Kirsty Buchanan.

A boy became a man in study - physically, emotionally and intellectually. A personality changed, an attitude matured. He no longer lived the dream of wedded bliss, instead he became a realist and focussed his attention on whatever task was at hand. He set himself clearly defined goals and pushed himself onwards until he reached them. He had erased the word failure from his lexicon.

Sometimes he pushed himself so hard that his instructors, be they academics, soldiers or coaches, had to reign him in. On occasion he would bite off more than he could chew, but he never complained and he always came back with a commendable result.

On top of French and German he learned Russian as a hobby and started conversational Mandarin until his head of department found out and ordered him to stop in case he lost focus. He argued that he had no intention of losing focus, but the tutor won.

He told his instructors he was leaving the UOTC to join the Territorial Army. But he astounded them by saying he would volunteer as a private rather than an officer so he could experience life in the ranks and be a better soldier for it.

And one Thursday night at Mulherron's gym, light heavyweight Dougie Donaldson, a rough diamond from the wrong side of the tracks, made the crass mistake of catching Fraser above the eye with an illegal elbow. The result was a flurry of punches which Mulherron hadn't seen since he'd been in Madison Square Garden. Seconds later, although far outweighing and outreaching Fraser MacLean, Donaldson was picking himself from the canvas with his chin, pride and hopes of going pro, severely dented.

The results of Fraser's drive were there for all to see. He passed every assessment he was set with distinction, quickly won credit and rank with the TA and was begged by Mulherron to consider going pro. But while he was working so hard at succeeding there was a part of him that he took great care never to show.

He stopped reading the Scottish newspapers because reports of old man's Buchanan's court cases ate him up with a burning agony. He stopped watching the TV news in case there was a story about the millionaire's latest legal triumph. He became withdrawn from his parents and forbade them from ever mentioning Kirsty's name. He made it clear to them that he would leave home for good and sever all ties with them permanently if they maintained any form of contact with Kirsty or her father.

His mother and Kirsty had been close. His father had enjoyed a Saturday morning round of golf with old man Buchanan. But Fraser told them straight – *her or me.*

His parents knew nothing of the details of the break-up.

It was just an end, nothing to it really. The time had come, that's all. It's a pity it had to happen on holiday though. And the extra few days in France? Well he was upset, naturally, but because he loved the place so much he wanted a few days on his own to enjoy the galleries and museums Kirsty wouldn't have wanted to see.

Had his parents known the full story, they would surely have severed all ties with Kirsty anyway out of loyalty to their son. But he couldn't tell them about that, Monique or the Foreign Legion. He was too ashamed.

Christmas without Kirsty Buchanan in his life came and went. It was a long three weeks for Fraser because Eilidh had gone back to Stornoway to spend the holiday with her family. He enjoyed a lovely meal on Christmas Day but spent the rest of the holiday in his room studying uncommon German verbs and infantry platoon attack tactics.

On New Year's Eve he suddenly developed a mystery 48 hour flu bug that kept him in bed while the rest of his family took visitors and went to see friends. *It wouldn't be fair to spread germs everywhere,* he said. *I'll house-sit. You go out and enjoy yourselves.*

But as the midnight bells chimed the start of a new year, a familiar old sadness crept up on Fraser MacLean and wrapped its arms around him. As he lay alone in the darkness of his attic room the tears fell like they used to.

He longed for Eilidh to return to start the new year. When she did, they stayed in bed for a whole day, exploring issues that had remained untouched for three weeks.

Relations were resumed and the routine of study, TA, boxing and togetherness lasted until his first year finals in May, when Eilidh Campbell was suddenly and unceremonially dumped.

There were several reasons. He needed time and space to cram for his exams and she would be going back to the Islands for the entire summer, which he didn't want. He also needed time to prepare for his TA summer camp in Germany.

But when he returned from two weeks on the German dust plain of Sennelager at the end of July, he wished Eilidh was still in his life.

He had flown, along with his 200 plus comrades, from RAF Bruggen in Germany to RAF Leuchars in Fife. A coach had taken them back to the TA centre in Maryhill where he had finally been dropped off. He'd returned his weapon to the armoury, said his farewells and cadged a lift from a fellow soldier to Central Station.

Weighed down by a massive bergen and grip bag he took a train home. But as he flopped down on the seat his eye caught a headline in a folded newspaper lying on the seat opposite.

"Glasgow's GI Bride," it read. Fraser picked up the paper and unfolded it to reveal a photograph and extended caption below telling the story. His heart jumped, then tears fell freely when he'd finished reading.

Giffnock girl, Kirsty Buchanan (19) of the Firs, Doune Crescent, has married Lt Eric Decker, United States Marine Corps, at the Marine Corps Chapel, Parris Island, South Carolina. Kirsty, daughter of Scotland's leading defence lawyer Jack Buchanan, had the most romantic of courtships after meeting Eric by accident in Paris last summer. The couple will settle in Georgia, because Lt Decker will be serving at Fort Benning for the next two years. They received a wedding present from her father of a trip on the Orient Express. They got married on July 30th 1984 – a year to the day after they'd met in Paris.

3

The picture of Kirsty, beautiful in white with flowers in her strawberry blonde hair, and Decker handsome in his dress uniform, tore into a heart only slowly healing. She looked so happy and he looked so dashing. He hated them both and wished them dead. He wished he'd never seen the picture. He wished he was going away on his camp and not returning from it.

He wished he was still lying in a hole in the ground in Germany with a rifle in his hands and his mates by his side. He'd grown to feel comfortable in the life of a soldier, the uncomplicated order of it all, the drills, the friendship, the humour. Now he was back in a world of pain and a year's good work had gone for nothing.

He had to start again, banish the demons and try to push onwards. Once again he had to return home with an empty heart to a house full of Kirsty. Once again he had to order his parents not to mention her name. And when his mother had said over dinner that night that the bride had looked beautiful and that Fraser should be happy for her, he'd stormed off to his room and cried for two hours.

The final twist had been the trip on the Orient Express – something he'd always promised her for their honeymoon.

Afterwards he threw himself into the bath and washed Germany out of his hair and the engrained dirt and gun oil from under his fingernails. Then he got dressed in the trendiest clothes he could find, which was quite hard because he didn't have many, and went to a nightclub in town. He wasn't much of a drinker but he forced himself to down a few pints of lager while standing alone at the bar. It didn't make him feel any better.

At midnight a girl came over to him and they started chatting. She was around his age, with short bobbed dark hair. She was very thin and looked nervous. He quickly realised why.

She asked if she could stand with him because she was alone and was being pestered by two men. Fraser agreed without a moment's thought. They chatted for a few minutes about nothing in particular. Shortly afterwards the men came over and challenged him. Both were bigger than Fraser. Both looked tougher than Fraser.

"That's my bird you're talking to," said the first, the accent rough Glasgow.

"Fuck off Paki," said the other, "she's with us."

There was something about the tone, something about the sneer, something about the hardness of the faces. But Fraser couldn't quite place it.

He was used to the racial slur. His dark features and eyes and the hooked nose meant he was often mistaken for an Asian. It bothered him the first few times it happened but not any more. This was different.

The girl was upset now. She started to scream above the music. "Leave me alone. I don't want anything to do with you," her voice was trembling now, tears were close. "I've told you before, leave me alone."

The taller man made a grab for her. His lunge was all Fraser needed. As the attacker leant forward, Fraser bent his knees then brought himself up as quickly as he could. His fist was only a fraction of a second behind his torso, but it was a perfect uppercut and caught the man under the chin. There was a sickening crack, which revellers would later say they heard above the noise of Michael Jackson's latest hit, and the assailant was lifted into the air before falling in a heap clutching his broken jaw.

The second threw himself at Fraser. But Jimmy Mulherron had taught him well. His feet were planted on the ground and he only needed to move his upper body to evade the move against him. Then he sunk a left jab deep into the soft belly of number two. Winded, the assailant doubled up. But his pain would only increase down there as Fraser brought his right knee crashing up into the man's face.

Both lay writhing on the floor. Fraser turned to the girl and nodded towards the door.

"I think we'd better go," he said, grabbing her arm. The pair ran downstairs and jumped into a cab dropping people off outside.

"Thank you. Thank you so much," she gasped once the taxi had driven a few hundred metres away down the road. "I'm so sorry for dragging you into that. They've been pestering me all night, groping me..." she stopped what she was saying and fished inside her bag for tissues to wipe away new tears.

Fraser was now tough enough to handle many things, but he still couldn't take a woman crying. He put his arm around her.

"Don't waste tears on them," he said, "scum like that don't deserve a thought." And she cuddled into his armpit like Kirsty used to do.

Lindsey was a nanny who worked for a couple in the affluent Bearsden area of Glasgow. She invited him in for coffee because the family were away on holiday. They sat chatting for a while in the large kitchen at the back of the house, then they moved to the comfortable living room and started on the red wine.

They were halfway through the second bottle when he checked his watch and said it was time he left. He excused himself and went upstairs to use the toilet. Minutes later he trotted back down to the front room and from the hall noticed the lights had been dimmed. Cautiously he pushed open the door.

Lindsey lay naked on the sofa.

"I don't normally do this," she said, "and you can leave any time you like, but I have never felt as aroused in my life as I did tonight when you sorted out those guys."

Her voice was soft, sensual. Fraser could feel himself growing bigger and harder in his boxer shorts. He walked over to the sofa, pulling off his shirt as he did so.

The second time they made love that night, they moved to the main bedroom. As they found each other in the darkness, he remembered where he'd seen the two men before. They were Parisians and they had knives and they'd laughed at him and mocked him and thrown his case in the Seine.

Fuck them. He thought. *And fuck you too* he said to himself, looking down at the face of Kirsty Buchanan.

In the morning he found that the sexual conquest and fighting off the two yobs had meant nothing to him. He'd taken Lindsey's telephone number as a matter of reflex, but had thrown it away almost immediately he'd left the house. He felt empty. There was no emotion. These things had happened; they were facts. Nothing more.

He went back home to a house full of Kirsty and an almighty row from his parents for staying out all night. He couldn't handle any of it and locked himself in his room again.

He looked at his diary and tried to remember where he'd been and what he'd been doing on July 30th. He recounted the events of that day and tried to picture how it had enfolded alongside Kirsty's wedding day.

He'd been on exercise in Germany and had probably risen at six am, washed and shaved in cold water and carried on with the platoon attack they'd been rehearsing. Given the time difference, they'd probably stopped for lunch at the time Kirsty would have risen. While she had put on the white dress she'd promised herself, he had been wearing camouflage combats. His make-up was cam cream and his hairdo was plastered under a kevlar helmet.

And that night when he and his comrades had been sneaking about in the dark, Kirsty would have said the words promised to him, to another man at the Marine Corps Chapel on Parris Island.

He thanked God that he would have been sound asleep in his foxhole when Decker had picked her up and carried her to their marriage bed and taken her again.

More tears.

The only redeeming factor was that in a few weeks time he'd be off.

Part of the arrangement for the start of his second year, was a two-month visit to a French or German city where he could immerse himself in the culture and language. He had chosen a French city, because he'd grown up in Germany and spoke German like a native. Even though France had been the source of so much pain, he adored it and wanted to be friends with it again.

But he was horrified to discover that the city earmarked for him was Marseille.

By now Fraser had been so indoctrinated by the military ethos that difficult things were quickly and effectively overcome. He would go to Marseille. He would stay there for two months. He would do what was expected of him. And if they wanted him to stay for longer, then he would stay for longer.

What he could not do, however, was apply the military maxim to forgetting about Kirsty.

He avoided Paris by flying to Nice then took the train to Marseille. He moved into the student halls of residence at the university and every day he cycled to a local High School and taught the pupils there the finer points of the English language. He used the textbooks on the reading list but he also used some books of his own. His teaching style was different, unorthodox, but the staff who sat in on his classes thought him to be an excellent teacher. More importantly, his pupils loved the dark young man from Scotland.

In the halls of residence were three female students who loved him too. They were attracted by his Scottish accent, his muscular arms and his dark eyes in turn, and he bedded them one by one over the two months. He quickly realised that the schoolboy who had devoted his heart to only one woman, had matured into an attractive young man who could have virtually any girl he wanted – and without trying too hard either.

But it didn't please him. There was no effort involved, no emotion. It was something that happened. It was a fact.

On his odd days off, Fraser would cycle around Marseille, taking in the sights. He did his best to avoid the railway station and he wouldn't go anywhere near Aubagne. But one morning, on a busy street on the outskirts of the city, he was sure he was passed by the coach bearing young would-be Legionnaires. He swerved up a sidestreet to get out of the way. Because he only gave the vehicle a brief glance he couldn't swear to it, but he thought he saw Sergeant Littbarski sitting in his usual seat at the front.

One weekend in late October the second of the three girls, a flat-chested, rake-thin, oversexed medic from Nantes, suggested they go to Tunis for a couple of days. Fraser was starting to grow restless in Marseille. They spoke French in Tunisia and anyway he was fed up of his father banging on about the 51st in Tunisia during world war two. He would go. It would be an experience.

4

The ferry had hardly docked at Tunis harbour when Araby crowded Fraser's senses. He drank in the sounds and inhaled the scents. It was mystic, novel, uncharted and he was hooked. He couldn't wait to get ashore.

The people wore modern European fashions and traditional Arab garb. He smelled the tobacco and spices and heard the lilt of

Arabic and also the babble of heavily-accented French. The streets were a bustle of traffic and the markets a throng of people. It was a heady mix of France, Africa and the east and he felt instantly and surprisingly at home.

The medic wanted to find a hotel room so they could make love. She went into an instant and irreparable huff when Fraser dragged her into the main soukh in Tunis instead. He wanted to stop and have a small glass of thick sweet Turkish coffee in the tiny dark market place, but she wanted to go out into the sun. He won.

He loved France, but this was different. This grabbed him and where it went, it took him. That night he spent two hours sitting on the balcony of their cheap hotel room just looking out on the busy street.

Then to keep the peace he turned out the bedside lamp and made love to the sulking medic, whose face became Kirsty's in the moving lights of the traffic.

Fraser vowed to return to Tunis, but alone. And before he went back to Scotland to resume his studies at Glasgow, he travelled twice more to that frothing mass of humanity. And every evening he had left in Marseille, he went to the Arab quarter and sat in the cafes listening to the men and women who came from that mystical land across the Mediterranean.

At the start of the second term of his second year, Fraser asked to see the senior lecturer in the languages faculty. He told him that while he would continue to major in French, he wanted to ditch German, because he was so fluent anyway, and take Arabic as an additional language in his third year. Deals were done and promises made on both sides. If any other student had asked, the department would probably have said no. But because it was Fraser, and he was by far the most talented student they'd had for years, they agreed.

For the rest of his second year he worked hard in and out of the classroom. He declined the advances of several girls at the university and instead took a supermarket job in the evenings to raise cash for his next adventure. His TA evenings and weekends also raised money for his grandest project to date – a four month-long journey across the Sahara during the next summer holidays.

When he was bored or tired or just sexually frustrated during his stark, self-imposed regime, he would go to the student union or a nightclub and pick up a girl. But no matter how much he drank, or how hard he tried to fight it, they all became Kirsty in the darkness.

The day his second year exams ended, in April 1985, he declined invitations to numerous parties and carrying a small rucksack, boarded the overnight train to London instead. There he spent some time in the British Museum's Egypt room, studying the Rosetta Stone, the cipher for all hieroglyphics, before taking another train that lunchtime to Gatwick airport. In the early afternoon he boarded a charter flight to Gibraltar and there sought out ferries to North Africa.

Using bus and train and sometimes covering miles on foot, he left Tangier in Morocco and headed for Casablanca and Marrakech. Over the next four months he travelled east across the Sahara through Algeria, Tunisia and Egypt to Jordan.

Casablanca was dirty and full of tourists looking for Rick's café and all its *play it again* clichés. He'd headed out almost as soon as he arrived and also quickly ditched the jeans and trainers for the dish-dash, shamagh and sandals of the Arab. He knew by now how much more comfortable they were – cool and beyond the penetration of sand by day, warm and comforting by night.

His journey took him east, paralleling the Atlas Mountains and across five borders. He lived the life of the Arab nomad, sleeping rough and only touching civilisation when he ran out of food or water and had no option but to head for the nearest town.

On many occasions he'd joined local people as they travelled and listened in marvel to their tongue. He was only interrupted from his journey when over-officious Libyan border guards took him into temporary custody because they thought he was a spy. He looked and spoke like a nomad, but he carried a full British passport and had all the visas he needed.

After he crossed from Libya into Egypt he travelled by bus to Cairo and allowed himself the luxury of checking into a youth hostel where he had his first experience of relative comfort in weeks. He washed his body and his clothes but didn't wash his hair or shave off his dark, straggly beard. He wore khaki shorts and sandals and a ragged old t-shirt to explore the wonders of the ancient city. He stayed for a week but decided to move on once his carefully-budgeted money began to run out. He found he couldn't sleep in a bed anyway.

He knew he would have an unpleasant experience when he crossed the Sinai peninsula and into Israel but gritted his teeth because the highlight of his trip awaited him. He was interrogated and searched repeatedly by the Israeli police, and he was certain the

Mossad too, at the port of Eilat, because they also thought he was a spy. But after several hours of questioning, during which he insisted he was heading for Jordan and not Tel Aviv or Jerusalem, they eventually waved him on. He avoided the crowds of people, mainly Red Sea scuba divers, heading for the popular tourist resort of Aquaba and instead turned north for Amman. There he joined a package tour for the ancient city of Petra.

It was the treat he'd been promising himself to end his trip. He'd adored Cairo and the magnificence of the pyramids and the Nile, but Petra had captivated him since he'd first read about it in the National Geographic. He stood in awe outside the ancient treasury building and marvelled at the intricacies of the beautiful red sandstone. He wandered for the rest of the day and the next and the day after, and when it got too hot, he sat down and cooled off by drinking the sweet, green tea of the Arab in small cafés hewn out of the stone.

And then he went home. He had wanted to walk Lawrence of Arabia's railway but had to head back to Amman instead because time and money were running out.

While he'd been away, he'd hardly bathed and had neither shaved nor cut his hair. By the time he caught the flight from Amman back to London, he looked and spoke - and thought - like an Arab.

On his trip he'd been touched by the magical serenity and beauty of the desert. He discovered that although it was scorching hot and the dust and sand were everywhere, he did not suffer. The desert was cleaner than he'd imagined, and though he sweated he did not stink. He had walked by day and as the sun dipped away to the west in the evening he would stop to set up camp. He would roll out his sleeping bag and build himself a small fire to take away the evening chill.

And he would sit and watch the rolling sand dunes change from gold to burnt auburn, to pink then blue and black. And then he would tuck himself into his sleeping bag and gaze at the vastness of the heavens. After a time he would drift off peacefully like the shifting sands and sleep like he never slept in any bed, a deep peaceful sleep, protected by the timelessness and beauty of the unspoilt desert.

The third year of his five-year course would be spent abroad so he could immerse himself in the language and culture of his choice.

Before he'd left on his summer adventure, he'd tried hard to get sent back to Marseille but university rules forbade it. He was offered Lyon but in the end settled for Nice because it was the closest he could get to the Mediterranean and the mystical lands beyond.

He worked in three secondary schools in the modern concrete new city far from the tourist-kitsch of the port, promenade and old town. At every opportunity he jumped on a train and headed west to Marseille. If he had more than a couple of days off he would cross to North Africa and spend time in Algeria. The year passed too quickly.

He returned to Scotland and continued his studies, sailing through his third year exams. That summer, the summer of 1986, he flew back to Jordan to resume his adventure. This time he did walk the length of Lawrence's railway and spent more time at Petra before hitching through Iraq and then back into Syria and Lebanon before catching the ferry back to Cyprus and flying home.

His fourth and fifth years at university were long and boring, but the summer in between was fruitful. He spent two hot but enjoyable months in Moscow, polishing his Russian while working as a translator for a publisher of technical manuals. For the last three weeks of his break he travelled by train to Tashkent and Alma Ata, following the footsteps of one of his heroes, Fitzroy MacLean, along the great silk road.

MacLean was a Scot who'd lived a life of great adventure and Fraser had a copy of his book 'Eastern Approaches' tucked in his rucksack. He read avidly as he travelled through the same places, fell in love with James Elroy Flecker's poem, 'The Golden Journey to Samarkand', which was quoted at the start of each chapter and began to hanker after a lifestyle similar to MacLean's.

His bread and butter at Glasgow was now Arabic and Russian and in 1987, his last university summer holiday, he travelled to Iraq where he could indulge his passion for both languages and cultures.

The Soviet Union and Iraq shared strong economic and cultural links. Moscow also armed Iraq and trained its military, a military which was locked in a bitter war of attrition with Iran. It was this war and the hardships it brought which meant Iraq needed people with Fraser's linguistic talents.

He lived in a guest house in the Al Rashid area of Baghdad. Every day he travelled to the university where he worked as one of four assistants to the librarian. He loved every minute of the job, but whenever he got the chance he went to the thronging mass of the city's bus station and on board a rickety old bus, travelled to the ancient cities he'd first heard about when Kirsty had quoted from her bible.

Iraq was once called Mesopotamia – the literal translation means 'between two Rivers'. He traced the routes of those rivers – the Euphrates and the Tigris and walked in some of the holiest sites on earth. He visited Nineveh, the ancient Assyrian capital, near the modern city of Mosul. He travelled to Babylon, 100 km south of Baghdad and searched in vain for the hanging gardens. He went further south to Al Qurnah and stood in the grounds of a hotel, said to be the site of the Garden of Eden, and stared at what locals believed was the tree of knowledge. These were Christianity's holy of holies, yet he was there and she wasn't. She was shacked up with some Marine on the other side of the world.

Where's your God now Kirsty?

But while he enjoyed the beauty and rich culture of Iraq, he also knew the downside. He knew about the President, Saddam Hussein, before he'd ever reached Iraq. He'd read the stories, heard the testimonies. He knew a despot when he saw one. Fraser frequently saw the presidential motorcades roll past, and noted the frightened expressions that quickly followed the forced cheers of a cowed, brutalised people. He heard about the disappearances, the purges, the bestialities and the summary executions.

The war meant he was followed everywhere he went in Baghdad by the Muqhabarrat, the secret police, who assumed he was a spy. But his documentation from the Iraqi Interior Ministry, inviting him to work in the country for the summer, was perfect. Suddenly he'd had enough of Baghdad. The massive triumphal arch of crossed swords, moulded from the weapons of soldiers killed in the war with Iran and modelled on Saddam Hussein's own arms and hands, repulsed him. Thieves Market no longer captivated him and he knew it was time to leave.

Through a friend of a friend at the university he heard of a temporary job as a translator in the south of the country. After getting the necessary documents and visa stamps from the Interior Ministry, he said his farewells to the staff at the library and took the bus to the oil city of Basra.

He worked in an office there for a Soviet oil company that had won a contract to service the pumps of the massive refineries. Then he was sent to the nearby port of Um Quasr, where he lived at the docks in a hostel for workers, most of whom were Indians or Bangladeshis.

He was popular with his Arab bosses and the Soviet engineers because of his excellent knowledge of their languages and cultures.

In the evenings he would wander off alone along the once tranquil banks of the Shatt-al-Arab waterway – the disputed Arab River at the centre of the disagreement with Iran that had started the war in 1980.

Sometimes he would cycle through the mud brick villages where the tomato farmers lived. He would stop and play with their children or sit with the men beside their plantations and talk about the weather or the soil, but mostly the war being waged on the Faw peninsula, just a few miles away to the east.

When he returned to Glasgow for his fifth and final year at university, he craved travel and a life out of the ordinary. But he knew that he'd have to bite the bullet and shortly start looking for a career. His original plan had been to become a French teacher and settle down in Glasgow and marry Kirsty. But the idea of marriage and urban bliss appalled him now – instead he needed something to satisfy his new hunger. He wanted only one thing from life now and that was adventure and he'd already made up his mind where he would get it.

5

When his tutors found out, many were privately deeply upset, others outright and openly angry. He was the best student they had seen for years, the brightest, the broadest thinker, the keenest appetite for culture, the finest ear for language.

No, he couldn't. What a waste. Surely not that, surely not someone as bright as Fraser becoming something as uncouth as that.

They begged him to change his mind. They dangled all sorts of carrots in front of him and made him offers of research fellowships in Jordan, exchanges with Algerian students, sabbaticals in Egypt. But what they wanted more than anything was for him to take a teaching qualification and return to the university as a member of the staff.

It would be a huge honour, he admitted, a great privilege even. But Fraser MacLean said no thank you to them all and intimated instead that as soon as he graduated, he would join the Army.

When Fraser MacLean's application and CV filtered through the Army's various branches and arms, it too made various overtures. The Intelligence Corps made a big pitch for him. A young man who spoke fluent French and German, but more importantly fluent Arabic and Russian, would be a huge asset to them. They too dangled carrots in front of him. Perhaps he would like to work at the ultra secret signals intelligence listening station at Ayia Nikolia in Cyprus? Or would he like to work as an analyst at GCHQ, the secret communications centre at Cheltenham? Or would he be interested in taking a short service commission and then going on to something altogether *more shady* instead?

But Fraser MacLean made it quite clear that he would not spend years sitting in front of a radio set wearing headphones, analysing SIGINT. Neither did he want to join MI5 or MI6 and become a spy.

He said a polite no to the offers and told the recruiting sergeant at the Army careers office on Queen Street in Glasgow, that if he could not join his family regiment, the Queen's Own Highlanders, he would withdraw his application and seek a commission with the Royal Navy or the Royal Air Force and become a helicopter pilot. Army recruiting sergeants are not stupid men. Fraser MacLean's application was duly annotated before it went through the system.

The first hurdle to gaining a commission in the British Army is the RCB – the Regular Commissions Board. The Saturday after the end of course party when, to a man, Fraser's university classmates were in bed nursing mammoth hangovers, he was at a country house at Westbury in Wiltshire to begin three-and-half days of assessment.

Shortly after he arrived, Fraser found himself standing in a drawing room before a handful of men. Having grown up in a military environment, he knew when to speak and when to listen at times like these. The board comprised some people he already knew. He recognised one man as being a close friend of his father's, a man in whose house he'd enjoyed many Christmases as a child in Germany. A slight panic rose when he saw him. But it died quickly because he remembered such panels care not a whit about who you are, only how you perform.

Each of the four men, dressed in battered old suits, threadbare shirts and regimental ties, had a copy of Fraser MacLean's CV and application in front of him. They were impressed with his academic qualifications, how and where he'd spent his holidays and how he'd given up being a potential officer in the UOTC to join the TA as a soldier.

They chatted with him for half an hour about why he wanted to join the Army and noted that he didn't once mention his father or brother. Fraser had heard enough about this situation from both men to know how to handle it himself. He trotted out the appropriate answers about desiring a life of adventure, a career that was different and one that made a difference. He expressed a love of the outdoors and a passion for languages.

Over the next two days he was rigorously tested.

He stood in front of a large map of the world and was asked to identify the Dominican Republic, Chad, Uruguay, the Solomon Islands and Madagascar. He was also asked to name the capital cities of another half dozen countries and explain why they had been in the news recently.

In another classroom, to test his communications skills and reactions under pressure, he was asked to deliver a 10 minute speech on a loaf of bread, unaided by notes.

But the main part of the test came when Fraser and the rest of the candidates started their command task. They left the comfort of the house and walked out to the large, leafy back garden. On the grass before them were arrayed half a dozen empty oil drums, a few coils of rope and some scaffolding poles. They were urged to get themselves and a small, but very heavy, ammunition box across the crocodile-infested river marked out by two lines of orange mine tape.

One of the other young men immediately took over. This was a test of initiative where every aspect was noted by the DS, and this guy wasn't going to be second in command of anything. Fraser watched with interest, as the well built lad of around 20 delegated jobs to the other candidates. It became apparent to Fraser that the leader was the captain of a rugby team given his build and manner. It also became apparent that he wouldn't be offered the Queen's Commission.

His intricate structure of poles and ropes collapsed at the first stress of weight from the ammunition box, and the leader spent the next five minutes screaming at the other candidates, belittling them for their lack of effort and commitment. When there was the first hint of tears in the young man's voice, Fraser took his cue.

"Right gentlemen," he said, firmly, walking to the front of the group, "let's give it another go. Why don't we try this..."

The four DS noted the tone and the use of the word "we". Teamwork - they liked that, they were impressed. They were impressed further when Fraser called the candidates together and outlined his plan. He appointed leaders to various aspects of the operation and encouraged each man to do his bit towards the team goal. After 10 minutes the box and each of the candidates were on the other side of the river. The crocodiles went hungry that afternoon.

The weekend is regularly visited by civilian management consultants complete with sharp suits, flipcharts and buzzwords. They study each aspect of the course in depth, suck the ends of their Mont Blanc pens then make their expensive recommendations. The Army politely ignores the advice. The board has worked very well down the years, thank you.

Fraser MacLean wanted to take his last lengthy summer holiday in 1988. If things went to plan it would be some time before he would get another. He wanted to explore Damascus and travel north through the rest of Syria and into Turkey, returning from Istanbul at the end of his trip. The day before he left Damascus, he phoned home to receive the two pieces of news he'd been waiting for.

The first was that the University of Glasgow had much pleasure in awarding him a Master of Arts Degree with First Class Honours in Modern Languages

The second was that having passed RCB, Fraser MacLean MA (Hons) had been selected to join the Army's commissioning course, and at the end of August 1988, would report to the Royal Military Academy, Sandhurst.

SANDHURST

The British Army is the best in the world. It makes this claim not out of bravado, but from reputation. That is why nations from around the globe send their young men and women to the finest military training establishment on earth – the Royal Military Academy, Sandhurst.

The Academy occupies around 900 acres near the small town of Camberley on the border between the counties of Surrey and Berkshire. Visitors are greeted by a beautiful sweeping tree-lined drive, which opens out to reveal playing fields and a series of buildings behind them. The most inspiring of these is Old College, a long white neo-classical entrance complete with columns and cannons.

Beside it stands New College, a red Edwardian structure with a clocktower whose timings are sacrosanct for hundreds of Academy cadets. Inside, the corridors are lined with shiny green and brown tiles and Fraser understood why the building was labelled the biggest public toilet in the country.

But he was disappointed to learn that he would stay in neither building during his year at Sandhurst. Instead, because he was a graduate, his residence would be Victory College, a hideous H-shaped concrete monstrosity built in the early 70s. He consoled himself with the fact that his second floor room looked out onto the sports fields and he had an exquisite view of the buildings where he would rather have stayed.

The room was small, long and narrow, but functional. He didn't care about being uncomfortable, he was there to learn. On his left as he entered was a wardrobe with a rack at the bottom for boots and shoes. Next to that was a wash basin and mirror and beyond that a line of a dozen coathooks for the myriad changes of clothing he'd require every day of the course. On the right was a single bed with a reading lamp on the small table beside it. Underneath the mattress were three drawers. One contained a long thin compartment with a padlock haft which would hold his rifle when it wasn't in the armoury. The only feature that had any element of comfort about it was an easy chair, already positioned at the window. At the far end of the room was a cork pinboard; above it were three bookshelves and below it a wide desk and reading lamp.

Propped against the reading lamp were two letters, one in the hand of his father, the other, his brother. He ignored them and unpacked his kit.

He'd heard so much about Sandhurst from both men that he knew what to take and what to leave behind. He carried as few personal belongings as possible. He was here for one thing only, to pass the course. There could be no distractions.

He hung up his suit and changed into a Scotland Rugby jersey and jogging pants. He knew he would be issued with kit by the QM, but he wanted to keep his own boots because they had been well broken in during his TA days. He placed them on the rack with his brogues. He had a couple of spare dress shirts, some underwear, a sports jacket and trousers and a Glasgow University tie. The only personal belongings he had with him was a book of German poems, with one surviving photograph of Kirsty secreted inside the back cover.

There was a knock at the door and a smiling brown face appeared in the room.

"Hello old chap. We're going to be next door neighbours for a year, so I thought I'd introduce myself." The voice was straight from public school.

"I'm Hassan, Crown Prince of Oman, nephew of the Sultan himself, but don't worry about that," he said waving his hand dismissively. "Please call me Hassan."

The young man entered the room and thrust out his hand. Fraser smiled and took it.

"Salaam al malakum," said Fraser in accentless Arabic.

Hassan had indeed been at an English Public School. After Eton he'd returned to the Gulf and had studied Politics and Economics in his homeland, before being sent back to England to complete his education by attending Sandhurst. When he returned to the Middle East, he would command his country's elite Special Forces.

Fraser took to Hassan immediately, despite the huge differences in their backgrounds and breeding. Regardless of his nobility and impeccable education, Hassan was like many of the Arabs Fraser had encountered down the years - an uncomplicated, kind man. In turn, Hassan was impressed by Fraser's travels, but more so by his mastery of language. For the next year Hassan would speak English to Fraser, but, much to the amusement of the Sandhurst cadets and instructors, the replies always came in Arabic.

Hassan stayed for an hour that afternoon. Far away across the playing fields could be heard a thousand feet drilling on the square to the accompaniment of screams from the instructors. The two men spoke about their lives and their plans. Fraser was circumspect. He was focussed on becoming commissioned a year hence and wanted no nostalgia this day. He stifled a smile when his new friend departed.

"Well pip-pip old chap, must dash." said Hassan, standing to leave. "I say, aren't you going to open your mail?"

The mail - the two letters he'd been avoiding. He didn't need to open them. He knew what they'd say, could predict them pretty well word for word.

After Hassan left he unpacked the remainder of his kit then sat in the easy chair alternating his gaze between the window and the two envelopes.

His father would say he was very proud and touched on his younger son's first day at Sandhurst, how it reminded him of his early days in the Army, and how he was sure he would do every bit as well.

His brother Euan, who'd been there two years previously, would say much the same thing. But would add some patronising advice – don't give up, it's about determination as much as ability and strength.

Fraser hadn't had a proper conversation with his father for years and had barely spoken more than a few words with his already-commissioned brother over the same period. He screwed up the letters and threw them into the bin, unopened.

Then he turned again to the window.

"You wouldn't understand," he hissed.

2

The instructors at Sandhurst are Colour Sergeants, infantrymen in the main, experienced men who have been soldiers for many years. It is considered a great honour for a soldier to be selected to go to Sandhurst as an instructor, because only the best of the best are asked. He is, after all, training the future officers of the British Army and the armies of many countries the world over.

The standards of the Colour Sergeant instructors are very high. There are no grey areas, only black and white. Either something is done correctly, or it is not. The instructors brook no criticism, their word is law and they never accept second best.

If an officer cadet is failing to meet the right standards, it usually becomes apparent fairly early on. They are given one warning and if they do not get themselves together, regardless of breeding, education, nationality or wealth, they are invited to leave.

Sandhurst is a place of great tradition. On their first day, cadets are shown the names of famous predecessors printed on the wall of Old College. Among them Churchill and Montgomery. The foreign cadets include the Sultans of Oman and Brunei in their number, along with King Hussein of Jordan. At this point cadets are told a famous, if apocryphal, story to show that nobody is above the summary justice of the instructors. It involved the Jordanian monarch, who was commissioned in the 1960s, being upbraided by a Colour Sergeant for some misdemeanour.

"You stupid King, Sir, " the instructor is alleged to have said.

Another tale which is now part of the Academy folklore, is of the instructor who wakes one morning at the end of term to find a brand new sports car sitting outside his home. It is a gift from an oil rich Sheikh for helping his son get through the course. The instructor drives the car straight round to the Sandhurst Commandant's office where he parks it outside and leaves the keys in the ignition. He may only accept a gift up to the value of £50 and even then it has to be declared. Anything above that value must be returned. The instructors cannot be seen to accept gifts in case they are interpreted as bribes.

Before being sent back to their rooms to prepare for the first day proper, the instructors teach their cadets the most important lesson they will learn at the academy.

"While you are here, I will call you 'sir' and you will call me 'sir'," they say.

"But you will mean it, and I will not. Fall out."

The Junior Term at Sandhurst is a short, sharp, shock to the system designed to turn immature young men into future officers. It is generally regarded as six weeks of living, sleepless, hell. The cadets enjoy no privileges during this time. They are confined to the Academy and are not permitted to wear civilian clothes. They are marched, or doubled, between the assault course and the rifle ranges, the drill square and the classrooms, the swimming pool and the running track. On Monday and Wednesday afternoons they are allowed a break - they take part in team games. Competitive fixtures take place on Saturdays.

It is at the end of the Junior Term that the instructors can tell who is and who is not on course for a commission. It is at this time that a few cadets get an unpleasant message from their instructors.

"Your hat, your feet, my office. GO!"

These Colour Sergeants see hundreds of cadets pass through the hallowed portals of Sandhurst. Speaking privately, never to any of the cadets, they would admit that they had never experienced a potential officer quite like Fraser MacLean.

While they bellowed at some cadets that they were "Oxygen thieves," or that their fathers had "wasted a sperm" on them, Fraser shone from the moment he set foot in the famous academy. Everything he did was first class, from drill to weapon handling, from the assault course to the lecture theatre.

His kit was always immaculate, his boots gleamed and his room passed every inspection. His instructors had long since resorted to inventing faults over which to criticise him, because it wouldn't do to give the boy a big head. They knew he'd been a private soldier in the TA and it showed in everything he did. They noted someone who thought and lived like a soldier, a young man who would be an excellent officer - a leader of men.

After he completed a task he would turn and help the man beside him and then the next man. On the stretcher races and log runs he would coax and cajole and encourage his team-mates onwards.

While his fellow cadets got lost and stumbled about on the Academy's Barossa Training Area, lost items of equipment and were repeatedly captured or killed by the enemy, Fraser was perfection personified. Although he only spoke if he had something to say, and apart from Hassan made few close friends, he grabbed people by charisma, by confidence and by ability. By the end of the course all the other cadets admitted that, even though they would one day be officers themselves, if Fraser MacLean was their leader, they'd follow him into hell.

He and Hassan shared a classroom and debated vociferously, but with eloquence, the merits and demerits of various battles and campaigns down the years. His modern studies and history lecturers noted a great intellect. Moreover he was a young man who worked very hard indeed to achieve the highest grades. He received straight

As in every subject.

One of the most important attributes of a cadet is his 'Officer Qualities'. This is a character assessment based on the individual's personality as much as his performance. Fraser MacLean was marked down as an excellent cadet who bore all the hallmarks of a fine young officer. Everything he did shone – the only place where his performance was average was on the sports field.

While he was a good boxer and badminton player, he enjoyed neither football nor rugby. But even though he was only moderately talented, they were team games and he played with far more enthusiasm and effort than skill. The instructors noticed how he would up his game and try for a winner if the match was level with only a few minutes left on the clock.

They marked him out as someone who would probably prefer to be a solo sportsman, but who played for the team with enthusiasm nonetheless. But there was something else, something they'd seen in other cadets down the years. He was driven. There was some silent motivator spurring him on. He wasn't an odd lad, far from it, he was very popular. But he just didn't shoot his mouth off, he just got his head down and got on with it. Whatever it was it wasn't doing him any harm. He was the best they'd ever seen.

What they could not know was that during the agonies of the forced marches carrying vast weights, when body and soul were screaming in agony and when any rational human being would simply stop and sit down, Fraser saw the face of Kirsty Buchanan, in agony then ecstasy, as Eric Decker took her virginity.

Then he gritted his teeth to shut out the pain in his legs and back and arms, pulled the straps of his bergen tighter about his shoulders and stepped up the pace.

Towards the end of their year at Sandhurst, Fraser and his comrades listed the regiments they wanted to join once they'd commissioned. There followed a series of visits and interviews. If the cadet liked the regiment and vice versa, that was it. If there was a family connection, then all the better. While his friends dithered between the Gunners or the Sappers or the Cavalry or the REME, there was only one regiment on Fraser MacLean's list.

It was no surprise to anyone at Sandhurst that at the end of his year at the Academy he won the coveted Sword of Honour as the best cadet on the course. He was presented with the award at the famous Sovereign's Parade, a lavish end of course celebration for those passing out and their families. The parade is attended by nearly every senior officer in the Army and is a carefully choreographed celebration of everything the British Army stands for.

Fraser and his comrades marched off the parade square, resplendent in their blues jackets and with silver bayonets gleaming. Then, in keeping with generations of tradition, with the band playing Auld Lang Syne, all those being commissioned slow march up the steps of Old College's grand entrance. They are followed inside the building, as ever, by the Academy's Adjutant on his horse. The Adjutant is always a Major in the Guards, the horse is always white.

Tradition says a cadet is commissioned when the doors are closed behind him. But in the mists of time a cadet is said to have tried to get his revenge on an instructor at this point by having him arrested. Nowadays cadets are officially commissioned at midnight on the night of the parade, when all the instructors have long gone.

On the evening of the parade the cadets attend the commissioning ball. It was the first time Fraser wore his new mess kit of scarlet jacket with buff lapels, blue collar and cuffs, and white piping, Cameron of Erracht tartan waistcoat and MacKenzie of Seaforth tartan kilt. On his gold braided shoulder cords he wore the single pip of a Second Lieutenant, covered with a ribbon of white silk tied in a knot on the top.

At midnight on May 31st 1988, Officer Cadet Fraser MacLean removed the ribbon and became Second Lieutenant Fraser MacLean, Queen's Own Highlanders.

3

Fraser didn't have a partner for the ball and after the dinner he drank one glass of champagne then slid away to pack his kit before the dancing started. He and Hassan were flying to the Gulf early the next morning for a last leave, traditionally called 'embarkation leave', before he joined his new regiment. He had already received his orders and he would be posted, as expected, to the Queen's Own Highlanders, based at Münster in Germany.

He couldn't bear the thought of going back to Glasgow for his remaining leave. The family had been at the passing out parade and that had been more than enough. His father had been impossibly pompous and nostalgic, his brother had cut around the old place looking for salutes from both cadets and instructors alike. And although he would miss his mother dreadfully, he would not go back to Scotland. Instead he would spend the next three weeks enjoying the culture of Oman as the guest of Crown Prince Hassan. Then he would travel to Germany.

At Hassan's insistence, and on his credit card, the two men flew to Muscat first class on British Airways. They were met at the foot of the airliner's steps by a convoy of black Mercedes limousines driven by moustachioed men wearing dark suits and sunglasses. The convoy took off and drove at speed through the domes and sidestreets of the Omani capital to a large townhouse on the coast. Two manservants removed Fraser's suitcase from the boot of the first car, carried it to his suite of rooms upstairs and unpacked it.

"You'll need a suit tonight," said Hassan with a broad grin on his face. Fraser knew his friend well enough by now to realise he was up to something. He only had one suit to his name so he showered and shaved and put it on.

Twenty minutes later the pair were back in the Mercedes heading into Muscat.

"Hassan, are we going clubbing?" asked Fraser innocently.

"Something like that," came the reply.

Shortly, with the sun setting in the distance, the convoy sped up the gravel driveway of a large house. The grounds were neatly manicured and there was an ornate water fountain in the centre. Armed soldiers patrolled everywhere. When the cars stopped, uniformed servants appeared and opened the doors. Hassan and Fraser walked inside the building, which was the most luxurious the young Scot had ever seen.

"Sorry old chap, but you'll have to stay here for a few minutes," Hassan said. Fraser sat down on a white leather sofa and waited.

Ten minutes later the double doors opened and one of the servants walked over to Fraser. He spoke in hushed English.

"Would you care to follow me sir," he said.

The two men walked out into the hall and then down a wide corridor which opened out into a much bigger room. There stood Hassan, with a handsome, white-bearded man wearing a long robe. In his belt he wore the ornate *Khanjar Haad,* the curved dagger of Oman.

"Uncle, this is the man I told you about. This is my friend from

Sandhurst. Second Lieutenant Fraser MacLean, this is my uncle Qaboos – the Sultan of Oman."

Hassan spent the rest of the holiday ribbing Fraser about the meeting with his uncle. The Scot hadn't twigged for a moment. For the first time in his life he had been lost for words. He had been touched by how regal, yet uncomplicated the Sultan was. In the few hours they spent together, he realised why his people adored the ruler so much. They dined at the palace that night and returned later to Hassan's townhouse in Muscat.

The next day they swam in the Gulf and relaxed before making final preparations to go out into the desert. For the next two-and-a half weeks Fraser and Hassan lived like Bedouin. Their adventure was only interrupted when Hassan had to make a brief visit to the Omani Army's armoured Corps HQ near Niswan. Fraser took the opportunity to explore the ancient capital and stock up on food and water, while his friend visited the special forces unit he would soon command. After visiting the souk and fort, he returned with Hassan to the silence and infinity of the sands.

It was with much regret that Fraser returned to Hassan's townhouse a fortnight later, stripped off his dish-dash and shamagh, bathed for the first time in weeks and left for the night flight back to London.

The two men shook hands and said their goodbyes at the airport.

"I will never forget all you have done for me," said Hassan. "There will always be a life for you here if you want it. You're a good soldier and, well, you could easily be an Arab."

The two men laughed and embraced, then Fraser boarded the plane.

As the Boeing climbed into the indigo Arabian night, a calm descended on him. He was never happier than when he was in the desert. He'd been to many places in the Middle East, but he'd enjoyed this trip to Oman most of all. He'd never known such peace, such contentment as he had in the sands.

The journey he'd plotted for himself was on course. Step one had been achieved, he'd passed out of Sandhurst and become an officer in his father's regiment. His father was wrong though. He assumed his son had followed in his footsteps out of pride and a sense of familial loyalty. He could not have realised what pushed the young man on and what his goals were.

Hassan was right, Fraser would slip in easily to the Omani military, just as dozens of British officers had done before him. But he couldn't, not yet, it wasn't part of the plan. He was being driven on, down a particular route, and it was a one way street with no exits, no diversions. He fell asleep gazing out the window at Kirsty's face among the stars.

The immigration officer at Heathrow Airport looked closely at Fraser MacLean's Passport when he arrived back in the UK the next morning. The youth in the photograph did not resemble the dark-haired, hook-nosed, black-eyed man standing before him. The officer asked Fraser to sit down while he called for his superior. Three weeks in the Omani desert had tanned Fraser's skin deeper than his normal olive. His hair was dirty and uncombed and his beard long and unkempt. He could easily have been an illegal immigrant.

He let the two immigration officials have their game before he showed them his Army ID card and invited them to make a telephone call to Sandhurst to check that he was who he said he was. The men apologised and Fraser went to collect his suitcase from the carousel.

He had three days leave left but couldn't face the journey back to Glasgow. Instead he booked into the Cottage Hotel, a cheap and cheerful place in the shadow of Euston Station, and relaxed. He spent the days in the British Museum and the evenings at the cinema or theatre. Afterwards he'd return to the hotel and dine at one of the many excellent curry houses round the corner, then go to a busy pub called the Jolly Gardener across the road. Every night he bedded a different Kirsty Buchanan.

Before he had left Sandhurst he had boxed his kit and in the three weeks of his absence it had been forwarded to his new address in Münster. All he had with him in London was the suitcase he'd taken back from Oman. The night before he left for Germany he emptied its contents onto the single bed in his tiny hotel room. The only clothing he had with him was the battered suit he was wearing and a couple of clean shirts and some underwear.

He put his soapbag, the clean shirts and the underwear back into the case and closed it. Then, using brown paper, string and tape he'd bought in Woolworths the day before, he wrapped the remainder of his possessions into a parcel.

He wouldn't need the dish-dash, shamagh, sandals, rough cotton trousers and assorted t-shirts ever again. But even though it was unlikely he'd return to the desert, he couldn't bear to part with the clothing he'd worn on his many trips there down the years. After he checked out of the hotel he walked to the nearest post office and mailed the parcel to himself at his parents' home in Glasgow.

MÜNSTER

A new officer joining his battalion in Germany usually takes a trooping flight from Luton airport to the RAF station at Gutersloh. Instead Fraser went overland. He took the tube to Liverpool Street Station and joined the boat train for Harwich. There he boarded the ferry to the Hook of Holland and five hours later the train to Amsterdam. He couldn't afford to stay the night there, so he took the overnight train to Hanover, changing early in the morning at Osnabruck for Münster.

It was bright and sunny when his train pulled in but Fraser felt the early morning chill when he stepped onto the platform. He expected someone to be waiting to collect him, but saw nobody. He went outside but there were no Land Rovers or men in fatigues there either. He sat in the buffet and waited.

The sun was deceiving. It was cold this morning and he was grateful for the piping hot coffee and toasted nussgipfel. It was a shade after seven AM.

The single pip of the Second Lieutenant would look very lonely on his shoulder for the first two years of his Army career, and Fraser knew this. His promotion to Lieutenant, and a second pip, would be automatic, but it would take two years.

Junior officers are called subalterns and they draw the jobs nobody else wants. He knew he would lose count of the number of times he would be asked to be duty officer or be nominated to escort guests. He knew he would have to stay awake for days at a time on exercises or man command posts while his seniors went to the mess for a drink. But it is during these years that a young officer learns a great deal about his job, and more importantly his men. Fraser knew this too. It was another milestone.

"Herr MacLean?" the voice was soft and questioning. Fraser looked up. The threat to the military from the Provisional IRA was great in Germany. Fraser had been expecting two Scottish soldiers wearing anoraks to hide their uniforms, or possibly an officer in a suit. Instead two men, middle-aged and apparently German, stood before him in shabby civilian clothes.

"We have come to collect you," said the second man.

Fraser hesitated - something wasn't quite right. He finished his coffee and picked up his suitcase. Outside the station stood a battered green Volkswagen van. The men opened the rear doors and gestured Fraser to put his luggage inside. He felt uneasy as he hefted his suitcase into the dark interior but was too late to do anything about it when two pairs of hands shoved him in after it.

The engine rasped into life. Fraser immediately tried to feel his way around the van, searching for a door or a window catch. This first of many attempts at escape was fruitless. His initial reaction was to panic. But he quickly overcame it and sat still instead. Shortly his eyes became accustomed to the darkness, as he knew they would.

But he could still see very little. The van's windows had been boarded up with plywood. The two rear doors had also been covered with a layer of wood that hid the interior release handle. There were no seats inside the van and no light. Then came the voice from the front passenger seat telling him he had been kidnapped.

"Ach just relax now Fraser and ye'll be fine." The accent was undoubtedly Irish.

Depending on how he held it, there was just enough light for Fraser to see the luminous hands of his wristwatch. He estimated he'd been picked up at around 7.30 and it was now nearly 10. The van hadn't stopped in that time. It had driven through the streets of Münster, making lots of turns, before reaching what Fraser assumed to be the Autobahn. He noticed also that it had kept to normal speeds, presumably so as not to draw attention to itself.

But why him? What on earth could he know that would be of any use? And why snatch him in broad daylight? That was pretty gutsy. Fraser thought there was something odd about this whole situation. The panic had gone. Now he just felt fear gnawing at him. He'd heard of this sort of thing. The IRA had targeted off-duty military personnel before. Usually they were just shot. They might torture him. But to find out what? He knew nothing that would be of any use to the IRA. Not yet.

The van stopped. It didn't screech to a halt, that would draw attention. Instead it slowed gradually, Fraser thought it also turned to the left. If it came down to unarmed combat against the two men in front, he knew he would be fine. But if there was anyone else, and they were armed, that was different. And if he did overpower the two in the front of the van, what then? Could he try to grab the keys and drive his way out of trouble? That sounded like a plan. He braced himself. He crouched at doors, waiting for the opportunity to burst out, feet and fists flying at whoever was out there. But the doors didn't open. His captors knew what they were doing.

After half an hour in his position he felt his limbs seizing up. He sat down in the corner nearest the driver's seat instead, his ear pressed against the wood in case he might pick up the slightest sound. But he heard nothing.

The silence of the next half hour threw him, disorientated him. Suddenly the doors crashed open and he felt many hands haul him out. But it was still dark and he was dragged from the van into what seemed to be a garage from the smell.

But the smell disappeared when a sandbag was put over his head. It had a peculiar musty odour of its own. His feet hardly touched the ground as he was taken down what he sensed to be a dimly-lit corridor and into a darkened room. He was manhandled a few paces inside then forced to sit down on what felt like a hard wooden kitchen chair. Then he felt himself being handcuffed to its arms.

He could see nothing and instead listened hard for any sign of what was happening. He was sure there were people in the room, a scrape here and shuffle there. The fear was back. And the confusion. Why him? The lights went on and seconds later the sandbag was removed.

He didn't know what to expect, but he certainly didn't expect the scene that met his screwed up eyes. Once the pain of the first bright light for nearly four hours had diminished, he looked around the room. The two men he'd last seen ushering him towards the van at Münster station that morning stood either side of him.

Before him was a desk, behind which sat a thin man wearing small round glasses. On either side of him stood two tall men armed with AK-47s. All three men wore the Feldgrau uniform of the East German Army.

East German?

The room was obviously an office. Its brick walls had been crudely smothered with light green paint. The windows were covered with Germanic shutters and the scene was completed by a single, naked lightbulb dangling above Fraser's head.

"Well now Fraser, it's really good to have you here," said the man by his side. The brogue was certainly Irish. Fraser's ear for language was keen, but he couldn't quite place the region.

"I'm sure you're wondering what this is all about aren't you now," he walked slowly round Fraser's chair as he spoke. He wore old brown cord trousers and a threadbare jacket. There was something odd about his shoes, something about them didn't make sense.

"You don't think we'd manage to exist here on our own do you? We have these guys to help," he stopped pacing and gestured towards the trio in front of him. The East Germans.

East Germans?

Fresh out of Sandhurst, Fraser knew the uniforms of the East Germans. Destined for a posting in Münster, the East Germans would be his enemy if the doctrine was right. The man who sat behind the desk was obviously an officer. He wore the flashes of a Major and on his forage cap Fraser could see the red, yellow and black roundels – the colours of the East German flag. The two guards wore coal scuttle helmets and highly-polished black jackboots. The AKs with their curved magazines were slung across their chests. They were the genuine article. But what were they doing here?

Münster, if that's where they were, was at the other end of the country. They were near the Dutch border. The East German border was hundreds of miles away in the opposite direction.

A safe house? With uniformed East German soldiers in it?

The question confused Fraser, but in his confusion, what struck him the most was the fact that the three men were expressionless and said nothing.

"I'm Paddy," said the Irishman, "but then you'd expect that." He bent over Fraser, his hands on the arms of the chair.

"I know all about you. Everything."

The voice was a whisper, almost a hiss. He stood up, blocking Fraser's view of the three East Germans.

"Our intelligence is every bit as good as yours, every bit. I know that in February the Queen's Own Highlanders will be going to Belfast. Ah, it's lovely in the winter."

Fraser sat stock still. At last they were getting somewhere, whoever *they* were.

"Oh yes, that surprised you didn't it? I know you'll be going as the Roulement Battalion to the Province. Depending on what platoon you get, you'll be off to North Howard Street Mill. Only, you'll be reporting to me and not your company commander."

Fraser spoke for the first time since he'd ordered coffee at the station.

"You can go and fuck yourself."

"Ah, the bravado! Sandhurst's a great place, sure and it is," said Paddy mockingly. Fraser struggled to get off the chair but the handcuffs held him tightly.

The Irishman was about 35 and looked fit. But Fraser felt he could take him – if only he could get the handcuffs off. The other three, all armed - two with machine guns, well that was a different matter.

"And what makes you think I won't be going straight to my company commander the moment you release me?" said Fraser.

Paddy stepped over to him and placed his hands on the arms of the chair again.

"Because I know all about Kirsty," he said softly.

The name thrust into Fraser's heart. The fear was back. The confusion had gone. He'd read about this kind of thing. It went on in the shady world of espionage; it happened to other people. It did not happen to him.

"We got to you, we can get to her," said Paddy again, "unless you help us."

Fraser raced through the dilemma. He had just arrived in Germany and had been kidnapped before he'd even got to his battalion. They knew what train he'd been on but hadn't come to pick him up.

What time would he be missed? How long would it take to work out what had happened? They'd probably think he was late, had too good a time in Amsterdam and had missed his train.

He hadn't even started with his new battalion and here he was being talent-spotted by the IRA. And they knew about Kirsty. They probably knew it all, chapter and verse. Where she lived, what she was doing now – the things Fraser never wanted to know, the things that would eat him up and the things he went out of his way to avoid finding out.

But could he bear the thought of her being hurt?

He knew the IRA were ruthless and could reach out across the world and kill her, or worse.

Did he want that? Was she still on that pedestal? Was she still that untouchable part of him, that part which must never be mentioned, never be thought of?

He hadn't seen her since that summer night in Paris six years before when she'd gone off with the American. And though he knew she was married now and lived her own life far away from everything they'd ever known together as schoolchildren, could he take the thought of her being in pain? Because that's what would happen if he didn't cooperate here. They'd get to her and it would be his fault.

The mention of Kirsty's name meant this was for real. Fraser had been struggling with the situation. The IRA man Paddy, if that was his real name, was a possibility. He knew the IRA had active service units all over the place; several in Europe. That was believable. The three stooges opposite him were hardly credible. The East Germans would have plenty of agents in West Germany, but Fraser couldn't imagine the circumstances that would see them in uniform. And armed? Never. But now Kirsty had been brought into the equation.

His head was bowed now. He felt very tired and closed his eyes for a few seconds. He couldn't let her be harmed. Even though she belonged to another man, he couldn't think about her being in pain. He could not stand it, even after all these years. But equally he couldn't cooperate either. He hated the IRA, not because he didn't agree with their cause, because part of him did. He hated any terrorist, anyone who put a bomb in a rubbish bin and killed innocent people for a cause. If they were real soldiers then let them fight a real fight, like real soldiers would.

Real soldiers.

He opened his eyes. Paddy stood before him, his feet apart. The shoes were black brogues, thick-soled black leather brogues. The toes had been bulled, but not this morning. Fraser had a pair of shoes identical to these, but they were brand new and still in their box.

These were old shoes.

Real soldier's shoes.

Barrack dress brogues.

He looked up and spoke slowly in German to the three uniforms.

"You're not really East German are you?"

The three men continued to stare blankly at him.

"Then who the fuck are you?" he yelled, "what the fuck is this all about?"

Paddy picked up the sandbag and hooded Fraser with it again.

"I'll fucking show you who we are," he whispered and dragged Fraser into the corridor again. But instead of going back into the smelly garage they went outside and Fraser could feel the warmth of the day on his body. Suddenly the hands left him and he felt the cuffs removed from his wrists.

Somewhere he thought he heard a stifled laugh. But that couldn't be so. And where was Paddy? Now that the cuffs were off, Fraser would be ready with his fists. He waited for a few seconds then pulled the sandbag from his head.

There, in uniform, stood his brother Euan. Behind him, on the parade square of Buller Barracks in Münster, stood the officers of the Queen's Own Highlanders.

"Welcome to the battalion Fraser," said Euan. "Thanks for being such a good sport."

2

As initiations went, it was a good one and would be remembered in the battalion for years. Officers would recount the tale to much laughter on many a mess dinner night. It became known as the day MacLean junior came to town and became part of regimental folklore.

Sometimes young officers arriving at their new battalions would be told to change into uniform straight away and were sent to man an overnight OP on a building, only to find in the morning that the building was part of their own camp. Another wheeze was to set up a mock HQ and leave the new officer alone in it for a while. As if by magic the phones would start ringing and radios receiving and details of some major event would come in, all fictitious of course. Before bullying allegations put an end to the more bizarre initiations, some cavalry regiments even tied up new officers and dangled them from the barrels of their own tanks.

A young officer is well advised to grin and bear it. It is an important part of his career. To be seen not to 'show form' is regarded as a black mark, almost on day one.

And to be fair to him, Fraser joined in. His first day with his battalion was a very important one and it wouldn't do to be seen not to take part. So he laughed with the rest of them and took the handshakes and the slaps on the back. For he was accepted now, part of the team, a member of the brotherhood. And to prove it, that very night in the mess, he and the rest of the officers began a champagne-fuelled plot for the next hapless subaltern scheduled to join them from Sandhurst a fortnight hence.

That afternoon the AKs, used to instruct soldiers on Eastern Bloc weaponry, went back to the armoury. The three East German uniforms were returned to the wardrobes of the officers who'd bought them for 200 Marlboros in East Berlin. And the dark green VW van went back to the rifle range where it was used to transport the Figure 11 targets back to the workshops for repair.

By eight that night the two East Germans became West German civilian rifle range staff and Paddy was reincarnated as WO2 Billy McLaren from Londonderry, Fraser MacLean's first Company Sergeant Major.

After the champagne had stopped flowing that first night, Euan walked Fraser back to his room in the mess. Outwardly he had partaken in all the bravado and drinking that went with such a special day in a young officer's life. Inwardly he felt much different. And Kirsty made the difference. It had obviously been part of the plan. And it had worked. But what else had been said? What other little pieces of trivia had been passed on by Euan? For trivia to anyone else meant just that, but to a soldier it meant intelligence.

They got to the younger man's door. Fraser opened it and gestured Euan inside, as though for a nightcap or to continue their conversation. But when they stepped over the threshold Fraser grabbed his brother by the scruff of the neck and hauled him forwards inside the room until his head battered against the opposite wall.

Euan collapsed onto the floor, confused in his drunkenness. A tiny rivulet of blood trickled down his temple.

"If her name is ever mentioned again," hissed Fraser, "I'll fucking cripple you."

3

Fraser MacLean spent less than a month in Münster with his new battalion before he returned to the UK to undertake the Platoon Commander's Battle Course at the aptly-named Wiltshire town of Warminster. While in Münster he'd had time only to learn 'jock bopping' – the Highland dance routines peculiar to the Queen's Own Highlanders.

But in Warminster, over the next three months, he learnt the specialized infantry tactics he would need to command a rifle platoon. As he did at Sandhurst, while crawling through the mud of Salisbury Plain, Fraser MacLean impressed instructors and fellow students alike. His thinking was lateral. he was the fittest student they'd ever seen and he led by example. He walked off with the best student prize.

He returned to Germany to take command of his first platoon. He ran with them and dug with them and fought with them on the plains of West Germany. He bashad up with them, brewed up with them and shared the same love/hate relationship with their old 432 armoured personnel carriers. He laughed and cried with them and shared the highs and lows of life in the British Army of the Rhine.

He learned to spot when one of his boys received a 'Dear John' letter or when another wasn't pulling his weight. He learned how to rely on his Platoon Sergeant, an older and more experienced soldier, but a man of lower rank. All the lectures and exercises and essays and tutorials fell into place. He practiced what he had learned, and for the first time it all made sense.

It is often said that the years spent at school are the best of one's life. In the Army, the years spent as a platoon commander draw comparison. It is a simple, uncluttered and incredibly fulfilling life. It is soldiering at its most basic and enjoyable level.

And as he loved his soldiers, they grew to love him. They quickly learned respect for him and saw him as an extremely talented and hard but fair officer who would expect them to do nothing he wouldn't do himself. They took pride in their work and quickly became regarded as the best platoon in the battalion.

Fraser returned to Buller from leave one Sunday to find his room in the mess emptied of every fixture and fitting. After scanning the floorboards and bare walls for a few seconds, he realized what had happened. It took an hour but he eventually found his room, reproduced faithfully from the curtains to the slippers under the bed, on the vehicle park. He laughed long and hard - it meant he'd been accepted by his boys.

Army humour is brutal and retribution swift. He got his own back when his platoon were attending a lecture on VD. With the accommodation block empty, he carefully urinated in every electric fan heater he could find – making sure they'd all been switched off first. When the time came to use them, the smell would be unbearable.

Fraser laughed aloud at his prank. He hadn't had so much fun since he'd got his revenge on the Sgt Major for his part in the initiation. Paddy had gone away on a course and Fraser had waited until dark before stealing into his room. Then he emptied a dozen packets of watercress seeds on the carpet and drizzled a watering can over the room for fully 20 minutes. Then he switched on the heating and left.

The Sgt Major was less than amused when he returned.

In 1989, a year after he left PCBC, he went with the rest of the battalion to Canada for his first major exercise. BATUS, the British Army Training Unit, Suffield, accommodates battlegroup training and live firing over the vast empty expanse of prairie. Fraser loved every moment.

From the day he joined the battalion, he was under the microscope. His superiors noticed he was an exceptionally hard worker, a gifted linguist and a fine young officer who was respected by his men.

They looked on admiringly as he joined in mess life and played his part in the regimental community with gusto. He was involved in games of mess rugby on dinner nights, where immaculate mess kit was often ripped and cutlery smashed, as two teams scrummed and rucked in the dining room. And he took part in childish challenges like trying to navigate round the outside of the ante-room using only the furniture - anyone touching the floor had to forfeit a bottle of champagne. They even suspected him of riding a motorbike up and down the mess corridors one night, although they could never pin it on him.

They knew who he was; his brother was now a Lieutenant in the battalion and his father had once commanded it. That was it. That was why he was so good. It ran in the family, the name, the tradition, the history – the regiment.

Fraser was quite happy for people to think his family connections drove him on. He knew nobody could really know why. They didn't understand that it wasn't simply that he wanted to follow in the footsteps of his father and his brother. No, there was much more to it than that.

He wanted to be *better* than them.

However, his main motivation was, even now, even after all these years, Kirsty, and what had happened in Paris. But he prayed that nobody in the battalion knew it.

Fraser MacLean was content that the milestones were passing slowly but surely. All that was missing was action, real action in which to prove himself before Kirsty and his family.

But his carefully considered plan, his career, the journey of his life, came unstuck on September 10th 1989.

That day Hungary opened one crossing point on its lengthy border with Austria and the first tentative step was taken towards pulling down the Iron Curtain. Thousands of people left East Germany and drove in their Trabants and Zastavas south into Czechoslovakia and then Hungary to queue for hours at the frontier before finally crossing into Austria and freedom.

After that, the people spoke across Eastern Europe. Hungary was first, then Bulgaria, then Czechoslovakia. Soon democracy touched the rest of the former Soviet Bloc.

In November, Fraser MacLean stood in the Buller mess with his brother officers and watched the historic TV pictures of the Berlin Wall coming down.

It was over.

The Cold War was at an end and the British Army in Germany was not now expecting to face the massive Soviet hordes sweeping west across the North German plain. In the space of a few months, decades of military build-up was rendered redundant.

The Queen's Own Highlanders undertook a rigorous programme of pre-Northern Ireland training ahead of their Christmas and New Year leave. The scenarios were all similar to those they'd have to deal with when they went to the Province in February. Life in Ulster was a wholly different prospect to that of an armoured infantry soldier in West Germany. The threat was different. The threat was real. The threat was terrorism.

Before they left for Northern Ireland, the world had changed yet further. Czechoslovakia had a new, democratically-elected non-Communist government and at Christmas the people of Romania rose and overthrew the despotic President Nicolae Ceausescu, executing him publicly on Christmas Day.

During the first months of their tour in the Province, the three Baltic states of Latvia, Lithuania and Estonia proclaimed their independence from the Soviet Union. On May 5th East and West Germany began talks to discuss their unification.

Fraser MacLean and his soldiers patrolled the scarred city of Belfast. They lifted suspected terrorists, they dodged blast bombs and they watched and they waited. They knew that when they returned to Germany their traditional enemies, the armies of the Warsaw Pact, would be gone and the closest they would ever come to any real action again would be here in Northern Ireland.

It was July 1990.

4

The Organisation of Petroleum Exporting Countries, or OPEC, is based in Vienna. It has no army and no weapons, yet it is arguably the most powerful body on earth. It controls the supply and price of oil and therefore impacts upon every consumer in the world. Decisions made by OPEC have bearing not only on fuel for domestic and industrial use, but on medicines, plastics and cosmetics.

From the end of 1988 and all through 1989, Iraq lobbied OPEC to save its economy. Iraq had just fought a hugely damaging war with its neighbour Iran and was struggling to balance its books despite being one of the richest nations on earth.

Iraq blamed another neighbour, Kuwait, for the problems. The Iraqi President, Saddam Hussein, complained repeatedly that the Kuwaitis were flooding the world market with cheap oil and were keeping prices artificially low.

The wider world paid scant attention to this. The west - especially the United States and the United Kingdom - did have its eye on the Middle East, but more particularly on Libya and Syria whom it suspected of carrying out the bombing of a Pan-Am airliner over the Scottish town of Lockerbie in December 1988. Events in the northern Gulf were not high on the international agenda, except for the ceasefire between Iraq and Iran after the 1980-88 war.

Britain enjoyed reasonable relations with Baghdad at this time, except when the Observer journalist Farzad Bazoft was arrested and sentenced to death for espionage. London kept an embassy in the Iraqi capital and its diplomats were able to travel freely within the country.

It was on one such trip, on July 16th 1990, that one of the consular staff at the embassy noticed heavy military traffic heading south along the Basra Road. A former troop commander in the Kings Royal Hussars, the diplomat counted the hardware and took surreptitious photographs. And when he returned to the embassy in Baghdad after his trip, he made a telephone call to a friend in the American Embassy who knew a man, who knew a man.

Minutes later the data had been encrypted and flashed by secure satellite link across the globe to the State Department and the Pentagon in Washington and the Foreign and Commonwealth Office and the Ministry of Defence in London. The message was simple. Three armoured Divisions of the Iraqi Republican Guard were lining up along the border with Kuwait.

There followed two weeks of intense diplomatic activity, and visits to the Iraqi President, Saddam Hussein, by friends in the Arab world. They all urged caution and they all came away from talks in Baghdad saying this was a show of force designed to worry Kuwait, nothing more. The world watched closely, but relaxed.

This is the Middle East. This is what happens here. This is how nations in this part of the world go about their business, they said.

It's only a bit of sabre-rattling, that's all. There's nothing to worry about.

But on August 2nd 1990, Iraq invaded Kuwait.

5

He was much scorned by his brother officers in the mess at Buller when he spoke his mind. Most of his comrades laughed aloud, others took apart his argument strand by strand and analysed it logically and militarily. The foolish made bets. But Fraser MacLean stood by his belief that the Queen's Own Highlanders would move from its base in Germany and go to the Gulf where it would fight to liberate Kuwait from the Iraqi invaders.

Some said the prospect of any British involvement was preposterous. Others said any military involvement in the Gulf would simply be to defend Saudi Arabia from the Iraqis. And even then it would involve the Americans alone, with any British contribution coming from the Royal Air Force only. The proponents of that argument felt vindicated when, a week after the invasion, the Ministry of Defence announced the launch of Operation Granby and the hasty despatch to Saudi Arabia of a squadron each of Tornado and Jaguar fighter bombers to help defend the kingdom.

Fraser MacLean stuck to his guns all through August when hundreds of thousands of US troops were moved to Saudi Arabia from their bases all over the world. And he refused to admit defeat even on September 15th when the government announced that Britain *would* send ground troops after all, but not the Queen's Own Highlanders.

The British Army's 7th Armoured Brigade, the famous Desert Rats, would move in entirety from Germany to Saudi Arabia, but the Queen's Own, part of a different formation, would stay put. He stood in the mess and told anyone who would listen that the Queen's Own Highlanders would eventually go to the Gulf too.

Iraq showed no signs of leaving Kuwait. In fact it strengthened its military positions and offended the world yet further by committing a string of atrocities against the civilian population. Soldiers looted the shops and banks, and civilians suspected of being involved in resistance were tortured before being summarily and publicly executed.

As time passed, the situation in the Gulf deteriorated. Diplomatic shuttles to Baghdad by the Jordanian King, Hussein, and the Egyptian President Hosni Mubarrak came and went without success. The Soviet Union, long an ally of Baghdad, did its best as did the UN Secretary General, Javier Perez De Cuellar. They all returned with the same simple response from Saddam Hussein – Kuwait belonged to Iraq and the invaders were staying put.

In November 1990 such a position prompted the United Nations to pass Resolution 678, which said that unless Iraqi forces left Kuwait by January 15th 1991, the allied coalition would be granted the power to use "all measures necessary" to remove them militarily.

Towards the end of the month the British Army had done its sums and realised that if the American plan to liberate Kuwait was to be put into action, 7 Brigade would need to be reinforced. The Ministry of Defence called for several more units to be brought forward.

Among them was the Queen's Own Highlanders.

Fraser MacLean took it all with good grace and didn't rub anyone's nose in it. His friends who'd made bets handed over their cash quietly. They asked how he knew. But he just smiled.

This prediction confirmed what his superiors had long suspected - Fraser MacLean was something special. He was an excellent young officer and arguably the best subaltern the regiment had ever seen. That he was capable there was no doubt; that he was talented was obvious. But there was something else.

The whole Gulf premonition was just an isolated example. They knew he'd lived in Iraq, studied the Arab lifestyle and was fluent in the language. Was that it? Is that how he knew Iraq would do it? No, there was more than that.

He was quietly confident about everything. It was as if he possessed some kind of second sight – he always had his eye on something in the distance, in the future, and that everything in between was irrelevant. No problem vexed him; no number of irritations diverted him from his aim. He stood head and shoulders above his contemporaries, including a proud, but rueful, brother.

The battalion would go to the Gulf in dribs and drabs, some elements before Christmas, others early in the New Year. That Christmas Fraser and Euan returned home to see their parents before leaving for what both men knew in their heart of hearts would be a war. Fraser dreaded the thought of going home to Glasgow, but while he didn't especially want to see his father, he was desperate to see his mother. He had deliberately cut familial ties but he missed her terribly.

They drove, largely in silence, from Münster to Zeebrugge in Belgium where they took the overnight ferry to Hull. On the long drive north, when they did speak, they spoke of things far removed from the Army and the impending war. There would be enough talk of those subjects shortly.

Their mother fussed over them as they knew she would, and they let her. It would be the last time for a while they would enjoy any comforts, far less the comforts of home. They ate and drank too much over the 10 days of their break and Fraser grudgingly admitted to himself that he actually rather enjoyed it.

There was still a minute chance he might bump into Kirsty, so he hardly left the house and on more than one occasion found himself alone with his father in the lounge. They skirted around any issue of real importance and Fraser made a point of avoiding discussion of the war. He forced himself to be convivial and managed to change the subject whenever his father started a conversation about when he'd been a young officer. He'd leave those chats to Euan.

The three men made a pact of not discussing anything at the dinner table which would upset their mother. But during their

Christmas lunch they paused to watch the Queen's speech which focussed on impending events in the Gulf. They listened in silence. Afterwards, when the national anthem was played, she burst into tears and ran from the table into the kitchen.

The 10 days were up. The brothers had to return to Münster to put the finishing touches to their platoons' preparations for the trip to the Gulf. The armoured vehicles, the low squat 432s that had been in service for decades and which would be in service for decades to come, had already been loaded onto ships at Emden harbour and were heading for the Gulf. Soon the soldiers would follow.

There were tears the morning Euan and Fraser left Glasgow. Their father did his best to placate their mother, but she wept as they said their farewells at the front gate. Tough fighting men they may have been, but they were taking a step into the unknown and they shed a tear too.

"I won't say good luck, because it's bad luck," she said, forcing a smile through the tears. "But you'll be careful. I know you will."

"You'll send us both food parcels, won't you?" asked Euan brightly, trying to take her mind off things. "Tins of sardines, tuna and the like? We'd really like that wouldn't we Fras?"

"Oh yeah. Sardines. Absolutely," replied Fraser, on cue. He didn't really know what to say. This was awful. Agony. He wanted to go, jump into the car and eat up the miles down the road to Hull, the ferry and Germany.

The brothers hugged her. It felt like she'd shrunk somehow; she was thin and cold.

"Don't volunteer for anything," she said and started to cry again.

They turned to their father, who shook their hands and smiled.

Fraser cringed. He was expecting to hear a speech about honour and duty. But his father's words were few.

"Cuidich 'n Righ," he said.

SAUDI ARABIA

Because of the complex nature of the war plan, The Queen's Own Highlanders didn't deploy to the Gulf as one complete unit. That would have been excellent for morale but such a move would have been far too simple for military planners. Instead, elements were sent piecemeal.

Battalion HQ would command the Armoured Delivery Group, a massive reserve of armour and armoured infantry reinforcements to be used to replace casualties.

A Company would be the guard force protecting the HQ of the British Division, if and when it deployed into Iraq. B Company would remain in Saudi Arabia and protect the Riyadh HQ of all British forces in the Middle East.

The regimental band had already gone to the Gulf. It had been sent out in October 1990 to take up its war role as medics.

Once in theatre, the rest of the battalion would stand by for orders.

Like most soldiers, while he had every respect for their pilots, especially the search and rescue helicopter boys, Fraser had quickly developed a loathing for the Royal Air Force. Although early in his Army career, he had lost count of the number of times he had been delayed because of technical difficulties on aircraft. He felt as though he had spent months of his life waiting at air bases around the world for the right part to come through from the UK so his journey could be completed. The airmen who worked in RAF parts departments only worked office hours – soldiers seldom did.

He also despaired at how it took the RAF twice as long as any civilian airline to load an aircraft and why it needed to cause as much hassle as possible for any soldiers travelling. He'd seen for himself how RAF personnel lived in hotels on exercises and operations, while soldiers roughed it in shell scrapes and bashas. He promised himself the next time an airman said to him "we check-in, you dig-in" he'd smack him in the mouth.

He'd also heard about the near mutiny on one flight from Canada when a battalion returning from a long and arduous exercise at BATUS had to wait on the tarmac and watch while a visiting RAF rugby team boarded the aircraft ahead of them and took the seats reserved for VIPs.

The commanding officer is said to have taken the pilot aside and hinted to him that unless everybody sat in the main cabin, there might be a bit of a fight.

It was therefore some relief to them that the RAF had no dealings in getting Fraser and Euan to the Gulf. They checked in together for the chartered Kuwaiti Airlines Boeing 747 which took the battalion from Hanover airport to Riyadh in early January 1991. Even the ropiest bucket shop charter flight would ensure matters ran far more smoothly than the RAF.

Apart from pleasantries and day to day military matters, until Christmas and the drive to Glasgow they hadn't shared a deep conversation since they were teenagers. Now it was real - they were going to war. As they sat together, they reminisced about their father's Army experiences and how he'd regaled them with the stories ad nauseum during their childhood. Euan said these stories made him want to join up.

If Fraser was being honest he would have said it was these stories, along with being an 'army brat', moving house a dozen times because of his father's job, which made him *not* want to join up and seek a career in academia instead.

If he was being even more honest he would have admitted that the real reason he joined the Army was to prove to Kirsty Buchanan that he was a man and to show his father and brother that he was a better soldier. But impending war or not, that was still a part of him he kept very much to himself. There would be no cathartic soul-cleansing, no confessional.

Many imagine a desert to be baking hot all year round. But in January 1991 Northern Saudi Arabia was mild and not unpleasant by day, but freezing cold by night. The officers and men of the Queen's Own Highlanders were processed into theatre at the air base at Al-Jubail where they landed. They overnighted at a transit camp there before beginning the long and uncomfortable road journey to their positions deep in the Saudi desert. There they would prepare for war.

Their first duty was to stand in long lines outside the medics' tents for the myriad inoculations they would need to combat the infections they might face in such an alien environment. Each man received up to eight injections for diseases ranging from hepatitis to plague to anthrax. As is often the way among tough fighting men, a number collapsed in embarrassed heaps before, during and immediately after the process. Fraser's fear of needles had long evaporated.

They also began taking anti-malarial tablets and were taken aside for a special issue of NAPS and BATS – the NBC threat was all too real. The Nerve Agent Pre-treatment Sets and the Biological Antibiotic Treatment Sets were specific drugs designed to be taken before and after a chemical or biological weapon strike.

The NAPS were made from bromide, the legendary chemical added to soldiers' tea to suppress their libido, and had to be taken every eight hours. A rumour started doing the rounds that the bromide was so strong in the 1991 issue that it made you impotent. Many Queen's Own Highlanders secretly dropped their issue down the field latrine.

The BATS were a very strong antibiotic called Ciproxin, designed to be taken after a biological strike. They had to be kept on a soldier's person at all times. Nobody wanted to contemplate using them, or the Atropine combopen syringes which each had to keep in his respirator haversack. These were to be used to inject a victim of a biological attack after he became infected.

At every possible moment it was drummed into the soldiers that Saddam Hussein had used weapons of mass destruction before.

Any soldier will tell you that being in a theatre of war but not being involved, is worse than not being in theatre at all. Fraser and his fellow subalterns were devastated when they learned the plans for their battalion, which were passed down the chain of command to them by the British Commander, General Sir Peter de la Billiere. The remainder of the Queen's Own Highlanders would be kept in reserve as BCRs – battle casualty replacements. As and when the ground war was prosecuted, they would stay in the rear. If they were called forward, it meant that something had gone very badly wrong.

Every one of the officers and men moaned and complained. But their protestations to de la Billiere's staff fell on deaf ears. Someone had to be held in reserve. They were relative newcomers to theatre. All the other units were in place, acclimatised and fully up to speed with their training and preparations. It made military sense. The battalion did the Army thing, bit the bullet and got on with it.

The Queen's Own Highlanders was part of 33 Brigade, an element of the 3rd UK Armoured Division, normally based in Germany to counter Soviet invasion. It was a mechanised infantry battalion and would go to war in its 432s. Home for the battalion was a series of tents and defensive positions just south of the

TAPline road, which marked the border between Saudi Arabia and Iraq. The Trans Arab Pipeline had been built by the British in the early days of oil exploration in the Middle East. The men who built it would surely never have envisaged the masses of men and material lined up on the southern side waiting to go to war.

The Americans had nearly half a million personnel ready to fight to liberate Kuwait. The UK had a fraction of that. And while the rest of the British contingent readied themselves to take part, Fraser MacLean and his brother officers sat in their tents and brooded. They would be idle.

As soldiers do, for reasons of discipline and morale, the Queen's Own Highlanders formed a routine. The men would rise at 6 am and exercise before it became too hot. This was usually a run followed by some press-ups and sit-ups. Others would skip; a few rigged up a punchbag; some even managed to mark out a football pitch on the shale sand of the desert floor and kick a ball about. Then they would rinse off the sweat and dust under communal showers fashioned from plastic buckets distributing tepid, but usually cold, water.

Clean, refreshed and ready for the day, the soldiers would then line up in the mess tents for a breakfast, which was usually less than healthy. But as Napolean pointed out, an army marched on its belly. Then they would return to their tents and prepare their equipment for the day's activities.

It still wasn't especially hot during the day but the desert environment was alien to the battalion and acclimatisation training was critical. They would drive down to the makeshift ranges and fire their weapons or practise debussing drills in their 432s. They would eat lunch out on the ground, growing more used to the heat and the sand every day, and return to the camp at night.

Each evening the men would clean their weapons and equipment and prepare for the next day's training. While the soldiers relaxed by playing cards, reading or writing letters, the officers would sit around their radios listening to the news on the BBC World Service. They hoped for a suggestion that de la Billiere's plan had changed and that they would be used in the battle and not kept in reserve. But each night they climbed into their sleeping bags frustrated.

Time was passing. Each day they got closer to the January 15th deadline imposed by the United Nations for Iraq to withdraw from Kuwait. Each day came and went without word of the Allies' move to the front line.

Their frustration was echoed by every other unit in the Gulf on January 9th when it looked as though there might be a diplomatic breakthrough. To come so far and not be involved was a hard pill to swallow for any military man. Despite the hundreds of thousands of men deployed to the region and the millions of vehicles and aircraft ready to liberate Kuwait at the drop of a hat, it looked as though the suits would win the day.

There was only one TV set in the Queen's Own Highlanders camp and that was in the main messtent. It was tuned to the American news channel CNN and hundreds of people crowded round it that night to see the late bulletin.

2

It was cold three time zones away. Dressed in a heavy overcoat and Astrakhan hat against the bitter evening chill, Foreign Minister Tariq Aziz descended the steps of the Iraqi Airways Boeing 707 at Geneva airport. A motorcade took him to the Intercontinental Hotel where the American Secretary of State James Baker was waiting.

The men had a six hour-long meeting in the hotel's presidential suite. Secretary of State Baker held a letter from President George Bush to the Iraqi President, Saddam Hussein. It exhorted the Iraqi leader to comply with UN resolutions and remove his forces from Kuwait immediately. It also contained a reminder for Saddam Hussein in case he was considering the use of weapons of mass destruction, in other words nuclear, biological or chemical weapons. It was a stark one - the US possessed these weapons too. It also warned Baghdad that it could not expect to dictate the terms of any war with the US and its allies as it had done in the war it had fought with Iran between 1980 and 1988.

Tariq Aziz told James Baker in response that Iraq was the cradle of civilisation and was more than 6,000 years-old. He conceded that the US had a massive military and would inflict serious losses on the Iraqi armed forces. But he told James Baker that his country would survive and the current leadership, and not the US, would dictate the country's future.

Mr Aziz read the letter but politely refused to take it to Baghdad. He stood before the flashguns and TV lights of the world's media a few minutes after the talks broke up and explained why. Millions of people across the globe stopped what they were doing and watched the most eagerly-awaited news conference the world had known for years.

He said he had declined to carry the letter to Saddam Hussein because it contained a threat and was not written in the kind of language one would expect in a communication between the leaders of two great nations. The letter stayed in Mr Baker's briefcase. Mr Aziz returned to the airport and flew back to Baghdad. War was now inevitable.

The news was greeted with a perverse sense of relief by coalition soldiers all across the Gulf. While nobody relished the prospect of what would doubtless be a bloody war, equally, they didn't want Iraq to wriggle out of Kuwait without being held accountable for its actions.

The next day, January 10th, the United States Congress started three days of debate about whether or not to rubber stamp the President's war plan. George Bush could not give the green light to his forces without Congress's say so. To do so would risk his impeachment. He needn't have worried. Geneva swung it. Even the doubters realised that if Baghdad had been remotely serious about a peaceful solution, it would have acted in Switzerland.

After the vote, Vice President Dan Quayle told the house the result. The yeas were 52, the nays 47.

In a final attempt to prevent the war, the Jordanian King Hussein again travelled to Baghdad for talks with his old friend Saddam Hussein. The two countries have long been allies and he tried to persuade the Iraqi leader to pull out of Kuwait. But that day the King's words fell on deaf ears.

"God is with us," said Saddam Hussein, and the King returned to Amman empty-handed.

The UN deadline for Iraq to begin withdrawal from Kuwait was January 15th 1991. That morning at dawn President George Bush signed the order for the US-led coalition to go to war.

3

At one am on the morning of January 17th 1991, Task Force Normandy took off. It comprised a flight of Apache Attack Helicopters armed with Hellfire guided missiles. They lifted into the inky Gulf sky from their base in Northern Saudi Arabia and headed low over the border into South-west Iraq. Their target was not the massed infantry positions surrounding occupied Kuwait or the armoured divisions dug into the desert sands. Instead it would strike the first blow of the war against two radar sites in the southern Iraqi desert.

At eight miles out the commander called the aircraft into line abreast formation and ordered them to hover. Each pilot ignored the blackness beyond their windshields and instead studied the TV screens on the control panels in front of them. Infra red cameras in the helicopters' chins cut through the night sky and illuminated the targets. Each aircraft painted the dishes and buildings of the target sites with a splash of energy from its on-board laser target designator. The Hellfire missiles, whose laser-sniffing noses would seek out the splash, were already warming-up on the weapon pods beneath the helicopter's stubby wings.

Once all the targets were "lased and acquired," the commander keyed the radio transmit button on his control column and spoke the pre-arranged codewords to start the Gulf War.

"Get some," he said.

The attack last four minutes and was a complete success. The radar early warning system, which would have alerted the Iraqis to the oncoming armada of 1,700 coalition warplanes, was totally destroyed. The first waves of aircraft could leave their bases in Saudi Arabia or aircraft carriers in the Gulf and fly for Baghdad with impunity. Once there, the primary targets were more radar dishes and communications centres – the eyes and ears of the Iraqis. When these had been destroyed, the allies could pick and choose the rest of their targets safe in the knowledge that the Iraqis couldn't see them, far less touch them.

But while the Iraqis couldn't harm the allied air forces, they had a shock tactic of their own. Shortly after Baghdad erupted in explosions that night, Saddam Hussein ordered eight Scud missiles to be fired at Israel.

This was the allies' worst nightmare. Israel had so far stayed out of the war, but that night it launched a flight of F-16 fighter-bombers to retaliate. But by doing so it endangered the coalition of Arab countries lining up to fight against Iraq. If Israel joined the war, countries like Egypt and Syria would not fight with the Israelis against brother Arabs. This fact was not lost on Saddam Hussein.

There was a further complication. The jets would have to overfly Jordan to get to their targets. Jordan had so far remained neutral, but was deemed to be pro-Iraqi. If Amman realised the F-16s had used its airspace, it might join the war - on Iraq's side. The whole situation was fraught with problems for the coalition.

In the end the Scuds killed nobody in Israel, apart from one woman who died from a heart attack. Some high level wheeling and dealing on the hotline between Washington and Tel Aviv saw the F-16s turn back and return home with their weapons still attached to the underwing pylons.

The next day the US ordered as many Patriot anti-missile missile batteries as it could spare to be sent to Israel.

But that night Saddam Hussein also launched Scuds into Saudi Arabia, and although destined for Riyadh and Dharan, the sensors set off the NBC alarms as they overflew military encampments in the desert en route to their targets. Fraser and his comrades were in and out of their NBC suits and respirators dozens of times from then on.

Saddam Hussein had used WMD in the past. However this time, with the world's mightiest arsenal facing him, he would only fit his Scud missiles with conventional high explosive warheads. But nobody was to know that, and every soldier carried his respirator on his hip, and NBC suit in his daysack, everywhere he went from the latrines, to the showers, to the cookhouse.

Despite the repeated NBC alarms, and even though they could feel the vibrations of the millions of tonnes of high explosives detonating on the other side of the border, and hear thousands of jet aircraft overhead every night, war still seemed incredibly far away for the Queen's Own Highlanders. Fraser MacLean and his brother officers felt more and more like Cinderellas. Nobody in his right mind wanted a war, yet a huge part of him longed for some personal involvement.

On February 1st, two weeks into the air war, he got his wish.

Just after breakfast that morning the RSM tapped him on the shoulder and asked him to report to the Commanding Officer's tent. He stamped to attention, threw up a salute and did what all soldiers do in this position - wondered what he had done wrong.

Lieutenant Colonel Iain MacLaren was 43 and a career soldier. He was fit and capable and Fraser respected him immensely. He was no fool and realised immediately what was on his subaltern's mind.

"Relax," he said, "you haven't been cashiered or anything. Quite the reverse in fact." Fraser untensed his muscles and exhaled, too noisily for his own liking.

"The Fusiliers battlegroup is short and has trawled for augmentees. I've given them men to augment their Milan and mortar platoons – and I'm giving them a rifle platoon," he stabbed his finger out over the desk, "your platoon."

Fraser's heart jumped. The Fusiliers were in the front line and would be in the thick of any ground war.

"Thank you very much indeed sir, I won't let you down," he said.

It was trite, it was a cliché, it was what was expected.

"It makes sense," said the CO. "The reputation of the entire regiment rests on whoever I send. I'd rather that was you. You've lived in Iraq, you know what's what there. You know how they think, how they feel. Also, you speak the lingo, which can only be an asset in a scheme like this, and," he paused and fidgeted with his pen, "well, I know it shouldn't matter, and in all honesty it doesn't in this case, but I'm an old friend of your father's."

Ordinarily, in any other circumstances, the remark would have angered Fraser. He'd worked very hard indeed to be his own man and wanted to get as far as he could in his father's regiment by his own actions and not by reputation. But this time it didn't bother him. He didn't care that unknowingly his father had helped him in this venture.

A million thoughts raced through his mind as he sat in the CO's tent. First and foremost was that he would be going into action and that his brother wouldn't. At last it was happening for him. At last he'd have something to say during those excruciating meals when his father spoke about the Seaforths and Camerons surrendering to Rommel at St Valery in 1940, or crossing the Irrawady five years later.

Euan was visibly shocked by the news but put on a brave smile when they met in the queue for lunch. "Good for you," he said shaking Fraser's hand briskly, "I know you'll do well. For the regiment I mean - and for Dad." The two young men held each other's eye for a second longer than was comfortable. Euan knew of the tension between Fraser and their father. They said their farewells after lunch and Euan went back to his platoon. Fraser returned to his tent and packed his kit.

His platoon would move that night to the final assembly area, known as 'Ray' which lay north of their position and close to the Iraqi border. Fraser would be accompanied by a buckshee Captain from the Battalion HQ, a Sergeant from a different platoon and a Company Sergeant Major to work as a liaison team with the Fusiliers. Fraser was delighted. The Captain was a complete buffoon and although he was older, of higher rank and talked a good game, Fraser knew he would easily outshine him when it came to the nitty gritty. He was even more delighted about the Sgt Major.

As was the way with many men of his rank, 38 year-old Walter Cameron was of diminutive height. He was fully five feet three inches tall, and arguably as broad. But what he lacked in height he more than made up for in talent, enthusiasm and voice.

He was also fearless and had a huge reputation as a Jap-slapper, winning the Army's karate championships twice. The men knew not to cross him but they also had huge respect for him as a soldier. He grew up on the rough Ferry estate in Inverness and left school at 15 to join his local regiment. He had served on a dozen tours in Northern Ireland, had been shot at, bombed and mortared. He was also hotly tipped to be the next RSM.

Fraser knew there was no better man to go to war with.

4

The Royal Regiment of Fusiliers is a proud old regiment which recruits from London, Birmingham, Liverpool and the North-East of England. They may have been highly-trained, well-equipped, twentieth century soldiers, but their roots were still in the hard-working environments of the mines, mills and shipyards of their homeland. Their reputation went before them. They were excellent soldiers - very fit and exceptionally well motivated.

Fraser MacLean noticed this as soon as he and his platoon arrived at Ray. He was grateful he'd had the opportunity to sit his men down beforehand and talk them through a few dos and don'ts. The opportunities to foul-up were huge here. Theirs was also a proud battalion; there could be no room for indiscipline, for fault, for failure.

He and the Sgt Major saw the men bedded down in their new accommodation, three tents in the middle of the Fusiliers' lines. Toilets, showers and cookhouses were pointed out, stag rotas drawn up. It was the start of a period of integration. The Scots would have to learn quickly if they were to be part of the team.

Fraser, the Sgt Major and the Captain who was to be the Liaison Officer, went to the Fusiliers' HQ to get their orders. They would join C Company of the 3rd Battalion, the Royal Regiment of Fusiliers whose Company Commander was a big bluff Geordie Major named Tony Greaves.

He was balding and had a build and face that might lead some to think he was lugubrious. Instead, he was a tough, intelligent soldier who called a spade a spade and who lived for his men. Fraser took to him instantly.

He also took to Michael King - a young English Lieutenant, also recently-arrived, who was commanding another newly-formed platoon of augmentees. The two subalterns sat through their first meeting with their new commander and listened carefully.

A training programme was quickly worked out and a routine established. The warplan was the least of it. Details of the mission, the wheres, whens and hows would come later. What was more pressing to Fraser and his platoon was the job of joining seamlessly onto the Fusiliers as though they'd always been there.

It started at five the next morning. Reveille, then a short sharp PT session. After showers and breakfast, the Queen's Own Highlanders were introduced to their new means of going into battle – the Warrior.

To a layman, a Warrior looks like a small tank. It is tracked and has a turret with a main armament. But there the similarities end.

The main armament is a relatively small 30mm cannon and the armour is light and for this campaign would have to be augmented with extra plates along the sides. The body of the vehicle is a steel compartment containing an infantry section of eight heavily-armed men. At the back is a heavy, hydraulically-operated door which gives access and egress. In the turret sits the commander and gunner, who operates the weapons systems – the main armament, and a 7.62mm coaxial chaingun. The Rolls Royce-powered Warrior is capable of around 75 kph over the ground. It's an awesome piece of equipment, loved by the soldiers who use it.

But Warriors were vastly different from their own 432s and Fraser and his men had to spend every waking moment working on the Warrior with the Fusiliers. It was a novelty, but it was a deadly serious one. One slip, one confusion, one error, could have horrendous results. They trained long and hard in the dust and heat of the day on the Devil Dog Dragoon training area.

To bring home the severity of the situation, as if it was needed, they used live ammunition. The health and safety regulations, which often hamper training exercises in the UK or Germany, were quietly ignored. The Highlanders debussed left and right from their new chariots, with live rounds dropping within 30 metres of them.

As part of the training, every day, at no given time, the hated scream of "GAS! GAS! GAS!" would come from somewhere and the men would scurry into their thick, charcoal-lined protective NBC suits to avoid agonizing death from a nerve agent, a blood agent or a blister agent. They had nine seconds to get their respirators on. If they didn't, they faced a death beyond contemplation. And once inside the mask, suit, gloves and overboots, despite the scorching heat of the desert day, the training continued.

At night, after a tepid shower and their evening meal, the men cleaned their weapons and studied every pamphlet and manual about the Warrior. They could not get this wrong. When he finally rolled into his sleeping bag each night, Fraser said a prayer of thanks for Robson and Winstanley, the gunner and driver of the Warrior he would command. As Fusiliers they had worked with the vehicle for years and knew it inside out.

All the time they were training on the Warrior, the air war continued.

There was little love on show on Valentine's Day 1991 as the mightiest armed force the world had ever seen was putting the final preparations to its warplan. That day, February 14th, saw the start of the final diplomatic effort to avert a land war. As Fraser MacLean and his soldiers were training in the hot sand of the Northern Saudi desert, 300 miles away to the north the Soviet special envoy, Yevgeny Primakov, was visiting Baghdad.

Mr Primakov was driven round the city by Iraqi officials and shown the downed bridges and shattered infrastructure – the result of four weeks of relentless allied bombing. That night he was taken to a freezing government guest house in the Mansour district of the city where he was met by Saddam Hussein himself.

Mr Primakov, by his own admission, was no soldier. But he'd been briefed by enough of them before he left Moscow and he knew what he was talking about when he spoke to Saddam Hussein. Once the platitudes had been exchanged, he told the Iraqi leader that his country faced annihilation by the US-led coalition unless it complied with the UN resolutions and withdrew from Kuwait.

To the astonishment of the Russian diplomat, Saddam Hussein said he would pull out.

Once again hundreds of thousands of soldiers, sailors and airmen sat transfixed as they watched TV or listened to their radios for the latest scrap of news. It was beginning to look as though the air campaign might have been enough. Public opinion across the world was starting to turn against the coalition anyway. The video game war, with gun camera footage of bombs going down chimneys, was showing all too accurately how a state of the art military was tearing apart one of the world's most ancient civilisations.

A week later Tariq Aziz flew to Moscow for talks with the Soviet President, Mikhail Gorbachev. The world held its breath. Moscow and Baghdad had long been friends and trading partners. They had a special relationship and one which was in danger now that the Soviet Union had tacitly sided with the US-led coalition lined up against Iraq. Mr Aziz was driven in a motorcade from the foot of his aircraft's steps to the Kremlin. It was 48 hours before the deadline set by the Pentagon for the Iraqi withdrawal from Kuwait.

Tariq Aziz was noted for his diplomacy and no little cunning. While the world watched and waited for a Soviet-sponsored peace deal, Aziz told Gorbachev Iraq would withdraw its 400,000 men from Kuwait but it would not comply with the UN resolutions demanding Baghdad recognise Kuwaiti independence and pay reparations.

Gorbachev thought this was a start and retired to his private office to use the hotline with Washington. He told George Bush his news and urged the American President to stop the war. The two men spoke for an hour, then Gorbachev returned to his guest. Bush called a meeting of his war cabinet.

To a man, they advised the President to ignore Aziz's proposal. Bush slept on it and called Gorbachev at dawn the next day, February 22nd.

"No deal," he said.

The French Foreign Legion, among them a very tough German sergeant whose name was once Hans Jedele, were among the allied forces lined up along the TAPline Road. But like many other countries across the world, the French were growing weary of the pictures of misery coming from Baghdad and Kuwait. They wanted a diplomatic solution and believed Aziz's proposal should be acted upon.

The French President, Francois Mitterrand, also lifted the phone to the White House that morning to urge Bush to think again.

As they spoke, a White House press officer slid into the Oval Office and switched on the TV. He flicked the remote control's mute button so the President's call would be uninterrupted by noise. But he wanted Bush to see the images. He managed to attract the President's attention and gestured towards the set.

The pictures showed hundreds of oil wells ablaze across Kuwait.

5

The air war had lasted for six weeks. In that time the military and civilian infrastructure of Iraq had been shattered. Night after night thousands of coalition warplanes flew into Iraqi airspace and bombed at will.

The ground war plan had been on the table for months. Soldiers tweaked it here and there, politicians had their say, but at the end of the day it belonged to one man.

General H Norman Schwarzkopf, the American commander of the operation, was a bear of a man - with a temper to match. He was born in Trenton, New Jersey in 1934, had an IQ of 170 and was a member of the International Brotherhood of Magicians. At 57 years of age and with 35 years service, he was a combat veteran of Vietnam. He had seen war at first hand and knew soldiers, knew how they thought, how they lived. He was a soldier's soldier and didn't suffer fools at all, never mind gladly. While his plan was brilliantly simple in its concept, it was fantastically complex in its execution.

The United States Marine Corps would smash north into Kuwait and mount a full frontal attack. But this was partially a deception operation designed to fool the Iraqi defenders into believing it was the main assault. Instead, a 'Left Hook' of heavy armour and massed infantry far out in the Western Saudi desert would storm north over the border then punch east into Iraq, encircling Kuwait and cutting off fleeing invaders on the Basra Road.

The diplomatic moves had failed and with military preparations complete, the final order was given from General Schwarzkopf's HQ in Riyadh.

The ground war would begin at H-hour, 0400, on G-Day, Sunday February 24th, 1991.

Among the soldiers who had tweaked Schwarzkopf's plan was General de la Billiere. The British 1st Armoured Division had originally been part of the USMC orbat for the attack on Kuwait city. While he liked and respected Schwarzkopf, privately de la Billiere thought the nature of the British involvement in the invasion was a mistake.

The British Division was heavily armoured, its tanks more suited to the vast empty expanses of desert than the street to street fighting envisaged in Kuwait. De la Billiere, known to many simply as DLB, was an ex-SAS man and much preferred the SF solution to problems – think laterally and go for the unexpected option. Privately he disliked the gung-ho American attitude and thought the full frontal assault would result in hundreds of British casualties.

Using charm and subtlety, over a considerable period of time, DLB managed to convince the volatile Schwarzkopf that the British armour would do more damage in the desert than in the city. Two months before G-Day the American finally agreed and the entire British Division moved west into the desert. DLB was elated and relieved. Elated because he'd won something of a victory, relieved because he'd saved hundreds of his soldiers' lives.

At H hour, 0400, on G-Day, Sunday February 24th, the ground war started.

Ahead of a massive two division US Marine Corps invasion force, were a handful of brave men armed with fibreglass rods on their bellies they prodded and probed their way from northern Saudi Arabia through the miles of minefields between them and Kuwait. Just behind them were snipers suppressing the Iraqi trench systems across the border.

As this was happening, miles away to the north-east, US Navy Seals swam onto the beaches of Kuwait and planted explosives. Shortly after they detonated, ships out in the Gulf began a massive bombardment of the shoreline. This, along with the broadcast of radio traffic recorded during an earlier exercise, was designed to make the Iraqis believe the main assault was coming from the sea.

As the USMC stormed north into Kuwait, it reported Iraqi forces heading for the coast to reinforce defences against a non-existent beach landing.

Twenty four hours later, the left hook would move.

The 3rd Battalion of the Royal Regiment of Fusiliers would be part of that left hook. The battalion was just one of one hundred and one coalition units strung out along the Saudi-Iraqi border, counting down the hours.

Their orders had started high up as big picture tactics. They'd filtered down the chain from formation to formation, getting smaller but more focussed at each level. When they'd reached the Fusiliers HQ, they had been translated into specific objectives – namely a series of Iraqi positions.

Shortly after lunch on February 24th, with the US assault on Kuwait city underway, Fraser sat through his first wartime O Group. He took the same notes he'd taken a thousand times on exercise - only the detail was different. The procedure was identical every time; it was drilled into young officers each time they went on exercise. This is why the British Army doesn't lose battles, far less wars.

But this time of course it was different. This time it was for real. As he checked and double checked every detail of the plan and how it would affect him and his men, he wondered how he would react. His cold, steely determination was one thing in peacetime but could he cope under fire?

It's called a drumhead service because in times past, the Padre would build a small altar out of the regiment's drums. But tonight there were no drums and the Padre made an altar out of a couple of 10-man ration boxes. He covered it with a piece of MacKenzie tartan cloth that looked to Fraser like a travelling rug. He took heart from that – the Padre used what he could find; he wasn't to know that MacKenzie was the Queen's Own Highlanders regimental tartan. When he saw it Fraser whipped round and caught the Sgt Major's eye. The older man had seen it too. He smiled.

But it didn't matter what the Padre used that night, or what he wore. The men crowded round him only to hear what he said. Fraser noted that the change in his soldiers was palpable. Men who were usually garrulous fell silent. Men who drank and fought and boasted about the pleasures of the flesh, were like children before him. They laid their weapons on the ground and knelt.

The Padre spoke softly and the hymns were sung slowly and falteringly, because minds were elsewhere. Men were alone with their consciences now. They thought of home, of loved ones, of the impending battle - the noise, the smell, the killing. And more than one felt the icy hand of fear touch his heart.

The light was just starting to fade from the winter sky when the Padre finished. The men wandered back to their tents to make final preparations to their kit before they went into battle. There would be an extra ammunition issue shortly; those who wanted it could stock up on more rounds for their weapons, or grenades. They would top up their water bottles, check radio batteries, secure body armour. Then they would do it all again because the nerves were starting. Some would eat their evening meal in the cookhouse tent as usual, others would eat nothing. Some wrote letters home, most tried to rest.

Fraser had already done his battle preparation. His webbing belt kit was full and heavy and his daysack was pre-packed and at hand. His weapons, automatic rifle and pistol, had been stripped, cleaned, oiled and reassembled.

He went to Mike King's tent and chatted for a while. Then they shook hands and Fraser left. He wanted to be alone now and went for a walk along the sand berm behind the tents.

It was all so real in his young man's mind, yet it all seemed so *unreal*. One minute he was sitting in his mess in Germany, the next he was in the desert. First his battalion was in the rear unlikely to see any action, suddenly he was in the front line about to go into battle.

His demons started again. Could he cope? Could he hack it? He knew he was the best young officer in the battalion, but that was on the training areas of the German plains. What would he be like under fire for real? What would his father think if he didn't perform? He surprised himself because he wasn't frightened of being killed or wounded, his only fear failure.

And then he thought of Kirsty. It was nearly eight years since he'd seen her, since he'd held her close, since he'd smelt her perfume, felt the warmth of her body against his. He closed his eyes and saw the strawberry blonde hair, the peaches and cream skin, the freckles on her arms. His heart leapt, then all too quickly the sadness of realisation was upon him. Girlfriends had come and gone down the years and he realised that they had all meant absolutely nothing to him. Kirsty was the only reason he lived. Even though she wasn't in his life any more, nor ever would be again, even though she was married to the American and was thousands of miles away in a happy household surrounded by the children she always wanted and a husband she loved, she was all he lived for.

Fraser looked up. Daylight was dying. Far away to the west the winter sun was setting and high above him a thin moon was coming into view. In a few minutes the sky would be dark and the heavens would be out in all their majesty. He loved the skies in this part of the world, they were infinite and wondrous. He sat down against the berm and watched the fading sunset. The light of the day had changed into a candyfloss pink and a pale blue. Soon the pale blue would be dark blue then a black and in a few hours time it would be February 25th – the day they'd go to war.

Somewhere, on the other side of the tents, Stewart the piper started to play. The notes drifted across the desert and found Fraser sitting in the twilight. Usually the pipes were met by good-natured howls of derision from the English soldiers' tents. "Stop strangling that cat," someone would shout, then there'd be howls of laughter from many men.

But on the eve of battle, there was silence from the lines – the Fusiliers knew what the pipes meant this night.

Fraser was not a religious man and hardly ever went to church. He wasn't Godless, he considered himself a Christian, but after his experience with Kirsty and her version of religion, he was ambivalent to it.

The Queen's Own Highlanders Regimental Lights Out tune was 'Sleep Dearie, Sleep.' But that night Fraser instantly recognised the gentle melody of 'The Day Thou Gavest Lord is Ended'. He remembered telling Stewart once that it was his favourite hymn. The sombre music fitted the mood of the moment perfectly.

He looked up again at the sun racing away to the west and wondered if it would be the last sunset he would ever see. He thought of the coming battle, but most of all he thought of Kirsty. And he wept.

"Surr." It was the Sgt Major. Fraser leapt to his feet and wiping away tears, turned towards the voice.

"What is it? What's wrong?"

The Sgt Major looked him up and down. In the half light

Fraser thought he saw a look of disgust on the older man's face. He wondered how long Cameron had been standing by the berm.

"Surr, there's a lot of young lads back there who're frightened, they're going into the unknown tonight," his voice was low, soft. Then it hardened.

"They'll be looking to you for leadership, for strength. They wouldn't want to see you out here greetin' like a lassie. Can I suggest sir, with respect, that you fuckin' pull yourself together."

The Sgt Major was right. Fraser couldn't afford to show any weakness in front of his men. Not tonight. Tonight counted for more than anything.

Fraser nodded and the Sgt Major disappeared into the darkness.

6

Fraser wore a pair of beige suede and canvas desert boots and issue desert pattern camo trousers and shirt. On top he wore an old but very comfortable green cotton gaberdine camo smock and on top of that his body armour.

In his smock pockets he crammed field dressings, torches, tracer rounds, pens, sweets, chocolate and chewing gum. In his top left hand pocket he kept his two morphine syrettes. In the right hand pocket, tied to his button hole with a length of paracord was his compass. The body armour was heavy. The Kevlar vest carried two ceramic plates in pockets designed to protect the heart, front and back.

Over this he threw his webbing, a belt and braces combination with pouches containing vital equipment. He wore four ammo pouches, each carried three magazines of 28 5.56mm rounds for his SA-80. He had another four magazines in his daysack and two bandoliers of ammunition. The belt also carried four utility pouches. One of these held a full water bottle. The others contained rations, a small hexamine stove, a space blanket, a woolly hat, gloves, matches, another torch, paracord and miniflares - enough food and equipment to keep him alive and fighting for 48 hours.

Attached to his left hand side by a thin webbing strap was the haversack containing his respirator and atropine combopen syringes. At the top of his daysack, loosely folded in case he needed to get into it in a hurry, was his NBC suit. Saddam Hussein had promised

'The Mother of All Battles' and consequently the threat of chemical or biological weapons was high.

He checked his weapon again. As a reflex, his thumb brushed against the safety catch to make sure it was on. He checked the selector was on R for repetition and not A for Automatic and slipped off the magazine. He pulled back the working parts and looked inside the breech. It was empty but he could see where he'd carefully oiled the mechanism earlier in the day. He took his tool roll from a webbing pouch and looked out the oil bottle. It wouldn't do any harm to oil it again.

Fraser and his men stood at their Warrior. To a man, they had been unable to sleep and had agreed to RV at their vehicle earlier than scheduled. Remembering what the Sgt Major had said, he called his platoon together for a final briefing.

He'd given them a few words of encouragement, cracked a few jokes and told his men that the drinks would be on him back in Germany. One or two of the soldiers asked for permission to smoke. The brief and flickering half light from the matches and lighters illuminated the faces of his men in an eerie gloom. Fraser noticed for the first time how young his men were. He knew them all so well by now, knew the football teams they followed, what they drank, even the names of their wives and girlfriends. But tonight he would get to know them better than ever before.

Tonight, when the rounds started coming in, when they had to debus and fix bayonets and close with and kill the enemy, they would be brothers. In the darkness, as the black humour of the soldiers washed over him, he wondered if they would all make it out the other end.

"Did you ever think it would come to this boss?" asked MacIntosh, the young private from Nairn.

"I guess not," replied Fraser candidly. "But once you start building up armies, it's very difficult to stop."

"Why aren't we going all the way to Baghdad?" asked Stewart, the piper. "I'd love to get my hands on that bastard Saddam Hussein."

"Well it's not part of the UN mandate," said Fraser, starting to feel more and more like a teacher, a father. "Our mission is to liberate Kuwait."

"I'd love to have that fucker on the end of my bayonet," he replied.

Fraser managed a philosophical grin in the darkness. "You'll get all the bayoneting you want in a few hours," he said, checking his watch.

"OK guys, listen in," he raised his voice now, no longer a teacher or a father, he was their commander again. His soldiers, the 30 men he would lead into hell, gathered closer.

"You know I'm not big on speeches and I'm not going to change that now. But I do want to say a few words because tonight is different." He paused.

"We're going to war. We've been trained for this and now we have our chance to show what we can do. If you are scared, that is only natural and you won't be alone. Remember your friends, your brothers, your regiment. Remember we are attached to another battalion. The Fusiliers are a fine bunch of men and we must not let ourselves down. Remember your enemy are conscripts, treat them kindly if they surrender, but if they want a fight…" he paused again and scanned the dark assembly of men before him, "then fucking give them one."

There was a murmur of approval then the men fell silent again.

"Cuidich 'n Righ," said Fraser.

"Cuidich 'n Righ" replied 30 voices.

The 550 HP Rolls Royce Diesel engine purred beneath him.

The platoon was divided up among three Warriors. Eight heavily-armed soldiers sat four along each side of the vehicles' darkened compartments. Fraser sat high in the turret of his Warrior, Sgt Major Cameron in the second and the Platoon Sergeant MacDonald in the third.

Fraser could see nothing without his NVGs but when he put them on he was overwhelmed by the size of the formation surrounding him. His Warrior was well down the chain amid hundreds of armoured vehicles. The noise and the fumes from the idling engines were overwhelming.

He lowered himself inside the turret and by the shaded light of his pentorch, checked the map for the hundredth time. He scanned the hand drawn diagram telling him his platoon's place in the Orbat and flipped open his notebook and re-read his orders. He checked his watch repeatedly as he counted down the minutes to H Hour.

The goosebumps were out all over his body and he could feel the small hairs on the back of his neck stiffen moments later when his radio headset crackled into life with the Company Commander's voice.

"All call signs this is Zero Alpha. Move now. Out."

The still night air reverberated with the throaty roar of 200 armoured vehicles bursting northwards out of Assembly Area Ray towards Iraq. It was a full 12 minutes before Fraser could see the Warrior in front of his move away into the distance. Robson the driver eased off the brakes and he felt his own vehicle roll forward. At first the speed was minimal but as the distance between the vehicles grew, the pace quickened.

Fraser experienced a rush like he had never felt before and thought he never would again as the battlegroup stormed towards Iraq.

But for the first 50 minutes they were still in Saudi Arabia. Then the column slowed, the path narrowed and Fraser realised they were about to cross the border.

He looked out to his right and to his amazement saw the Fusiliers' commanding officer standing beside his stationary Warrior. His right hand was at his temple, saluting his boys as they went off to war. Draped over the side armour of his Warrior was a huge black sheet of cloth with white writing on it.

"Good luck and God bless you all," it said.

Seconds later they stormed through the berm.

Fraser keyed the intercom button.

"OK boys, we're over the border. We're in Iraq."

There was a loud cheer from the belly of the Warrior and then the soldiers started to sing at the top of their voices.

"Oh Flower of Scotland, when will we see your likes again."

IRAQ

The singing was so loud, Fraser had to shout over the intercom to warn Robson, and Winstanley the gunner, to be extra vigilant now that they were in enemy territory. Intelligence had reported that the Iraqis had laid five miles of minefields as part of their defences.

The engineers of the American 1st Mechanised Infantry Division had breached the berm earlier that night and created a major highway that the allies were now pouring through. It was 16 lanes wide. At the side was a huge sign that read, "Welcome to Iraq, courtesy of the Big Red One".

Despite the stress of the moment, Fraser managed a wry smile at the Americans' expense. Even in wartime they couldn't help being cheesy. But he was chilled later when he learned that in clearing the route, the American armoured bulldozers had simply filled in Iraqi trenches burying alive the occupants.

More Americans were waiting on the other side of the barrier, known as Phase Line Vermont, and escorted the Warriors forward. The Americans drove Humvees with huge, illuminated "Follow Me" signs on the roofs. The Fusiliers battlegroup followed the Americans for 17 km until they reached a track codenamed "Line Cherry". There the Fusiliers met up with their own recce elements who'd gone in ahead of the main body to scout for routes to their objectives.

There had still been no contact with the enemy. Fraser traversed the turret and scanned his arc of fire with the Warrior's night vision gunsight. All he could see were the silhouettes of other British vehicles, black against the eerie green of the sky and sand. The tension in his Warrior was palpable. As well as conventional weapons, Fraser knew well the dangers of an NBC strike.

Saddam Hussein had weapons of mass destruction and had already used them on friend and foe alike. He'd killed 5,000 of his own people in the Kurdish village of Halabjah in 1988 by using the nerve gas Sarin, Cyanide gas and Mustard gas. It was a version of this latter substance, named Yperite (because of its use in the trenches near Ypres in the Great War) that he dropped on the Iranians during the war between 1980 and 1988.

If Fraser was the Iraqi commander there would be one place and one place only he'd target for a WMD strike and it was here – the bottleneck breach in the defences - where the coalition forces were pouring through. His hand went down to his left side and touched the respirator haversack firmly attached to his belt. He shuddered.

Then the radio sparked into life again – reports from the point elements of the column. Not contacts with the enemy, not engagement, not fighting to the death - but surrender.

Fraser strained to hear above the roar of the Rolls Royce. At first he couldn't believe it, but then he saw it for himself. First a handful, then dozens and finally hundreds of Iraqi soldiers were walking towards the British vehicles with their arms in the air. The coalition forces had been told that the Iraqis would fight to the death, that their regular battalions like the Republican Guard, were well trained and highly motivated. Instead, the enemy was surrendering in droves.

Fraser wanted to pop the hatch and take a photograph but he knew he couldn't. Instead he scanned the Iraqis with his night sight. They looked pathetic. They were thin and wore ragged clothing. Their equipment was in tatters and they moved in a rabble. But then he thought that the best army in the world would look like a rabble if it had sustained six weeks of bombardment like the one meted out by the coalition.

To stop and take the Iraqis prisoner would have been a mammoth task. Instead the HQ element radioed the column to keep going; the MPs could deal with the prisoners farther down the line. Nothing could interfere with the objective. They had to be ignored, the column had to keep moving.

Fraser was beginning to wonder if the whole thing was going to prove to be a huge overestimation. If this was the enemy, hadn't the allies over-reacted? If this was the calibre of Iraqi soldier then wasn't the coalition using a sledgehammer to crack a nut? Perhaps this would be over in days and not weeks or months as was first thought.

The column continued its punch north. Then, without a shot fired in anger, it swing round to the east – the left hook. The vehicles rolled on for another 20 minutes, and at shortly after five am they were ordered to stop.

The men dismounted while their commanders worked out what was happening. The soldiers did what soldiers do whenever they get the slightest opportunity – they brewed up tea. It seemed the British thing to do.

Inside the rear door of every Warrior is a piece of equipment called a boiling vessel which provides water for cooking and drinking. Each man got out his mug and soon everyone was enjoying a much welcomed drink, while the officers discussed what was happening or rather what was *not* happening.

The Iraqi soldiers were not fighting as they'd been expected to. Instead they were surrendering in their thousands and the battle was well ahead of schedule. Much more ground was being taken more quickly than had been anticipated. This had its pluses and minuses.

The plan had been for the infantry-heavy 4 Brigade to enter Iraq first and clear the Iraqi positions to allow the armour-heavy 7 Brigade, the Desert rats of WW2 fame, to punch deep into enemy territory. While the absence of any fight by the defenders was welcomed by everyone, there were inherent dangers.

The mass surrender was all good and well but it could result in complacency among the British who might yet came up against an objective where the defenders would not give up, but fight to the bitter end. There was also the danger that by advancing too far too quickly, the British units would stretch the logistic tail upon which the tanks and armoured vehicles relied. Challengers and Warriors were regarded as the best in the world, but without fuel and ammunition they were useless lumps of metal.

Fraser was glad of the break and he jumped down from the turret of his warrior and set foot on Iraqi soil for the first time. In the distance he could hear the ongoing rumble of battle and overhead helicopters clattered back and forth. It was cold and damp. There was a chilly wind blowing and he was grateful for all the layers of clothing he was wearing. He was grateful too for the cup of steaming tea he drew from the BV.

"It's going OK boss intit?" smiled Stewart, exhaling cigarette smoke through crooked teeth.

"Piece of piss sir," added MacIntosh. Both men beamed broad smiles from beneath the smeared camouflage cream and encrusted grime of war on their faces.

"We can't assume it'll be like this all the way in," said Fraser in cautious tones. "We'll have to keep our heads together. Some of them are bound to fight, bound to."

Fraser stood at the rear of the Warrior drinking tea and chatting with his men for about an hour. It was a happy time – but it would not last.

"Hello foxtrot two zero, this is Zero Alpha, over." The radio crackled and hissed into life. Recognising their own callsign, as one the men stubbed out their cigarettes and poured away the dregs of their drinks onto the sand. Fraser leapt back onto the Warrior and climbed into the turret.

"Hello Zero Alpha, this is Foxtrot Two Zero. Send, over," he said.

The war was back on.

2

For 24 sleepless hours they rolled on through freezing, driving rain. The weather was closed in, it was dark and damp. The skies were all the darker and more menacing because of the clouds of smoke from the battle and the burning oilfields. Twice Fraser's platoon was sent away to the right of the advance to scout areas of desert thought to contain Iraqi positions. Carefully the Warriors patrolled round the areas but reported nothing seen and returned to the main formation.

Fraser listened to his radio in frustration as other elements of the battlegroup were involved in action, while he and his comrades in Charlie Company, remained on the periphery. All the Iraqi-held objectives had been given the codenames of metals, Cobalt, Tungsten etc. Fraser tried hard to concentrate on the ground ahead of him as the rest of the unit tackled Copper South.

The Iraqis kept around 20 T72 Tanks dug in around Copper South, their western-most defensive position. They were laagered up, hull down so as to reveal as little of themselves above ground as possible. But they were no match for the Challenger tanks of the British Army.

Each tank was equipped with TOGS, the Thermal Optical Gunsight. This enabled the crew to see in the dark, regardless of the light state or weather conditions. The British crews could pick up the heat signature of the Iraqi tanks, which showed up in green, white and black on their monitors, and engage them.

Once the crew had selected a target on the TOGS, they sent a laser beam onto it. This then bounced back to the tank with an exact range and compass bearing. This data was then processed by the Challenger's computer and its main armament, a 120 mm gun, automatically locked onto it. A complex system of gyros ensured that regardless of either vehicle's speed, movement or position, even if they were reversing away from each other, even if they were both turning, or rolling over hilly ground, the gun never left its target.

The crew could fire the main armament from two-and-a half kilometres away and destroy the enemy armour without the Iraqi crew even knowing they'd been seen, far less targeted.

The T72s were Soviet tanks with rounded turrets and good armour. They were generally considered to be excellent tanks and among the best kit the Warsaw Pact forces had to offer, but it had nothing to stop the Challengers. As the war progressed, the Allies began to understand how it might have been if they had ever had to go to war against the Soviets back in Germany.

The British tanks carried various types of ammunition with which to despatch their opponents. Favourite was APFDS, or Armour Piercing, Fin-stabilised, Discarding Sabot. Known as "Fin" to the crews, this wasn't an explosive round, but a dart of Depleted Uranium, chosen because of its density and weight. It passed clean through the armour of a targeted tank and out the other side, its wake creating a vacuum in the turret that sucked the crewmen out of the dinner plate-sized exit hole in a slush of flesh.

The other round in the armoury was the HESH – or High Explosive, Squash Head. This round didn't penetrate the armour of the turret but smashed against it. The fearsome concussion of the explosion caused the equipment and people inside to reverberate around the confined space at the speed of sound. It was equally as lethal as Fin.

If the gunner and commander got their shot right, the turret of the target tank would be blown clean off and even though it weighed several tonnes, it would fly through the air and land yards away. The impact usually caused the immediate detonation of the ammunition and fuel inside. The crew never had any chance.

To die in a brewed-up tank was to die an awful death.

Once the Challengers destroyed the T72s, the Warriors rolled forward, stopped just short of the objective and debussed their infantry to close with and kill the remaining enemy. There were very few left at Copper South by the time bayonets were fixed. In the end, most of the British soldiers took prisoners and gave first aid to the Iraqis who were wounded, many of whom were in a shocking state from maltreatment by their own officers as much as the allied campaign. They had no food, no water and their clothing and equipment was in tatters. They'd endured weeks of abuse from their superiors, relentless bombing and now an invasion. Copper South fell after a brief and ultimately futile defence by the Iraqis.

The allies rolled on towards Kuwait.

3

"Hello Foxtrot Two Zero, this is Zero Alpha. Over." The Geordie burr of Tony Greaves came clear as a bell into Fraser MacLean's headset. The Company Commander wanted to talk to his callsign.

"Foxtrot Two Zero, send over," he replied, anticipation in his voice.

"Warning order. Brass will be our next objective. Mission, to destroy the enemy and his infrastructure there. Concept of operations, details to follow. O Group at Grid 2987 4793 in three zero minutes."

Fraser was now buzzing. He could hear SITREPS over the radio net involving other units. The attack was moving at such speed, it was clear that all elements were being rotated to give everyone a taste of the action and as many people as much rest as possible. Other elements of the Fusiliers battlegroup had been involved in taking objectives. Now it was his turn.

The Company Commander's O Group took place half-an-hour later at a location a few km away. The three rifle Platoon Commanders' Warriors reversed into position around the Company HQ element vehicles. Their turrets scanned the horizon in case any Iraqis rolled through the thick smoke of the burning oil fields to attack what was undoubtedly a juicy target.

The O Group took place at the open rear door of the Company Commander's Warrior and lasted less than 10 minutes. Greaves had built a rough model of Objective Brass on the ground using his water bottle and mug, a few lengths of green string and couple of stones he'd found in the sand.

Stuck onto the inside of the Warrior's door, with the thick black masking tape without which the British Army would not function, was a satellite photograph. It was printed on a sheet of paper the size of an OS map and on it in grey and black were the outlines of the Iraqi positions taken from outer space.

Fraser sat with Mike King and the third Platoon Commander, Will Holden. He and Mike knew they were the outsiders here. They listened intently, took notes and said nothing. He expected his to be the reserve platoon while the others went into action, but he was wrong.

Referring to the photograph, and notes he'd written at the O Group he'd attended earlier with the battlegroup commander,

Greaves talked his officers through the enemy positions.

"Int tells us there is an artillery brigade with G5 155mm guns and some armoured vehicles in defence here. Green slime have satellite imagery of the area and this is how it lines up. The objective is around 40 square km but our target is down here to the left, a complex of buildings, bunkers and trenches. A Company's to the right, Two Company in depth behind. The Challengers of D Squadron, the King's Royal Hussars will go in line abreast at the front after the artillery barrage. We will close with and kill any enemy who survive.

"This part of the model is accurate to the satellite picture." He pointed down.

Fraser and the two other officers carefully sketched their own maps from it. Their papers rustled in the growing wind. The rain had stopped but a dust storm was growing. Greaves spoke of the weather next.

"The wind is from the south, we'll be heading right into it. There is a chance that the preliminary artillery bombardment might tickle up their ammunition stocks. Int suggests that given this is an artillery brigade, they might have Mustard gas shells there. That said, the NBC threat is all the more real."

There was a solemnity to his voice. Any war was bad enough, but one that might involve that unspeakable aspect of the modern arsenal made everyone focus their thoughts all the more.

"He's used gas before, as we know. He's used it on his own people, at Halabjah, and he's used it on the Iranians. He wouldn't hesitate to use it on us. Don't lose sight of that."

Nobody would, today of all days.

"If the wind is right we'll have a Gazelle up ahead scouting. I'll be on the blower to him at all times.

"H Hour is 0945. This will be a phased attack led by armour and artillery, once the donkey wallopers and dropshorts have done their bit. It's down to us."

The remainder of the O group was spent on the details of the plan, coordinating instructions with other units, boundaries and radio frequencies. Then came the nitty-gritty.

"We'll have two up, bags of smoke." He paused. "Jock, I want you and your boys up front on the right," he said, drawing a cross in the sand with his propelling pencil, then pointing it at Fraser.

"Mike, your platoon's on the left," he lifted his eyes to Lieutenant King, the second platoon commander. "And yours Will, back in reserve. Hopefully, if the slime have done their sums right, we won't need you."

"Any questions?"

Greaves stood up. There were none.

"Right guys, this is our first show," said Greaves. "Let's make it a good one. Mount up."

The plan was straight from Staff College. Artillery, way back in the rear, would pour fire down on the position before the shock of armour went in. Hopefully by the time that phase of the attack had been completed, the enemy would have surrendered or been killed. If not the Warriors would manoeuvre close enough for the infantry to debus.

Fraser's apprehension and emotion during the bagpipe moment had been replaced now by raw aggression. The last 24 hours of nerve-screeching, adrenaline-pumped, relentless, sleepless movement had dissipated it all. He was at war. He had survived the first 24 hours of it. His comrades had been blooded, but not him. Until now.

He chatted briefly with his two fellow platoon commanders and returned to his men to backbrief them on their part of the assault onto Brass. As he walked back to his Warrior he sought out the Sgt Major.

"How are the boys?" he asked.

"Fine boss, raring to go," said Cameron.

Fraser nearly asked, "*and how am I doing?*" but he stopped himself just in time. Before Paris he might have fished for compliments, but never since, and certainly not here.

"See you at the reorg," he said and walked off to his Warrior.

4

Objective Brass was the southern-most of the Iraqi positions. It was around 50 miles from the Kuwaiti border and 20 from the Saudi border. It comprised a command bunker, a communications tower and control room and a series of smaller bunkers and slit trenches. These were all designed to support the brigade's role as a major artillery position. As such, it also contained dozens of gun emplacements.

The intelligence units and planners had done their stuff. The recon satellites and pilotless drones had transmitted back priceless images of the Iraqi positions and strengths at Brass. These were analysed and passed down the chain to the commanders on the ground, who planned their assaults accordingly. Not surprisingly, the Iraqis were ready to repel the invader and every gun barrel they had was pointing south.

This was food and drink for the British Army, which trained on the manoueverist doctrine. If the Iraqis were prepared for an attack from the south, the British would attack from the north.

But there were delays. The tanks of D Squadron, The King's Royal Hussars took more time than estimated to complete their earlier objective and had to backtrack 20 km to rejoin the Fusiliers. The pre-attack artillery barrage on the target was to have lasted two hours but because of the delays it lasted only 15 minutes. However in that time six batteries of guns and a number of MLRS units gave the target a massive pasting before the ground forces went in.

The confusion caused by the Iraqis' attempts to move defensive forces from the south of Brass to the north, was nothing like the confusion caused by the Challenger tanks of the Hussars. Using TOGS the 14 Challengers, racing forward line abreast, quickly identified then engaged the hull-down T62s and T72s of the defenders. In little more than a minute the first line of defence lay shattered, each tank had huge gouts of flame bursting from the turret ring as the ammunition inside cooked off. The turrets themselves, some with the commanders still hanging from the hatches, lay smouldering yards away. What caused the most confusion to the defenders was the noise.

Although they couldn't see more than a few metres outside their perimeter, they could hear the crump two km away to their rear, as the 120mm main armament of the Challengers opened up. A micro-second later came the deafening crash as the round impacted on the target. Then followed the rapid whooshes and pops of the exploding ammunition inside each hull.

The staccato small arms fire from the defenders' rifles was futile. It only interrupted the screams of their dying comrades.

All around was smoke – a black-grey fog from the oil wells and the acrid clouds from the burning defending tanks and APCs. Soon Brass was a hellish place to be.

Fraser MacLean listened to both the platoon net and the company net on his radio. He tried to follow the bigger picture battle and relate it to his own. Charlie Company was in a holding position to the north-east of the target. It was raining again and the drops falling through the oil smoke brought a black drizzle. Visibility was poor even with NVGs. But he didn't need artificial aids to hear the battle and feel its awful vibrations through the ground.

Ahead of him, the Hussars' tanks punched on into the area behind Brass. The Iraqi tanks were dug in hull down facing south and couldn't traverse their turrets to counter the attack from the rear. The armour at the back of any tank is lighter than at the front and the sides and the HESH and Fin rounds shattered line after line of defences until the only outgoing fire from Brass was small arms.

The tanks rolled closer. Their Iraqi counterparts had ceased to exist as a cohesive force. There was no danger now from armour, but a well-aimed anti-tank weapon fired by an infantryman could still knock out a Challenger. They punched into Brass's outer perimeter and loaded HESH to tackle the buildings and bunkers.

Hundreds of Iraqis had already run south, away from the attack. The bodies of their comrades who had either been too slow or unlucky, lay strewn across the ground. Some had been dismembered and lay grotesquely shaped in death. Others seemed blessed by sleep.

Around 30 Iraqi tanks and APCs lay burning or upsides down. Artillery pieces that once pointed towards the Allies in Saudi Arabia were destroyed. The communications tower had evaporated, all that was left was a smouldering stub of twisted metal and wires that sparked and shorted in the moist air. The bunkers and command post had been pummelled with HESH and raked by the 7.62mm coaxial chaingun of a dozen Challengers. The tanks prowled around inside the base, their turrets traversed back and forth like the heads of Daleks, seeking new targets. The buzzing of the movement a gentle, benign sound amid the awful cacophony of war.

"Foxtrot two zero, two one and two two. This is zero alpha. Move now. Golf Lima. Out."

The Geordie accent seemed to Fraser to be more at home on a football terracing, but here it was finally sending him into action. Inside his turret Fraser acknowledged the radio signal and nodded down to the driver. The 550 HP Rolls Royce engine growled in anger and the Warrior slipped the leash.

Golf Lima, GL, *good luck.* Fraser liked that. It wasn't standard procedure, in fact the rules expressly forbade the use of critically valuable radio air time for personal use. But this time it was necessary. It was the English Company Commander recognising that the Scottish soldiers were far from their own unit. It was a message saying, 'good to have you aboard boys, you won't let us down.'

The Challengers had gone firm inside Brass. Their turrets continued to traverse. The main armaments were now silent to conserve ammunition, but the coax machine guns spurted fire every few minutes when the gunner spotted movement among the smoking debris of the bunkers.

The Warriors raced across the shale and sand towards the smoking objective. Visibility was still very poor but after a few minutes the outlines of the rearmost Challengers came into view. Then Fraser saw the objective.

On the road a Warrior can touch 75 km per hour. The terrain here was flat, sand and gravel, and the vehicle was travelling close to its maximum speed. Soon it was inside the rear perimeter of Brass and Fraser and his colleagues took stock.

Greaves came on the net again from his Warrior, slightly behind and to the left.

"Hello foxtrot two zero, this is zero alpha. Your target is the cluster of bunkers to the right of the stub of the comms mast."

Fraser acknowledged. The commander then ordered Mike King's platoon onto targets to the left of the mast. He was using the obvious feature as a boundary between the two attacking platoons. It made sense to use something visible to all as a reference point because the fog of war could cause no end of confusion.

Fraser ordered Winstanley the Warrior gunner to traverse the turret and scan the area with his own sights. Seconds later he'd identified the cluster of three bunkers which would be the platoon's target.

"Target front! Two o'clock. Range 250 metres," he screamed.

"Engage," ordered Fraser and the Warrior's 30mm Rarden cannon sent three rounds lancing into each bunker. Then the chain gun sprayed them for good measure.

In the back of the Warrior the section of infantrymen sat nervously. They'd readied themselves for action several times over the past day and a half, only to be stood down. In their heart of hearts they knew that this time it was happening, this time it was for real. In a few seconds time they would be out there. They sat facing each other imagining the battle - they could see nothing of it from inside the steel can. Their only contact with the outside world was the intercom with their commander.

"Three-hundred metres, two-hundred metres, one hundred-metres…stand by," Fraser's metallic voice crackled into the steel chamber of the Warrior. There was a pause, the Warrior crashed to a standstill and then he gave the order.

"DEBUS RIGHT! DEBUS RIGHT! DEBUS RIGHT!"

The hydraulic arm that controlled the rear door rammed it open and the eight men leapt from the Warrior's protection.

The first pair sprinted in a zig-zag for a few metres to spoil the aim of the defenders, before diving to the ground behind what little cover they could find. Then they rattled off a few rounds into the bunkers from their SA-80s. Behind them the rest of the section did the same and when the first pair heard these rounds going in, they leapt to their feet and ran towards the target.

Fraser sat in the turret of the Warrior and watched the action through the smoke and murk using its 8x magnifier nightsight. In his headset he could hear both the Company net and his own platoon net. The latter screeched in his ear.

"Hello Zero Bravo, this is Mike One Charlie. Contact Front. Wait. Out."

The leading section of the platoon was meeting fire from the bunker complex. Fraser traversed the turret to try to get a better view, but the smoke was still too thick to get a clear picture. In this case, he told himself, nothing would be better than the mark one human eyeball.

"I'm debussing. Hold the fort," he shouted to Robson and Winstanley over the intercom. Then he jumped out of the turret into hell.

5

Outside the sterile protection of the Warrior, Fraser's senses returned to him. Instead of staring through a gun sight or tiny observation slits, he could see the whole awful panorama of war. But it wasn't the vista that had the deepest effect on him, it was the noise and the smell.

Somewhere out there in the desert, Saddam Hussein had blown hundreds of the pressurised oil wells that littered the country and torched the fluid as it spurted out. It was drizzling a thin mist of rainwater and oil, a mixture of heaven and hell. What fell to earth stank the sharp odour of poison. All around was the acrid smoke from the burning of metal, rubber, explosives and flesh. The industrial mixture caught in the back of Fraser's throat as he sprinted to catch up with his platoon.

For what seemed like days now he'd been wearing a headset with radio nets crackling in each ear. Now all he could hear was intermittent small arms fire crackling off in the near vicinity. Further away he could hear the heavier crump of a Challenger's main armament, then the terrible crash of the round impacting. Everywhere, men were screaming.

Then he heard a weapon he could not recognise. It felt close, yet sounded far away. It was a *ba-boom*, followed seconds later by another *ba-boom*. Weapons that were fired, or which impacted close by, caused variations in air pressure that could usually be felt in the thoracic cavity in the chest. This was one of them. As he raced forward, a million thoughts charging through his mind, his senses filling, he tried to work out what it was.

By the time he caught up with the rearmost fireteam of his platoon, he realised the noise was not a weapon but the beating of his heart.

The four-man fireteam was crouched in a small crater and he crashed down into the sand beside them. He gasped for breath in the poisoned air but in an instant his reflexes and training brought up his rifle and pointed it towards the target.

"What's the fucking hold-up?" he screamed.

A soldier turned towards him. Through the cam cream and dirt Fraser could see fear etched in his face.

"Effective fire from the right hand complex," yelled the soldier.

Fraser paused. Amid the bedlam, all was silent for a split second. *Assess. Act.*

"When I signal, you and your section follow me. Got it? We need to make this fucking good and fucking fast." He was screaming again.

He was driven on by an adrenaline rush like he'd never known. This *had* to work. His men could not afford to get bogged down on the first stage of their first attack.

He rolled onto his back and keyed the pressel of his radio. He snapped an order to Robson back in the Warrior, which growled into motion a second later and rolled towards them. Then he fished into his smock pocket and removed four tracer rounds.

He'd cocked his rifle the instant he'd stepped out of the Warrior so there was a live round in the chamber. In a flash he pulled the magazine from the weapon, cocked it again so the round tipped out onto the sand. He slid the red-tipped tracers inside the magazine before slapping it back in its housing. He cocked the weapon a third time, bringing the first tracer round into the chamber.

"OK guys, let's fucking do it." A scream again and he rolled out the side of the crater and sprinted forward towards the bunker.

In a nanosecond he took stock of the situation. The bunker was in fact two small buildings, one slightly behind the other. A shallow trench connected them then fanned out into the flat area that Fraser and his men were sprinting towards now. He remembered that they were attacking from the north-east, that the Iraqis faced south, and that this was the *rear* of the complex.

Then he saw the muzzle flashes from the defenders' weapons. Two, possibly three, AKs were rattling rounds towards him.

He slid to a stop in the oily sand and dropped to one knee, his weapon levelled towards the target. His left hand moved to the radio pressel attached to his webbing strap and he spoke to the Warrior again.

"Winstanley. Watch my tracer. Put 10 rounds after it."

Then he lifted the rifle to his cheek and held his breath. Through the SUSAT sight he could see the outline of the doorframe of the nearer bunker. Somewhere inside that building there were men determined to defend that complex. They were his enemy. They were slowing up his attack. They had to be swept aside. If that meant killing them, then that's the way it had to be. He would worry about the moral argument later. He could not afford to be slowed up by this. Charlie Company depended on him. He could not let them down. By letting them down he would be letting down his own regiment. That could not happen.

His right hand held the pistol grip of the rifle, his index finger caressed the trigger. His left hand cradled the stock. Slowly the middle finger of his left hand slid back a centimetre and a half and clicked off the safety catch.

He squeezed the trigger a fraction more and felt the rifle punch into his shoulder as it sent two tracer rounds arching into each of the open doorways, lighting the air in between for a split second each.

Fifty metres to the rear, Winstanley had an even better view. He watched where the red slugs hit the target and traversed the

Warrior's turret to make a microscopic change to his aim. Then he sent 10 30mm cannon rounds after the tracer.

By this time Fraser had dived for cover and was making himself as small as he could. He rolled away from the position he'd held when he'd fired his first shots of war, in case someone had spotted him and thought about firing back.

He fished about in his equipment and looked up to see his men in the crater watch him expectantly. They'd followed him forward and were waiting for the next move.

Slowly, deliberately, his eyes not leaving theirs, he drew his bayonet from his webbing belt and fixed it with a snap onto its housing on the end of his rifle. His men did the same. No words were needed.

From a webbing pouch he took a smoke grenade and hefted it in his palm.

"Once this goes in lads, pour fire on the target and follow me."

He peeped round the corner of the cluster of concrete-filled oil barrels he'd been using for cover, and watched the two bunkers. He was certain he could see movement coming from one. He wriggled into a position that was less uncomfortable and took a final quick glance at the bunkers. Again he held his breath and pulled the pin.

Before the smoke started to spew from the tiny aperture left by the pin, he'd lobbed the canister towards the target. He'd aimed for a point about 10 metres away from the doorway. The idea was to block the defenders' view of the attackers and give his men the chance to move undetected, and more importantly, unmolested.

The green plume brought an unusual dash of colour to the drab grey skies and burnt oily sand of the desert. Before the pressurised cloud of sickly sweet-smelling smoke billowed more than two metres into the air, a dozen British rifles clattered rounds into it.

Fraser felt the kick of his rifle butt in his shoulder again as he poured rounds down on the target through the smoke. Then he stopped, applied the safety catch and stood up.

"NOW! FUCKING MOVE NOW! MOVE!" he bellowed again as hard as his clogged lungs and throat would allow.

He set off at a sprint once more and zig-zagged towards the bunkers. Out of the corner of his eye he saw the main body of his men race for the front door; he could hear their awful screams as they ran, bayonets fixed, inside. He peeled off to the right in case any of the enemy tried to get away to the side or rear of the position. Suddenly he was cresting a rise. It was totally against all tactics but the adrenaline thrust him on. The berm that flanked the bunkers was about six feet high. Anyone on the other side would have had a perfect view of him outlined against the sky. But there was nobody there.

He hurdled the berm and ran down the other side into the flat area beyond the bunker complex. As his feet hit the flattened sand he realised he was probably in a mined area. Too late now. His momentum took him onwards. He skidded round to the left and felt, more than heard, the explosions made by two grenades his men had rolled inside the bunker.

He pulled a grenade from his webbing pouch and ran for the rear of the bunker. On the south facing side there were three narrow apertures from where anti-tank weapons protruded. Beside them was a hole that could only have come from an allied tank round. Fraser slid to halt beneath it. His hands shook as he pulled the pin. He did what every instructor had taught him down the years on the ranges and checked both hands to ensure one held the grenade, the other the pin, and posted it through the hole.

There was a muffled crack from inside the bunker then, rifle first, Fraser leapt through the gap and into the smoke.

Once inside he did an instant sweep. He was in a room about 10 metres square. But for the anti-tank weapons, it was completely empty. To the rear was a dark communicating passage leading back inside the bunker. Fraser stopped for a few seconds. He knew his men were attacking the bunker from the other direction; he could hear their weapons, their yells. He did not need to bump into them coming the other way.

Suddenly he heard footsteps from the passage. It was a panicked run, a sprint hampered by the darkness and the confined space. The footsteps were heading straight for him out of the blackness.

Fraser lifted his rifle to his cheek.

A split second later the running man was in the room.

Fraser had read somewhere that many Iraqis styled themselves on Saddam Hussein. This man was obviously one of them. He wore the dark green fatigues of a soldier, but on his shoulders were green rank slides with the three yellow stars of a Captain. He was in his late 30s, of medium height and wore his hair and moustache in the style of the leader himself. His eyes were wide with fright when he emerged from the corridor and saw Fraser MacLean standing there.

The Iraqi held an AK in his right hand and in slow motion he began to raise it.

The first millimetre of the movement was all Fraser needed.
His brain, his eye, his finger were one.
His rifle's sight was centred on the Iraqi's chest.
He didn't need to aim.
He squeezed the trigger.
Click.
Nothing.
Click.
Stoppage.
Click.
The dead man's click.

HEAVEN

The idea had been his guidance teacher's. Even at 15, Fraser MacLean would have preferred to study more French or German, but he was pointed instead towards the art class. Yes he could take photographs, and indeed had been commended for the composition of some of his landscapes, but he was the first to admit his drawing was poor. He went infrequently to Glasgow's art galleries, but he did not enjoy the visits. And while he loved books and plays and the cinema, painting, sketching and sculpture were lost on him.

But he had little choice. The spare periods had to be filled somehow and his guidance teacher had stressed, somewhat haughtily, that Fraser's planned career in academia would not be quite complete unless he left Newton Mearns Academy, without at least an O Grade in Art. Even Mr Bridges, the Modern Languages master, agreed. Fraser went grudgingly, but without comment, to his art class on the first day of the school year that summer of 1979.

The classroom was on a side of the building that appeared to catch the light all day. It was said that the head of the art department had insisted it be there for that very reason. He was a fierce looking man of about 50 who hailed from the Western Isles and spoke with a pronounced accent. Fraser was terrified of him at first - he thought he looked like the devil with his goatee beard and dark swept back hair. But he quickly found him to be a sensitive, pleasant man and he grew to like him immensely.

While Fraser had no future as an artist, and both he and the teacher accepted this, the pair got on well. Fraser's ear was far more gifted than his eye and the teacher would speak in Gaelic whenever the opportunity arose. Two years hence Fraser left the class with a bare pass in art, but an excellent command of Scotland's ancient language.

Late in 1979 Satan, as Fraser had nicknamed him, was forced to take time off because of a heavy cold. Fraser was certain the noxious pipe tobacco the man smoked had more than a little to do with it. The teacher from the classroom next door came in at the start of the Friday afternoon period and gave the pupils some work. He said that in the absence of the regular teacher, he would pop in and out to keep an eye on things and warned that anyone caught misbehaving would be dealt with summarily and severely.

This was a nod towards the hard leather two-fingered belt that lurked menacingly in a desk drawer.

There were about a dozen people in the class. As soon as the teacher had gone back to his own lesson, three of the rougher pupils left the room gauging, correctly, that he had not done a proper head count and they could leave without being missed. The rest of the afternoon would be spent enjoying a packet of 10 Gold Leaf behind the science labs.

The remainder of the pupils sat in silence. Fraser was struggling with a book about the impressionists. The concept troubled him. He could not see the point of painting a picture that did not look anything like the subject. He was toying with ignoring the chapter altogether and going instead to the section describing the artists' lives in Paris. He would find that far more interesting. Paris fascinated him.

"I dare you," came the whisper from one of a bunch of boys to his left, "I'll give you my Sex Pistols badge if you do," said another.

Fraser ignored the disturbance and flicked through the book. There was movement among the boys, a flurry of colour, then an angry shout.

"Ow! Leave me alone!"

Fraser looked up. One of the boys had crossed the room and was standing in front of a desk where the only girl in the class sat. Fraser couldn't see clearly but he was sure he was groping her breast.

The group of boys on his side of the class began cheering crudely. Their hero returned to his own side of the room punching the air. Fraser saw the girl was clutching at herself, her face red with embarrassment.

Five minutes later the second boy crossed the room and confronted the girl. She crossed her arms to protect herself and the boy turned away at the last minute. But instead of going back to his seat, he circled round behind her and attempted to undo her bra through her blouse.

"Get out of my sight, you scumbag," she yelled. The boy laughed and returned to his mates.

Then they both ran over and began lunging at her. One tried to pinch her breasts from the front, the other attempted to undo her bra at the back.

Fraser put down his book and looked on in shock. He'd seen the girl around the school but didn't know her. *Wasn't her name Kirsty?*

He'd heard her mother had died a couple of years before and he was sure they said her father was a famous lawyer and very rich, but he didn't know her. She seemed nice enough but he would never have spoken to her. God no, if you spoke to a girl everybody automatically assumed you were her boyfriend. The ridicule would be agony. Anything more than a mumbled "Hi" was deemed to be a marital dialogue. No, he'd never spoken to her.

But he wanted to speak to her right then. Her face was red and tears rolled down his cheeks. Her arms flailed helplessly as she tried to shield herself and fight off her assailants.

Courage came from somewhere. He leapt to his feet, the chair fell to the ground behind him, and he strode across the room.

"I really don't think you should be doing that. I'm going to tell the teacher," he said, fighting to keep his voice steady.

"I'm going to tell the teacher," repeated one boy in an effeminate voice.

"Fuck off you Paki swot," hissed the other.

Fraser hated it when people called him that. He was dark, yes, and got darker when he'd been in the sun. Sometimes he was taken for being Spanish or Italian. Being mistaken for an Asian didn't bother him in the slightest, but he didn't like the word 'Paki' used in that context.

"Leave her alone," he said and grabbed the first assailant by the shoulder.

In later years he would learn to read a punch, to feint, to weave, to ride its contact on his chin. But he never even saw the fist that caught him square in the face. His nose exploded in a mist of blood and snot and he was sent sprawling across the desks and chairs.

He looked up and saw the strawberry blond hair, the head bowed in embarrassment and the tears falling on the grey school skirt. Her arms were still crossed over her front and he could see her shake as she cried openly now. He rose.

Before he'd taken a pace, a boot caught him in the groin and he fell back again, screaming in agony as the pain crashed through him. It was his turn to cry now - tears of frustration, tears of pain, tears of humiliation.

Despite the numbing spasms coursing through him, he knew he couldn't leave this situation alone and he rose to face his attackers again.

The bell rang. The room emptied.

"Are you ok?" her voice was soft. She was a gentle person, a kind person. She had been the victim but now her attention was turned to him.

"Am I ok? More to the point are you ok?" he said hoarsely.

Fraser's eyes fell to her school blouse. The top three buttons had been torn off and the white cotton garment lay open. He could see the white lace of her bra and the cream skin of her breasts. The area above her cleavage was a mass of freckles. He'd never seen anything like it in his life. She saw him looking at her and she folded her arms again in embarrassment.

"I…I…I'm sorry," said Fraser, looking away. "I wasn't…I didn't mean to…"

"It's ok," she said, I know. Thank you for helping me. I hate those guys. I always have."

"I wasn't able to do very much. I'm sorry. I'm not very good at fighting." Fraser stood up and walked stiffly back to his seat. He picked it off the floor and removed his grey school jersey from where it lay beside it on the ground. He walked back over to the girl and handed it to her.

"You might need this," he said.

She smiled and thanked him.

Fraser returned to his desk to find that someone had spat on his book at the page that described the artists' quarter of Paris. He put his handkerchief inside and folded it closed.

His home in Ballantrae Crescent was not far from the school, but Fraser had to walk home gingerly because every pace brought a grinding pain in his groin. He went upstairs to the bathroom and cleaned himself up as best as he could before his mother saw the mess his face was in. He turned to use the toilet before he went downstairs.

But when he saw blood in his urine he fainted.

Secretly his father was very proud of Fraser that Friday night. The old soldier believed his son was too soft and needed to toughen up. That the boy had been involved in some minor skirmish and had been blooded was no bad thing, he thought.

His mother was of a different view.

"Scrapping is not gentlemanly," she said haughtily as she dished up dessert. "Why are you at a good school if you are going to waste time fighting instead of concentrating on getting to university? You should have gone to one of the local high schools instead."

Fraser ate in silence. He'd explained the bloodied face was the result of a fair and frank exchange of views with another boy. He said it had been a scoring draw, no winner, no loser. He omitted any mention of the girl with strawberry blond hair whose smile had been beautiful through the tears.

He hardly slept that night because of the pain in his groin and his blocked nose. His mother was adamant that if he passed any more blood over the weekend he'd have to go to casualty at the Victoria Infirmary. The prospect of a doctor, or worse, a nurse, examining his private parts was mortifying.

But what kept him awake most of all was thinking about Kirsty.

He spent the next day the way he spent most Saturdays, surrounded by books. His father had long since given up on Fraser joining him for a round of golf at Haggs in the morning and a rugby match at Hughenden in the afternoon. Fraser's older brother Euan was the more sporting of the pair.

Instead Fraser would rise, help his mother with whatever jobs needed to be done around the house and garden, then read for the rest of the day. In his father's study, amid the military books (which he ignored) he found an old tourist guide to Paris and started to read about the artists' quarter. It fascinated him. After dinner he thought he would explore the attic where he was certain he'd seen another book about Paris that might yield more information.

2

He'd been in the attic for only 10 minutes that evening when the doorbell rang. He heard his mother shout for him to come down because he had a visitor.

Fraser was confused. *Who would be visiting at this time on a Saturday?* His best friend William had gone hillwalking on Skye with his parents that weekend. He trotted down the stairs and his jaw dropped when he saw Kirsty standing waiting in the hall.

"Thanks for letting me use this," she said holding out a carrier bag.

Fraser thought for a moment - *The jersey, of course.*

"Would you like a cup of tea Kirsty?" His mother's voice.

Oh Christ, thought Fraser. *Say no, say no, say no, please say no*. He was facing enough ridicule on Monday morning as it was after the events in the art class. What if somebody had seen her walking up the path or ringing his doorbell?

"Well, only if you're putting the kettle on."

The next two hours passed in agony for Fraser. His mother and father made small talk with Kirsty while he sat and squirmed. He hardly spoke. He wasn't sure how to play this. He was 14 and a half. He didn't know what to say to a girl. Boys were different, they were easy. *What music did she like? What TV programmes did she watch?* Something like that?

At last it was time for her to go. *Get her out quick. End this hell.*

"Thanks for what you did," she said at the door. The smile was back. "It was very…gallant, that's the word." She said it in a French accent, emphasised the second syllable. He liked that.

"See you around," he said.

"See you," she replied and stepped outside.

Fraser's father strode across the hall holding a jacket.

"Don't be such an oaf Fraser," he said thrusting it into the boy's hands, "walk Kirsty home."

He died a hundred deaths as he stepped into the night air. When they got to the end of the drive he quickly scanned up and down the road in case he saw anyone who knew him. He couldn't afford to be seen with a girl. It would be the end. He was thankful for the darkness, if it hadn't been for that he'd have asked her to walk a few steps ahead of him in case anyone spotted them together.

Kirsty's house was a large, detached bungalow called "The Firs" in Giffnock, another exclusive area of the city. The walk took around 20 minutes, during which they chatted about school, their favourite subjects and teachers. They both laughed when they agreed that art was not something they enjoyed. Fraser felt awkward because he had never been in this situation before. He didn't have many friends and they were all boys and they did boys' things. But by the time he and Kirsty reached her gate, he felt better. They stood awkwardly for a few seconds. He wanted to glance at her breasts but didn't dare.

"I'd better go in," she said. "Dad will be wondering where I've got to."

Fraser nodded in understanding, then looked at his feet.

"He'd like to meet you. I told him what happened. Why don't you come over next Saturday night? About eight? We could listen to some records?"

Fraser's heart jumped, first in panic then anticipation.

"Love to," he heard himself mumble, his feet still holding a fascination for him.

"It's a date then," she said.

A date. The magic word. *A date.*

She took a pace forward, placed the palm of her hand on his chest and kissed him gently on the cheek.

"You're my hero," she said, and walked off into the darkness.

3

The week passed in a haze. Every morning Fraser walked to school and looked for her among the crowds of grey skirts and cardigans. He wasn't sure of her timetable and didn't know her movements. His heart jumped into his mouth when he passed her unexpectedly in the geography corridor on the Wednesday morning. He didn't know whether to acknowledge her or ignore her. He was with a couple of his friends and if he spoke to her in their company, the embarrassment would be a killer. He looked over and their eyes met as they passed. She smiled, he smiled back. Nobody noticed. It was beautiful.

He counted the minutes until the next Saturday night. He thought of her at every moment, the softness of the peck on his cheek and the sweet scent of her perfume.

He was her hero.

She said it, she actually said the words. She also used the word "date." And then she'd kissed him.

The incident in the art class evolved in his imagination. He fantasised about some ridiculous scenarios where she would be in danger again and he would rescue her, only this time he would win the fight. She would be a nurse in a field hospital in the trenches of World War One and he would be a dashing soldier. Or she would be working in a blazing office block and he would be a fireman.

On the Thursday night, he realised he'd been fantasising so much throughout the week that he'd lost track of time. He'd forgotten that he would share a classroom with her again at art the next day.

The next day.

It would be a week since the incident that brought them together. He'd be in the same classroom as her for the first time, which was exciting beyond belief. But at the same time the two neds who'd groped her would be there too and the whole ugly scene would be replayed.

How would she react? How would he react? How would the two thugs react?

He'd kept his head down all week and avoided contact with the pair. Few people had mentioned the incident to him and when they did he managed to change the subject.

But if it all started again how would he cope?

He wasn't nearly tough enough to take them on. And this time they'd have their friends with them.

Nerves gripped Fraser as he walked to school that Friday. The morning passed without incident but he could hardly contain himself between excitement and fear as he walked into the art classroom after lunch.

Antibiotics are wonderful things. Sitting behind his desk at the front of the class reading a book about Glasgow's Art Deco buildings, was Satan. Fraser was overcome with relief and took his seat. He looked over at Kirsty and noticed she was wearing a white poloneck sweater under her blouse. She lifted her eyes from a charcoal drawing she'd started and smiled at him. It melted his heart.

The rest of the afternoon passed in ecstasy for him. When he was sure she wouldn't notice, he stared at her, transfixed. Her hair was light red, although he'd heard it described as strawberry blonde, and she had clear, pale green eyes. Her nose was turned up at the end and her mouth always seemed to be smiling. Her teeth were shining white and perfectly straight.

He saw her tongue dart out of her mouth and quickly moisten her lips. He was overcome by the urge to dive into the shining wetness. He knew he shouldn't but he couldn't help looking at her breasts. They were bigger than those of any of the other girls in the school and his mind flashed back to the previous week when he saw the freckles on her cleavage.

There was an uncomfortable erection in his grey flannel school uniform trousers when the bell went to mark the end of the day. His mind flashed back to the tableau of the same time the previous week and he blushed with embarrassment. What he'd done had been a huge gamble, but he was glad he'd taken it. It didn't matter who the girl was, whether she was pretty or not, nobody deserved to be treated like that.

He packed away his books and stood up to leave. If he timed it right he'd manage to walk out at the same time as Kirsty and maybe steal a word or another smile.

He watched out of the corner of his eye as she tidied away her books and pencil case. *Was she dallying so she could leave at the same time as him? Did she feel the same way too?*

They reached the door at precisely the same time and left together. They walked along the corridor talking about nothing in particular and this time Fraser didn't care who saw them.

"See you tomorrow night?" she said as they were about to part at the school gate.

"Looking forward to it," he replied.

Fraser's Saturday started badly. His elder brother Euan managed to elicit from him his movements that night and proceeded to tease him all morning.

"Fraser's got a girlfriend, Fraser's got a girlfriend," goaded Euan until 11 o'clock when their father took him out for 18 holes and a lecture on etiquette. As ever, their mother was the complete opposite.

"She seems nice," was all she said, but with a look in her eye that spoke volumes. He spent the rest of the day helping her in the garden and reading a French novel called 'Thérèse Desqueyroux'. It was really for fourth year pupils but Mr Bridges had given it to him anyway and he found he could follow the plot so long as he kept a verb and vocabulary book handy.

Euan decided to make a pest of himself that night too by hogging the bathroom until 7.30 and taking an extra long shower, even though he planned to sit in front of the TV all night. Secretly he also hoped to use all the hot water and therefore stymie his young brother's attempts at wooing. Sensing the situation in advance, as only a military man could, their father ordered the older boy out of the steaming room to allow the younger one in.

"Don't forget to wash your willie," sneered Euan as they passed on the landing.

"You're willie's still got handles on it," came the reply.

"Enough!" shouted their father, "move, the pair of you."

Fraser wasn't sure how to play Kirsty's father. He was desperate to see her and spend time with her, but her father was different. His own father wasn't slow to inform him that Jack Buchanan was a millionaire defence lawyer and a fellow member at Haggs. He was obviously no fool. But what would he be like? Secretly he was glad that she'd told him what had happened. Fraser was desperate that Buchanan liked him, but he was agonising over how they would discuss the subject.

He jumped into the shower and washed thoroughly. He was about to switch it off when the water started to run cold. He swore revenge on his brother, but that could wait, he had a more important issue at hand.

He wasn't quite 15 and because he was very dark he already had the downy beginnings of a moustache on his upper lip. It had never been important before, but now it was.

What if she kissed him again, but on the mouth this time? What if he had to kiss her back?

He had never kissed a girl before. He didn't even know how. But he was certain that if it got to the kissing stage the moustache would have to go.

He rummaged in his father's soapbag, removed the razor and studied it carefully. As a young boy he'd watched his father shave many times. Surely he could remember how. The blade looked old and a bit rusty in places so he dismantled the razor and removed a new blade from its packet. Gingerly, remembering how his father did it, he put the whole assembly back together again.

Then he found the can of shaving foam and squirted some onto his hand. He didn't know how to judge the flow and poured out far too much. Some fell on the carpet. He tried to rub it in with his foot but the stain grew worse. Things weren't going to plan – his mother would kill him for this. He smeared the rest onto his face.

Not realising the benefits of holding a razor blade under the hot tap for a few seconds to expand the steel, Fraser MacLean passed from boyhood to manhood with a cold and bloody sweep across his face.

He yelped in pain and rummaged again in the soapbag for the aftershave his father used. He remembered being told it acted as an astringent and would stop the bleeding. Again he misjudged things and poured more on the floor than in his hand. He splashed some of the green liquid onto his face and cried in agony as the aftershave reached the cuts. The pain was so intense that he jogged on the spot for a few seconds to try to alleviate it. When it had died away, he looked at himself in the mirror. *There wasn't too much blood*, he assured himself.

Before he'd gone into the shower he'd lain out his carefully-chosen outfit on the bed. When he went back to the room it had disappeared.

It took some cajoling, two thinly-veiled threats then finally a plea, before Euan returned the neatly-pressed trousers, shirt and v-necked sweater from their cache in the garden shed. After a final and futile argument with his parents over his choice of footwear, Fraser MacLean left to go on his first date with a girl - a warning to be back by 10.30 ringing in his ears.

His nerves had been at fever pitch all the way from his house to hers but when he finally walked up the drive and plucked up the courage to ring the bell, they went off the scale. Kirsty answered, bright and breezy in jeans and a sweatshirt.

"What happened to your face?" she asked as she let him into the wood-panelled hall.

Fraser needn't have worried about her father. Top lawyer he may have been, but he was far more relaxed than the boy could have imagined. He instantly wished his own father could be this way.

Jack Buchanan wore cords and a checked shirt, the sort Fraser had seen farmers wear, and slippers. The front room was untidy in a way Fraser liked. He hoped to have a study like this one day. There were books and newspapers strewn everywhere and a log fire roared in the hearth.

He shook Fraser's hand and thanked him for helping his daughter.

"I'm sure those guys will be clients of mine one of these days," he joked. He looked at his watch. "Anyway, I've got work to do on a case for Monday so I'll leave you two in here. Don't make too much noise with that thing," he said nodding towards the music centre on a low table beside the window.

Kirsty turned to Fraser and smiled.

"Ultravox or the Stranglers?" she asked.

She made coffee and the pair sat at either end of the sofa in front of the fire. They spoke about school, their hobbies and their favourite books and records. After a while she told him how her mother had been diagnosed with cancer and had died inside six months. Kirsty had been just 10.

He could see from the brief meeting in the hallway that Kirsty and her father were very close. He imagined her doing the cooking and cleaning and Fraser felt so sad for her. He didn't think that she would have had much of a childhood. He wished he'd been there to comfort her when she must have been in so much pain.

Fraser was certain she'd only asked him over out of politeness and to meet her father. But as the evening passed he found that they got on well and he felt relaxed in her company. He had wound himself up into such a state of anxiety already that night, that asking her if she wanted to go to the cinema the next Saturday wasn't a problem.

He couldn't contain his delight when she accepted. At the end of the night it was Fraser's turn to kiss Kirsty on the cheek. He wanted to kiss her on the mouth but he didn't dare and anyway, he didn't know how.

He floated home. She was so, so what? *So nice.* Nice was a horrible word, but she *was* nice. No, wait. She was *nicer* than nice. She was lovely. When he let his mind wander off onto something else, then thought of her again, he felt a small kick in the pit of his stomach.

When he got home he washed his face and brushed his teeth before jumping into bed. In the dark he lay pretending to hold Kirsty Buchanan the night her mother died. He wanted to make it all better, to protect her, to be there for her. He slept long and deep.

The next day he didn't say much. He ignored his brother's taunts and his parents' questions. Instead he wandered aimlessly around the house pretending Kirsty was there with him. He would have silent conversations with her, like a young child with an imaginary friend.

Because of traffic, by the time their bus reached the Odeon cinema on Renfield Street on Saturday night, they'd missed the start of Alien, the film they were originally going to see. They risked trying to get into the Deer Hunter instead. Both films were 18 certificates and by rights they shouldn't have been anywhere near either of them.

But they got in and after an hour Fraser was glad they had. Whenever Robert de Niro or his comrades came under fire in the jungle of Vietnam, Kirsty would turn and bury her face into his shoulder. When De Niro and co were imprisoned in a bamboo cage, partly-submerged in a rat-infested river, Fraser made up his mind to act.

Minutes later the suspense of the Russian roulette scene became too much and Kirsty burrowed into his armpit again. He was nervous but he knew he wouldn't get a better opportunity and threw his arm around her shoulder. It stayed there for the rest of the film and the entire journey back to Newton Mearns on the bus.

By the time they'd walked from the bus stop on Ayr Road down the leafy avenue to her house, his senses were full of the sweet smell of her hair and the warmth of her body. They ambled along, discussing the film. In truth he wasn't paying much attention to what they were saying. Instead, his mind was on what he knew he would do in a few minutes time.

He was still nervous, but determined, when they finally reached the driveway of Kirsty's house. Deliberately, he walked her past the gate and into the shadow of the tall hedge beyond. His right arm was still around her shoulder and when they stopped and turned towards each other, he slipped his left hand round her waist and pulled her close.

Her fringe was level with his nose, her pale green eyes looked up into his. Her lips were shiny and her teeth sparkled white between them. Slowly, nervously, he lowered his mouth to hers.

Then fireworks exploded and church bells rang.

Their mouths were closed and their eyes wide open the first time, but after a full 20 minutes of experimentation, the process was reversed and they became experts. Fraser got a row for being late when he got home that night, but he couldn't have cared less.

And so it began. Two children becoming adults and enjoying the first burgeoning feelings of pure teenage love. Each Friday and Saturday evenings they would visit each other's homes or go to the cinema. Gradually they met each other's friends and became involved in a wider circle of people. But in truth they were only interested in each other.

At school they quickly learnt each other's timetables and would look out for each other as they passed in the corridor. They would seek out each other at break times and walk home together each night.

When he saw her with her friends he wondered what they spoke about. He didn't think they'd be talking about him, why would they? They always seemed to be giggling. When he heard a snatch of conversation that wasn't meant for male ears, he couldn't understand any of it. He wondered what girls discussed, how they reasoned. To Fraser, women were a mystery, they were complicated, sophisticated, more advanced than him, even at the same age. In the end he gave up. Women, he conceded, were simply from a different planet.

The art class that had thrown them together became a kind of shrine for them both. They each moved seats so they could sit together. It was the only time of the week when they shared a lesson and they both wished their days away until Fridays so they could be together. Fraser actually became quite interested in art and did his best to draw and paint well. But his efforts with pastels, brush and pencil were to impress Kirsty and not Satan.

It became obvious around the school that they were an item and the childish taunting started as expected. To Fraser's surprise he wasn't as bothered by it as he thought he would be, and in fact he became proud of it. All he cared about was Kirsty and being with her. He could shut out everything else. And when the whistlers and name-callers realised they were having no effect, they stopped, as much through jealousy as anything else.

Older boys he didn't even know would stop Fraser in the corridor and ask him if he was "screwing" Kirsty Buchanan. The notion angered him. His girlfriend was above that kind of language, that kind of suggestion. She was good, pure, kind. He would swallow his fear of the bigger boys and reply in his haughtiest tones that yes, he was *seeing* Kirsty Buchanan, and what about it?

"You're a lucky bastard," was the invariable reply.

4

The Christmas holidays were coming and Fraser felt like he had never felt before. School was ending, which was cause for celebration in itself. But what he was looking forward to most of all was spending time with Kirsty during the day. They planned to go into the city centre and wander around the shops, go to George Square and look at the Christmas decorations or simply sit drinking coffee somewhere nice.

How adult was that?

There was no art class on the last Friday afternoon before the break. Instead there was a much anticipated Christmas dance in the gymnasium. The pupils were allowed to wear what they liked and the Scottish country dance music blaring out over the public address system was interspersed with music from the charts. For two weeks beforehand, the normal games of the gym classes were replaced by rehearsals for country dancing. And while the other male pupils were dreading the event, Fraser couldn't wait.

Kirsty stole the show and mouths gaped around the hall when she made her entrance wearing a long dark green velvet dress, which complimented her colour perfectly. She looked very grown up in the outfit, which was enhanced by a trace of make-up. Fraser didn't like make-up on girls and didn't really think Kirsty needed any, but he had to admit she looked fantastic and he told her so repeatedly.

They danced to every tune and when his friend William took Kirsty up for one dance Fraser stood at the side of the gym and watched in envy. As soon as they'd finished, Fraser grabbed her and took her back onto the dance floor. Other boys asked her to dance later but she always said no, she was Fraser's partner.

The last dance was a waltz and even though his mother and father had tried to teach him in the living room, he hadn't been able to master the steps. Instead he held Kirsty close and they shuffled around the floor, vaguely in time with the music - their first slow dance together. His arms were around her tiny waist, his nose was full of her scented hair and he could feel the firmness of her breasts pressed into his chest. He hoped she couldn't feel the rock hard bulge in his flannel trousers.

He couldn't have been happier, or prouder as they walked home that evening.

They shared a magical snowy Christmas Eve walk through Queen's Park, wrapped up warm against the chill. When they stopped to admire the frost on the leaves in the golden glow of the sunset, he produced a sprig of Mistletoe and they kissed long into the evening.

Her present to him that first Christmas was a warm woollen jumper, chosen simply because she knew he needed one. It came neatly wrapped in bright Christmas paper with small strips of tape precisely placed to hold it all together. There was a rosette of ribbon and a small card in her neat writing.

While her present to him had been simple, and borne out of need, the process of him buying a present for her had been far more complicated and angst-ridden. He had agonised for weeks over what to get her and had discussed the matter with anyone who would listen. He had debated between clothes or a record or perfume. But he didn't know her size or what style she would like and he couldn't face the thought of her displeasure if he bought an LP she didn't like. As for perfume, his mother had said that kind of present was a bit too personal, because girls had their own favourites and Fraser didn't know what Kirsty's was.

In the end he went for something far more personal than perfume. He bankrupted himself of all his savings, borrowed money from his brother, father and two friends, and purchased a necklace from Fraser's, Glasgow's top department store. In later years he would shake his head at the cost of that first Christmas present, but he knew she was worth every penny.

Kirsty and her father had been invited by Fraser's parents to their home for drinks on Christmas night. Fraser thought he had done well by purchasing a box of golf balls for Kirsty's dad – they seemed to go down well. Fraser himself was surprised and very grateful for the present he received from Jack – a book of poems by the French writer Rimbaud. Mr Bridges would be impressed when he started quoting from it in class.

While he had been genuinely touched by that present, Kirsty was overwhelmed by Fraser's gift to her. The parcel had been neatly wrapped by the staff in Fraser's and it took some time for Kirsty to open it. Everyone's eyes were on her when she eventually removed the long thin silver chain with green stones embedded in it.

She gasped and tears sprung into her eyes as the stones sparkled and flashed in the light.

"Oh, it's beautiful Fraser," she whispered, and his face went beetroot when she kissed him in front of everybody.

A week hence the MacLeans were invited to the Buchanan household for a New Year party. Fraser wore his new jersey and Kirsty her necklace. They both felt very grown up as they sat listening to the adults' conversation, Fraser drinking a lager shandy with far more lemonade than lager, and Kirsty a Vermouth so weak it hardly managed to leave the glass.

At midnight they all wished each other the best for the New Year and the new decade. At five past midnight Fraser and Kirsty escaped for a walk along the deserted streets to be alone for the first time that evening.

"I want to spend every New Year like this, with you," he told her.

"That's what I want too," she said.

He fumbled in his pocket and removed an empty cigar packet he'd taken from an ashtray in Kirsty's house. He took from it the cellophane wrapper that had contained the brand of cigar enjoyed occasionally by Jack Buchanan. Kirsty watched him in confusion as he gently prised open the clear plastic and removed the paper band that had once been wrapped round the top of the cigar.

"One day I'll buy you a proper ring, but in the meantime this'll have to do," he said, sliding the paper onto her finger.

"Oh Fraser you're lovely," she whispered and kissed him again.

After a moment he broke off and his eyes fell to the ground. He was searching for something, the words, the moment, both.

"I love you," he mumbled.

It was something he would never have said to anyone, those words were for other people, older people, people in films, not people like him, 14 year-old schoolboys. But tonight he felt different. Tonight he felt like a man. This was what it must be like, being an adult.

"Oh Fraser, I love you too," she said and again they were locked in a tight embrace, kissing frantically. A car approached and they ducked off the pavement into a long dark wooded driveway. They kissed on until their mouths were sore.

Fraser had his hands around Kirsty's waist and after a time he began to feel the bitter cold. He unzipped her jacket and put his hands inside, clutching her around her tiny waist again. It was much warmer here. They kissed on.

Snow began to fall around them adding to the magic of the moment. He kissed the nape of her neck and felt her shudder, she moaned when he nibbled her earlobe. Spurred on by this, his right hand rose an inch and he could just feel the weight of her breast against the web of skin between his thumb and forefinger.

He waited for her objection, but none came and they continued kissing. Minutes later boldness got the better of him and he lifted his thumb to caress the fullness of her breast. He was surprised how large and firm it felt. He knew she had large breasts from glances he stole while he thought she wasn't looking, but only in his wildest fantasies he could he imagine what they felt like.

Again there was no objection and he shortly placed his whole hand on her breast through her bra and jumper. All she did was moan with pleasure.

Feeling bold now, he slipped his hand up the inside of her jumper. Her skin was warm and silky soft. Soon he was caressing the lace of her bra – he was in ecstasy, he assumed she wouldn't let him do this, he assumed she'd object.

He had imagined this moment in long, tumescent fantasies. Now he was doing it. This beautiful, sweet, lovely girl was his girlfriend. They had spent the perfect Christmas together and now New Year was the icing on the cake. He had his hand inside her clothing and was caressing her breast, and not only was she not saying no, she seemed to be enjoying it.

But Kirsty did say no and squirmed away from him when he made a clumsy attempt to undo her bra.

"I think we'd better go back," she said adjusting her clothing, "Dad will be worrying about us."

They walked back to the house, only the crunching of their feet in the snow broke the magical silence.

By Valentine's Day Fraser had managed to get both hands inside Kirsty's blouse and discovered that a woman's nipples hardened when she was aroused. The thought had never occurred to him before.

It was on midsummer's night when they joined half a dozen friends on a camping expedition to Loch Lomond, that Kirsty let Fraser undo her bra and touch her breasts for the first time.

He wanted to go further that night but she wouldn't let him. "God wouldn't like it," she said. And because he loved her, completely and utterly, he let it go.

A year passed since they started seeing each other. By then they spent most of their spare time together and if they weren't in each other's company they were on the phone. Kirsty loved children and that summer of 1980 she went to Delaware in the United States to work as a child carer at a summer camp for local kids. She was away for a month.

Fraser hated it. He was lost without her and moped around the house. He wrote her endless letters and spent as much time on the phone to the hall of residence in Delaware as his parents would allow. He missed her but he was also petrified that she would meet someone else while she was away.

He couldn't bear the thought of his girl in the arms of another boy and lay awake at nights worrying. When she wrote or called he would hang on every word and listen to every nuance of conversation for a hint of trouble. He would ask her repeatedly if everything was ok between them and if she missed him. He was hardly assured when she said yes, but spent hours worrying instead.

His father had had enough after two weeks of this and frogmarched Fraser to a supermarket in Giffnock and ordered him to apply for a vacancy as a shelf stacker. The job paid a pittance and was mind-numbingly boring for someone of his intellect, but it got him out of the house.

Eventually Kirsty returned from Delaware. To prove that she *had* missed him, on their first evening alone not only did she let him remove her bra, she allowed him to put his hand inside her pants and feel the soft fuzz of hair at the top of her firmly shut legs.

They returned to school happier than any other pupils. This was their world – holidays had to be shared with parents. At Newton Mearns Academy they could resume their little secrets, the codes, the smiles and the hidden touches.

They studied together in each other's homes for their O Grade prelims, which they sat in October of that year. They would test each other and help each other memorise formulae or verb endings. Kirsty's favourite subjects were Chemistry, Biology and Physics. Fraser had no interest in the sciences, instead he was fascinated by language. He would sit English, French and German. He also enjoyed History and Geography but these were mere sideshows. And while he loved the art class and what it stood for, he had no interest in it as a subject. He was aiming to go to Glasgow University to study modern languages with a view to one day teaching French and German. She would go to Edinburgh University to study medicine.

The last exam was on a Friday. That night Fraser went to Kirsty's house and because her father was at a dinner in town, and the house would be empty for four hours, they quickly undressed each other in front of a roaring fire in the lounge. He had never seen a completely naked woman before - Kirsty had only ever let their petting take place in total darkness.

But there she was in all her teenage glory, lying for him in the glow of the flames. He saw the fire of hair at the top of her legs for the first time and wondered why it was red. He wondered also why she bothered wearing a bra, because her breasts seemed to stay in the same position without it.

He had never been naked in front of a girl before and was cringing with embarrassment when Kirsty slid down his y-fronts. He had been aroused every time they'd as much as kissed and he knew she must have felt his hardness digging into her. This was the first time she had seen him though, and he began to panic in case she would think he was too small. He'd heard all the stories about size being crucial. What if he wasn't big enough?

But he needn't have worried. She smiled up at him as her soft, inexperienced fingers explored his most sensitive part.

They studied together for the rest of the academic year and walked hand in hand to every O Grade exam when they came around shortly after the Easter of 1981. Kirsty excelled at science, Fraser at language. Neither found the exams particularly troublesome, though Fraser struggled with his art practical.

Neither would continue with art as a subject beyond O Grade and they bade a grateful, if emotional, farewell to Satan and his classroom after the exams. He wasn't blind and he wasn't stupid. He knew what was going on between them, though he would never know how they came to be together and his fateful part in it. He wished them well for the future with a knowing smile.

As he left the classroom for the last time, Fraser turned to look at the desk in the corner where it had all started. It was his turn to smile.

5

Kirsty got straight As in every subject, as did Fraser - apart from Art where he scored an expected C.

She returned to Delaware to work again at the summer camp. Although he hated it and wanted nothing to do with it, Fraser went back to his supermarket job. It earned him some money and made his days pass more quickly. But what cash he earned he had to give to his parents to pay for the phone calls he made to Delaware every other night.

Fraser was still scared stiff that she would meet another boy in the US. He listened carefully to every word, and more importantly every silence, of their telephone calls and read between the lines of every letter. But when she came back to Glasgow it was clear she had missed him as much as he had missed her. For the remaining few days they had left together before they returned to school, they explored each other's bodies as never before.

The first night, with his hand to guide her, and after a few minutes of painful practice, she managed to rub his manhood until he ejaculated.

Later, she took his hand and guided his fingers around and inside her until he felt her shudder and heard her moan his name.

Then they lay in each other's arms in front of the fire.

They returned to school to join the fifth year and study for their Highers, a more complicated set of exams that would determine their futures after they left. Fraser continued to study French and German as his main subjects under Mr Bridges, but he would also sit English, History and Geography. Kirsty's subjects would be Chemistry, Biology, Physics and Maths.

They followed the same pattern, in the autumn of 1981, of sitting prelims then going on their Christmas holidays. By now Fraser and Kirsty were inseparable. Both largely shunned the company of their friends and ignored hobbies so they could spend every moment together.

He was secretly very happy one Friday evening when she scolded him for being a few minutes late for a date. "That will stop when we're married," she said.

He was also very proud when Kirsty opened her purse in a shop or restaurant and he saw the ring from the cigar placed neatly inside the clear plastic pocket containing his picture.

Fraser hoped Kirsty's Christmas present to him would be to allow him to make love to her. But while she had grown accustomed to pleasuring him and allowing him to bring her to climax manually, she said a firm no to anything more.

Their chances of being alone together were few and far between and when they had them, they quickly undressed and leapt into bed or lay in front of the fire. And whilst he would never dream of forcing the issue, he was growing increasingly frustrated with their love life.

When they discussed it, she said she wasn't ready to have sex. She said she was too young for that part of their relationship and was worried about becoming pregnant. And anyway, she said, she was saving herself for Fraser on their wedding night.

But most of all she said it was a sin before God for them to have sex before they were married.

Christmas 1981 came and went. Her present to him was not her virginity, but a shirt and tie in a box.

The Higher exams were by far the hardest tests either had encountered. Again they prepared together, walked to each sitting together and waited outside the main hall afterwards to quiz each other on the detail of the papers. Fraser had no interest in science and was happy to let Kirsty's knowledge wash over him. But he was secretly proud that he knew so much more about his subjects than she did.

He liked to fantasise about taking Kirsty to France or Germany where she would be totally reliant on him because he could speak the language. He imagined some crisis where he could save the day by saying the right thing to the right person at the right time. Then at night they would return to their luxury hotel where she would relent and allow him to make love to her.

In the spring of 1982, Fraser was far more interested in the events of the Falklands War than he was in the forthcoming World Cup. Being an old soldier, his father corralled the family around the TV every night to watch the news. Fraser followed every battle in rapt attention.

Kirsty was less than enthused. She hated the idea of a war and couldn't contemplate one involving Britain. Wars were things her grandfather had fought in. Although not a football fan she sought escape in the World Cup about to be played in Spain at the same time.

When they met, he would talk about the battles for Goose Green and Tumbledown. She was more interested in Scotland's chances against Brazil. Fraser wasn't a football fan and couldn't understand why Scotland was playing football in a tournament involving Argentina, when young men from the two countries were bayoneting each other thousands of miles away.

But he relented and they sat together to watch Scotland play Brazil on TV. Kirsty became very excited when Scotland scored first. But though he knew little about football, Fraser said that all Scotland had done was anger the far superior Brazilians and that retribution would be swift. He reminded everybody of his prescience when the South Americans outclassed his countrymen and eventually ran out winners by four goals to one.

The defeat meant nothing to him but Kirsty's open admiration of the footballers' physical attributes did. It confused him. She was showing overt sexual interest in men, yet she wouldn't let him make love to her. And he became angry when she suggested to him that he take up football or rugby.

She had once told him that she loved him because of his brain, his mind, his intellect. She had told him she thought he was handsome and that she liked his hairy chest. But she had never said she found his body attractive.

Fraser didn't hate sport, but he didn't like it either. He wasn't interested in football. He thought football fans violent, drunken, bigoted cretins. The game itself was simple enough and he couldn't understand what the fuss was about.

He despised the way Glasgow was divided up into Protestant or Catholic football fans who supported either Rangers or Celtic accordingly. He'd long given up trying to fathom out why events in Ireland centuries before had any bearing on a sport.

He was slightly overweight and had no real coordination for games. At school PE sessions he was usually made to go in goals by bigger boys in the team and he spent many frozen hours standing around having heavy leather footballs blasted at him from close range.

He liked the idea of rugby though. It was a sport played at the better schools and watched by a better class of spectator. But he'd played the game only the once and older boys had treated him so roughly it was nearly a week before he could walk properly afterwards. He tried to learn the rules but found them too complicated. His father had taken him to Hughenden to watch a game one Saturday, but he had been bored stiff and frozen to the marrow.

His father never tired of telling Fraser he needed to toughen up, become a man. "Why don't you try a bit of 'Jap-slapping'?" he said repeatedly, referring to Karate in Army jargon.

But the only sport Fraser enjoyed and at which he was quite competent, much to the bewilderment of his father, was badminton. It required more skill than speed, more guile than brawn. He had once asked Kirsty to play as his partner at the school club but she had declined. He had hoped she would come and watch him play but she didn't even do that. She wanted him to play football or rugby, but there was no way he was going to oblige. He didn't have the inclination and with their final and critical school year approaching, he certainly didn't have the time.

They reached an impasse on the matter. He concentrated on his books and enjoyed a game of badminton once a week. To his annoyance, Kirsty began buying magazines about football and sticking pictures of the players she fancied on her school folders.

"He's cute," or "he's handsome," or "he's got a nice bum," she would say.

Each had collected A grades in their Highers that summer of 1982. Fraser had applied, and had been accepted for, a five year Master of Arts degree in Modern Languages at the University of Glasgow. Kirsty had also been successful with her application and would study medicine at Edinburgh University.

They could have gone up to university that year, but their parents thought they were too young at 17. And anyway Fraser and Kirsty wanted another year together at school before they had to be separated. They went back to the Academy to finish their studies by sitting one last set of examinations. The uniquely Scottish Certificate of Sixth Year Studies is by far the hardest examination in Secondary education. Fraser sat English, French and German. Kirsty took Physics, Chemistry and Biology.

Most of the pupils their age had left school by this time and they were close to what few friends remained. It was nearly Christmas when Fraser realised that he and Kirsty were the only couple among their peers who were not in a full sexual relationship. While he loved Kirsty and wanted nothing more in his life than to be with her, the lack of sex embarrassed and angered him.

It was the only stumbling block in an otherwise perfect relationship. She was beautiful, intelligent and well-liked. She didn't have a dark side, she was open and honest and didn't seem to play the mindgames he'd heard that some other girls played. She was deeply religious, which he liked, she went to church every week and was involved in the Sunday School. Even her choice of career was ideal – a doctor, a GP, what could be better than that? It was respectable, it was safe. She was always scrupulously clean and fashionably dressed without being flamboyant. She loved children and animals and got on very well with Fraser's parents. She could do no wrong. Even though her father was fabulously wealthy, she was the proverbial girl next door. She was perfect. He adored her. He put her on a pedestal.

But early in the new year of 1983, they had their first big fight.

Fraser and Euan had gone to Giffnock one Saturday morning to pick up some shopping for their mother. As they walked down the main street Fraser saw Kirsty in the distance. But before he could call out or catch up with her, she stepped into a coffee shop on the other side of the street. He felt as though somebody had kicked him in the stomach when he walked past and saw Kirsty sitting at a table with another boy.

6

He spent the afternoon in his room, alone. *Who was he? What was Kirsty doing with him? Was this the end of them?* He couldn't think about that – that notion would not compute. His head and heart were a swirl of their most romantic, most private moments. He thought back to the whispered conversations they had had about getting married, about living together, about being a teacher and a doctor, about becoming parents. *How could she throw all that away*?

His heart was on fire and tears sprung to his eyes. He felt suddenly alone and worthless. His life would be empty without her. Then he thought about her with another boy, a boy who played football, who was handsome and had much more to offer than he had. And he cried again.

That night he walked round to Kirsty's house as planned. Normally he would have a spring in his step and joy in his heart. But tonight he felt awful. He hadn't eaten anything since breakfast. He was starving but the thought of food made him feel sick.

He wondered how he was going to handle the situation.

Would he ignore it? Would she mention it? Was there some innocent explanation?

And when she opened the door and smiled and hugged him and kissed him as she always did when she saw him, his heart melted. Of course there would be an innocent explanation. There had to be.

He hadn't wanted to broach the subject at all but as soon as they were alone in front of the fire he couldn't hold it back and his fears blurted out. His heart raced, his voice was a growl.

"I saw you today with another boy. Who the fuck was he?"

Her face was painted with surprise.

"I met my friend James for coffee. What about it?" she said.

"James? James? Who the fucking hell is James?" he hissed, leaping to his feet.

"He's a friend and there's no need for swearing like that from someone who claims to be so expert at language."

"A friend?" Fraser was incredulous. He was struggling to keep control. "A fucking friend? How do you know him? How long have you known him?"

"Fraser calm down. Don't you have any female friends?"

He thought for a few seconds. He didn't have any female friends. He didn't have many male friends either. She was his best friend. At least that's what she told him.

"No I don't, you're the only girl in my life," he said. "Are you going out with him? I bet you are. And I bet you let him do it to you, don't you?"

"Of course I'm not," she screamed. "He's just a friend. I've known him since last summer. He's nice. He's funny. We met in the states. He wants to be a GP too." Tears filled her eyes and when she turned to speak again, he saw her flash a look of pure anger.

"And no we're not doing it. Why does it always come down to sex? Is that all you think about? You're obsessed."

She was crying now. He moved over to her and put his arms round her. He couldn't bear to see her weep. But she didn't want him to touch her and she shrugged away.

"Why didn't you tell me about him before now?" he asked softly.

"Because there was nothing to tell. He's a friend, and anyway he has a girlfriend." She sobbed for a moment, then she went to him and leant her head on his chest.

"I knew you'd react this way so I never said anything. It's sweet that you're jealous," she said, then after a long pause added, "but sometimes you can be a real pig."

They stood silently, in a troubled embrace.

"Are we still together then?" he asked after a time, because for him that was the bottom line.

"Yes of course we are," she sobbed, "but right now I'm not sure why."

He held her until she stopped crying, then he said goodnight and walked home early.

Now there were tears in his eyes.

That January night marked a turning point in their relationship. Fraser would never be able to put his finger on it, but something had broken between them.

They fell out every month from then on. He put it down to Kirsty's pre-exam nerves and worries about going to university. But when he confided in his older brother, Euan knowingly put it down to something else.

Fraser knew girls had periods but he'd never heard of PMT. He was certain Kirsty had periods but she never discussed them, she was far too modest and private about her body and that was something about her that he liked. He studied books in the public library and stole glances at women's magazines in shops. The diagnosis was complete. The moods, the tears - Kirsty was obviously a sufferer.

But he knew PMT couldn't be to blame for her starting to ration what little sex life they had. On the few occasions when they were intimate, she once again insisted that the light remained off. Then she began to ask Fraser not to touch her in a certain way or in a certain place.

In the month before they sat their final exams she dropped the bombshell that she thought they should stop being intimate, for a while at least. She had a lot on her mind with the exams, she said.

Fraser started to panic. He took this as a sign that there was, after all, a problem between them. His fears were confirmed when, the night before the first exam, she confirmed that the physical aspect of their relationship had ended.

"I'll miss it too, but it has to stop," she said. "God doesn't like it."

The day after the last exam, Fraser MacLean left school. He visited every classroom at Newton Mearns Academy and said his farewells and thanks to the teachers, especially Satan and Mr Bridges, who had done so much for him down the years.

Then he got the bus into town and went to his building society on St Vincent Street where he withdrew his life savings in cash, less £50 rainy day money. Then he walked along to the big Post Office on George Square where he cashed the Savings Certificates and Premium Bonds his grandfather had given him when he was a child.

Afterwards he walked round the corner to the foreign travel centre at Central Station and put his plan into action.

HELL

Do the drills.
Do the drills.
Do the drills you've done ten thousand times since you joined up.
Do the drills.
The drills you've done blindfold, in the rain, in the cold, in the dark.
Do the fucking drills.
The drills that take seconds.
And maybe you'll live.
Maybe.
Do the FUCKING drills.
Drop to one knee, make yourself a smaller target.
Drop.
Drop you spastic, drop.
Left thumb, safety catch to safe.
Do it.
DO IT!
Left thumb and forefinger, select lever to repetition.
Flick it.
Flick the switch.
Flick the fucking switch.
Magazine off.
Left thumb on the release.
Get the fucking magazine off.
MAGAZINE OFF!
Clear the stoppage.
Get your fingers into the chamber, boy and clear the fucking stoppage.
Move the working parts, back and forth.
Move them.
Grip the cocking handle.
Left thumb and forefinger again.
Hurry.
Fucking hurry.
Your arse is twitching isn't it?
Like they said, like they joked, all those times in the mess, the old sweats.

When you're frightened, really frightened, your anus contracts and expands.

Sixpence half a crown, sixpence half a crown.

And now your hoop is twitching like a good un.

Move the bolt back and forth and clear the chamber of whatever's causing the stoppage.

Why won't the working parts move?

Fucking cunt.

Fucking cunt.

FUCKING CUNT!

They've seized.

They can't have fucking seized!

It's like rubbing two pieces of sandpaper together.

You cleaned and oiled it.

You know you did.

You never stopped cleaning it or oiling it.

But you didn't do it well enough, did you?

Did you, you stupid fucking cunt?

And now you're fucking dead.

Dead.

Fraser knew it would be his last living action. His useless rifle cradled in his hands, he looked up.

The Iraqi stood with his AK pointing down at him.

Fraser could see the detail on the curved magazine and the chipped varnish of the wooden stock and butt. The Iraqi's shocked expression had been replaced by one of curiosity. Now he understood what had happened to the British soldier who'd confronted him. He waited, taunted. The lips, once open in the shock of anticipating his own death, curled into a thin smile.

He lifted the AK to his cheek.

Fraser screwed shut his eyes and turned his face away.

"Oh Kirsty," he said.

BRRRRRRRRRRRRRRRRRP!

The deafening sound, like ripping cloth.

The blinding flash of yellow light in the dingy bunker.

Then the silence.

In death he felt nothing, no searing pain as the AK rounds lanced through his flesh, no hammer blow of impact spinning him round, no feeling of release or heavenly white light at the end of a tunnel.

He felt nothing.

He opened his eyes.

Before him the Iraqi's chest and throat blossomed red. He trotted backwards like a drunken marionette, before crashing into the rear wall and slumping to the floor. He lay there for a few seconds, twitching in death. Blood gushed from three chest wounds and the ragged hole where his Adam's Apple had once been. A grotesque wheezing, wet death rattle filled the room.

Fraser stood up.

What?

Who?

He spun round.

"What the fucking hell are you doing in here? Are you totally fucking stupid? Get the fuck out of here. I'll fucking deal with you later."

Through the smoke Fraser could see the Sgt Major standing outside the ragged hole in the wall made by the tank round. His face was contorted in rage and his left forefinger stabbed repeatedly towards his officer. Smoke wafted from the barrel of his rifle.

Fraser spun round again, he could hear more footsteps in the corridor. Many footsteps, many men. His men. They'd cleared the rest of the bunker complex and were coming through from the front.

He screamed as hard as he could before the dryness of his throat reduced his voice to a croak.

"Room clear, room clear, British officer in here, British officer in here. Check fire, check fire."

Peeking out of the darkness towards him he saw a bayonet on the end of an SA80 barrel. Behind it was one of his soldiers, a young man, keyed up, nerves stretched to breaking point, high on adrenaline.

"Easy mate," he shouted, "Lieutenant MacLean and the Sar'nt Major in here. Room clear. Check fire. Check fire."

The Jock entered slowly. It was Stewart the piper. His eyes darted round the room to make sure things were what they seemed. His blackened face was streaked with sweat, his hands, clothing and equipment caked in the filth of war. He glanced round the room and saw the dead Iraqi lying on the floor. Then he looked up at Fraser and smiled.

"Fuckin' good shootin' surr," he said.

2

Infantry tactics and doctrine demand that once an objective has been taken, the platoon must move off it and reorganise. When the enemy has lost a position he tends to call in a mortar or artillery barrage or an air strike on the new occupiers.

But today there would be no response from the Iraqis. Their Army had either surrendered or been vapourised. Their Air Force had long since been destroyed on the ground, in the air or had flown to safety in Iran.

Fraser took a long swig from his water bottle to wet his parched mouth, then screamed to his men to rally a few metres away beyond the bunker. His soldiers sprinted towards him and skidded to a halt, spraying sand and dust into the air. They circled their position with their weapons pointing outwards, in case of attack. But even in all round defence, their eyes combing the horizon, they were all ears to what Fraser had to say.

He went through the routine of checking for casualties and organising a replen of ammunition and water for those who needed it.

As he spoke, he tried to clear his jammed rifle. It took some force, but he managed to pull the magazine out of its housing. The metal container made a grinding noise as it eventually slid free. Then he struggled to cock the weapon and shook it to remove the live round lodged in the chamber.

He pulled out the pair of pins locking the rifle together and broke the weapon into its two main parts. Inside, it was caked with dried sand that had turned into a glass-like substance with the heat of firing. He cursed aloud and rummaged in a webbing pouch for his tool roll. He removed the wire brush and scraped out the worst of the glass. Then he took his oil bottle and emptied half of it onto the SA-80s working parts. He snapped the weapon back together and slid the cocking handle back and forth a dozen times to make sure the movement had returned. Then he squirted another liberal amount of oil into the chamber. He put the old magazine inside his smock, took a fresh one from his ammunition pouch and slapped it onto the weapon. He was armed again.

He wouldn't be the only British soldier to have problems with the rifle in the desert. But it would be some time before the stories came through. When a soldier ran, his equipment tended to bang against the magazine release catch. The last thing a soldier needed in the heat of battle was the magazine dropping off his rifle. Sand got everywhere and could never really be cleaned out. There were problems with the cocking handle and the gas parts, which took the efflux of a fired round back into the rifle and brought a fresh round out of the magazine using a system of springs and pistons.

While most soldiers admired the SA-80's telescopic sight, few liked it as a weapon. Like many others, Fraser wondered why the British military hadn't bought off-the-shelf instead of developing a new weapon that was so unreliable.

The men remounted their Warriors, blooded. The platoon could return to their English hosts with a proud success. They had cleared their objective quickly and effectively with no losses. They had killed three Iraqi defenders and taken another dozen prisoners. The battlegroup intelligence officers were already poring over the bunkers and trenches of Brass. Each find, of maps or documents, added a scrap of colour to the bigger intelligence picture.

Satellite imagery, aerial photographs and the mark one human eyeball showed that the battle for Objective Brass resulted in 30 Iraqi tanks and 50 armoured personnel carriers destroyed. Overall, a further 400 Iraqi soldiers were taken prisoner and 80 were killed or wounded.

The next position to be taken was Objective Steel, the first part of which was really an extension of Brass. The battle group continued its north-south axis and moved onwards with its companies in line abreast formation across a 5km-wide front.

The remaining outposts of Brass posed no resistance to the advancing British, who quickly swung west to east again to attack Steel. The next objective was thought to be an Iraqi logistics centre lightly protected by small pockets of infantry and artillery. The battlegroup changed formation and put C Company on the left flank with the squadron of tanks in the centre.

The tanks led the attack and Fraser was impressed with the pace of it all. The armour punched into Steel with the infantry-carrying Warriors racing to keep up.

While the tanks fired at will towards the bunker and trench complexes, it became evident that the enemy was by now in no mood for a fight. They surrendered in their droves. Fraser's company didn't fire a shot but took hundreds of prisoners instead.

He was humbled by the gratitude of the Iraqis when they realised they were not going to be lined up and executed, as they'd been told they would by their officers. Their clothing and equipment was in rags, they were starving and literally dying of thirst. Many of them spoke perfect English and told of how they'd been conscripted into the Army and then beaten and in some cases shot by their own superiors.

In the end there were so many prisoners, the British stopped accepting their surrenders. Instead Fraser and the other commanders leant out of their turrets, ordered them to drop their weapons and pointed in the direction they should walk. The Iraqis looked so bedraggled, Fraser could only feel pity for them. He remembered the proud, cultured people he'd met when he was a student here and spoke in Arabic to them whenever he could.

At 1445 the battlegroup stopped at the edge of Steel to allow the Royal Engineers to come onto the objective and destroy the Iraqi guns. C Company was ordered to face east in line abreast formation, the tanks of the Hussars formed a protective arc 500m away to the south.

Each unit was told to mount their vehicles and close the hatches because the Sappers were about to blow the Iraqi guns. But there were problems with the explosives and the order went round for the Warriors to open hatches and debus, so the soldiers could get some much welcomed fresh air and a leg stretch.

By now shock was just starting to set in to Fraser's body. He'd been so busy in the immediate aftermath of the bunker incident, he'd had too much to think about to dwell on events. Now he could feel himself starting to shiver and his bowels loosen. Less than an hour previously, he'd been about to be killed, was seconds from death. An enemy soldier had stood above him pointing a loaded weapon in his face. He'd closed his eyes expecting to die, but had lived. A split second later he, and not the Iraqi, would have been lying against the wall with his guts hanging out.

He was not a religious man but Fraser said a quick prayer of thanks to God for his survival. Then he thought of the Iraqi. He knew that as a Moslem, the other man believed that to die the way he had, meant he'd be a martyr in paradise. Fraser said a prayer for him too.

He relived every moment of that situation. He knew the images flashing through his mind would never leave him. Although he thanked God for his life now, at the final moment he hadn't pleaded to God to save him, or promise to him that he would turn to religion or change his life if he was spared.

No. He'd thought of Kirsty.

Kirsty, Kirsty, always Kirsty.

He shook his head and jumped out of the Warrior's turret. After his feet hit the sand he felt his knees trembling. He was both hot and cold at the same time and badly needed water – the effects of shock.

He heard himself speak.

"Right guys, relax. We'll probably be here for a while. Have a brew, get a scoff on. You've deserved it."

He walked off a few metres into the desert. He didn't smoke, hadn't touched a cigarette since the time he'd been sick in Paris, but he badly wanted one right then. He bummed one from one of his soldiers and instantly felt guilty because he knew he earned much more than they did and their cigarette stocks were precious. He dragged the smoke deep into his lungs and his head immediately started to spin. He coughed and spluttered but carried on even though he had the beginnings of a headache and felt sick. He wasn't sure if it was the cigarette or his reaction to what had happened in the bunker.

Whatever, Sgt Major Cameron had saved his life. If he hadn't turned up, Fraser would have been killed. No doubt. He owed Cameron his life. He should go and speak to him, to thank him. But judging by the way Cameron had spoken to him in the bunker, he'd have to choose the moment carefully.

He'd be dealing with his own demons at that moment, his own shock. You don't kill a man every day and carry on as normal. No, Fraser would wait for a while before he spoke to the Sgt Major.

But Walter Cameron was no fool and had been thinking precisely the same thing. Fraser turned and saw the stocky Warrant Officer striding towards him. He braced himself. This would not be easy.

"Sergeant Major," he began in a trembling voice, "we should talk."

"You're darn tootin' we should talk," said Cameron through gritted teeth.

Fraser didn't like the tone. A Sgt Major doesn't talk to an officer in that manner, not even in wartime. He waited for a "sir" at the end of the statement, but it didn't come.

"What the fuck was all that about? What were you fucking playing at back there?" His voice was a low growl now.

"Something to prove have we? I remember your father. He was a good officer, a good CO, respected. Want to be better than him do you?"

Each word was a hammer blow. Fraser didn't know how to respond, what to say.

"You want a medal don't you? You want to be a hero. You want to go home to dad with a gong to say you're better than him. You went charging in there to win the fight without telling anyone where you were going or what you were doing. It's just as fucking well I saw you."

His face was contorted in anger again and Fraser could see his chest heaving.

"I wanted to thank you for saving my life," Fraser said, finding words at last. "I know that sounds corny, but there it is."

"Or maybe it isn't your father you're trying to impress. Maybe it's that girl of yours, the one you lost."

Fraser stopped trembling. Shock countered shock.

How could he be so right? How could he know about Kirsty? Nobody knew about Kirsty. She was his secret. He never spoke of her.

But Euan knew about her and they knew about her at his initiation when he joined the battalion. It wasn't beyond the realms of possibility. In fact it was probably an official regimental rumour.

Cameron saw Fraser's face, saw the resignation. He carried on.

"That's it, isn't it? It's her." He took a pace forward until their faces were just inches apart, his forefinger stabbed into Fraser's breast. "I'm watching you son. You keep your fucking wits about you."

He gestured towards the cluster of men behind them. "These boys' lives depend on you. Now clean your fucking rifle."

Cameron stomped back to his Warrior.

3

Fraser had cleaned the weapon after Brass had fallen, but he immediately stripped it and cleaned it again. His fingers darted over the parts by reflex, but his mind was elsewhere.

Cameron had been right about it all. Fraser winced as he remembered the incident with the bagpipes, when he had cried the night before they went into battle. The Sgt Major had witnessed that. He'd also heard Fraser call Kirsty's name when the Iraqi was about to empty his AK into him. And his father? Of course Cameron would remember him, he'd served under him. Fraser winced again.

"Look guys, we've got air cover."

Stewart's shout broke Fraser's concentration. He looked up and saw two planes circling overhead. A-10 Thunderbolts, American tankbusters.

You're a bit late, he thought, *you've missed the action.*

Suddenly one aircraft banked steeply and went into a dive. From its belly popped a dozen phosphorous flares. These were countermeasures designed to attract enemy heat-seeking missiles away from the aircraft's scorching hot engines.

But why do it here?

The other A-10 made a low pass over the Warriors and it too released flares. Then it climbed before diving again.

Fraser was puzzled.

His eyes dropped to his rifle again.

Someone took a photograph.

He saw the flashgun go off in his peripheral vision.

Who had a camera out here?

Why hadn't they asked him to look up and smile?

"Smile boss," he would have said.

The flashgun was bright.

Brighter than they usually were.

And noisy.

Noisy?

They were never noisy.

The flashgun rent the air with a dull thud then a deep, loud crack.

He looked up suddenly, a soldier again.

The flash from the explosion was blinding for two full seconds.

It silhouetted the Warrior, matt grey on black.

Then the fire changed the light again.

The fire from the burning Warrior.

It lit the sky a bright, angry orange.

Then the screaming started.

Fraser grabbed his rifle and sprinted for the Warrior. The front looked normal, the turret was intact and the Rarden cannon pointed straight, as it should.

But the rear was an open, burning pit. Inside he could see the blackened forms of wounded men struggling in grotesque slow motion to move in the tangled molten metal.

Around him, scattered on the sand, lay the bodies of his men.

Other soldiers were with him now. He dropped his rifle and tried to get closer to the inferno. The screams were louder, shriller. They could be heard easily, so easily, above the roaring of the flames. Somebody clambered up onto the turret and began trying to pull men out that way.

He had no thought, only reflex. He felt himself grab a limb and pull a man, but the soldier's webbing straps were caught on a burning snag of metal somewhere.

The fumes choked him, the acrid, gagging industrial smoke of burning metal and plastic. But he couldn't go back, he couldn't let go, mustn't. He was their officer, he was their commander, he was their leader. He pulled again, harder. He saw another soldier at his side dive in to Hades and grab the man by the other leg. They heaved together in despair. There was a twang and suddenly the webbing belt gave way and the man was free.

He was free, but he was still on fire. His hair and face were a mass of flames, his uniform was black and smoking - like a Guy on a bonfire.

And he was screaming, screaming, screaming.

The man stood up suddenly and started to run around comically, like a headless chicken, two paces there, then two paces back. But his comrades kicked him down onto the sand, the cool, welcoming sand. Despite his wounds they roughed him up, rugby tackled him, rolled him into the ground to put out the flames.

It was then Fraser lost the smell of the fire and instead sensed the stink of burning flesh, burning soldier, burning man.

"Mines! Mines! Mines!" someone started yelling. "We're in a fuckin' minefield. Don't move! Don't fuckin' move!"

Fraser stood stock still, as the training told him to do when he heard that word screamed that way. He glanced at the ground around him and saw a black plastic mug lying in the sand. The boys had been standing at the rear door of the Warrior drinking tea when it exploded.

Mines? Could a mine to do this?

He glanced at the Warrior. It was a sturdy piece of kit. This kind of damage could be caused by an anti-tank mine but the Warriors had been stationary and the weight of a man wouldn't detonate such a munition. A man's weight would detonate an anti-personnel mine though, but the explosion from one of them would just have bounced off a Warrior. This wasn't caused by mines. Couldn't have been.

Was it a tank?

A T-72 could brew up a Warrior, no problem. But were there any around? The Iraqis had surrendered in their hundreds. Was there a rogue tank crew left out there? Fanatics, ready to strike one last suicidal blow for Saddam? Fraser scanned the horizon but could see nothing.

Someone else had the same idea and he saw a pair of Challengers roar off into the desert, plumes of black diesel smoke billowing from their exhausts. The turrets traversed across the horizon seeking revenge.

An Iraqi prisoner stood watching, mouth agape in horror. Some British soldiers instantly assumed he'd been responsible, had somehow fired an RPG at the Warrior. They jumped on him and started to beat him up, ignoring his screamed pleas of innocence.

The Warriors had been up-armoured with a new secret weapon called Chobham. Long ceramic plates designed to absorb explosive impact had been bolted onto the Warrior's sides. If he'd done it right, taken his time, aimed properly, there was a chance the firer could penetrate the Warrior's skin where it wasn't protected by the Chobham armour.

By now the rest of the platoon's Warriors had rolled round the inferno, like animals protecting a wounded member of the herd. Men spilled out of the crew compartments to help their friends. But there was little they could do.

A new sound – ammunition inside the burning turret began to cook off.

The Challengers roared around in the middle distance, still looking for the T-72.

Still the smell, still the screams.

Four minutes later a second Warrior 200 metres away was engulfed in a gout of flame.

Fraser watched in horror as the bruised armour bent and buckled in and out like a pressurised can of food. A microsecond later it exploded, spraying the area with white hot shards of shrapnel.

The men inside, men from Mike King's platoon, died in an instant.

The roar was louder than the first explosion and scattered the men, stunned, to the ground. These were seasoned soldiers. They knew what explosions sounded like, which were close, which were terrorist bombs, which were mortars.

They'd never heard an explosion like this before.

Fraser watched as Mike King dived into the burning wreckage to try to save his men. Soon he was joined by other Fusiliers and Highlanders. But it was all to be in vain.

To a man, they looked up and saw the A-10 again, fly lazily, low across the sky.

To a man, they realised what had happened.

Above the two burning Warriors the aircraft did a victory roll then flew off to the south.

"Murdering bastards," screamed Fraser.

The medics and their vehicles were on the scene within minutes and dozens of men scurried about tending to the wounded. An emergency field dressing station was hurriedly set up, bandages were applied and drips raised.

For those who were beyond help, there was the Padre.

Fraser walked over to the area behind the ambulances where the bodies had been laid out on a groundsheet. One of the medics had covered them with a poncho.

There were nine of them, in two neat, regimental rows – six Fusiliers, three Queen's Own Highlanders. A few metres away their helmets were laid out in the sand in the same order.

Gingerly he lifted the poncho. He tried not to look, he didn't want to see. He focused on the charred stubs of the feet, the burnt boots, hoping only his peripheral vision would pick up the faces.

But somehow he couldn't *not* look. He stood there knowing he would never forget the indignity of that last image.

Corporal MacDonald from Aviemore - a quiet man, a nice man.

Stewart the piper, the poor young piper from Dingwall, who played his favourite hymn for him, and who wanted to go to Baghdad and bayonet Saddam Hussein.

And at the end of the row, as if even now keeping his men smartly in line, lay the body of Sgt Major Cameron.

In the distance, Fraser could hear the rotors of the casevac helicopters clattering towards them. He walked off into the desert and after a few paces stopped and vomited repeatedly.

When he had nothing more to throw up, he sat down in the sand and cried.

The war continued. The Fusiliers battlegroup's next objective was Tungsten, the last and eastern-most Iraqi defensive position on the border with Kuwait. The CO arrived at the scene of the devastation and took the Company Commander aside. He asked him if he would rather C Company was rested, given the scale and manner of his losses.

Tony Greaves braced up and stamped to attention in the sand in front of his CO. He declined the offer. Forcing back the tears he said his men would fight on.

But Fraser MacLean would not. A medic found him at last light, sitting shivering in the sand. At first Fraser resisted the help offered to him. But the medic saw the burns to the young officer's face, the shreds of lifeless skin hanging off his hands, the scorched uniform and the violent trembling of deep shock.

Fraser's last conscious memory was of his smock pocket being opened by the medic, who removed from it the syrette of morphine kept there. Then he felt the long, thin needle being stabbed through his combat trousers into his thigh, lifting him gently out of hell.

4

He was flown out on a Sea King that night and taken to 33 Field Hospital at Al-Jubail in Saudi Arabia – the place where the Queen's Own Highlanders had landed from Germany all those weeks before. There, his hands were treated, bandaged and placed in protective plastic bags. His face was only superficially burned; the eyebrows would grow back in time.

But he could not speak.

The nurses were female, soft and gentle and kind. He could smell their perfume, their cleanliness. He could see their smiles, feel their touch as they dressed his wounds, or moved his pillows.

He wanted to talk to them, to thank them, to explain what had happened. How the Americans who were supposed to be protecting them, had burned them, killed them.

But he couldn't speak. The trauma was too great and anyway,

each nurse looked too much like Kirsty Buchanan.

They knew his story, heard how the brave young officer had dived into the burning Warrior to rescue his men, how he'd sat in the desert refusing medical care. How three of his boys had been killed by the Americans, their allies.

On his second night in the hospital, the dreams started. The ugly shape of the A-10 buzzed around his bed. The planes weren't nicknamed 'Warthogs' for nothing. They were short and fat with stubby wings bristling with weapons. The engines were at the back, hidden from heat seeking missiles by the twin tail fins. In the nose, surrounded by a world war two style painted shark's mouth, was a Gatling gun the size of a Volkswagen Beetle.

And at the controls was Eric Decker.

After a few seconds of flying round the ward, Decker laughed uproariously in the cockpit and before he did a victory roll, the wings would spurt fire.

The fire was hungry, all consuming.

And this time there was no morphine to take Fraser away.

The ground war lasted only 100 hours and it was long over and Kuwait liberated by the time Fraser's condition improved enough for him to take visitors. His strength and appetite grew by the hour and the RAMC doctors told him he would soon return to his unit.

But he was still very tired and didn't speak much.

It was the dreams.

When he woke sweating from a fitful afternoon nap on the last day of February 1991, he was shocked to see his brother and Colonel Iain MacLaren, the Queen's Own Highlanders CO, sitting on canvas chairs beside the bed.

"Friendly fire" said the CO, breaking the heavy silence that followed the pleasantries. "It's happened down through history."

Fraser heard the sadness in the voice. MacLaren looked tired. He'd aged since Fraser had last seen him.

Euan sat in silence. Fraser suddenly noticed the three pips of a Captain on his brother's rank slides. Newly-promoted, and in the field too.

Not bad, Euan.

Fraser saw how clean his brother's desert combat uniform was, how well-fed and rested he appeared.

"Do we know what happened? Why it happened?" asked

Fraser after a few moments. It was more words than he'd spoken in a week.

"A full inquiry's been promised," said the CO, quietly. "All we know is that the American pilots mistook you for Iraqi tanks, T54s or T55s. Maverick missiles, infra red, 125 pound shaped charge. One hit the first callsign, your callsign, on the left side.

"The second targeted Lt King's platoon. The missile went right through the top of the Warrior's turret…" his voice trailed off.

"But…but…Warriors don't look anything like Iraqi tanks. There wasn't any Iraqi armour for miles," said Fraser, not comprehending.

He thought for a moment. The weather had been awful overnight and early that morning a sandstorm, mixed with rain showers and the gunk from the oil fires, meant visibility would not have been good. But after the attack on Brass it had cleared up and it was fine and sunny for the assault on Steel. The skies were clear, the planes were low and made several passes.

Surely they couldn't make such a mistake? And anyway, what about the victory roll?

"We had our orange identification panels on top of the Warriors for that precise reason," said Fraser, "and we flew Saltires and Union jacks. They couldn't have confused us."

He found a surge of strength from somewhere and sat up in bed.

"What are we going to do about it?" he asked. "Will there be a court martial? I mean, we have to prove negligence here."

Euan fidgeted and stared at the floor.

"I'm afraid there's nothing we can do," he said.

Fraser was all too familiar with his brother's resigned tone.

"What do you mean there's nothing we can do?" he said irritably. "Of course there is, there are tribunals for this sort of thing. It was fratricide, it was deliberate, it was, it was," he searched for the words, "it was fucking murder, that's what it was."

"I'm afraid it was an accident, a tragic, awful accident, which happens in every war. I'm sorry Fraser. I feel as bad about it as you do."

Euan stopped. He realised too late how crass the last part of the statement sounded.

Then the truth dawned slowly on Fraser.

"You've been got at," he whispered, "you've been fuckin' nobbled, hushed-up, haven't you? It's to be swept under the carpet."

"It's not like that at all," replied Euan, but Fraser saw his brother's eyes and realised it was.

"We don't want to piss off the Americans, that's it isn't it? We don't want to rock the boat," said Fraser.

"We can't do nothing. We can't just sit back and do nothing. We owe it to these boys, and their families."

"Fraser, now is not the time. You're not fit enough yet. You shouldn't be getting concerned about this. We have to leave it just now. We'll look at it later, back in Germany."

As the visitors left, Fraser closed his eyes and saw the row of blackened bodies lying in the sand.

Three days later the staff took off his bandages and Fraser began to use his hands again. The scarring wasn't too bad and the plastic surgeon said he'd make a full recovery.

At night the dream plagued him and he lay awake for hours. There were very few casualties and the hospital was all but empty. He had nobody to talk to during those long dark sleepless nights and he didn't want to bother the staff.

Instead he lay weeping for his men.

But during the days, when the sun warmed the tented hospital, he felt better. The light was his guardian, the heat his friend. In daylight he could snatch a few moments of shallow, but blessed sleep.

Eric Decker didn't fly his A-10 in daylight.

No, it was far too dangerous. Better to fly at night when nobody could see him and the targets were easy prey to his night vision devices.

During the days Fraser lay and dissected events. He remembered every detail of the incident, and short, graphic snapshots of it came back every few minutes. He pieced them together and analysed them and held them in one hand while the other tried to grasp for the unknowns, the variables, the improbables.

So what had happened? What had gone so badly wrong?

He examined the facts.

The war had been nearly over. The Iraqis had been routed. There was no question that the allies would win. It was only a matter of time before they swept round the back of Kuwait, cut off the occupiers and rolled into the city.

So why had they been targeted?

They were static. They'd just fought through objective Steel. They had orange panels strapped over their Warriors and each coalition vehicle flew national flags and had an inverted V painted on the side, as per the SOPs, to show they were allied.

Was the Americans' vehicle recognition so poor? Did they not know what a Warrior looked like? It looked nothing like an Iraqi tank. The pilots should have known that.

Fraser knew what a Bradley looked like, and an Abrams. He and the rest of the battalion had attended interminable lectures on the various equipments in theatre – friendly and enemy. They had pored at length over recognition manuals and memorised the distinguishing features - a whip antenna here, a rounded turret there. It was hard work and yet another thing they needed to remember at a stressful time, but it was critical. It was good skills. It was what a soldier needed to know.

And anyway, the Iraqi armour hadn't moved for days, weeks. It was laagered up, in burning piles of metal. And they couldn't even blame bad weather. The skies were crystal clear and the planes flew low.

It wouldn't compute. The mis-identification of the British Warriors for Iraqi tanks just didn't wash.

By the third day the sad truth dawned on Fraser. The explanation was simple.

The pilots realised the war was nearly over and they probably hadn't seen any action. Their comrades had but they hadn't. They didn't want to return home without firing their weapons, without being blooded, without a kill. They'd seen the stationary Warriors beside Steel and thought the target too good an opportunity to pass up.

It was probably Iraqi, they thought.

Probably.

They hadn't bothered checking and had gone for it.

Probably was good enough for the Americans.

And if they were wrong? If the target had been friendly? Blame the fog of war. It would be ok. Shit happens.

Fraser thought the pilots bloodthirsty, gung-ho cowboys, just like in the movies. In fact, life to the Americans, especially the servicemen he'd met, was one big movie. They lived a John Wayne film fantasy, where the American killed the bad guy, saved the world, got the girl and came home a hero.

Except this time he hadn't killed the bad guy. He'd killed Fraser's innocent men, men who were on the same side. And while the pilots went back to bed in their nice comfortable airbase in Saudi, fire engulfed the victims.

And inside Fraser MacLean's breast, fiercer and hotter than ever, burnt the flame of hatred of all things American.

5

A Land Rover from the MT pool came to pick him up from the hospital and took him back to the Queen's Own Highlanders location. The driver was Colour Sergeant McHardy, the CQMS from B Company. The journey along the TAPline road passed in silence. McHardy and Sgt Major Cameron had been close friends. They'd grown up together in the Ferry estate in Inverness and had played football for Clachnacuddin Boys Club.

Two hours down the road, the vehicle stopped at an RMP checkpoint where Colour McHardy had to log the details of his journey with the traffic controllers. The numbers of logistics vehicles rolling along the MSR had once been vast but had dwindled now the war was over. However, procedures had to be followed and checks still had to be made.

Fraser watched McHardy jump out of the Rover and walk over to the Redcaps' tent. He was inside for a few minutes. By the time he returned, Fraser had had an idea.

"Are they busy in there?" he asked.

"Nah. All they'll have to deal with now is convoy cock."

Both men smiled. Army humour abated their sadness for a moment.

He followed the path taken by the Colour Sergeant and walked into the tent. A young RMP Corporal sat struggling with a tabloid crossword. On the desk lay a flyswat and an electric fan whirred in the corner. He looked up when he heard Fraser's footsteps on the plastic matting.

"Can I help you sir?" he asked.

"I'd like to report a war crime," replied Fraser.

He slept the rest of the way back, as though a kind of peace touched him. He'd done the right thing. He'd done right by his boys. He wouldn't let them down. Not now.

But the Corporal had taken some persuading, had thought it

was a joke at first. Then he saw the resolute expression on Fraser's face. Anyway, he'd heard about the incident at Steel. Who hadn't? American bastards. The SIB boys were going to look into it, eventually.

Fraser had been serious all right. He'd demanded the Redcap log his complaint, watched him write down the details in the book, took the carbon copy of the incident report and wrote down the crime number in his notebook.

Fraser was a good soldier. In the aftermath of the incident, despite the horror and his shock, he had the presence of mind to mark the position using his GPS to get an eight figure grid reference. He'd even written down the names of the soldiers present and noted their Army numbers so they could be called to give evidence at the inquiry.

And now that he'd reported the incident as a war crime, it was in the system and would be actioned. There would have to be an inquiry now.

Wouldn't there?

NORTHERN IRELAND

Fraser MacLean did what many soldiers did when they returned to their base in Germany from the Gulf War late in that March of 1991 – he got married. But by the time he walked down the aisle in Salisbury, he'd seen enough churches.

The three funerals had done it for him. There he was, a man who had few dealings with God, a man who hated the rules of religion, its credo, sitting in churches across the north of Scotland on consecutive days, saying goodbye to his men.

Piper Stewart's was first. Fraser had to bite his bottom lip and ball his fists to stop himself becoming hysterical when the piper played 'The Day Thou Gavest Lord is Ended' as the coffin was carried from the church in Dingwall. The last time the 19 year-old played the pipes he'd played that tune, and he played it for Fraser. It had been his favourite too.

He waited outside but Stewart's family was too upset to stand and talk. They were whisked away by the undertakers.

Corporal MacDonald's family didn't want a military funeral and Fraser and his comrades sat uncomfortably in suits at the back of the tiny church in Aviemore. It was the lull before the storm – the hardest moment was yet to come.

Fraser loved Inverness, the Queen's Own Highlanders regimental home and recruiting heartland, but on the day of Sgt Major Cameron's funeral, he couldn't wait to leave.

A high sun split the electric blue spring sky and lit the twin pink sandstone towers of the St Andrew's Cathedral, which stood in Gothic majesty beside the racing River Ness. And after the bearer party had slow marched past with the coffin, smart in their number twos, headgear off, he'd stood outside with the family.

"What is the Army doing about it?" asked Liza, Cameron's widow. She spoke the way the civilian partner of a soldier always spoke to their man's officer.

"We'll be compensated of course," she said, "but so what? What about the pilots?"

Fraser looked down at the mousy figure in black. At her side were two sons, aged about eight and nine, their hair already cropped short - soldiers to be.

Liza was in many ways like Cameron, short and feisty.

Fraser wondered if she knew. Wondered if she'd got a letter

from her husband telling her of the officer who wept the night before the battle, who ran off trying to win a medal and grab the glory under fire. The same officer he'd had to rescue and who'd cowered before death and in his last living moment shamefully uttered a woman's name.

He wondered if she sat there at night in their quarter up on the patch beside Cameron Barracks reading the Sgt Major's last bluey home.

Did he have time to write one between Brass and Steel? Then give it to somebody to post? Is that how he whiled away the hours sitting inside the Warrior as they prowled around Southern Iraq?

Did she know? Did anyone?

Fraser felt a biting shame when he realised, there and then at the funeral, the hearse just about to head up to Tomnahurich Cemetery, where the firing party would send volleys of blanks over the coffin and where the piper would play the regimental lament, 'Flowers of the Forest' that Cameron's death had been convenient.

Convenient. His death had been *convenient*.

"There will be a full inquiry Mrs Cameron. I'm sure if there was any negligence, it will be proved and the appropriate action taken." Fraser's voice was low and calm. It was a class thing. It was how officers spoke to soldiers and their families. It was expected of them. It was the way.

"Your husband was a fine man Mrs Cameron. He was an excellent soldier. The boys loved him and I trusted him with my life."

He waited, waited for her to say, *yes she'd heard how her Walter had saved his life.*

But she said nothing – tears fell instead.

On his wedding day Fraser felt little joy. Admittedly his bride looked radiant as she walked down the aisle towards him, and her smile melted his heart. But he couldn't wait for the service to end, the organ to stop playing and the minister to stop speaking.

It reminded him too much of the funerals. He and his best man, a brother officer from the regiment, but not his brother, stood where the coffins had stood, draped in the Union Flag. He wanted to be out in the sunlight.

And when they left the church, man and wife, their new life together began as they walked under the archway of swords held aloft by Army guests, buttons, brasses and medals glinting in the sun.

2

The courtship had been short and interrupted by a war. Anna Winterburn was a decent girl and had decent ideals. She was a teacher, with strawberry blond hair and a skijump nose, and they had met at a house party in London in the summer of 1990 while he'd been on weekend leave from Belfast.

She had been secretly very impressed by the dark, quiet Scotsman who'd bumped into her in the hall, who'd spilled her drink and who went to fetch a cloth to mop it up and who'd returned instead with a bottle of wine and two glasses.

She thought he was handsome, in an unusual way. She deliberately didn't stare at his hooked nose, instead concentrated on letting his soft Scottish accent wash over her. She wanted to listen to it all night, and she did. And at the end of the evening when he asked her for her phone number, she was delighted, although she tried not to show it.

He took her to a summer ball at the Royal Artillery mess in Woolwich and she'd been speechless at the extravagance and beauty of it all. The tables were bedecked with silver, candles were lit and a military band played gently in the background. And Fraser looked so dashing in his mess kit, the scarlet jacket with buff lapels, collar and cuffs, the MacKenzie tartan kilt.

And he wore a medal, a small one at least, with a green and blue ribbon. She thought he must have been a hero, won it for some act of bravery. She didn't like to ask him. She'd read somewhere that men who won medals seldom spoke of it, something to do with the trauma they'd suffered.

They danced long and slow that night and later, in the narrow single bed of his room in the accommodation block, they made love for the first time.

She didn't learn until much later that the medal was the General Service Medal and was awarded to any soldier who'd served in Northern Ireland for 31 days. And she didn't realise either that his promotion from Second Lieutenant to Lieutenant that summer came automatically two years after commissioning.

She was sure it was down to some outstanding feat of soldiering.

Anna's home town was Amesbury in Wiltshire. She'd grown up on Salisbury Plain and had become accustomed to tanks and Land Rovers on the roads. But she had no interest whatsoever in the Army – until now. She'd left Wiltshire for a good job teaching Geography at a London school. She'd had a few boyfriends, but none was like Fraser, a soldier, a hero.

They'd meet infrequently, when Fraser came over on leave. She watched the news every day and read the papers. The events in Northern Ireland appalled her. She realised Fraser was in danger every time he set foot outside his barracks, but she could put that to the back of her mind. Instead she focussed on his letters and phone calls and forthcoming leaves – the romance.

And she learnt quickly from him how and where to talk. When they were out in London, or on the Underground, they would never discuss the Army. She was told never to speak about Fraser, or what he did, to anyone she didn't know well.

He explained to her that the IRA had active service units all over the place and one slip could be fatal. They could be followed, their movements noted, addresses remembered. If she told a stranger what Fraser did and that stranger was an IRA sympathiser, she could be in danger and the threat of danger to her could be used to blackmail him.

It was common sense to Fraser. It was routine. It was what a soldier did. But to Anna it was an adventure, like something out of a romantic novel.

In July 1990 the Northern Ireland tour ended and after a lengthy leave, Fraser and his comrades returned to Münster. While Anna was forbidden for security reasons to travel to Belfast to see Fraser there, she was welcomed in Germany. She attended mess dinner nights, or wandered the streets and shops of Münster with her boyfriend. Sometimes they would meet in Amsterdam or Brussels and enjoy naughty weekends away. It was all so romantic.

When Iraq invaded Kuwait on August 2nd 1990, Anna couldn't have cared less. Fraser was in Germany. What could it possibly have to do with him?

She wasn't in Germany to see the battalion preparing for war. Fraser kept her away. He knew it would hurt her. But they met up where and when they could and throughout the autumn of 1990 he felt happier than he had for a long time.

His career was progressing nicely. He'd already served a tour in Northern Ireland and he was certain his battalion would have some involvement in the forthcoming events in the Gulf. He was popular and respected among his brother officers and he had a girlfriend to be proud of. She would one day be a perfect regimental wife and the fine mother of his children. It was all going to plan.

Fraser would work away until he proved his point. One day he would command this regiment, his father's regiment. He'd be a husband and a father and get the respect he deserved.

And when the war came and the battalion flew out, she'd been there at Hanover Airport with the tears, his fiancée now. She'd waved the chartered jumbo into the sky and went back to London where she became the centre of attention of all her friends, colleagues and family. There was a war on and Anna's man was out there, in the thick of it. A war? In 1990?

She was the perfect partner. She wrote to Fraser every day and every week sent him a shoebox with his favourite chocolate, tins of boot polish and bottles of deodorant. She also sent photographs of herself. But while the Jocks and the Toms received pictures of their women in states of undress, Anna kept her clothes firmly on. Neither would her letters ever stray towards the 'sports pages' sent to the soldiers by their wives and girlfriends. Anna would do her talking in the bedroom.

And she'd been rewarded upon his return from the Gulf with a ring. He'd been on full pay all the time he'd been away and of course had nowhere to spend it. When he returned, his bank balance was very healthy. They went to Amsterdam where he told her to choose a diamond that was then cut into shape and mounted on her engagement ring.

They went on honeymoon to the South of France and took two weeks to drive along the Cote D'Azur from Cannes to Monaco. Anna knew Fraser had been wounded, she could see the scars on his hands and some slight marking on his face. And she knew there were scars she couldn't see. She held him close at night, during the nightmares, when he lay sweating and murmuring. She knew about the friendly fire incident, but he never talked about it much and she hadn't asked too many questions. She didn't want to pry. All she knew was that Fraser was a hero and that she loved him. The questions could wait.

That summer she left her job and moved to Münster to be with him. Fraser moved out of the mess and they took a small quarter on the patch near Buller barracks. It was damp and cramped, but they were very happy.

Anna spent the long hot summer days looking for a job. She had one interview, at the British school in nearby Bielefeld, but she was pipped to the post by a Brigadier's daughter.

The A-10 still flew around the bedroom from time to time. But once he'd wakened, and lay sweating in the darkness, he found he couldn't talk about it to Anna, or anyone else.

3

Fraser had been a Platoon Commander for three years and it was time to move on to another post. Normally young officers do the job for only two, but the war had thrown a huge spanner in the works. He would miss the day to day dealings with his platoon, but he knew he would have to fly the nest sometime soon if his career was to progress him to the top job in the regiment.

At this stage in a young officer's career, he or she is normally sent away from the battalion for their next job. Many go off to be instructors at training establishments or begin staff jobs at a headquarters. The idea is to give a young officer more experience and taste life away from the regimental family.

But Fraser was older than the battalion's other Lieutenants because he'd spent five years at university. He was also much brighter than any of them and in addition he was judged to be more mature. His experience in the war was also a factor. The CO wanted Fraser to stay.

He would be promoted Captain and become the next Regimental Signals Officer, a crucial job dealing with every aspect of the battalion's communications systems.

Fraser was delighted with his new job. But his wife was not. Becoming the RSO was dependent on attending an intensive six month course at the Royal School of Signals at Blandford in Dorset.

While Anna was less than happy with the fact that her new husband would be spending the next six months in the country she had just left to be with him, she was proud of his new rank and status. A Captain, even a junior one, carried a lot of sway in the battalion and the RSO was a critical job. His increase in salary was also very welcome.

But when she waved him off for the first time she found herself quite alone. A job would help, but without one she was no longer Mrs Anna MacLean, she was 'wife of Capt MacLean.' Still, at least she had the Christmas ball to look forward to.

It was ironic how the tables had turned. Now he lived in England and she in Germany. They'd meet up again in London or Amsterdam whenever they could. One weekend she suggested they should go to Paris but he had flown into a rage and the subject was never raised again.

Between the end of the summer of 1991 and New Year 1992, Fraser and Anna saw each other a handful of times. He missed her when they were apart but focussed on his studies.

The instructors at Blandford had never seen anything like the new Captain. The skills and drills on the various radios and signals kit were as good as it got. They knew all about the friendly fire incident in the Gulf and when they heard it had been Fraser's platoon, they thought they knew why he was so driven.

At the end of the course, shortly before Christmas, he graduated with the highest score ever seen at Blandford and returned to Germany ready to take up his new post.

Fraser didn't recognise the quarter the night he arrived home. In his absence Anna had had the place gutted, redecorated and refitted. He had to admit it looked fabulous but he was livid when she told him how much it had all cost.

The Christmas ball was a major social event in the regimental calendar. Fraser donned his mess kit, which now had three shiny new pips on each shoulder and the Gulf War medal on his breast. Anna looked stunning in a brand new designer ball gown.

For Christmas he'd bought her a bracelet from a shop on Bond Street. It had been expensive but not overly so. Her present to him was a Rolex watch, which, even with the forces' duty free discount, cost well in excess of £1,000.

As the RSO, the new year of 1992 was a busy time for Fraser MacLean. There was new kit to deal with and lessons to be learnt from what happened during the war. He immersed himself in his new job but his mind was never for a moment far from the friendly fire incident. He had pestered the CO and the Adjutant with repeated pleas to act on his behalf to try to get something done.

They nodded and agreed and said the wheels were in motion but in the end it appeared they'd hit a brick wall. On the third week of January Fraser was summoned to the CO's office, to find Euan already there.

He sat down beside his brother at a low magazine-strewn coffee table.

"There are a few things you should know," said Colonel MacLaren.

"An interim report from the int people has crossed my desk. It appears the A-10s were in contact with the RAF before they attacked you. They were looking for business and radioed an AWACS circling the area. The controller in the AWACS has sworn to a statement he's given saying he spoke to the pilots and directed them onto a target with a 10 figure grid reference." He paused.

"It was 20 km away from your location."

Fraser felt as thought he'd been struck by lightning.

"Twenty K? They were 20 kilometres off target?" he said in disbelief.

MacLaren nodded.

"Fucking useless septics," hissed Fraser.

He stood up and paced around the CO's office for a moment then sat down again and crossed his legs.

"Well that's negligence. We can prove it now. This must get out, there must be a public inquiry. These pilots must be tried for murder, manslaughter at least." Fraser felt good about things for the first time in nearly a year.

"There'll be an inquiry and you will of course be called to give evidence, but..."

"But what?" asked Fraser.

"But it's an internal Army Board of Inquiry, it's held in private and the full details won't be made public."

Euan spoke next.

"As for prosecuting the pilots? I've been looking into it. Forget it."

"What do you mean forget it?"

"It'll never happen."

"Why not?" Fraser was angry now.

"Think about it," said Euan soberly.

"I fucking well haven't stopped thinking about it," snapped Fraser. Then he remembered where he was and added a "sorry sir" to the CO a moment later.

"Look, I want these guys to be hung out to dry as much as you do," said Euan. "But what I'm saying is this. Don't expect too much action against the Americans. It simply won't happen, I know it won't. This goes to a much higher level, governments, special relationships, the lot."

"But we have to try, we can't just let it lie. We owe it to these guys, to their families," the tremble was back in Fraser's voice.

"Go to the inquiry, give your evidence. Do your best for them. Just don't expect the Army, the MOD, the government, to go chasing after the pilots because it won't happen."

4

Fraser travelled with Mike King to London the following Monday and in a dark room of the MOD's main building on Whitehall, gave evidence to the inquiry. There were around a dozen suits sitting at tables forming three sides of a hollow square. Fraser sat alone at a table on the fourth side.

The suits scribbled furiously. Fraser was puzzled that there was nobody in uniform in the room. He didn't recognise any of the men and was told only that they were members of a board of inquiry. He was asked to tell his story from start to finish. He'd prepared for this moment. It took three hours.

There was a break for 20 minutes then he was questioned on parts of what happened by two of the men who sat opposite him. He understood them to be senior civil servants or lawyers for the MOD.

"Are you certain the aircraft did a victory roll?"

"Yes I am."

"Which aircraft? The first or the second?"

"Whichever one hit the second Warrior."

"From which direction did it fly?"

"From the west."

"Did you see the missile leave the wing?"

In his dream he did, most nights, but did he see it on the day? *Think. Think! Think reality not dream. You can't confuse them, not here.*

"No I did not."

"Did you see the pilot?"

Yes it was Eric Decker you fucking moron. He still flies the A-10, around the bedroom of my quarter, most nights. You should come and see it, then you'd understand. Then you'd understand the fire, the heat, the smell.

Fraser and Mike walked up Whitehall afterwards, crossed Trafalgar Square and found a pub and stayed there until closing time. The next day, still massively hungover, they flew back to Germany.

While an internal Army Board of Inquiry could do and say what it liked without scrutiny, the Coroner's Court was a public place and its deliberations were open. More importantly, it could call whatever witnesses it liked.

Because the bodies of the nine soldiers who died in the incident were flown home to RAF Brize Norton in Oxfordshire, the Oxford Coroner was bound to hold an inquest into the deaths before a jury of 12 good men and true.

Fraser would give evidence again. More importantly, so would the pilots.

Along with Mike King, he spent the next two months re-interviewing the men from the Queen's Own Highlanders and the Fusiliers who'd been on Steel. He was still the RSO and had to divide up his life accordingly. With what little spare time he had left, he tried to take his marriage a stage further.

Anna still hadn't been able to get a job and while the quarter was now immaculate, she found herself easily bored. Wife of Captain MacLean wasn't such a glamorous title now, and there seemed to be fewer social functions to attend in the bitter German winter. Anna busied herself with helping out the Families' Officer and the PMC and learned to ride at the Münster Saddle Club, but she was still bored and often lonely.

Fraser worked late most nights and even if he came home early he still had paperwork to do. She felt he was obsessed with the inquiry, although he seldom discussed it with her.

But what they did discuss was starting a family.

It was what young officers did. It was part of the plan. He was a Captain, a war veteran and the RSO and had eyes on command one day. He would soon play his part in nailing the A-10 pilots and once the inquiry was out of the way and the deaths of his men had been avenged, he could return to the battalion, mission accomplished.

Then he could refocus on the battalion. He was already a married man, his wife was accepted and liked and was the perfect regimental partner. What could be better than the patter of tiny feet to complete the picture?

They began trying for a family as soon as Fraser returned from London. But the process was interrupted in early May when he travelled to Oxford for an undisclosed period of time to attend the Coroner's Inquiry.

The night before it started he found he couldn't sleep and tossed and turned in his Oxford B&B. Over the previous weeks he'd whipped himself up into a frenzy about seeing the pilots in the witness box, hearing their evidence, their excuses.

But what he relished most of all was seeing them found guilty for killing his boys.

He wondered what he'd say to them if he ever met them, bumped into them in the corridor.

He was tired the next morning but adrenaline and expectation spurred him on. He rose, showered and shaved and dressed in a dark suit, white shirt and regimental tie. It was a glorious spring day and he felt better than he had for a long time as he walked down the road towards the Crown Court.

As he approached he saw a cluster of people. Among them was Liza Cameron, the Sgt Major's widow. She looked as determined as he was that day - determined to see justice done. They stood on the steps chatting for a few minutes before going in. But their enthusiasm would not last.

Sitting around the table in the well of the court were the seven lawyers and a QC representing the MOD at the Taxpayers' expense. The families had been refused Legal Aid by the government and were represented by a keen young lawyer who had agreed to waive his fee.

Among the first business heard by the jury was a written statement from a senior Pentagon official. In it he said the two pilots would not be appearing to testify. They had given their evidence in sworn written statements, which would be made available to the court. Neither would they be named or in any way identified.

Fraser's heart sank. It sank further on the third day of the inquiry when he read the pilots' statements. They were lengthy documents that could have shed light on precisely what happened that day a year before. But as far as Fraser was concerned they were useless - large sections of the 25 page testimonies had been blacked out.

He gave his evidence and sat through the testimony of all the wounded soldiers. He'd heard them before of course, but informally, personally. Now they were spoken in hushed tones in the solemn environment of a courtroom.

But he had to leave when the medical witnesses were called and he took Liza and MacDonald's wife and Stewart's mother out for a coffee so they couldn't hear either. That his men had been murdered was bad enough, he didn't want to hear precisely how. Neither could he look at the photographs of the incident's aftermath being passed round the court as evidence.

However he enjoyed the testimony of the RAF controllers who had been circling high above the area in their AWACS that awful day more than a year before.

The senior controller stood in the box and swore under oath before the court that he had vectored the A-10s to an Iraqi target 20 kilometres away from Steel and that the pilots had acknowledged the position of that target.

"Are you certain the pilots acknowledged?" asked the Coroner

"Yes sir I am," replied the controller

"Are you aware of the consequences of this?"

"Yes sir I am."

They'd even acknowledged it!

Fraser was elated. He checked the pilots' written statements and found that they denied ever speaking to the AWACS.

He sat transfixed listening to the RAF officer's testimony. By the time the young forward air controller had finished and left the court, Fraser had counted 104 inconsistencies in the evidence of the Americans compared to that of the RAF.

He was happy to be with the boys again and every night he and Mike King took the soldiers to the pub and had a few drinks to try to take their minds off the inquest. The soldiers came and went, some were already out of the Army, and had their own lives now. Others clung to Fraser somehow, as if he would see them right. He hoped and prayed he could.

They sat together in a group at the back of the public benches. They would listen in animated silence, and make faces to each other if they heard evidence they either didn't like or didn't understand. At the end of a lengthy inquest the jury retired to consider its verdict. Fraser went outside with the rest of the survivors and the families of the victims.

While he had been struck by how young they had seemed in the desert, every one of them now appeared so much older. The youths he went to war with were now battle-hardened veterans who'd seen so much. The friendly fire incident had aged them.

But there was more. Many British soldiers now complained of illnesses with no apparent cause. Some suffered from chronic fatigue, others physical deformity. They blamed the radioactive Depleted Uranium tank rounds, choking fumes from the burning oil wells or the cocktail of drugs and injections they'd been forced to take in case of NBC attack. The Army doesn't respond well to illnesses without cause, especially when they are given a name like "Gulf War Syndrome" in the media. So the men kept quiet and soldiered on.

Fraser's men stood clustered together smoking and laughing nervously in the sunshine. The last time these boys had surrounded him like this had been on a dark night in Saudi Arabia more than a year before when they had been just about to mount the Warriors and head into Iraq. It had been a fight then, it would be a fight now.

But then the fight had been against an enemy, the Iraqis. Now the fight, arguably much harder, much more hurtful, was against their own side.

Fraser watched the soldiers and their families shuffle into court and stand with their heads bowed waiting for the verdict. They were downtrodden, cowed, already beaten. As if that was their place.

The women, three bereft women, were dressed in their best clothes, tired clothes, unfashionable clothes, clothes seldom worn. Their money went on other things, food, children's shoes, heating, running a car. The women were tired too. They were spent, exhausted. And here they were at the final hurdle, the last and almost certainly futile obstacle.

They couldn't expect justice, they couldn't expect the system to help them. Instead it had stood solidly in their way since the morning a year before when the families' officer and the Padre had knocked on their doors and asked if they could come in for a quiet word.

And since then the system had offered tea and sympathy but no justice. Far from it. The regiment looked after its own, that was always the way. But there was no British campaign to have the pilots brought to book. No, that would rock the boat, that would upset the Americans.

The Americans!

And while you're at it Mrs Cameron, could you leave your quarter please? Yes we know your husband died a hero, we know he died in a war, but it was an awful, terrible accident and not a result of enemy action. But he's dead now and we really need your three-bedroomed house on Wimberley Way in Inverness. Can you not go back to the council house down the Ferry? And can you do it quickly? quietly? Like a good soldier's widow?

No, there would be no justice from the system.

But the roof nearly came off the court when the jury returned a verdict of unlawful killing. They had been told by the coroner before they retired that such a verdict could mean one thing and one thing only - Manslaughter.

The cheer was huge. There was laughter, laughter like Fraser couldn't remember, smiles and hugs. And tears, there were tears too. The joy spilled out onto the steps of the court where the TV cameras rolled and the flashbulbs popped.

He walked off with his thoughts. He couldn't stand with the families, didn't want to be filmed. He took himself away to the pub where they met every night. He would see them all there later. But for now he had to be alone. His elation was complete but silent. His disbelief surrounded him. It couldn't be true, could it?

The jury had been bang on. Fraser couldn't have written the script better himself. The foreman said there had been clear evidence of a failure by the Americans to recognise procedures in engaging the enemy.

Clear evidence of a failure.

A verdict of Manslaughter would have to be passed on by the Coroner to the Director of Public Prosecutions. It was then a matter for him to decide whether the two pilots would be extradited to the UK and stand trial in the criminal courts.

The pilots, the murdering bastards, the murdering American bastards. They hadn't been named, hadn't had the decency to apologise far less give evidence in person. Could they be forced to stand trial? To travel from America or wherever they were now to the UK and stand trial? Fraser's gut reaction was that it would never be allowed to happen. But then he had never anticipated the jury would return the verdict it did. He returned to Germany, his farewells complete, in a buoyant mood. His quest for vengeance was on course.

The battalion was quietly jubilant when he got back to Buller. Publicly no comment was made but privately the officers and men were elated. The regiment had had a good war but obviously the friendly fire incident had been a devastating blow. Now everybody waited for the DPP to decide whether or not to move against the two pilots.

For the rest of the summer Fraser and his comrades lived regimental life as before. There were exercises and courses in Germany and beyond. In October there was special training ahead of the battalion's first operational posting since the war – its eighth tour of duty in Northern Ireland.

That November the battalion moved to Belfast and took control of the west of the city as part of 39 Infantry Brigade. Fraser MacLean, as RSO, was part of the HQ element and was based at North Howard Street Mill for six months. It was an unaccompanied tour so Anna stayed in Münster.

Fraser got home on leave whenever he could and once again they would meet in London for weekends. When Fraser got back to the flat in Germany he noticed that Anna spent most of her time painting and decorating rooms that had only recently been done. He questioned her about it but she said it kept her busy while he was away – which was most of the time.

Anna still had no luck in finding a job and spent her days reading or helping the Families' Officer. Fraser said it wouldn't matter because she would soon have their baby to deal with and that would surely keep her busy. But even though they couldn't keep their hands off each other when they were together, Anna had no luck in getting pregnant either.

At Christmas 1992 Fraser bought her a long leather coat from a designer shop on the King's Road. It was expensive but not overly so.

Anna's present to him was a Hi-Fi stacking system with one of the new CD players in it. Even with the forces' duty free discount, it cost well over £1,000.

5

Fraser left Germany after Christmas leave and returned to Belfast. His room in the mess was so small there was no space for the Hi-Fi so it stayed in Münster. Anna enjoyed playing the new

CDs she bought in the NAAFI to replace Fraser's much prized collection of LPs, which she'd thrown out because they spoiled the look of the living room.

He and his superiors were so busy in Belfast they didn't have time to devote to pressing politicians, civil servants or Army top brass over the DPP's deliberations. Fraser had daily dealings with the soldiers who'd been wounded in the friendly fire incident; he kept in touch with Mike King and his men and wrote and telephoned the families of those killed. He did his bit, he hoped those in the system were doing theirs.

At the end of April 1993, the battalion prepared to pack up and leave Belfast to return to Münster. Two weeks before departure, Fraser was called in to see the CO.

Space is at a premium in Army bases in Northern Ireland and the office was tiny compared to the one in Münster. There was no sofa, no coffee table. Fraser marched in, saluted and stood to attention as per the rules. Colonel MacLaren was not alone. Euan stood by the door and gazing out of the window behind the seated CO's desk, was a civilian, aged around 50. Fraser thought he recognised him as one of the suits from the Army Board of Inquiry in Whitehall the year before.

"Fraser sit down. We need to talk to you. This is Brigadier Samson, from the Army Legal Service."

The man turned round and caught Fraser's eye. Fraser nodded a greeting.

"You won't like what you're about to hear. I'm afraid the DPP will not be pushing the issue and there will be no attempt to extradite and prosecute the pilots."

The families, the widows, the mothers, the children. Fraser's mind clicked like a camera, he pictured snapshots of Liza Cameron, of Stewart's mother, MacDonald's twin daughters. They had trusted him to get something done. The Coroner's Court verdict had been too good to be true.

Of course.

They had been foolish to expect otherwise.

Fraser surveyed the detail of the wallpaper in the far corner of the room. Their last chance had disappeared, the last flicker of light, the last glimmer of hope, gone.

The Brigadier spoke next. He was still staring out the window as a watery sun tried vainly to brighten Belfast's grim skyline.

"It ends here," he said softly, "there will be no campaign for justice, no lobbying of MPs or speaking to the press. It ends here."

Samson turned round.

"This has come down from the very top, MOD, FCO, Number Ten. The Americans are our allies. You'll know all about the special relationship we have. That has to be maintained. What happened was a tragic accident, nothing more."

Fraser stood up.

He noted Euan's smug expression, saluted the two senior officers and left.

It was a sombre cookhouse for the rest of the tour. The word had got out among the boys. Their comrades would not be avenged by the extradition and prosecution of the two pilots after all. The soldiers' already healthy dislike of the American military deepened. They barely hid their anger.

Fraser vowed to fight on, but in his heart he knew there was little that could be done now.

As preparations were completed to leave Belfast and return to Münster, the regiment was dealt a further hammer blow in a leak to the media from an MOD document.

In February 1990, long before Iraq invaded Kuwait, Defence Secretary Tom King, himself a former infantry officer, realised there was no need for such a large defence budget given the collapse of the Soviet Bloc. As a result cuts had to be identified to reduce defence spending by 25%. Because the threat of the Soviet Army rolling across the North German plain had disappeared overnight, plans were afoot to reduce the number of infantry soldiers by a quarter – nearly 120,000 troops from BAOR. The process would be called "Options for Change."

One of the cuts being considered was the axing of the Queen's Own Highlanders.

The leak caused uproar. Officers and soldiers alike were outraged that the government could send the regiment to war, to fight, and lose men, while at the same time secretly plan its demise. A campaign had started at home to save the regiment – politicians, ex-soldiers and the media were now lobbying with vigour.

Fraser mulled it over for the remaining fortnight of the tour. His burning desire to have the pilots extradited and tried for Manslaughter would not now happen. He could try going through official channels from now until Domesday, but as he knew from Brigadier Samson and his own understanding of the system, he would face a brick wall. To carry on with it would no doubt damage his career and hamper any chance he had of ever commanding his regiment.

But if everything he read in the media was true, there would soon be no regiment at all. The Queen's Own Highlanders was among a dozen famous old regiments facing the axe under Options for Change. He wasn't naïve enough for a moment to think there could be a reprieve. He'd been among the military long enough to know what was what. All the speculation in the papers, from people who should know what they were talking about, pointed to at best an amalgamation with another threatened regiment, or at worst a disbandment.

Traditionalists in the regiment had seen it all before. The Queen's Own Highlanders had already been through an amalgamation in 1961 when the Camerons and Seaforths had joined together. It had been uneasy at first but slowly the new regiment had blossomed. After less than 35 years in existence it would disappear.

Some old sweats recounted the tale of the Cameronians, another famous old Scottish regiment facing disbandment in the 60s. It could trace its roots back to 1689, was present at the siege and relief of Lucknow and fought in the Zulu wars. It had served with great distinction in the Boer War and among its honours were the World War One battles of Mons, Ypres and Gallipoli. It was evacuated from the beaches of Dunkirk and fought in Italy and Burma in World War Two.

But when faced with amalgamation, its members declined and volunteered to be disbanded instead. And so, on May 14th 1968, after a long and glorious history, it paraded for the last time at Douglasdale in Lanarkshire. Afterwards the battalion flag was lowered and the CO marched up to the General commanding Scotland at the time, to ask for permission to disband. When this was granted he said, "Sir, we'll have to go now," and the battalion marched off into history.

Traditionalists said they would rather the Queen's Own Highlanders did the same than merge again.

The battalion was regarded as among the top three in the Army, it was fully recruited and had seen action in wartime. The cynic in Fraser believed it was being targeted because of the friendly fire incident and was being axed to shut it up. Morale was the lowest it had been for some time.

Fraser quickly realised that if the regiment disappeared, he had two options. He could re-capbadge, in other words join another regiment, or leave the Army.

He didn't want to leave the Army. It was his life now. And anyway he still had points to prove. But equally he didn't want to leave the Queen's Own Highlanders and join another regiment. The Queen's Own Highlanders was his family's regiment, his father had commanded it, and he wanted to command it one day too. But he couldn't command a regiment that didn't exist.

Anna was less than happy to see him when he returned to the quarter. The rumour factory had been working overtime in and around Buller Barracks. She had been climbing the walls with worry about the regiment disbanding. What would happen to their quarter? Would Fraser still have a job? What about the social life? Would there be any more balls? Ladies' dinner nights?

Fraser and Anna use to joke about there always being two bangs when he came home on leave, and the second was his bergen hitting the floor. But instead of the great sex they usually had the moment he was across the threshold, they had a row.

Parked outside the flat was a brand new black VW Golf GTI. When he saw it he assumed there were guests waiting for him in the house, ready to welcome him home from his tour. Fraser bit his lip when Anna said it was hers.

He went upstairs to the bedroom and dropped the grip bag containing his entire worldly civilian possessions from his Belfast tour. He opened the wardrobe to hang up his jacket and saw that it was full of Anna's designer clothes.

He noticed the room had been redecorated since Easter, when he'd been home last. But when he looked in the spare room on his way back downstairs, his jaw dropped. The brand new king size double bed they'd bought for guests only the year before had gone.

In its place was a cot. The wardrobes and dressing tables had disappeared to be replaced by a playpen, complete with toys and hanging mobiles. This room too had been redecorated.

The row started after Fraser demanded to see the bank statements for the past six months. He'd been earning good money as a Captain in Belfast and had had nowhere to spend it. That problem had been overcome by Anna.

She'd been bored, she said, bored without Fraser, without a job, without a life of her own and had redecorated the flat as a hobby as much as anything else. The car? Well, she needed a car to get around. And the clothes were to make her feel better, to feel attractive. There had been a few social nights with the other wives at the mess and the NAAFI.

Fraser wasn't especially jealous. His feelings of jealousy, possessiveness had been confined to Kirsty all those years before. He wasn't really jealous of anyone being with Anna. But now he thought about it, the doubt crept in. *Would she? Could she?*

He knew how some wives left alone for months on end while their husbands were away on ops would leave a packet of OMO soap powder in the kitchen window.

It meant 'On my own' or 'Old man overseas'.

Anna wasn't like that, was she?

But the real row started when she admitted she'd spent a thousand pounds on creating a nursery when she wasn't even pregnant.

"You have to have sex to get pregnant," she screamed as she threw the first object that came to hand. Twenty of Fraser's hard earned pounds disappeared in shards of glass as the cut Caithness crystal decanter smashed against the wall.

"And we never have sex because you're never here." A glass came next. The remaining three glasses and silver tray were thrown as she detailed Fraser's shortcomings in the bedroom.

"Maybe you're firing blanks," she screamed, "we've been trying for a year and nothing's happened. You're hardly ever here and when you are you can't even deliver."

She slumped down at the kitchen table sobbing.

Fraser had heard how some of the soldiers who'd been in the Gulf had fathered children with webbed feet and hands, or heart defects, thought to be linked to the conditions in the desert. Others couldn't father children at all. He wondered if the Depleted Uranium, the Bromide, or the cocktail of drugs he'd taken, had rendered him infertile.

"I'm beginning to think you love the Army more than you love me," Anna said coldly.

Fraser looked round the kitchen at the new cooker and fridge freezer, he saw the bank statements and smelt the new paint.

"I love the RAF more than I love you," he said.

That night as he lay alone in bed, Fraser weighed up his options. He'd been contemplating his future for a while now, since the campaign to prosecute the pilots had failed, since a question mark had appeared over the regiment. The next morning he would set the wheels in motion to do what most soldiers contemplate, many attempt but few actually achieve.

He would formally apply to undergo selection to join the Special Air Service – the SAS.

HEREFORD

The CO took Fraser's news with a resigned nod and a thin smile. The young Captain hadn't been alone in announcing his desire to leave. Many of the officers and men said they wanted no truck with a new regiment formed from the merger of the Queen's Own Highlanders with another doomed battalion. Many said they would join a different regiment or corps before they became part of a hybrid with no history whatsoever. Others said they would leave the Army altogether.

Iain MacLaren didn't stand in Fraser's way, as many COs might, when he learnt of his plans. He knew what his RSO had endured down the years and agreed to rush through his paperwork.

Fraser moved out of the empty, but beautifully decorated, quarter and returned to a room in the mess in Buller. He went through the ignominy of selling the car and all the furniture through the usual Army channels, which meant sticking up 'For Sale' postcards in the NAAFI and notice boards all over camp. The loss of face was humiliating and many officers would have crumpled. Fraser just got on with it.

The sale of the marital belongings hardly covered the credit card bills, now arriving with alarming frequency since Anna's departure. She had spent a fortune on clothes and make up as well as on furniture. She had taken the designer wardrobe and cosmetics with her but Fraser sold every stick of furniture and every fitting in the quarter, except the hi-fi and the cot. He took the hi-fi into his room in the mess. He couldn't bear to sell the cot, even though it cost a thousand Deutschmarks. Instead he gave it to a young Private in B Company whose wife had just given birth to their third child.

Like the majority of soldiers, Fraser went for a run every morning. The day after Anna left, he rose and filled a daysack with bags of sugar and followed his usual route. In the evenings, instead of joining his brother officers in the mess for a drink, he would go to the gym and skip, press weights or lay into the punchbag for an hour. Then he would cycle back to the mess.

He gave up the fried breakfasts and mountains of toast for fruit and porridge. He gave up chips and sweets and ate lots of pasta, rice, steak and fish instead. He gave up alcohol for pints of water and fruit juice. Every morning he ran a little further carrying a little more weight. If he had a long weekend off he would head down to

Bavaria and climb in the mountains with as much in his bergen as he could carry.

Slowly but steadily he increased his strength and stamina. All the time he was training he continued as RSO at Buller. But it was a thankless job now. All anybody cared about was the future of the regiment – or the lack of it.

The public campaign, dubbed SOS for Save Our Soldiers, had been mounted and MPs and ex-soldiers, the media and Uncle Tom Cobley and all had become involved to try to save the regiment. In the end, despite massive pressure being applied and huge public support being voiced, it came to nothing – as Fraser had guessed.

In November 1993 the Queen's Own Highlanders left Münster and came home for the last time. For the final few months of its existence it would be based at Dreghorn Barracks in Edinburgh.

By then the future had been mapped out in the dark corridors of Whitehall. The Queen's Own Highlanders would amalgamate with another fine old Highland regiment, the Gordon Highlanders, to form a new regiment called simply 'The Highlanders'.

The campaign had failed.

Fraser's mother thought her son's return to Scotland would mean she would see a lot more of him. She was very wrong. Every Friday lunchtime he would throw his bergen into his car and drive into the mountains. With everything he needed to survive, food, water and shelter, on his back, he would spend two full days climbing in Torridon, the Grampians or Glencoe.

Regimental duties had been abandoned in preparation for the amalgamation, so his workload was very light. While emotional debates raged on about which items of dress would survive the amalgamation, Fraser's mind was elsewhere. As the committees of the Queen's Own Highlanders and the Gordons met in Edinburgh to debate whether to wear the blue hackle or the Cameron of Erracht tartan, Fraser continued with his preparations.

When he wasn't training hard, he was studying hard. He read, re-read and memorised pamphlets on the minutiae of signalling, foreign weapons, astral navigation and survival skills. Then he would get out his old university books and revise as much Russian and Arabic as he could.

On July 22nd 1994, the Queen's Own Highlanders held a service of thanksgiving in St Giles Cathedral in Edinburgh. The next day they paraded for the very last time as a regiment on the square at Dreghorn. It was review parade, a farewell, and a little piece of history died when the Queen's Own Highlanders marched past Prince Philip, the Colonel in Chief.

That afternoon a farewell gathering was held on Dreghorn's playing fields to mark the occasion. As the glorious summer sun split the sky, grown men cried.

The Gordons, whose regimental heartland was the north-east of Scotland and the Shetland Islands, had no desire to be part of an amalgamation either and its soldiers were as emotional about it all as the Queen's Own Highlanders.

The River Spey, which runs roughly south to north through Morayshire, marks the geographical boundary between the Queen's Own Highlanders and the Gordons homelands. Fraser donned his regimental service dress for the last time on the 14th of September 1994 when the two regiments marched onto the tall, arching bridge over the Spey at Craigellachie.

The two COs met in the middle. They saluted, shook hands and drank from a quaich full of Speyside single Malt Whisky to cement their new relationship.

Three days later there was an amalgamation parade back at Dreghorn. After a brief drumhead service the colours of the two regiments were grouped together to mark the moment.

Then the new regiment, the 1st Battalion, The Highlanders, marched off the square to start its life.

Fraser stood in the crowd at Dreghorn watching events that day. Officially he'd left the Queen's Own Highlanders at Craigellachie. He was now on extended leave, so he was ineligible to be on parade. Not that he would have wanted to be part of it anyway. Instead he stood with his father and brother and watched in emotional silence. For once the three men agreed on something.

The next day the Highlanders would begin training for their first operational posting to Northern Ireland. Instead, Fraser went to the Quartermaster and handed in his kit. After he said his farewells, he left his room in the mess and packed his few civilian belongings into his car. He drove through to Glasgow where he said his farewells to his parents.

Then he headed south, then west and didn't stop until he got to the small Welsh town of Brecon, where he took digs in a farmhouse belonging to an ex-soldier and his family who knew precisely why he was there. Every day for the next three months, except for a few days at Christmas and New Year when he went back to Glasgow, he went climbing in the Brecon Beacons and the Black Mountains – the proving ground of the SAS.

2

There are two selection courses to join the best special forces unit on earth – summer and winter. Each is as hard as the other, the only difference is the weather. The courses attract thousands of men from all corners of the Army each year. But only a few, a very special few, ever pass.

During the long, hard months he'd spent on his build-up training, Fraser MacLean got back into the driven, obsessive mindset. He'd eradicated the word 'failure' from his lexicon by the time he walked into Stirling Lines in Hereford in January 1995.

By then he knew his paperwork would have been filleted and his background vetted by the SAS system. He knew they would have studied every detail and checked every fact, figure and date. They would realise he had wartime experience and had been involved in the friendly fire incident in the Gulf. They would be aware that he had been the RSO at his old battalion, because signalling skills were crucial to the SAS. And they would know, and be impressed, by the fact that he had an excellent degree and spoke a dozen languages – among them, importantly, Russian and Arabic.

But that degree would also count against him. The five years he spent at university meant he was now 30 years of age, old for even an officer candidate.

Stirling Lines is named after David Stirling, the man who formed the SAS during the North African campaign in World War Two. The sprawling camp is on the A49 Hereford to Ross on Wye road. It is not signposted, it is not advertised. Anybody who needs to go there should really know where it is.

Those who don't need to go, don't need to know.

It was just starting to snow that February Sunday evening when Fraser reported at the gate. His name was ticked off a long list and he was shown to his quarters. Fraser was a 30 year-old Captain. He'd been in the Army for six years and had been on many courses and exercises. Arriving somewhere new, even somewhere as auspicious as this, did not daunt him. He did what all soldiers did at times like these, he found where he was to eat, where he was to sleep, and where and when he had to be on parade the next morning.

His accommodation was a long Victorian barrack room with four beds either side. There was a handful of men of all ranks already preparing themselves for the first day of selection. They were passing round bottles of isotonic drinks and rolls of surgical tape for their feet. As Fraser unpacked his grip bag and placed his shaving kit in his locker, he listened to their chat.

"Kev said I could be in G Squadron by the summer," said one.

"Nah! I want the black kit. I want to kick in windows and slot a few towelheads," said his mate.

Fraser smiled to himself and carried on unpacking. The SAS owed a great deal of popularity among soldiers to the events of May 5th, 1980. That bright spring evening, 12 SAS soldiers stormed the Iranian Embassy in London's Princes Gate where Iraqi-backed terrorists had been holding hostages since the siege started on April 30th.

Only one hostage was killed in the assault - only one terrorist survived.

The startling images of men in black boiler suits and balaclavas blowing in windows were flashed around the globe as they happened. It emerged later that the Prime Minister, Margaret Thatcher, had insisted the TV cameras be given unfettered live access to the events. She wanted the world to see how Britain dealt with terrorists.

There was a huge spin-off. The media had hardly ever heard of the previously secretive special forces unit based at Hereford. Now they wanted to know all about it. So did every soldier in the Army. And while the media's attention was unwelcome, the boost to recruitment was immeasurable.

Political correctness has not yet reached the Special Air Service. No women may apply. The Regiment only takes men aged between 19 and 34 who have served at least three years and who have at least three years left to serve.

Soldiers who join may stay with the Regiment for the rest of their Army careers, but they drop a rank when they enter. Officers may join for an initial period of three years then they return to their original units. If they are good, and more importantly popular with the Regiment, they are invited to return later in their careers.

But all of this is dependent on passing what is without doubt the most demanding military selection course in the world.

Fraser knew what was ahead of him so he went to bed early that night. Many of the others in the room stayed up and chatted into the night. Fraser drifted off to sleep as they discussed their desires to dress up as trees in the bandit country of South Armagh or disguise themselves as Arabs in order to assassinate Saddam Hussein in downtown Baghdad.

3

He woke early the next morning and dressed, as ordered, in t-shirt, shorts and training shoes. He paraded, as ordered, in the main gymnasium, with 200 other prospective candidates.

Fraser had had dealings with the SAS many times down the years and was always surprised by how ordinary they appeared. The popular image of the SAS is that they are devilishly handsome, muscle bound, hyperfit, dashing, superheroes. In fact they looked just like any other soldier - the difference was on the inside.

What the SAS seek in a candidate is basically the qualities of a very good soldier - someone who is fit, keen and capable. A man who is a talented, self-confident individual, but who is not flamboyant or headstrong and therefore incapable of working as a part of a team. Fitness and skills aren't enough, these can be taught, honed. Is he resourceful? Keen? Determined? Or does he give up at the first hurdle?

This was the first hurdle on day one of the winter selection course to join the SAS. It wasn't an abseil down the side of a building, it wasn't unarmed combat against three karate experts and it wasn't jumping out of a Hercules at night. It was the BFT, the basic fitness test of the British Army – a three mile run that every soldier should be able to pass. The rules were simple, the first mile and a half was to be done in a squad in a time of under 15 minutes. At the halfway point it became individual best effort for the rest of the run.

Fraser hardly broke sweat and was back in the showers before most of the candidates reached the two-mile point. Thirty of them, those who limped home wheezing, coughing and spluttering, were taken to one side by the DS and ushered onto a four tonner destined for platform four – where the trains to London left from Hereford Station.

Fraser was aghast. If civilians had done the run he wouldn't have been surprised. But these men were all serving soldiers and the BFT was just that, the basic fitness test. They'd done it in PT kit and trainers, not wearing boots and carrying bergens – that would come. While back in the Queen's Own Highlanders, he took his platoon on a BFT every week. It had been a team building exercise as much as anything, but there were also the fitness implications.

While he was surprised, the SAS DS, senior NCO instructors from the Training Wing, were not. Every selection brings a quota of Walter Mitty types, fantasists, who talk a good game but who are in reality of little use to the Regiment. These people are usually found out at the beginning of day one and are on their way home before the course really starts – the same policy of the Foreign Legion. Fraser looked at himself in the bathroom mirror and thought back to the young man in Marseille all those years before.

Failed candidates get another chance though. Very often borderline failures know to work on whatever fitness or military skills they need to get through the second time. Sometimes candidates get right to the end of the course and fail because of an injury. They get their second chance but if they are injured again, or are delayed by helping a casualty for example, that's it - even if it isn't their fault. The SAS standards are so high, and because it gets so many applicants, it can afford to take only the very best.

Fraser got out of the shower and padded back to his room. As he towelled off and dressed, the Armagh tree and the Baghdad assassin packed and left quietly.

The course started in earnest the next day. Other ranks do a three week-long build up phase, while the course for officers lasts two weeks. It comprises a series of road marches or route marches across the Brecon Beacons. These are done in groups but as a few people fail or give up every day, the candidates quickly find themselves on their own.

They march in full kit and carry bergens that, at the behest of the DS, increase in weight as the days pass. In the bad old days the bergens were filled with bricks to get the desired effect. Sadly so many candidates died of exposure on the hills, that the weight is now made up of food, water and survival equipment. And if a bergen is to weigh 25kg, then it must weigh 25kg at the end of the march, so food and water must be carried as extra weight.

The weather was vile as Fraser and his colleagues set a cracking pace across the crags of the Brecon Beacons. It was colder at night and more difficult and dangerous in the dark. But Fraser's map reading and night navigation had always been excellent. He already knew to climb hills as quickly as he could and run down the other side.

The candidates would rise at 0400, and start their day. They'd jump into four tonners and try to rest until they reached the drop off point. Then they'd be given a map and compass and told to be at a certain grid reference by a certain time. Each day the distance increased while the time allowed for the march decreased. To check the candidate's mental agility during such a punishing schedule, they were given problem solving exercises along the way. One might be asked to strip an AK-47 or another foreign weapon, another might be asked about the last geographical feature he'd passed. Some were asked to name the capital of Tasmania, or solve a mathematical problem. If they got it right they were given the next RV and timing for the leg.

It was platform four if they got it wrong.

The surviving candidates got back to camp around 10 each night, soaked, frozen and exhausted. But they couldn't go to bed before they'd cleaned and prepped their kit for the next day's ordeal. The failure and drop-out rates were high.

But Fraser MacLean gritted his teeth and got on with it. He thanked his lucky stars that he'd had nearly a year to train and prepare and that so far he'd been spared from injury. He was still confident he could get through selection - but all the training and positive mental attitude in the world wouldn't help him if he fell and broke his ankle.

Every night he soaked in a long hot bath to ease the aches, then he checked himself for injuries. The bergen burns on his shoulders he could do little about. These opened up every time his rucksack carried more than a few pounds. He was resigned to them now - he'd had them since he was in the UOTC. All he could do was lather on antiseptic cream and hope for the best.

But he paid special attention to his feet. He pumiced away rough skin, rubbed foot oil on soft skin and took special care of his toenails. Other soldiers tore theirs off in the bath when they got too long, but he clipped his carefully. He didn't want to fail selection because of a toenail. He dried carefully between each toe then splashed talc on them to ward off Athlete's Foot. In the morning, after a cold shower, he bound his ankles with sticky tape to support them for that day's battering.

While other ranks did their third week of build up training, officers made up the time difference by undertaking a little slice of hell called Officers' Week.

On the first day Fraser had to stand up in the packed Training Wing lecture theatre and give a presentation about himself. He did this with only scant mention of the friendly fire incident and no mention at all of his brief flirtation with the French Foreign Legion. Every day he and the other officer candidates were given a series of exercises to tackle. There would be a written problem to overcome, usually staff work exercises related to special forces duties, and a more practical task to be carried out every evening.

During this time the marches and cross country navigation exercises continued. One evening Fraser was asked to plan a mission to snatch a terrorist leader. He was told what resources he had at his disposal and the timeframe during which the raid was to be mounted. Then he sat alone for half an hour with a blank notepad in front of him and planned his mission.

He'd heard all about the 'Chinese Parliament' before he came to Hereford, but now he found himself in the middle of one. It's a uniquely SAS concept where the officer or senior rank in charge briefs his men on a mission and outlines his plan. Then, regardless of rank, the men sit and discuss it and put forward their own views. It very often ends in the officers' hours of work being binned and a new plan made.

A slight panic rose in Fraser's breast when he realised he might be thrown out if the DS didn't like his plan for the snatch. Candidates were being RTUd for the slightest fault. He was confident in his own fitness and abilities as a soldier, but it wouldn't matter whether or not he could run all day if the DS didn't like his ideas.

The fear grew when the half dozen DS sat and tore holes in the plan and asked him to defend every aspect of it. One Corporal spotted a flaw in Fraser's supply chain. And the man had been right – Fraser had never considered that particular aspect of his logistics. He didn't care about being humbled in public by an NCO. He was more worried about the effect it might have on his chances.

He admitted the fault, quickly thought through his options, and made a new plan.

Improvise, adapt and overcome.

He'd long since given up trying to work out the DS. They were an odd bunch, yet at the same time they were incredibly normal. The varied in age and they all looked average, some positively unsoldierly. He was sure he even saw a small spare tyre on one man, and many of them smoked like Beagles.

Yet they were all very fit, highly competent soldiers. Underneath, each man possessed that SAS thing, that self confidence, self reliance, calmness under fire - that magical x-factor that every candidate aspired to.

Fraser worried all that night about the way his plan had been treated by the corporal. He expected to be sent to platform four first thing in the morning. He feared the worst when he was told to throw his massive bergen in the back of a four tonner and climb in after it. But instead of being driven to the station, he found himself once again in the mountains. He was ordered to march to an RV farther away than the last one, in a time eight minutes shorter.

After build-up training and officer's week, the remaining candidates were allowed the weekend off to rest and prepare themselves and their equipment for Test Week – the period when the course really hots up. The pressure on candidates is deliberately increased by the Training Wing DS then, with longer route marches to be completed in shorter times.

Fraser looked around him and studied his opposition. They weren't friends, they weren't colleagues, they certainly weren't comrades. The other men doing selection were the opposition. Every time a man dropped out, and there were a few every day for various reasons, Fraser felt no sympathy. Instead he cheered inwardly. He was still there and going strong. He had no intention of quitting, and only an injury or some improbable factor would stop him.

The other men were, in the main, Paras. There were a few assorted infantiers and even a couple of gunners and cavalrymen. The rest were engineers or signallers. Fraser was on nodding terms with the 60 or so left on the course. He knew few names because there was no time for socialising. At the end of every day it was a case of preparing kit for the next day, treating any injuries and getting as much sleep as possible.

Men were dropping out as the weather closed in and minor injuries became open sores. Fraser kept his head down and his mind on the job. When he slackened he made himself think of the poncho in the sand covering his men, his friends, Decker's grotesque Red Baron features in the A-10 and Kirsty's sickly sweet smile.

At the end of one gruelling leg through the Brecon Beacons he came across one of the DS sitting on a rock smoking a cigarette. Fraser nodded a greeting then checked the map. This wasn't the RV he'd been ordered to go to.

"All right mate? How's it going then?" said the man.

"Fine thanks," replied Fraser suspiciously.

"Take a break if you want, you're well ahead of the game here, well ahead of time. I've been watching you. You're good."

Fraser stole a glance at his watch. The DS was right, he *was* well ahead of time for the leg and he could do with a break. But he knew that any candidate who dallied, far less sat down, would be on the train to London by lunchtime. He thanked the DS, declined the offer and carried on.

It was a ploy. They would pay you a compliment, flatter your ego and offer you the chance to sit and talk about yourself. Others were asked by the DS if they wanted to dump some of the weight from their bergens. Any takers were binned on the spot.

And there were the sickeners too. Fraser was prepared for his and managed to take it in his stride when it came. He'd just finished an 18 mile leg as the light was fading. The RV was a four tonne lorry parked at a T-junction. When he was only a couple of metres short of it, the engine coughed into life and the lorry rolled off. He had no option but to follow it until it stopped, which it did - 12 miles later.

Many candidates had enough when this happened and simply dropped their bergens and sat on them. Some sobbed, a few whimpered, others sat in silence waiting for the safety vehicle. By this time Fraser had shut out the burning agony in his calves and knees and the scalding hot barbed wire someone was dragging through his spine. He just gritted his teeth and set one foot in front of the other.

He knew it wasn't just about physical ability, he knew it was about mental ability. It was about the ability to shut out everything, the pain, the emotion, and focus on the mission. The mission was everything. Nothing else mattered.

Test Week finished with the Fandance, a 60km forced march over the Brecon Beacons. Among them was the highest, Pen-y-Fan, thus the Fandance. The candidate carried a bergen weighing 25kg plus his weapon. The weapon had no sling so couldn't be supported around the neck – it had to be carried. He had to complete the course in under 20 hours and if he did not, even at this late stage, he would be thrown off the course.

Fraser had done the Fandance four times in training and it held no fears for him. What worried him was the prospect of falling and getting injured or delayed if bad weather set in, which was a distinct possibility. He stood outside the block the night before and looked up at the stars. He knew that 24 hours hence it would all be over.

The Fandance came and went and Fraser and the 20 other survivors were told they'd passed the initial section of the course. Inside, each man was bursting with pride and relief. Outwardly they showed no emotion. Every action, every word was examined by the DS. The wrong thing said at the wrong time would mean endex for any of them. Fraser said nothing. He returned to his room to sort out his kit.

4

For the next 14 weeks Fraser and his fellow candidates moved from Hereford to the Pontrilas training centre on the A465 Abergavenny road. There the atmosphere was totally different. This was continuation training. As long as you had the basics of soldiering that was fine. The SAS would teach you the rest, their way.

Over the following three months Fraser learnt the special forces skills not taught in any manuals. Highly skilled SAS instructors took the remaining candidates through the intricacies of a hundred foreign weapons, how to handle explosives and save lives with intensive first aid training. They were also taught perhaps the most critical skills of all, how to use the myriad communications kit that keeps the SAS in touch with Hereford wherever it goes in the world.

It was summer by the time the last major test took place. While the build-up and test week had been all about the physical, what lay ahead was all about the mental.

Escape and Evasion and Resistance to Interrogation training started gently enough. Civilian experts were brought in to Pontrilas to show the candidates how to build shelters, set snares and tickle trout. But the nature lesson did not last.

One day in June, Fraser was unexpectedly ordered into a room in the Training Wing and told to strip. He removed his comfortable boots, combat trousers, shirt and smock and was thrown ancient battledress shirt and trousers. The shirt had no buttons and the trousers no belt. Each was far too big for him. Then he was given an old pair of hobnailed boots, minus the laces. These too were too big. The ensemble was completed by a beltless army greatcoat, again too big by far.

He knew what was coming. Before he was allowed to put on his new outfit he was made to touch his toes.

He grimaced as he heard the snap of latex, then a DS voice said, "sorry mate," and Fraser felt a gloved finger enter his anus.

A favourite trick among candidates was to wrap some matches, a thin candle stub or some chocolate-coated raisins in a condom then secrete the package inside his body. The search of Fraser's inner self had proved negative and the DS looked disappointed when he removed his finger and threw the glove in the bin.

"It's only a sin if you enjoy it," he cracked. "The next time you see me I'll be wearing a white armband. Then it'll be all over either way. Now do us a favour mate and call in the next victim."

Fraser managed a grim smile and hobbled towards the door.

But there were no smiles over the next week as the candidates were chased high and low all over the Brecon Beacons by a hunter force comprising men of the Parachute Regiment. The Paras loved finding soldiers they knew, who'd decided their regiment wasn't good enough and who'd wanted to try SAS selection instead. The Paras' company commander had upped the ante by telling his men that anybody who found a candidate would automatically get a week's leave.

Fraser heard the screams as Paras found candidates and administered summary justice before they were handed over to the DS. By this time he'd lived successfully off the land and had avoided capture. He'd stumbled upon some mushrooms and had eaten them to keep going. He hadn't been certain they were safe but rubbed one on his lips, then gum, then tongue. When there was no reaction he ate a small piece and when he felt no ill effects he ate a larger piece. Eventually he ate a dozen.

It was warm by day but cold by night. Fraser found a creeper that, when doubled, proved strong enough to lace his boots. He stole a roll of garden twine and a pair of secateurs from a shed behind a farmhouse and fashioned himself a belt. He made a mental note of the house's location so he could return the spoils later.

He used the secateurs to cut branches and build himself shelters. He drank from streams and he ate berries and mushrooms where and when he saw them. He almost caught a rabbit innocently sunning itself near its burrow. But Fraser was more tired and disorientated than he thought and though he managed to grab the beast's ears, its legs were full of power and it sprinted for safety.

Fraser made the final RV four hours before the cut off time. There was no point in hiding now. He sat on a boulder and waited, waited for the ultimate test.

The Land Rover pulled up and two men got out. They wore combats with no rank or insignia and had no headgear. They approached Fraser. He stood.

"You're MacLean," said one. "You're the last. You've done very well. All the others were caught ages ago."

Fraser said nothing. He turned to the other man, expectantly. Had he been stronger, had he eaten properly, rested properly, he might have put up more of a fight. Instead, the punch in his kidneys felled him. He tried to rise but all he managed to do was thrust his head into the waiting sandbag. Then he smelled the musty odour of the German sandbag in Münster a world before, and felt the bite of the cable tie on his wrists. A kick hit him behind the knees. He crumpled and was bundled into the back of the vehicle.

He tried to sleep but the journey was too fast down a bumpy road and his head crashed repeatedly off the cold steel floor. *Soon,* he told himself, *it would all be over soon.*

He tried to count the number of hands that grabbed him, slid him out of the Rover, dropped him off the tailgate onto the concrete floor. But he couldn't. Pain replaced fatigue now. Pain in his lower back from the punch, pain in his legs from the kick and the thousands of miles he'd walked over the past six months, pain in his head from the Rover floor and pain in his heart from everything.

Why? Why had he done this? What was it all about? Why didn't he just leave? Go back to a school somewhere and teach French? That's what he really wanted to do wasn't it? What was all this soldiering nonsense all about? Why go through all the agonies of the Gulf, seeing his boys killed by their own side, then watching as nothing was done about it? See his regiment, his beloved family regiment neutered by his own government? What the fuck was that all about?

Pity. Time for pity.

No!

This was no time for pity. Get a grip.

Get a grip.

Sleep.

Sleep? Fuckin' doubt it.

Rest then.

Silence.

Recover.

You're still in control here.

Fuck them.

Fuck 'em.

Fuck 'em dead.

Fraser found himself spreadeagled against the wall, or squatting on the ground. Every few minutes he was moved into an even more uncomfortable posture. These were stress positions, designed to unbalance him, to disorientate him, to make him fail.

Fail.

That word.

That word he did not recognise.

That word he would not recognise.

Not this day.

Not after coming this far.

Fuck you.

Fuck the lot of you.

I'm gonna return that man's secateurs.

And I'm going to do it badged.

Fuck the lot of you.

Fuck you.

Fuck you all, dead.

The room alternated between icy cold and unbearable heat. He tried to listen for sounds he recognised but there were none. The men must have been in the room with him because he could hear no footsteps. He would wriggle about in the various stress positions for what he thought was a few minutes then they would be changed.

The hood was still on, his wrists still bound. He badly needed to pee. While he had not eaten very well he had drunk long and slow from every stream he had passed. His bowels did not need to move but he thought his bladder was going to burst. If push came to shove he'd have to do it, let it go. But he'd try to time it so that the handlers were moving him when he did and hopefully he'd get some on them, the bastards.

He had no watch, not that he could see it even if he wanted to. He had no concept of time and no idea how long he'd been there. In his confusion he was certain he'd slept, well dozed at least, but for how long?

Then, from what sounded like the next room, he heard another man's voice, in pain.

"Oh fuck this," he shouted and began sobbing. "Let me out of here, I've had enough, I've had enough. Endex, endex." The sob became a wail as another candidate gave up.

Fraser wanted to scream at him to hang on, not to give in, not now, not at this late stage. But he was terrified to speak, frightened to give the DS something to bin him with.

The hands grabbed him and hauled him up. Now! He tried to pee, let it go, pour from him, drench the men. But he couldn't. He was elated. He was still in control. They hadn't debased him enough yet for him to give in.

Fucking chew on that you bastards, he tried to say. But his mouth was so dry, nothing came out.

He thought he was being dragged into another room. The vine lace in his left boot snapped and it dropped off in what felt like a corridor. There was a draught, but a nice one, a mild one. The outer door was open and it was summer outside.

It's fucking winter in here, but it's summer outside lads and all I have to do is hang on for another wee while and this will be over and I'll be in.

The sandbag was ripped off his head and the bright lights caused his head to spin. A rough male voice ordered him to strip.

Was it a Glasgow accent?

You see, I still have my faculties. I can still think this through. I can still recognise a Glasgow accent, even now, even after all I've been through. Maybe not Glasgow, possibly Clydebank. West of Scotland anyway.

Well fuck you, wherever you're from.

Stripping wasn't a problem. His ancient clothes were ripped and hanging off him. He kicked off the remaining boot and stepped out of the trousers and shirt. He was dizzy. The MOD issue wallpaper was tumbling before his eyes.

"Is that it? Is that all you've got? You won't do much damage with that." It was a female voice. A giggling female voice.

Fraser turned slowly. There was a desk. Behind it sat two girls, pretty girls, wearing jeans. They were pointing at him, pointing at his waist.

"You're a fucking pencil dick aren't you?" said the girl on the left.

Blonde, not bad looking, about 30? Nice tits.

That's it. Focus on her. Don't let her make you focus on you. Don't rise to the bait. You're nearly there.

"I bet you could walk into a wall with a hard-on and break your nose," said the other girl.

Darker. Smaller tits. But firm. Nice.

Both girls giggled.

"No wonder your wife left you," said the first. "There's no way you could satisfy her with that."

She pointed at his groin again. Fraser ignored the barb, didn't react as he was meant to, didn't look down. Throughout selection his body had needed fuel and had eaten away at every spare ounce of fat and because there had been precious little of that, it started on his muscle. His eyes latched onto his ribs. They stood out through the dark hair on his body like he'd never seen them before. His belly was taught and below that his manhood. A shrivelled acorn in a black forest.

The black forest.

The black forest gateau is a very nice pudding.

I don't really like puddings but I do like a Black Forest Gateau.

And when I get out of this I'm going to eat four of them.

And you girls can't because you'll be watching your precious fucking figures, so you can attract some fucking SAS hood.

Well I'm going to eat my puddings and I'm going to enjoy them.

And I'm going to do it badged.

They wanted Fraser to react, to get angry, to give something away. Even now they could fail him. Even after all this time. But they wouldn't, he wouldn't let them. They were nothing.

Nothing.

He was everything.

Selection was everything.

Badged.

They were only a couple of squaddie bikes wheeled in for this. Given fifty quid and a quick shag off some moustachioed, badged fucker, behind the sheds.

Fucking slags.

Bet you've got fannies like the fucking Clyde Tunnel anyway. Either that or you're fucking dykes.

That's it isn't it? You're lezzers. A couple of beanflickers, gaplappers, switch hitters.

He managed a laugh, a dry, sore laugh.

The two girls rose and left the room, still giggling. They'd known about his failed marriage. They'd have read his file.

Would he have reacted if they'd mentioned Kirsty?

Would he? With all this at stake?

Would he have failed selection because of her?

He was hooded again and dragged back down the corridor into the other room. For an hour, or was it two hours, he was back in stress positions. They changed every few minutes. Somewhere near, somebody had switched on a radio. It was very loud. Then he knocked the dial off the station and all Fraser could hear was static. Whoever it was placed the radio beside Fraser's head.

He was deaf in one ear and half demented by the time he was dragged away down the corridor and into the room again. Suddenly the sandbag was ripped off his head.

A man in civvies came in carrying a clipboard. He sat down behind the desk and looked up at Fraser.

"Well done. You're in. Congratulations. MacLean isn't it?"

Fraser felt drunk. He swayed. The room was spinning. He slumped back against the wall, felt his legs buckle, caught himself in time. Forced himself over the screeching agony of his knees and stood up straight. Against the sandpaper in his throat, he spoke.

"I'm sorry. I cannot answer that question." It was a whisper, a croak.

"Oh for goodness sake. You're in man. You've done it. You've passed selection. You're in the SAS. It's over. Now you've got to help me with the paperwork. Are you Mac or Mc?"

Fraser's bladder was about to explode. He couldn't see straight, he was starving, his body ached as it never had in his life. He wanted this to be over. He wanted to die.

But he would die before he answered anything other than the big four – name, rank, number, and date of birth.

If he spoke outside of that mantra he was out, even now.

Out.

"I'm sorry I cannot answer that question."

"Well what is your name?"

That question he could answer.

"Fraser Andrew MacLean."

"And let me get this straight, are you married?"

"I cannot answer that question."

"What's your blood group"

"I cannot answer that question."

"You're not being much help. What else can you tell me to help me get this done, get this over with, end this agony for you."

"I cannot answer that question."

"You're fucking useless. What are you?"

"I cannot answer that question."

"Did your mother give birth to you or did you slop out of the bucket?"

"I cannot answer that question."

Fraser used every iota of being he possessed to concentrate. This was make or break. He was so close now. To fail here would be beyond agony.

To say yes or no now would mean instant failure, and they'd love to fail him, love to.

Stick to the big four.

Stick to it man.

And you're home free.

If you're ever doing it for real, like the boys in Iraq in '91 and you get captured you'll almost certainly be sat in front of a video camera.

The question would be, "are you a British serviceman?"

Innocent enough. The answer is of course "yes".

But a crafty edit on an audio or video tape could make that the response to a question like "have you come here to assassinate our President?"

Then a "yes" would hang you.

So stick to the big four.

"Where do you live?"

"I cannot answer that question."

"It's Scotland I know that. You're Scottish aren't you?"

"I cannot answer that question."

"What is your rank?"

"Captain."

"Are you sure?"

"I cannot answer that question."

The man tutted and scribbled on his clipboard.

Then the door opened and a second man came in.

This time, instead of a latex glove, he wore a white armband.

5

In July Fraser and the other survivors went to Brunei to undergo jungle training. It was a totally new environment to him and though he didn't particularly enjoy the damp heat and the insects, he listened and learned.

Jungle survival skills came first, then navigation, then ambush drills. Soon he felt at home and after a while he even began to enjoy it.

The DS treated the survivors as adults because they were very nearly the finished article. The SAS is the best fighting unit on earth and can afford to take only the best of the very best. Even now a candidate could be binned for the slightest transgression. Fraser didn't want to suffer the humiliation of being sent back to his battalion having undergone nearly six months of special forces training, only to fail at the finish line because of some tiny fault. That could not happen. He drove himself on.

The final hurdle came upon the survivors' return to the UK at the end of the jungle phase. For the next four weeks they attended the Parachute Training School at RAF Brize Norton near Oxford. The first jump was from a balloon lashed to the ground, the other seven were from the ubiquitous C-130 Hercules.

One of these was at night, another under operational conditions where the Herc flew low and fast and performed aerobatics to disorientate the jumpers before they stepped out.

When Fraser MacLean's boots hit the soil of Salisbury Plain that morning, he had successfully completed selection.

That afternoon the six survivors from the original 200 applicants lined up outside the Training Wing back at Hereford to be badged.

Each man now wore an electric blue stable belt around his waist and on his right shoulder he sported sabre squadron wings.

The CO came out of the building and walked down the line of men, shook their hands and handed each man his coveted sand coloured beret.

"Remember," he said coldly, "these are harder to keep than they are to win."

Fraser fingered the beret's soft material and studied it closely. The colour represented the desert sands of North Africa where the

Regiment had been born more than 50 years earlier.

In the midst of the beige was a flash of black material. Upon it, in light blue, was the famous winged dagger badge of the world's most elite special forces unit. Below it, in dark blue, was the motto of the Special Air Service.

"Who Dares Wins".

BOSNIA

There is no such thing as a fully trained SAS soldier. In fact Fraser didn't stop learning from the moment he passed selection until he left the SAS at the end of his three-year tour as a Troop Commander.

The SAS, or the 'Regiment' as it's known in the Army, comprises Sabre Squadrons of 64 men each. Each squadron, A, B, D, G and R, is commanded by a Major and is made up of four 16-man troops commanded by a Captain. Each troop has its own particular speciality. Boat troop is made up of men who have trained in all aspects of amphibious warfare, Mobility troop goes to war in any vehicle from a motorbike to an armoured car, Air troop is made up of parachute experts and Mountain troop is at home in the hills or Arctic snows. Each troop is further sub-divided into four, four-man patrols – the basic SAS fighting unit.

The Regiment looks on its young officers to provide planning and operational staff work. It doesn't need them to charge spitting machine gun nests – there are plenty of soldiers to do that kind of thing.

There is no bullshit in the SAS. Soldiers seeking bullshit should join the Guards. Scant mention is made of rank at Hereford. People are judged on their abilities rather than the number of pips or crowns on their rank slides. Whilst nobody was disrespectful to Fraser, few people called him "Sir". He was occasionally called "Boss", sometimes "Jock" but more often than not, Captain Fraser MacLean, Special Air Service, was known simply as "Mac".

Mac joined G Squadron and became Mountain Troop Commander. On his first day back at Hereford after a weekend leave, instead of going straight on ops, he began yet more training. Cross training is designed to hone each man's individual abilities, with emphasis on demolition, signalling and medical skills.

Mac found himself on a week-long attachment to the A&E department of a Manchester hospital. There he shadowed medical staff and, under supervision, dealt with various casualties, including several men with gunshot wounds.

Then he spent a further week at the London Hospital for Tropical Diseases studying the symptoms and treatment of some of the more exotic conditions he might come across on his travels.

He was also down to spend a month at the Defence School of Languages at Beaconsfield in Buckinghamshire. But when the instructors there realised he could speak so many languages so well, he was sent back to Hereford after a week.

And while his time with the SAS saw some varied training, he climbed in the Himalayas, spent weeks in the jungles of Belize and undertook Arctic exercises in Norway, his operational experiences over the next three years were no more than absorbing. He spent some time on OP work near Crossmaglen in the bandit country of South Armagh in Northern Ireland, but didn't taste real action until G Squadron was sent to Bosnia.

But there too his duties were confined to OPs and he spent an uncomfortable tour in a deep hole in the ground, eating cold rations and defecating in plastic bags while watching Serb traffic on an approach road to Gorazde. It was vital work but not very fulfilling. If Mac had been honest with himself he had imagined fast roping from helicopters and storming besieged embassies. But he kept those thoughts private and stagged on.

The only incident of note during Mac's tour came when he was on his way back to his HQ at Split in Croatia after a week-long leave in Rome. He'd reported, as ordered, in civilian clothing to the NATO air base at Gioia Del Colle near Bari on the Achilles heel of Italy. He'd checked in at the guardroom and sat in the transit lounge of the air terminal waiting for the ferry flight to Split.

Part of the SAS way was to be the grey man, go unnoticed, not be there. To say or do something made you stick out in a crowd. That wasn't how the SAS worked. Anonymity was the key.

Mac sat among a group of men in the lounge, reading a newspaper. He wore Timberland boots, a pair of baggy beige cargo pants, and a frayed denim shirt. There was an hour to kill.

He didn't look up but sensed two men wearing green sit down beside and opposite him. A few moments later, when he turned a page, he clocked them. They wore all-in-one flying suits and black flight boots. Their hair was held in place with wet gel and they wore sunglasses. Their suntans were deep and their teeth, film star perfect.

Their flight suits were adorned with patches telling the world that they flew the A-10 Thunderbolt.

Mac would have paid them no attention but for that fact. Now he focussed on their conversation, not his crossword. He tried not to look at the patches, the caricature of the plane, nicknamed the Warthog because it was so ugly. But a morbid fascination overtook him.

The image was so like the grotesque plane flown by Eric

Decker in his nightmare. A short ugly nose containing the Gatling gun hidden in the Shark's mouth. Behind that the stubby wings bristling with death and at the back the two engines which stuck out like a racing dog's bollocks.

At the bottom of the patch, beneath the cartoon picture of the aircraft, was the inscription 'Hawnk like a Hawg.'

They spoke in drawls. They spoke of nothings. They were glamour boys, jet jockeys, who lived in a hotel and took to their ugly steeds every once in a while, but only if it wasn't too much trouble; only if the weather was good; only if they had fighter protection and only if the targets were British.

Mac wondered if they were the pilots who killed his men.

The Americans spoke again. Louder. They were always loud.

Why were they always so loud? Did they want everybody within 10 miles to hear them?

But in truth Mac *wanted* to hear them. He wanted to know everything about them.

He guessed they were in the lounge waiting for their aircraft to be refuelled, perhaps they were transiting back to their own base. Mac didn't think they would be on his ferry flight – not dressed like that.

The A-10s were tank busters. They'd be used to attack Serb armour now that the UN had given the all-clear.

"And that tin-can? That BMP? Boy what was it like when it went up?" said the pilot beside Mac.

The man opposite laughed and nodded.

"Yeah. It brewed like a Brit."

Mac checked his watch. His flight would leave in 20 minutes. He read and re-read the paper. He read the financial pages and the sports pages even though he had no interest in any of it.

The American beside Mac also checked his watch then stood up.

"Gotta go pee," he drawled.

"For sure," said his friend.

The pair headed towards the men's room in the far wall of the crowded terminal.

Mac continued to read. He made himself count to 20 before he folded his newspaper slowly and followed them. He glanced sideways into the plate glass of the terminal window to make sure there was nobody behind him.

The grey man entered the toilet.

One pilot was standing at the urinal, the other was washing his hands at the sink.

"Hi," said Mac brightly.

The man at the urinal looked up from his handiwork and smiled.

"Hi," he said.

The right jab caught him full on the mouth and Mac felt the man's front teeth disintegrate against his fist. He fell back, startled, against the wall. Mac saw the man's penis wave a stream into the air. It fell on the green of the flying suit, staining it.

"What the fuck?" exclaimed the other man, turning towards Mac.

He fired a left jab at the second American and hit his nose, knocking his Raybans to the floor. The pilot appeared more concerned about his sunglasses than anything else and stooped to pick them up. As he bent down Mac's right foot came swinging up and caught him full in the face. Blood sprayed across the white tiles.

He turned back to the first man who was struggling to get up. His flying boots were slipping on the urine-soaked floor, his leg was outstretched.

Mac jumped into the air and brought both feet down on the man's knee. There was a soggy crack as the joint snapped like a damp twig under his full weight.

Mac quickly checked that no blood had splashed onto his clothes, then he turned to look at the Americans.

One lay in the corner, his nose and mouth a red mush. The other sat in shock staring at his lower leg, which jutted out at a right angle.

"Cuidich N'Righ," he said.

The grey man got out just before the screaming started.

He joined the queue for the flight and was well over the Adriatic before the Italian MPs, not noted for their alacrity, tried to establish who had been responsible.

By the time Mac arrived in Bosnia the trail had gone cold. He'd been swallowed up by the SAS operation in Split then on-passed up the secret chain. He had gone, disappeared, didn't exist any more. It had never happened.

As he settled into his OP, he felt elated at his small victory. The men had been A-10 pilots and that had been good enough for him. They were unlikely to have been responsible for killing his men in Iraq five years before, but they would have known the pilots who were. They would certainly have heard of the incident.

Mac wished he'd had more time with the men. He would have beaten the details out of them then gone after the pilots himself. The Army wouldn't help him, the system couldn't care less and the MOD would have tried to stop him for fear of upsetting the Americans.

The fucking Americans.

But his victory was greater than he'd imagined, although he would never know it. One pilot's knee had been totally dislocated, his cruciate ligaments ruptured. The joint could never again take the pressure of the hydraulics of the A-10's rudder pedals. The other had suffered a detached retina in his left eye and would wear glasses for the rest of his life.

Neither man flew again.

2

Mac completed his tour in Bosnia and returned to Hereford. Once again he went on ops in Northern Ireland and when he came back, his three-year tour with the SAS was over.

Soldiers can stay with the Regiment but officers have to move around to create opportunities for newcomers. Mac's career was mapped out ahead of him. He said his farewells to the finest special forces unit in the world and returned his kit to the QM. He packed his bags and went on a short leave to Tunisia, where he explored the ruins of Carthage, before he went on to his next job.

If they're good enough, and if they're liked, the SAS will ask officers to come back later in their careers. Nobody told him, but the headshed at Hereford had been impressed by Mac from the moment he'd crossed the threshold on the first day of selection. Every candidate goes under the microscope and is subjected to minute examination. Mac had been perfection.

They couldn't tell him of course. They'd seen fit guys before, they'd seen excellent soldiers before, but Mac was among the best candidates they'd ever seen. They watched him on the hills, when the going got tough. They saw his reaction to the sickener, to the interrogation.

They saw that he had that drive, that something invisible in his make-up spurring him on. He had that x factor that the SAS needed. He had it in spades – but they would never know why.

They'd have Mac back all right. They'd have him back in a minute.

But for Fraser MacLean to go back to the SAS he'd have to be a Major and to be a Major he'd have to attend staff college. It's a defining time in many officers' careers. They give up the soldiering, they give up getting their knees dirty and they hang up their combats, put on barrack dress and sit in a classroom for a year. For many people it is just too much to stomach and they leave the Army as Captains. But for those career-minded officers who want to climb the ladder, they must attend staff college.

Fraser found he actually quite enjoyed the course, which started at the Royal Military College of Science at Shrivenham before moving to the staff college itself in the grounds of the Royal Military Academy Sandhurst at Camberley. It had been a considerable length of time since he'd used his brain in such a way. His thesis on the role of infantry in the armoured battle group tied up the DS for weeks and copies of it landed on some senior desks in the MOD.

He graduated in 1999 with a distinction and was promoted Major. He knew that with a grade like that and a CV like his, the Army world was his oyster.

By now he'd had plenty of contact with his brother officers from the new regiment, The Highlanders. After a few teething problems they found they loved it. Fraser had monitored the new unit's progress all the time he'd been with the SAS and he had been quietly impressed.

He might have asked for his brother's views, but Euan wanted to be the Commanding Officer too one day and had gone off to the MOD to be a staff officer and wouldn't return to the Highlanders for some time. Fraser thought Euan, now also a Major, was jealous of his being in the SAS. He didn't know – they never spoke.

So, with no Queen's Own Highlanders to join, he would join the Highlanders. His new crown on his rank slides, Major Fraser MacLean left Camberley and moved to the grim surroundings of Somme Barracks in Catterick. There he took over as the commander of A Company upon the battalion's return from its tour of Bosnia.

He won his spurs early as a company commander that July

when the battalion went to Canada and took part in Exercise Pond Jump West. He was a sponge. He soaked up the experiences. He transferred his man management skills from platoon to company. The SAS had taught him many things. He excelled.

In June of 2000 the battalion moved to Northern Ireland. For once Fraser was glad to give it a miss. Instead he was posted with A Company to be the garrison company in the Falkland Islands. The tour lasted until November when he returned to Catterick.

Things were going to plan. He had long since overcome any resentment about the Highlanders. The merger had happened and people were now getting on with it. Fraser could see for himself that morale was high. The battalion was fully recruited and highly motivated and he was enjoying himself immensely.

3

Fraser was delighted to learn upon his return to Catterick from Stanley that DSF, Director Special Forces, had been in touch. He was in charge of every matter relating to the SAS from selection to ops. The wheels were already turning to get Fraser back to Hereford.

It was June 2001. Three years had passed since he'd left. In that time he'd got all the ticks in the right boxes. He was now a Major with an honours degree who'd attended staff college and graduated with the best mark possible. He had operational wartime experience and had served with Special Forces before returning to his parent unit for a two-year tour as a company commander. Now he could go back to Hereford.

There was a slot waiting for him. Fraser MacLean would return to the Special Air Service and command G Squadron. They knew all about him but he went through the formalities of the interviews anyway.

After two years with the Highlanders he felt very strongly about the new regiment. Despite some early Queen's Own Highlanders versus Gordons rivalries, it had become one of the best in the Army. He once again harboured the desire to command his own regiment one day and said the right things to the right people and wrote the right letters at the right times.

The system would do the rest, beginning with a Military

Secretariat board at the Army Personnel and Manning Centre in Glasgow. It looked at all the Majors in the Army whose careers had reached a certain stage and who had the specific qualifications to be promoted to Lieutenant Colonel. The administration is carried out on pink paper and therefore the successful candidates are placed on what is called the Pink List.

In a separate annual process, a number of those newly-promoted officers are placed on the command list having been selected to fill any command vacancies that arise.

Fraser thought he stood a good chance of being picked up with a CV like his. But once his paperwork was in the system, he could do nothing but wait.

At Hereford there was no marching up and down, no kit inspections, nobody yelling at you to get your hair cut. Soldiers wore combinations of uniform; many wore tracksuits, others jeans and t-shirts. It was what was inside the clothes that mattered. But Mac was a traditionalist. He dug out his old SAS beret and stable belt and polished his boots every morning.

The job was a big one. There was a 64 man sabre squadron to deal with. Some men were off on ops, the others were back at Hereford preparing for the year's main effort, a massive series of manoeuvres in Oman starting in the summer and slated to last until the end of November. Mac would lead G Squadron to Oman on this exercise, his first big test back at Hereford. But before that happened there was a mountain of staff work, planning and preparation to be done. It would take months. From the moment he arrived back at the Regiment, he hardly set foot outside his office in the Kremlin – the nickname for the HQ block.

Since he'd left, the SAS had moved from the original Stirling Lines to a new base at the former RAF station at Credenhill. It was just as anonymous, just as secretive, but this time there was a huge pan and hangars for the Regiment's helicopters and storage space for mountains of kit.

While the headshed was based in the Kremlin, each squadron had its own admin area, accommodation and interest room. The interest room had always been Mac's favourite place at Stirling Lines and the one at Credenhill was no different. There were a few chairs and a couple of desks, but the walls were the focus. High up on one was a large TV permanently tuned to CNN or Sky. The other walls were crammed with photographs, newspaper cuttings and mementoes from previous operations.

If someone saw something of interest in, say, a fishing magazine, up it went. If it added a new skill or gave someone food for thought about the way he did something, it went on the wall of the interest room. Anything to help went up, anything to improve - an SAS soldier is never fully trained.

It was a glorious, golden day in early September. Mac had meetings about the Oman exercise in the afternoon but found himself free for most of the morning. He went for a run along the perimeter and at around 1.15 wandered over to the G Squadron block for a shower. Afterwards he stood alone in the interest room gazing at the walls and eating the fruit he'd brought for lunch.

His first meeting was back at the Kremlin at two. He glanced at his watch. He would catch the news headlines on the half hour then go back to his office.

Mac turned and looked up at the TV.

His mouth dropped open in disbelief then horror.

Then the phone in the interest room rang angrily.

AFGHANISTAN

The metallic voice of the loadmaster could barely be heard over the roar of the Herc's four turboprops. It didn't matter to Mac, he knew the script. A split second later the cabin lights went out and he felt the aircraft begin its long shallow descent. They were now in Afghan airspace.

The lights went out for two reasons. There were many people in the mountains forming the border between Pakistan and Afghanistan who would enjoy nothing more than to shoot them down. They could hear the Hercules's distinctive engine noise but couldn't see the aircraft. Why help them by showing them cabin lights?

Also, if the aircraft had to crash-land, the lights would go out and there would be a panic as people scrambled around in the dark. Better to put the lights out early and allow people's eyes to get accustomed to the darkness.

Once over the border mountains the Herc was in SAM country. One man down there with a Stinger and a grudge could do untold damage. Mac couldn't see them but he knew that as the aircraft settled onto its final approach into Kabul, dozens of phosphorous flares would be streaming from the bird's portly underbelly. They would burn hot and long and hopefully distract any heatseeking missile warheads away from the scorching exhausts of the engines.

They'd taken off from Thumrait in Oman that afternoon and left the heat and the sand behind. Now they were heading for the bitter, thin altitude of Kabul. Oman had been a great foil for this operation. The Gulf Sultanate was in many ways the spiritual home of the SAS. Twice, in the Jebel Akhdar in the 1950s and Dhofar in the 1970s, the Regiment had been involved in conflicts there. In the first, the SAS helped repulse a local insurrection against the Sultan and in the second, the SAS fought against Communist-backed rebels from neighbouring Yemen.

The battle of Mirbat in July 1972 was part of SAS folklore. That day nine SAS soldiers held at bay 250 'adoo,' the Arabic word for enemy. Oman and the UK were therefore great friends and the Sultan was very pro-Britain.

Early in 2001 he had invited the UK to conduct a major desert exercise called Saif Serrea, the Arabic words for 'swift sword'. Cynics would say that exercise was purely preparation for a future Gulf War against Iraq. Whatever, that autumn thousands of UK servicemen and women were rolling across the desert practising their drills and skills, and while they were holding the media's attention, the SAS slipped anonymously into the country to make final preparations for Operation Veritas – the name given to ops in Afghanistan.

Two full sabre squadrons, A and G, would deploy. They flew in from RAF Lyneham in C-130s and stopped en route at the huge Royal Air Force of Oman airbase at Thumrait in the south of the country. There the soldiers rested, checked and tested their equipment and weapons while the officers, including Mac, continued the planning phase of the op.

He had only one night off and travelled to Niswan to meet Hassan, his old friend from Sandhurst. Hassan was now the CO of the Omani Special Forces and knew enough about world events to realise what Mac was doing in his country. He didn't pry.

At the end of an evening spent drinking tea beside a campfire in the desert, Hassan reminded Fraser there would always be a place for him in Oman. The pair shook hands, then embraced.

Mac's G Squadron was destined to be disappointed. The early part of their mission would not be spent closing with and killing AQT. Instead their mission was surveillance, reconnaissance and intelligence gathering operations with the Northern Alliance, the anti-Taleban fighters already being groomed by the CIA and US special forces.

It would mean more OP work. The soldiers were far from happy and Mac felt for them. His entire SAS career to date had been spent on such operations. They were unglamorous, but vital. Like his boys, Mac wanted to get his teeth into proper special forces tasks after the horror of September 11th.

And as he and the command element worked on the plans for Op Veritas while in Thumrait, he got his wish. CO SAS ordered him to delegate his OC G Squadron job to his second in command while he worked on something altogether more interesting instead.

The pilot throttled back and raised the Herc's nose slightly to bleed off excess airspeed and the aircraft's tyres squealed onto the threadbare concrete of the main runway at Kabul airport. The Herc turned off onto a taxiway and rolled to a halt outside the terminal. The tailgate dropped and the chill night air crept inside the aircraft.

The crew didn't care. Their turnaround would be brief and

they'd be heading back to Oman in 40 minutes or so. It was different for the passengers – they were here for a war. Mac rose from the red canvas bucket seat, picked up his bergen and grip and walked down the ramp. He felt a rush of excitement the moment his feet hit the tarmac.

To his left, silhouetted dark brown against the inky blue of the dark night sky, was a craggy line of hills overlooking the airport. Beyond it in the moonlight Mac could see the snow-capped tips of the Hindu Kush. Above him stretched a magic carpet of stars. It was very cold.

The night air carried the aroma of Kabul. It was a mixture of heavy, oily diesel fuel, the mud from a billion housebricks and from somewhere the smell of drying nan bread.

Mac had travelled alone. G Squadron's infil had been wholly covert. On October 24th a shuttle run of US Air Force Hercs had flown them from Thumrait to various bases inside Pakistan. After they'd checked and tested their kit, they headed for rough landing strips hewn out of the rock of Northern Afghanistan. There they'd RVd with the Northern Alliance.

The rest of the passengers on Mac's flight were service personnel, about to start a six month tour of duty. Every one of them would count the days until they could get on the Herc home. But Mac was in Kabul for a specific mission and he didn't know how long it would last.

The other passengers were in uniform. Mac wore Timberland boots, baggy beige cargo pants, his favourite frayed denim shirt, a dark blue fleece and on top of that a green puffer jacket. Despite his layers he felt a tremble race through him. *Was it the cold or excitement?*

Kabul airport was no international hub. The tiny terminal building had no windows and in places, no roof. It bore the pock marks of millions of small arms rounds. All around lay the wreckage of dozens of aircraft, civil and military, destroyed in various battles.

But the airport had everything the RAF needed – a long, reasonably sound runway and plenty of hard standing for aircraft to park on. When the British arrived a few weeks previously, they brought their own landing lights and generators

The others stood shivering on the apron waiting for the four tonner which would take them to Camp Souter, the UK HQ in Kabul. Mac stood in the shadows a few yards away from the main group and waited for his team from G Squadron to pick him up.

"Welcome to Kabul," shouted a burly Military Policeman above the din of the Herc's ground crew.

"Whatever you do, stay on the concrete. The airport is the most mined area of the country. The grassed areas between the runways and the taxiways are alive with nasty surprises."

The white 4x4 sped out of the airport towards downtown Kabul along a deserted road. It was lined by hundreds of tin shacks, each one guarded by a solitary naked lightbulb. Mac thought they were shops, but he could only imagine what they sold. He'd find out tomorrow.

The 4x4 cut sharp left through a ramshackle housing estate bristling with satellite dishes. It reminded Mac of some parts of Glasgow. He smiled. From Glasgow to this.

Behind a high, barbed wire-topped wall, sat Camp Souter. It was a cluster of a half dozen buildings erected around what appeared to Mac to have been a factory in a previous life. It had been named after Captain John Souter, the only survivor of a massacre of British soldiers by the Afghans in the 19th Century. They found him lying wounded, wrapped in the Colours of his regiment, the 44th of Foot. The Afghans believed the flag to be a robe of great value, indicating Souter was a very important man. So instead of butchering him, as they would normally have done to any wounded enemy, they nursed him back to life.

Camp Souter possessed a main HQ complex, which the SAS ignored, a large cookhouse and accommodation blocks behind it.

The Regiment had its own HQ and comms cell at the British Embassy in town. Most of the SF work was mounted from there or Bagram Airfield, half an hour to the north. But special projects were executed from Souter. Mac and his team had a very special project to undertake.

The two G Squadron men who'd met him at the airport, showed him to his room in the SF block. They had mixed feelings about their job here. They'd basically be Mac's security men and drivers, running around Kabul with him. Would they rather do that or lie in a rocky hole in the ground in the hills around Mazar-e-Sharif, counting lorries and shitting in plastic bags? At least here they'd be busy. And anyway, Mac was a good guy – even if he was a Rupert.

When the trio opened the door to Mac's room, they found a

stocky Captain in his mid-twenties sitting at the desk. He leapt to his feet.

"Hi I'm Andy Barwell. I'm the Adjutant here. Welcome to Souter."

Mac shook hands and smiled. He knew an SAS spotter when he saw one. The Army was full of wannabees, whether they wanted to drive tanks, fly helicopters or be Paras. Many men in the Army harboured a secret desire to join the SAS.

Mac studied the Adjutant closely. He was slightly overweight, wore neatly pressed, clean combats and sported a good tan.

"Good to meet you Andy," said Mac.

"I guess we'll be working very closely together. If there's anything you need, anything at all…"

Mac said nothing. The Adjutant sensed his cue.

"Well I'll leave you to it then. I'll be in the HQ if you need me."

The Adjutant is the commander's right hand man when it comes to administration. He is a key player in the HQ and has to be very good at his job. But his strengths are very much behind the scenes. He would be working for the regular service personnel in Kabul and would have absolutely nothing whatsoever to do with SF operations.

But the adj had come over for a looksee anyway. Fair enough thought Mac, but that would be as far as it would go. The two G boys started to laugh as soon as the adj left the room.

"You can't get peace to enjoy a brew in the cookhouse without that fucker interrupting," said Lofty, so called because he was five feet four in height.

"He was so far up my arse last night, you wouldn't believe it," added Bob, so called not because his Christian name was Robert, but because his surname was Hoskins..

"Wanted to know all about you, who you were, what your op was all about. What a wanker." He made the universal shifting fist motion with his right hand.

"That'll do guys, he's an officer," said Mac, pretending to scold them. They laughed again and left him to unpack.

After he'd emptied his bergen and grip, Mac lay on his bunk with the light out and stared up through the window at the stars.

2

The finger of blame for the September 11th attacks on the US had pointed almost immediately to Osama Bin Laden and his terror network, Al Qaeda – the Arabic term for base or foundation.

The mystic Bin Laden was born in Saudi Arabia to a Yemeni family, it's thought, in the 1950s. He worked for his father's burgeoning construction business there and quickly became a multi millionaire. So outraged was he by the Soviet invasion of Afghanistan in 1979 that he left Saudi Arabia and travelled to fight in the 'Holy War' against the non-believing Russians. Ironically, while fighting with the Mujihadein, he received training and weaponry from the CIA, who were anxious for the Soviet occupation to fail but for very different reasons.

In Afghanistan he founded the Maktab al-Khidimat, which recruited Moslem fighters from all over the world to join the war against the Soviets. They came from as far afield as Indonesia and Algeria, each one delighted to have the opportunity to die for his cause and become a martyr to Allah against an enemy who had no God.

When the Soviets had been defeated, Bin Laden and his fighters turned their attention to America and her ally, Israel. He was expelled from Saudi Arabia in 1991 because of his opposition to the government's decision to allow US troops to be based on holy ground during the war to liberate Kuwait. To Bin Laden, Christian (or worse, atheist) American servicemen being in the same country as the holy sites of Mecca and Medina, was the last straw.

He fled to Sudan where he planned the bombings in 1993 of the World Trade Centre in New York and the US Embassies in Kenya and Tanzania in 1998. After pressure from Washington, Sudan expelled him and he fled to Afghanistan again. There he plotted the attacks of September 11th using a satellite telephone and a complex series of numbered offshore bank accounts, which held his vast fortune.

The main supporters and hosts of Bin Laden and his terrorists were the ultra fundamentalist Islamic Taleban regime, which had ruled Afghanistan with an iron rod since 1994.

It was no surprise that on October 7th, 2001 America and Britain launched an aerial bombardment on the dozens of AQT training camps across the country. Satellite-guided Cruise missiles flew from US and UK ships and submarines in the Gulf. American bombers mounted raids from aircraft carriers and some even took off from land bases as far away as Diego Garcia in the Indian Ocean and Missouri in mainland USA.

The Taleban resolutely refused to hand over Bin-Laden, by then the world's most wanted man, or give any clues to where he might be. This even when President Bush had declared that he would take Bin-Laden "dead or alive" and offered a $25 million reward.

The CIA and US Special Forces had backed the moderate Northern Alliance in its campaign to overthrow the Taleban. The ultra strict rulers forbade women from leaving their homes, far less working, men from shaving and even the children from their traditional game of flying kites. Music and theatres were banned as were TV and radio. Under Islamic law, they were deemed to be idolatry. Anything that could be interpreted as going against the teachings of Allah was forbidden.

The brutal Sharia Islamic law had been enforced vigorously. Limbs were lopped off at will and those condemned to death were publicly executed on the centre spot of the Olympic stadium's football pitch.

On Friday October 19th, 2001 a full scale land assault had been launched on Afghanistan by American forces. Some were helicoptered in from the forward operating bases in Pakistan used by A and G Squadrons to infil, others parachuted in from Hercs. The aerial bombardment continued throughout.

A combination of the armed struggle between the Northern Alliance and the Taleban and assault by the most powerful war machine on earth, eventually forced the rulers from power in a brief but bloody conflict.

But there was still no sign of Bin-Laden.

It was now November 20th and events had moved on considerably. The two SAS Sabre Squadrons were already well-established up-country. Their secret work had begun.

After breakfast Mac drew his weapons from the wardrobe-sized steel flight case in the room opposite his. It had been flown in from Hereford the week before and contained his specialist kit, including satellite comms gear, weapons and a significant sum in cash and Gold Sovereigns.

He lifted out his Browning High Power, the standard issue 9mm pistol of the British Army. While it was standard issue, the training that the SAS did with it was not. He clipped one 12-round magazine into its housing in the butt and slid a second into its compartment in the black nylon shoulder holster under his jacket.

Then he removed his main weapon, a Heckler and Koch MP5 9mm machine gun. It had a devastating rate of fire and in the right hands there was no better close range weapon in the world. He drew five magazines, slid one onto the weapon, checked the safety catch was on and placed the others in the top flap pocket of his daysack.

Into his myriad cargo pants pockets he crammed various bits and pieces. First went three small torches, a pocket knife, a Leatherman multitool, a bundle of US Dollar bills, some sweets, morphine syrettes and a shell dressing. It was early days for the last items, but you never knew.

The engine of the 4x4 was purring when Mac jumped inside. He clipped the HK into its housing in the passenger footwell. The pistol grip was uppermost, the butt collapsed, for ease of access.

The G boys, Lofty and Bob, drove Mac around the city on a brief orientation tour. He was spellbound. He'd read so much about Afghanistan, about the crushing poverty, the high mortality, the history. Now it lay before them, a seething, frothing mass of humanity.

People hustled and bustled, few were idle. Everybody seemed to be busy at something, trying hard to eke a living out of a few bits of scrap metal or bald car tyres. The tin shacks he'd seen the night before were now open for business. Some sold spices or sugar, others had joints of meat hanging in the chill bright air. There were workshops repairing almost anything, and bakers who turned out nan breads the size of table tops. He was spellbound.

The men wore tatty clothes and beards. They all seemed to sport photographers vests; sleeveless jackets with dozens of pockets. Despite the disappearance of the Taleban, nearly all the women still wore Burqqas, the long dark all-in-one garments covering the wearer from head to toe with only a narrow mesh slit for the eyes.

Occasionally you saw a pale skinned person, with fair hair and blue eyes. The Soviets had occupied Afghanistan between 1979 and 1988 and while the might of the Soviet war machine was engaged in an ultimately futile war against the Mujihaddein, many soldiers on R&R in Kabul found the local women irresistible, despite being totally out of bounds.

But best of all were the children. Most were dressed in rags and invariably had nothing on their feet. Few had material things like toys to play with, but their smiles made up for everything. Every child was dark faced and bright eyed, and most had days of encrusted snot on their noses. Mac was deeply touched by them all. They had nothing, but didn't care.

One of the G boys stayed with the vehicle while Mac and the other went for a walk. They strolled along Chicken Street, once the city's main poultry market, but which was now lined by running sewers and shops selling fabulous, brightly coloured carpets and Lapis Lazuli – the deep blue precious stone unique to Afghanistan. He bartered for a while with one Lapis salesmen over a fabulous blue and white chess set, but in the end bought only some clothing from a shop two doors down.

At one pm the 4x4 returned to the airport, but instead of going to the terminal, it turned left immediately after the guardroom and drove up the perimeter track to the RAF's SF hooch – a couple of ISO containers where the ground crew hung out when the SF Herc was in town.

They arrived as a Chinook touched down on the pan. The helicopter's twin rotors slowed to a halt and the tailgate dropped to disgorge three men in jeans, boots and open necked shirts. Two of them cradled HKs, the man in the middle carried a briefcase.

Mac shook hands with Colonel Sam, CO SAS, and nodded his greeting to the bodyguards. The group headed for the hooch.

As they ducked inside the ISO container, the sharp crack of an explosion rent the air a few yards away.

"Contact!" screamed a G boy.

"Where? Which direction?" yelled the second.

There was a flurry of people. The bodyguards grabbed the CO and hauled him behind the container. Mac and the G boys levelled their HKs. There was a rattle of oiled metal on metal as the weapons were cocked as one.

Everyone was now flat on the ground or behind cover. Mac looked around him, scanning the horizon over the sights of his HK.

Then he heard the screaming.

A child's.

A plume of dirty grey smoke still hung in the air and a shower of fine dirt started to fall around them. The screaming got louder. Mac leapt to his feet and sprinted from behind the hooch towards it. He was just about to leap off the tarmac of the apron and onto the grass when he heard a bellow from behind him.

"STOP!"

Mac had been a soldier long enough to know that shout. It was the kind of shout you got on a rifle range or on an exercise. When a DS screamed like that you did what you were told and kept the questions for later.

It was a G boy.

"Mac, don't even think about it. The grass here is mined all to fuck, stay where you are."

Mac turned back towards the screams. By now he could see where they were coming from. In the grass, between the tarmac of the apron and the perimeter fence, lay a small boy. He wore the Perahan Wa Tonban, the baggy shirt and trousers, that were the Kabul standard.

The trousers blossomed red.

Mac's mind raced. Of course the Soviets had been here, then the civil war, then the Taleban. The airport was a crucial piece of real estate. It would be mined all right.

The screams got louder.

Mac fished in his pocket, removed his Leatherman and extended the blade.

He dropped to his knees and began to prod gently into the grass. He covered an arc no wider than his body's width. Inch by inch he worked forward.

"Mac this is madness," a voice from behind.

"We can't fucking leave him can we?" he shouted.

The screams were constant. A young boy in agony. A child.

He hit something, he couldn't take the chance it was a stone. He diverted left then right. It seemed to take an age to clear a metre into the minefield. He removed a torch from his pocket, used it to mark the left boundary, a bar of chocolate the right.

Outside these boundaries was hot, sharp, crippling agony. If you were lucky. Quick sweet death if you weren't.

The screams.

Another 50 cms forward.

Hang in there son.

Hold on.

I'm coming.

His notebook left.

His compass right.

The channel extended outwards in slow motion.

In the distance he heard the screaming siren of the ambulance.

In front of him he heard the screaming of a small boy, bleeding to death, dying.

He saw the blood, he saw the shining white stump of bone.

The boy was about 10.

He hallucinated.

He screamed.

He writhed in agony.

"Don't move. Stay still," Mac screamed.

The boy could roll onto another mine. Kill them both. He'd probably stood on a small anti-personnel mine, not much bigger than a champagne cork. These were designed to maim not kill. They took three men out of the battle, the casualty and the two men needed to treat him. It destroyed morale. But it didn't kill. It didn't need to.

Clever bastard weapons mines.

A bouncing betty would kill you though. A jump-mine, a bounding munition, it would kill both Mac and the boy and possibly the guys behind as well. Movement triggered the release and a second-and-a half later the spring-loaded mechanism fired the mine three feet into the air.

Then it would detonate, spray shards of shrapnel, ballbearings, for 100 metres. Cut the first man clean in half. Kill.

The knife hit metal under the grass.

A last minute detour.

Left then right.

Mac's knees ached.

Onwards.

He reached the boy.

The brown eyes had rolled up into the skull. The screams had been replaced by a low moan. Shock was now at home. Mac fished into his pocket and removed the morphine syrette. He flicked off the plastic cap and plunged the needle deep into the boy's thigh.

Silence.

The stub of shinbone protruded from the ragged, blood-spattered trouser leg. Mac took out his shell dressing and ripped the packing open. He squeezed the gauze bandage onto the stump and tied the twin lengths of tape around the leg both to keep it on and to act as a tourniquet.

Then he fished into his shirt pocket for a pen and wrote a large 'M' and the time on the boy's forehead. The first thing the medics would do would be anaesthetise him. If they did so without knowing he'd had morphine, he'd die.

Mac was sweating now, but not from any exertion needed to lift the boy. He carried the pathetic bony frame of the malnourished body back over his own precise footsteps. To deviate even a centimetre could kill them all.

He looked down at the child, at the work-hardened hands, the rotten teeth, the snotty nose.

The medics met him at the safety of the concrete and stole away the limp body.

3

"I want you to go native on Monday." Colonel Sam fixed Mac with a stare and waited for a reaction. But there was none.

"You look like one, you talk like one. Christ you could be one. We can't buy that kind of expertise. Not here, not now. It's vital. You must go into Mufti on Monday."

Mac sipped his coffee. They were back at the Souter cookhouse, sitting in a corner, away from prying eyes.

He thought of the boy in the hospital. The boy who would never walk properly again; never run again; never play; never work; die young. Mac had been in Kabul for only a matter of hours but he'd seen the beggars, mostly children, rolling around the streets sitting on skateboards - double amputees.

Mines.

The worst weapons in the world if you're a civilian.

The best weapons in the world if you're an arms dealer.

And Afghanistan was alive with them.

"I know you wanted more recce time, more familiarisation time. But we need you out there on the streets. Our Kabul HUMINT isn't great yet. You're all we have here, for now anyway."

Mac eyed the other man, a full Colonel. He was a very fit and capable soldier and commanded the world's most elite fighting force, but he looked like your Uncle Jim.

"I've got to get back to Bagram." He rose. "I'll see you get a mention in despatches for what you did today."

Seconds later, the Adjutant slid over with a mug of tea and a sticky bun.

"Was that who I think it was?" he whispered conspiratorially, sitting down.

Mac smiled and went back to his room.

He switched on his short wave radio because the BBC World Service would be broadcasting shortly in Dari.

He opened the wardrobe and examined his purchases. In time, British soldiers in Kabul would buy these clothes, or Burqqas for their women, as souvenirs, something to wear to a fancy dress party at home perhaps. But Mac's reason for wearing them was deadly serious.

His outfit comprised a chocolate coloured Perahan Wa Tonban, a grey photographer's vest (de rigeur in Kabul that season) a shamagh scarf cum headdress and a Pakol - the brown roll hat with a flat top, favoured by supporters of the Northern Alliance.

Then he went to his soapbag hanging by the sink. He removed his razor and toothbrush and threw them in the bin.

Mac and the G boys spent the next three days driving around Kabul. His eyes alternated between the map and the boiling broth of people through the windows of the 4x4. His orientation would have to be completed quickly. Mac noted landmarks, military checkpoints and bus routes. He spotted the main areas of congregation, the markets, the places in the huge sprawling, bustling city where men gathered to meet and talk.

He saw the shanty town in the bed of the Kabul River, washed away every year in the spring floods.

He saw the ISO containers by the roadside, bent and buckled and peppered with holes. The G boys told him the story, how the Taleban locked enemies inside for hours on end in the heat of the day. Later they lobbed in a couple of grenades. Then, after a time, they unloaded their AK 47s through the steel to shush the cries of the dying.

He saw Victory roundabout where Kabul's menfolk congregated to talk, to barter or just sit and watch the world go by. He visited the shattered remains of the once fabulous King's Palace, drove past the massive Central Mosque and the Olympic Stadium, where the Taleban publicly executed people, or merely hacked off a limb or two, for breaches of Sharia law.

He saw the British Embassy, from where normal SAS Kabul ops were run. The G boys told him the story about the two local men who'd looked after it and kept all the paintings, furniture and silverware inside safe from the Taleban for nearly 13 years. They'd locked the gates and stopped people from getting in, including the SAS, when they'd reached Kabul only a fortnight before.

"They deserve the MBE," quipped Mac.

Nearby, he saw the European cemetery, the only place in the whole country where Christians could lie in peace.

He saw the old Soviet Officer's sports club, across the road from the US Embassy, the CIA building and the studios of Radio Kabul.

He returned to Chicken Street, which still bore no chickens, then drove along Flower Street, which had scant few flowers, then Electric Avenue, which, now that the Taleban had gone, sported TVs and radios by the thousand.

He and the G boys decided on RVs and fallback positions. They gave each location a codename and memorised together the emergency actions-on drills to be carried out if things went wrong.

On the night of September 11th, when everyone at Stirling Lines had sat glued to live TV pictures from the USA, he'd gone home to his flat in Hereford and retuned his radio from Radio Four to the BBC World Service and listened intently to the broadcasts in Dari – the dialect spoken in Kabul. He bought the books and the tapes the next day and started to study it in detail. Even then he knew he was heading for Afghanistan, where he would go into deep cover and try to find Osama Bin Laden.

After a few days without washing, shaving or brushing his teeth, Mac looked, and smelled, more Afghan than many Afghans he saw in Kabul. His growth was heavy and the beard grew quickly. His hair gleamed black; his dark, hawk eyes and hook nose completed the picture.

Colonel Sam came in from Bagram to give him a final briefing. It was short. There was scant intelligence on Bin Laden's movements. Little was known about him before the September 11th attacks. He never appeared in public, only ever gave brief statements to select Arab media outlets and never stayed in the same place for long. It was said he was in his 40s and had three wives, but details were limited. If he was an enigma before September 11th, he was an even bigger one now.

There were whispers he was hiding in the caves of the Tora Bora mountains, others said he was over the border in Pakistan. But if he was hiding in Kabul, Mac's eyes and ears on the ground could yield the vital piece of intelligence that would lead to the most wanted man on earth.

They shook hands and the CO returned to the airport.

The next morning Mac ate a hearty breakfast because it would be a very long, cold day. Then he returned to his room and dressed.

First of all he donned his thermal long johns, a long sleeved vest and a pair of thick Army socks. On top of that he wore the Perahan wa Tonban and the photographer's vest. Then he draped a heavy blanket poncho about his shoulders. On his head he wore the brown Pakol.

Inside his belt were taped the eight Gold sovereigns he'd signed for in Hereford and which he very much hoped he'd return to the chief clerk upon his return. In a vest pocket he kept his blood chit. This was the source of much grim humour within the SAS. It was a letter to any captor, written in a dozen languages, saying that if the bearer was returned alive from whence he came, and with all component parts attached and intact, the holder of the letter could keep the Gold. Because of the propensity of violent men in these parts to lop off captives' testicles and stuff them in their mouths, the blood chit could come in handy.

His concessions to military equipment were his dirty, but very comfortable, beige suede and canvas desert boots and the contents of the vest. In one pocket he carried a dozen or so jelly babies, chocolate covered raisins and boiled sweets, in another his torch and two bars of chocolate. The top zip-up pocket contained his Leatherman multi-tool and a Zippo lighter. Another pocket contained his Kabul map, several rolls of US Dollars and a bundle of dirty, threadbare Afghani banknotes.

Hidden beneath the poncho and clipped securely to his back, but not too securely to prevent quick and easy access, was his HK. He carried four spare magazines strapped to his left thigh, hidden under the long Perahan. In the shoulder holster under his left armpit he carried the Browning HP pistol. The two spare magazines for it were strapped to his right thigh.

Under his right armpit he carried a scabbard containing a razor sharp US Marines K Bar fighting knife. He didn't think he'd need any of the hardware, but you never knew.

But by far the most important item of equipment was the tiny radio transmitter/receiver mic and earpiece. The pressel was secreted in the folds of his clothing, the mic in his photographer's vest. The earpiece was so tiny it had to be inserted and removed using a pair of tweezers.

One call on the set would bring the 4x4 bristling with the G boys' guns to his rescue. It was a piece of kit perfected on the streets of Northern Ireland down the years. It had saved the lives of plain clothes operatives on countless occasions. He hoped it wouldn't be needed here.

The sun was higher now but the temperature was still barely above freezing. A few patches of ice glittered on the dusty paths of Camp Souter as he walked to the gate. When he got the nod from the sentry that the coast was clear, Mac wandered out of the camp and into Kabul.

4

On his left, beyond the burnt out Soviet BMPs lying beside the main gate, was an imploded building. It had been a food warehouse but was now strictly out of bounds. Live cluster bomblets were still scattered inside after the US air force had hit it. The Int boys at Souter told him that a couple of kids were blown up in there every week.

At the T-junction where the street reached the main Jallallabad Road, were a cluster of shacks and shops which one couldn't really describe as a village. Indeed the shops were made up of old ISO containers salvaged from previous conflicts and adventures. This area of Kabul is known as Qabel-Bey and the local saying has it that one should keep one's hand firmly on one's wallet here because of the proliferation of pickpockets. Anyone who tried to put a hand on Mac's wallet that morning was in for a nasty surprise.

He wandered past the half dozen bustling spice shops, and joined the rabble of people who were standing at the roadside. There was no shelter that he could see, but having passed in the 4x4 many times Mac knew this was where the buses stopped on their way into town. There were already a dozen or so people waiting. Mac joined the group.

The Millie bus that came 10 minutes later was like every bus in Kabul - a battered old Mercedes garishly painted and decorated with hanging ornaments of all kinds. Some imaginative soul had hand painted "Comfortable Reisen" in gold lettering along the side and "Frankfurt Dienst" on the door. The trip would be neither comfortable nor would it go anywhere remotely near Frankfurt. Mac smiled and climbed aboard.

The road paralleled the trickling stream that was the Kabul River. Along its filthy banks dozens of small shacks appeared, outside each was a pair of ramps fashioned from old PSP. Perched precariously on top were the ubiquitous yellow Toyota Corolla taxis being soaped and rinsed in freezing river water. Mac wondered how the vehicles could possibly be clean after being washed from that source. But he dismissed the thought - it was yet another of the bizarre mysteries of the city.

On the right was the sprawling mass of the Microrayon apartment complex that Mac had driven through on his first night in Kabul. Using the template design seen all over the Soviet Union and Warsaw Pact countries, Moscow had built thousands of these flats to house their officers and civilian officials during the occupation. Since then they'd been fought over dozens of times and bore the scars of millions of rounds of small arms fire. Now they were a complex mass of washing lines, TV aerials and satellite dishes. The bus rolled on.

Mac jumped off a few minutes later when it reached the Victory Roundabout. Relief washed over him as he pulled the bitterly cold fresh air into his lungs. The bus had been packed and stifling hot. What little air there had been inside was heavy with the stink of rotten teeth, soiled clothing and unwashed bodies. He walked on until he could inhale the magical mixture of spices and roasting chestnuts.

To his left the roundabout seethed with traffic. Cars, buses and lorries fought it out with pedestrians, cyclists and livestock. There were no traffic lights, there were no rules – you just kept going and hoped for the best. To add to the confusion, on the roundabout itself was a taxi rank with about 30 yellow Toyota Corollas. Surrounding it were a hundred men arguing about anything and everything. Mac stopped at the side of the road to watch, listen and smell.

It was the closest gathering point to Souter and it seemed the obvious place to start. Mac hunkered down to watch and listen.

The next day he took the bus to the old Soviet Officers' sports club on Akademie Prospekt. It would soon be the HQ of ISAF, the multinational peacekeepers of the International Security Assistance Force, but now it was an old empty building. It was across the street from the CIA HQ in Kabul and Radio Afghanistan and there were rumours that atrocities had taken place there when the Russians were at home.

He went to the Bozkashi that day, at the field next to the sports club. He joined the thousands who watched from the touchlines as the horsemen raced back and forth fighting over the goat's carcass in a bizarre polo match. He was mesmerised by the spectacle and struggled to concentrate on what the voices in the crowd were saying. He listened hard for word on OBL's movements, but all he learned was who the spectators thought were the best riders.

The day after it was Chicken Street, the next day the Noor Eye Hospital, the day after that the Olympic Stadium.

Every day for a month he went to places where he knew large crowds would gather. But all Mac got for his efforts was a chilling to the bone and aching feet from walking. He went back to Souter each night for debriefings with nothing to report but complaints from locals about the city's lack of food, medicine or electricity.

He wanted to jump into the shower every night, feel the warmth wash over him, shave off his itchy beard and brush his teeth, but he couldn't. He had to maintain the disguise. Instead he dressed in a fleecy jogging suit and tried not to be offended when people moved away from him in the cookhouse queue because he stank.

Victory roundabout was the most interesting place he'd visited. He went there more than anywhere else. He could lose himself there, attract no attention. He was just a face in a million – the grey man of the SAS.

But it was cold there and Mac was glad he'd invested in the thermal underwear. He'd hunkered down against the corrugated iron wall of a shack and managed to make himself comfortable even though the HK dug into his back.

It was late afternoon when he noticed the boy staring at him through the crowd.

The same dark eyes, the same snot on the nose.

But now there was a prosthetic limb.

The boy hobbled over to Mac.

He cursed silently, looked away, tried not to see. He wanted to get up, run away, but he couldn't. He was frozen to the spot. The boy was so pathetic, he couldn't leave him, couldn't bear to see the disappointment on a face that had seen enough disappointments.

The boy stood before Mac and studied him silently.

"Hallo meester Eenglish. Give me one Dollar. Give me one pen."

It's what the kids said to soldiers on patrol. They said it to civilians too. They'd said it to Mac when he'd been walking around Chicken Street in civvies before he'd become one of them. A Dollar, a pen. Life was simple here. A Dollar or a pen were riches beyond belief. Having his leg blown off didn't seem to matter, a pen and a dollar did.

"Give me one pen, one Dollar." The boy spoke English not Dari.

Mac fought the panic. *What if someone heard him?*

"I'll give you a boot up the arse if you don't fuck off," he hissed under his breath, his eyes scanning all around.

"You saved me, you carried me out of the forbidden field. The home of bouncing betty. My family thanks you," the boy looked down at him.

"If I give you ten dollars and some pens, will you promise to go away and never come back?" Mac's voice was a whisper, his eyes darted around.

The boy looked hurt. Mac felt a stab of pain. The kid had nothing, had even less now.

One leg? No job with one leg, sorry. Go out and beg like the rest of them.

"What ees your name? Are you a soldier boy?"

"Beat it, go on," Mac snapped in broad Glaswegian.

"I am Habib. I live here." He waved proudly over to the Microrayon complex behind the roundabout as though it was the King's Road.

"What are you doing here? Why are you dressed like that? You look like a man from Kabul, but you don't walk like one. You walk like a European." He started to laugh.

Mac could feel himself crumple. All that training, all that effort. He looked like a local, he could speak the language like a native, he was in the SAS for Christ's sake.

Yet his cover had been blown by a 10 year-old boy who'd seen him walk.

"Shut up you cheeky little fucker," he whispered.

He could feel himself starting to lose his cool. He reached under the Perahan and took a handful of notes out of a pocket and threw them on the ground.

"Take them and go away," he growled.

The boy lifted the money and hid it under his own shirt.

"Do you search Taleban? Do you look for the men in black?"

Lightning struck Mac. He was astounded. His eyes darted around the busy patch of ground beside the roundabout. It was getting dark now. Blessed night.

"Bugger off will you, leave me alone."

"I know where they are."

"No you don't. Go away, please Habib. It's dangerous to say these things here."

"It's dangerous for you if I tell the Taleban where you are."

He was silent for moment. Mac longed for him to go away.

"I saw a schoolbook once with the soldiers in red jackets outside the Queen's house. Is that what you are? Are you a soldier in a red jacket? Do you guard the Queen's house? I see soldiers at the airport every day. They give me sweets sometimes."

"Stay away from the airport, it's not safe to play there," scolded Mac.

"I know."

Mac felt the sadness again. *Of course the boy knew.*

Habib spoke of a schoolbook. At least he went to school. But he'd *seen* the schoolbook, he didn't *have* the schoolbook. And his English was good. Afghan school children used to be taught Russian as a second language after Dari. Since the hated Soviets left that had changed back to English. Maybe Habib *would* have a chance in life, even though he had lost a leg.

There was a pause.

"The Taleban are here?" Mac asked cautiously.

He thought the boy had been bluffing.

Kids fantasise don't they? Kids invent stories, invisible friends. He couldn't be telling the truth. Could he?

"Come with me," said Habib.

The boy took Mac's hand and led him, limping, behind the line of shacks.

The water had long gone from the low culvert and the brickwork was crumbling. The prosthetic limb didn't seem to hamper Habib as he clambered down into the mud. One brick, then two came away. He pulled out a package wrapped in black nylon sacking and handed it to Mac. He didn't need to open it, he could feel the launcher and elongated coca cola bottle-shaped warhead of an RPG-7, a Russian rocket propelled grenade.

"Are there more of these?" asked Mac.

"Many."

"And the Taleban are here?" he whispered the question this time. "Tell me the truth Habib, the truth."

"All around."

Mac fished into his pocket and gave Habib another wad of notes.

"You did not get this from me. I do not exist. Get away with you."

Habib grabbed the notes and hobbled off into the night.

5

The accommodation block's ablutions hadn't been plumbed in yet so Mac had to go outside to use a portable chemical toilet. As he walked towards the line of blue cubicles, a flash of movement caught his eye behind him and to his left. He whipped round and stared into the darkness. His sight was only slowly recovering from the brightness of the accommodation block and his night vision hadn't yet kicked-in. While he couldn't see what it was, he knew it was moving. He gave chase. Instinct.

It took a dozen paces before he caught up with the sprinting figure. For an instant he was back on the sports field and a perfectly-timed rugby tackle brought the Adjutant crashing to the ground.

"What the fuck are you playing at snooping around here?" he hissed.

The other man's mouth opened and closed like a Goldfish. "I was only…I was…."

Mac cut him short. "I can have your fucking pips for this. This part of camp is out of bounds to everyone, especially Walter Mitty types like you. Now fuck off."

Barwell scurried off into the night. Mac was livid. The last thing he needed after a hard day was that idiot on his case. He'd take great pleasure in mentioning it to Colonel Sam when he came in for the debrief.

Mac dressed in warm sports kit – white socks, trainers, a Scotland rugby jersey and the fleecy jogging suit. He wanted a good hot meal, a cold beer and several hours of sleep. Instead he would attend a debrief with the boss, who was due in from the embassy in half an hour.

To kill time Mac wandered into the small admin office under

the headquarters building that served as a bank, video library and Post Office. The young female Lieutenant who ran it knew who Mac was but never asked any questions. When he caught her eye she knew what he'd come for. Nothing was said – it didn't need to be. He smiled his thanks as she handed over the padded envelope from Hereford containing his mail. After he left the office she blushed.

He crossed the narrow road to the main block and walked through the gym and past the five-a-side football pitch into the cookhouse. He was too late for dinner but poured himself a cup of tea and walked back to his own accommodation block at the rear of the camp. It was bitterly cold and Mac was glad to get inside and under cover. He always felt the cold when he got back after an op.

He opened the envelope. It was no surprise that his mess bill caught up with him. Wherever he went in the world, from the densest jungles to the remotest deserts, even on the most secret of undercover missions, his mess bill would always follow.

There was other mail – bank statements, circulars and the like. But two letters stood out. One was blue, addressed in the handwriting of his brother. The other was the buff OHMS envelope with a Glasgow stamp telling him it was from the Army manning centre.

It was the letter he'd been waiting for. It would tell him he'd been pinked – selected for impending promotion to Lieutenant Colonel and offering him command of the Highlanders.

Mac threw the padded envelope on his bed and propped the two letters against a tin of unused shaving foam on the desk. He sat back in his chair and stared at them, sipping his tea. He wanted to savour this. It was what his career had been about from the start - all the tabbing, all the slogging, all the bollockings and beastings, they had all been geared towards this moment.

He was a 36 year-old Major. He'd commanded a platoon and a company in his own regiment. He'd fought in the Gulf War to liberate Kuwait and had been on countless operations in Northern Ireland. He'd done two tours with the SAS and had been on operations in Bosnia and now here in Afghanistan. He had graduated with distinction from Staff College. His CV couldn't have been better. He was pregnant for promotion.

He removed his penknife from his pocket. He'd had it since he was a young officer cadet and he'd used it for thousands of tasks down the years. But this one would be the most special of all.

His brother's letter could wait. It would be congratulating him, through gritted teeth no doubt, on his appointment.

He opened the blade of the knife, slid it into the buff envelope and removed the piece of pink paper he'd been expecting.

But when he started reading, the knife dropped from his grasp and clattered onto the floor.

1/12/01

From; SO1 Directorate of Army Manning
Kentigern House
Glasgow.

To; 546453 Maj FA MacLean SAS

1. This office is required to inform you that your paperwork has been processed by the Military Secretary.

2. Your application for promotion to Lieutenant Colonel and thereafter to command your parent unit, 1st Battalion, the Highlanders, has been discussed by the relevant departments.

3. On this occasion your application has NOT met the required standards.

4. This office would like to thank you for your interest.

GRA Hammond
Lt-Col
Directorate of Army Manning

In shock, numbed of senses and on autopilot, Mac picked the knife off the floor and opened the other letter.

5/12/01

Dear Fraser,

How goes it in the sunny 'stan? I trust this finds you well, and more importantly safe.

I have news. I've been pinked and will be a Lieutenant Colonel next June!! How cool is that? More amazingly, command of the regiment is mine next time round. I'm absolutely delighted as you can imagine. I know you wanted it too but it hasn't happened for you this time. I'm sorry. But your career in SF is much more interesting. Let me know when you're home next – the beers are most definitely on me.

Yours Aye,
Euan

"Mac, Mac, stand-to mate, there's a flap on." It was Lofty. Mac was lying on his bunk in the dark.

The years of planning were now worth nothing. The years of a thousand agonies on operations and exercises were scratched at a stroke. The superhuman efforts of passing selection and going on SF operations were nullified. He was rendered worthless and now wished above all other wishes that he'd followed his first love and had become a French teacher.

That he'd failed to be promoted and take command of his regiment was one thing. That his brother had won it over him was quite another.

"Coming mucker," he said, forcing enthusiasm into his voice as he rolled off the bed.

"The boss is here for your debrief, RV in the conference room," said Bob, who was waiting outside.

The three men moved silently through the darkness until they were picked out by the lights of the HQ building. They filtered in, avoiding the eyes of any of the soldiers in the busy foyer, and climbed the stairs to the first floor.

The conference room was down the dusty corridor on the right. Mac knocked twice and entered. A group of men was seated around the table. Mac nodded a greeting to Colonel Sam. Opposite him were two heavy set men with short cropped military haircuts and jackets, which surely covered weapons in shoulder holsters.

At the head of the table sat a man who was obviously their leader. He wore a photographer's vest over a black poloneck sweater. His hair was still golden blond and his eyes a bright piercing blue.

The years had been good to Eric Decker.

6

"Sir, this is my team," said Colonel Sam, introducing the G boys to the visitors. Decker leapt to his feet and thrust out his hand.

Mac remembered the last time he'd crossed a threshold to find Eric Decker in the room. His hand hadn't been so friendly then. He'd tried to kill the American that night in Paris and tonight, nearly 20 years on, he wanted to do the same. He was still exhausted from his days on the streets of Kabul, the shock of the letters had yet to sink in fully, and now this.

"Decker. Secret Service. Good to know you."

"I'm Mac," came the reply.

"Mac?" replied Decker. "Are you Scotch? My wife's Scotch. She even gave our kids Scotch names."

Colonel Sam spoke first. Mac was glad of that. Inside he was weeping.

"We're having a visitor the day after tomorrow," he opened. "Our friends here are from the American Secret Service. They want us to secure the airport for our guest's arrival then they'll take over. Mac?"

Mac had been listening intently to his boss, but now turned his head towards Decker. He could picture the film star good looks twist into ecstasy as he made love to Kirsty. Pain was welling up in his heart, his palms were sweating and he had a thousand questions on his mind.

He found the strength to ask only the one.

"Who's the visitor?" His voice was barely more than a whisper.

"The President of the United States," said Decker.

7

Every military organisation in the world has an orders process. That of the SAS is unusual to say the least. While every respect is given to the commander of the mission, his rank is largely disregarded and his view is only one of many. The team sits down around a table or a map board or a model and each member speaks his mind. In the Regiment this is known as a Chinese Parliament. The plan is usually an amalgam of everyone's input. The plan to secure the arrival into Kabul of the President of the United States was no different.

The members of G Squadron's Mountain Troop not on ops up north had flown down from Bagram for this mission and sat in the interest room in the SF block at Souter. On one wall was a map of North Asia, beside it a larger scale map of Afghanistan. On another wall was a satellite picture of Kabul and beside it a large scale map of the airport. All the seats in the room faced this map.

As missions went, this wasn't the most arduous, but the orders process was important nonetheless. In a nutshell the task would involve a constant recce of the airport, a sweep for IEDs and patrols of all nearby routes. Then Decker's Secret Service detail would take over.

Colonel Sam began the brief. But Mac's mind was elsewhere. This was a menial task, this wasn't a mission, this was an errand boy's job. Mac was disgusted. One minute he was hunting OBL, next he was acting as a sentry for the bastard septics and working for the man he hated more than anyone in the world. This was demeaning; this was a job for a dozen pimpled squaddies, not the SAS.

"Situation. The President wants to show face here to tell the world that Afghanistan is returning to normal after AQT." He paused.

"He will be here for two days, arriving early on Thursday morning. He will stay in the US Embassy on Thursday night and spend his time here visiting US troops and holding talks with officials from the Transitional Authority before leaving on Friday night.

"This visit is as much about Air Force One as the President himself. Air Force One is the icon. Its arrival is key. It will land in the dark and the idea is that come daylight everyone will see it and the message will hit home – that Afghanistan is slowly returning to normal now that the Taleban have left. It will leave under cover of darkness the next night.

“Mission. Our mission is to secure the APOD for its arrival and departure.” He repeated the mission statement so there could be no doubt. There was no doubt in Mac’s mind what the mission was. It was a fucking insult.

“Execution…” and the Chinese Parliament started. But Mac’s mind was on a different mission.

8

Wednesday morning dawned bright and bitterly cold. Mac noticed how the snowline on the high mountains surrounding Kabul crept lower every day. He’d heard from the rest of his boys what the conditions had been like in the rough ground around Mazar-e-Sharif. He shuddered at the thought of the icy, airless hell.

It had been a sleepless night, not surprising given the events of the previous evening. Two bodyblows in the space of 10 minutes had knocked the wind from him. He hadn’t even been on the ropes, he’d gone straight to the canvas for a count of 10.

And he’d had the dream. For the first time in months (or was it years?) Decker had flown the A-10 around the room. Outrageously large in the tiny cartoon drawing of the Warthog, he’d laughed grotesquely and pressed the tit on his control column sending Maverick missiles lancing into the British Warriors.

Mac had slept fitfully and woke shivering and sweating at 5.30 when his alarm went off.

He ate a hearty breakfast as usual and dressed in his normal local garb. He took the Millie bus to the Victory Roundabout and when he got there he sat on his haunches and waited. He hated the idea having to put himself in the hands of a child, but now he had no option. He scanned the skies for kites and each time he saw one he followed the string back to earth, but he did not see who he wanted.

In the end, just after 4 pm, it was Habib who came to him.

“You have returned Saheb,” came the small voice. Mac spun round.

“Give me one Dollar. Give me one pen,” he added, the words strung together as usual.

It crossed Mac’s mind to reply aloud in Dari, to front it out, but he knew it was useless – his cover had been well and truly blown.

"I'll give you my foot up your arse if you don't keep your voice down," he growled instead. He followed Habib round the back of a tin shack where they could be neither heard nor seen.

"I need your help my friend," he said in a kinder voice, fishing under his poncho and removing a bundle of Dollar bills. He held them tightly in his fist but he showed enough of the green and black to Habib to let him know he meant business.

"The package you gave me yesterday. Does it really belong to those people you said you knew? Those bad men? Did you mean it? Honestly Habib? The truth?"

Habib looked cold today. His body was pitifully thin and trembled under a ragged shirt and badly-fitting jeans. Over his shoulders and round his throat was wrapped a Longi, a cotton headdress cum scarf. His eyes were wide and dark. His nose and mouth were still crusted with snot. The prosthesis seemed to be part of him now.

"Why do you want to know?" he asked, not taking his eyes off the Dollars.

"It doesn't matter why, but I need to know if it's true," said Mac, peeling off a bill and handing it over. "It's important. It's very, very, important." He peeled off another bill then another.

"My father knows a man…" his voice trailed away and Mac threw another two bills at the boy.

"I need to know and I need to know now Habib," he said, urgency in his voice.

"My father knows a man, a stranger, a student."

Habib used the word student. Taleban meant students in Arabic. That would do. Mac placed his hand gently on the boy's shoulder.

"Habib, I need to speak to that man and I need to speak to that man tonight. I will give you more Dollars and pens than you could ever imagine. Go and tell your father that I must speak to this student, but don't tell anyone else. Hear me?"

Habib nodded, tucked the Dollars under his shirt and hobbled off. Mac returned to the roundabout and sat down to wait.

When night falls in Kabul the city becomes an eerie place. In the few minutes either side of darkness people apparently vaporise and what was previously a colourful, seething mass becomes a gloomy, silent, Stygian void. And it got colder in the dark too. Mac wrapped his poncho tight about him and shuddered against the chill.

There are very few streetlights in Kabul and they don't light the place as such, they colour it orange. There are also no regulations governing pollution and people who have fires burn whatever they can to keep warm. The result is that Kabul has nightly pea-soupers of which Victorian London would have been proud.

And it was through this gloom that Mac's highly sensitive ears picked up the faint odd beat of Habib's feet. One was a shoe, the other a shoe which contained a false leg. He turned to face the way he knew the boy would come, under his poncho his right hand gripped his pistol.

Habib waved when he rounded the corner of the tin shack. Mac nodded in return. A man dressed in an old suit and wearing an Astrakhan hat was with the boy. Mac took him to be Habib's father and nodded to him too.

"Thank you for what you did for my son at the airport," he said in Dari, then in the same breath, "Do you have Dollars?"

"Yes I do," replied Mac.

"How many?"

"Enough."

"This man wants nobody to know where he is. If you want to see him, it will cost you."

The man smiled in the darkness. Ordinarily this would have greatly angered Mac but tonight he had to go with the flow. His mission was critical.

"How much?"

"Five hundred Dollars."

"Half now, half later."

"Follow me."

The two men and the boy headed into the Microrayon complex and were quickly screened on all sides by the huge blocks of flats. Mac memorised the route in case he had to extract in a hurry and get back to the main road. They ducked down a couple of alleys and were soon in a tiny yard between two small buildings which reminded Mac of Glasgow steamies. In the days of rubbish collection, bins would have been kept here in this yard Mac supposed. Now rubbish just lay where it was dropped.

The party stopped. Habib's father held out his hand for Mac's banknotes then he and the boy disappeared.

It was just as cold here as it was at the roundabout but even the tiny pools of warming light from the few street lamps were missing. The yard was a perfect place for a secret meet - it was only about 10 feet square, nobody could see in, nobody could see out and there was only one path leading to it. Mac squatted down to wait once again, this time he'd slid the pistol from his holster, cocked it as quietly as he could and held it in the folds of his clothing.

Twenty minutes passed before he sensed that he wasn't alone. He heard nothing and his eyes strained into the darkness to try to make out the human form he was certain was near him. It was the almost imperceptible movement of the visitor that eventually gave away his presence. Mac was impressed. The man could have been there for ages and he wouldn't have known.

Presently the shape of his trunk became clear, then his arms and legs and finally his black turbaned head. He took half a pace into the yard and then stopped, facing Mac. He was about five feet eight tall and of medium build. He wore dark clothes, a robe over trousers and a heavy poncho over that. He said nothing.

The two men watched each other in the dark, weighing up the possibilities. Mac knew he was taking the gamble of his life. Get this wrong and it was finished – everything. It was all or nothing now. His career, his life, rested on it. Then he thought of Kirsty and of Decker and of his brother and realised he had only one card left and had no option but to play it.

"Who are you?" he asked in Dari.

"I am a student," the man replied, but in Arabic which surprised Mac. "Who are you?"

Mac thought for a moment and replied, also in Arabic.

"I am a Pilgrim," he said.

Back at Hereford there is a memorial clock tower where the names of every SAS soldier killed in action are listed. Also engraved there are a few lines of his favourite poem, 'The Golden Journey to Samarkand' by James Elroy Flecker.

"We are the Pilgrims master, we shall go always a little further.

It may be beyond that last blue mountain barred with snow,

Beyond that angry or that glimmering sea."

Mac didn't know it when he first read it as a student, but the poem was an SAS favourite. The word 'Pilgrim' had consequently become a nickname, a codeword, for soldiers of the Regiment.

"You speak Arabic. You are not an Afghan?" said Mac softly.

"I am a Saudi," replied the student. "I came here from the Madrasses in Pakistan to be part of the new Afghanistan. It is dangerous for me everywhere now thanks to the Americans. And you? You speak Arabic but you are not an Arab, although you look like one."

"I'm a European."

"A crusader?"

Mac thought for a moment. This wasn't a Christian war against Islam, although many would treat it as such. To him it was a war of right against wrong. Even now.

"No. Not a crusader, a Pilgrim."

"Why did you want to see me and want to see me so badly you would pay Sadiqqi 500 Dollars for the privilege?"

This was it. It was now or never. All or bust. His heart pounded. Could he find the strength, the words? He swallowed and took a deep breath and when he spoke the words came out in a long slow whisper.

"Listen very carefully. At 4.30 tomorrow morning, Air Force One will land at Kabul Airport. On board will be the President of the United States."

Mac stood up and walked towards the path.

"If I were you I'd use a Stinger," he said.

Tiredness hammered him now. He'd hardly slept the night before. How could he have? And when he had dropped off for a few moments he'd had the dream for the first time in ages. He'd passed the day waiting around in the cold without food, without comfort. He left the housing complex and joined the Jallallabad road at a shack with a sign outside it saying 'Punctur Repairment'.

As he walked back towards Souter, Mac threw down his remaining piece of chocolate and crunched the few boiled sweets he had left.

His job in Afghanistan was done. If his hunch was right the student would take it all the way and Mac would be blameless. They said revenge was a dish best served cold. His revenge on Decker was icy. Mac felt the slate was cleaned. Two wrongs didn't make a right, he knew that, but somehow his wrong had been the greater and 20 years of hurt hadn't eased in any way. Only now did he feel any better. Decker couldn't possibly have remembered him. There was nothing to connect the two men. The betrayal was complete and the revenge would be all the sweeter for its severity and the length of time it had taken to deliver. All he needed was for the student to deliver.

His loathing of the Americans had climaxed. His hatred of Decker and the two A-10 pilots manifested itself in the destruction of the most powerful man in the world. Decker equalled the pilots and they all equalled the President.

It was the Secret Service's job to protect the President wherever he went. When the President was killed America would weep. That pleased Mac immensely. But what pleased him more was the knowledge that the destruction of Air Force One and the death of the President would mean the end of Eric Decker.

Mac walked the length of the Jallallabad Road and it took an hour to reach Qabel-Bey. He turned left at the bizarrely-named 'No Lemon Repair Shop' sign and headed for Camp Souter. The lights shone in the distance and as he passed the burnt out shells of the old BMPs and BTRs he could smell the aroma from the cookhouse.

After changing into his rugby shirt, tracksuit trousers and trainers, he went to find the members of his squadron. But they were nowhere to be seen and he joined the queue to wash his hands and ate a hearty meal alone. If his guys had been around he would have gone for a couple of beers and enjoyed them all the more for knowing what the Students would be doing at the same time.

He returned to his room, set the alarm for 2 am and lay on the bed in the darkness. It was 9 pm, he would sleep for five blissful hours before rising to witness a momentous event.

But that sleep was barely three hours old when Mac was roused by a G boy.

"Stand-to boss," said Bob, "they want you across in the conference room."

His senses were on full alert as he walked through the camp. Everything seemed normal, the only thing to catch his eye was two strange vehicles parked outside the HQ block. They were white Toyota Landcruiser 4x4s, similar to the ones the SAS used, but he didn't recognise either of them.

He ran up the flight of stairs to the first floor, turned left and walked down the corridor to the conference room. He paused then knocked and entered. The room was nearly full.

A dozen men sat round the table. At the head was Eric Decker. Beside him sat the student.

9

Four Military Policemen grabbed Mac and wrestled him down onto the table. One man grabbed each arm, another his neck, the fourth his waist. His knees were pinned to the wooden leg and his cheek pressed against the varnished top. He felt a plastic cable tie bind his wrists.

Resistance was useless. He relaxed, a sob rising in his throat. He was thrust back into a seat. Head bowed, he lifted his eyes to scan the room. It was over.

Down one side of the table were four men Mac took to be American Secret Servicemen. They wore puffer jackets and poloneck sweaters. On the other side of the table sat the British. Colonel Sam couldn't look at him. Sitting beside him grinning broadly was the Adjutant.

"You guys in the SAS think you have the monopoly on deep cover. Well you don't," started Decker.

"Mac, I'd like you to meet Ben Burgess, CIA." He paused then laughed, "but I guess you've already met. He's been one of our deep cover operatives here in Kabul for three years. Not surprisingly he went active after nine eleven."

Burgess nodded, almost civilly. His disguise was perfect. The Perahan wa Tonban were jet black, a la Taleban. His beard was long and dirty and there was months of grime and oil engrained on his hands. His skin was dark brown.

"My father was Afghan and my mother Pakistani," he spoke in a broad Bronx accent. "He was a pilot with Ariana and met my mom on a trip. When the Sovs came in 79, they baled to Peshawar, then the States. He flew seven twenty-sevens for Delta." He stopped and lit a cigarette.

"I spoke four languages by the time I was eight. I got a scholarship. School. CIA. Bingo. Here I am." He exhaled smoke noisily.

"People like you make me fucking puke."

He turned to the Adjutant. "Got any coffee?"

Barwell snapped his fingers and one of the MPs left the room.

"Did you honestly think you could get away with this, this, this madness?" It was Decker again.

"Air Force One has the most comprehensive countermeasures suite of any airplane anywhere. A fucking Stinger wouldn't touch it." He laughed.

"She'll fly in here tonight and at lunchtime we'll hold a news conference at the airport to show that we mean business. We are the greatest country in the world. Never forget that."

Then he turned to the MPs standing behind Mac.

"Get this piece of shit out of my sight," he said.

The cable tie bit into his wrists and Mac could feel his hands go cold as the circulation was cut. He remembered the old trick of flexing his muscles as he was being bound so that when he relaxed them he would have some slack. It had worked, but not by much.

The MPs took him down the stairs and out into the freezing darkness. Two peeled off towards the vehicle park, the other pair escorted him towards the guardroom's cellblock.

Time was very much an issue for Mac. He could ignore no opportunity now. Two against one were far better odds than four against one. He waited a split second until he was sure the first pair of MPs were out of earshot, then he stumbled and fell.

"Up you get, you bastard," growled an MP. Mac did as he was bid, but not in the expected fashion. He rolled into a squatting position and rose quickly, his bound fists followed the rest of his body and caught the MP under the chin. Despite being a burly six footer, the force of the double-handed blow lifted him straight off his feet and left him sprawling on the ground. Mac followed up with the hardest kick he could muster and caught the redcap on the side of the face. There was a resounding crack as the policeman's jaw broke.

Mac swivelled round and caught the second MP with a double-fisted blow on the temple. He went down like a pack of cards. Mac's eyes darted about the camp. It was late, and dark - there was nobody watching. In the distance Mac could see Decker and the rest of the Secret Service team leave the HQ building and jump into the 4x4s. They were too far away to see him, but he crouched down in the shadows beside the two writhing forms of the MPs, just in case.

When the vehicles drove off Mac went to work. He ran, crouching, to a nearby Landrover where he hooked the cable tie binding his wrists on the sharp inside lip of the bumper. He pulled hard and felt the tight plastic band bite even deeper. Then suddenly it snapped and Mac was free. The bumper, however, was now buckled.

He hurried back over to the two MPs. The first one was gurgling and moaning and clutching his jaw. The other was still sound asleep, a bruise growing on the side of his face.

One by one Mac checked they hadn't swallowed their own tongues then dragged them off the concrete and into the shadows behind the cellblock. Leaving them in the recovery position, he secured each man to the other with their own handcuffs and thought that had they used these on him, he would never have escaped. He took the keys from each man's belt and threw them far into the darkness then gagged the unconscious man lightly with his own handkerchief. The MP with the broken jaw wouldn't be making any noise for a long time.

Mac stuck to the shadows and returned to his own accommodation block. But he knew he couldn't stay long there. The other two MPs were bound to check the cells and the alarm would be raised when he was missed.

Despite the urgency of the moment, his training wouldn't leave him. He stood in a doorway across the path from his block to wait and watch. He guessed, correctly, that the rest of his team were either at the airport or on their way there. He waited for eight minutes and when he was certain there was nobody in the block, he stole inside.

He cased the corridor for a further four minutes before he went into his room. He stripped off his tracksuit, rugby shirt and trainers and rummaged in his wardrobe and grip bag to find a set of combats, his smock and pistol belt. He groped around on top of the wardrobe for his old Queen's Own Highlanders Tam O Shanter. He wasn't superstitious but even though the regiment was long gone, he'd kept it as a souvenir and had taken it with him whenever he went on a trip. He thrust it into his trouser pocket.

Then he picked up his soapbag and ran to the bathroom where he quickly shaved off his beard.

On his way out he grabbed the baggy poncho and Pakol hat. The word would be out by now, the alarm raised. They would be looking for a bearded man in a tracksuit. Now Mac was neither.

Then he felt under the bed for Habib's package.

He spirited himself round the back of the accommodation block and once again stood in the shadows waiting and watching. He let his eyes grow accustomed to the darkness, then moved off.

Camp Souter is surrounded by a ten feet-high wall topped with razor wire. At each corner is a sangar housing a heavily-armed sentry. When he first arrived at the Camp, Mac had done what all good soldiers do and carried out his own recce of the ground. He'd found an area behind his block midway between two sangars which, because of the way a cluster of ISO containers had been situated, was a perfect blind spot. Weeks before, Mac noticed a battered old pallet propped against one of them. It was still there. And battered and old it may have been but it would suit him perfectly.

Silently he lifted it over to the wall and used it to climb on top. Gingerly he manoeuvred his body under the strands of the razor wire. He caught his trousers on the jagged edges, but managed to extricate himself before too much damage was done. He dropped down into the dust on the outside of the wall and made a dash for a huge crater a few metres away.

When he had seen these gouges in the earth for the first time he thought they were shell craters but it wasn't until he'd been in Kabul for a while that he realised what they really were. The first sign of rain would turn the earth into cloying mud and people, mainly children, would dig up lumps of earth and mould them into bricks. Brick pits lay all around Souter and tonight Mac was grateful for them.

He waited and watched and only when he was certain there were no patrols outside the camp looking for him, did he move. He pulled the hat down onto his head, wrapped the poncho round his shoulders, and hid the package under its folds. He cut across the open ground between Souter and joined the Jallallabad Road further west than normal. He broke into a trot.

Despite his pain and mental turmoil, Mac managed an ironic laugh. It was along this very stretch of road that one of the most ignominious moments in British military history took place. In the bitterly cold January of 1842 the retreat from Kabul began here. Sixteen thousand men, women and children were slaughtered trying to flee and in the end only one man made it out alive, Doctor William Brydon, who was later depicted in a famous painting arriving in Jallallabad on his exhausted horse.

Tonight was Mac's retreat from Kabul. But even in the shock and pain of the events, he was still thinking ahead. He would head for Oman and find Hassan. His friend would help him. He would join the Sultan's special forces. He would become an Arab, and disappear.

He checked his watch for the umpteenth time. It was a shade after three. He trotted along the darkened road. Every so often a vehicle would pass and Mac would throw himself to the ground or disappear into the shadows. Forty minutes after he left Souter he reached the junction at the

'Punctur Repairment' sign and turned right.

Over to his left was the huge Microrayon housing complex where he'd taken his last chance and lost. *Or had he?* He was free and all he needed was his freedom. His training would do the rest. He walked on.

"I'm sorry Saheb."

Mac stopped in his tracks. The child's voice had come from the darkness to his right. He strained to listen and followed a series of sobs to a bus shelter where Habib sat weeping.

"I'm sorry. I did not know. My father told me later," he said.

"Told you what? What did he tell you Habib?"

Even now, even at this late stage there could still be something Mac might benefit from knowing – the intelligence picture was never complete.

"The student. After you left last night, my father started to laugh. I asked him what was so funny and he said you were. He called you a fool, an idiot. He said the student paid much better than you. He said the student had told him he would pay big Dollars for anyone who asked about the Taleban or who wanted to meet him. I thought I was helping you but now I think you're in trouble because of me." He sobbed again.

"Why do you say that?"

"When you'd gone the student congratulated my father and gave him a thousand Dollars and said he'd helped put an enemy of Islam in jail. He meant you and I was sad because I put you in jail."

"But I'm not in jail, Habib," said Mac softly. "I'm a free man now and I'm going to make things right. Why aren't you at home?"

The boy looked up, tears glistened on his cheeks. "I couldn't be in the apartment with my father. He called you bad names and said you were a stupid man and had made him rich. You are the only man who has been kind to me. You saved me from bouncing betty. You are the only man who has treated me like a friend and not like an animal…" his voice trailed away.

Mac screwed shut his eyes. He remembered the traditional Afghan saying, "A woman is for babies, a man is friendship and a boy is for pleasure." He knew that in parts of Afghanistan young boys were still ritually sodomised.

Mac thrust his hand under his poncho and emptied the contents of his pockets. He had a small torch, his penknife, and a length of thin paracord. He might still need them.

But he crouched down beside the boy and handed over a bundle of 20 $100 bills, his last remaining money. He would have to get to Oman without cash, just the Sovereigns. And if that failed he would head north instead and use the coins to get to Uzbekistan. He smiled at the irony – if that happened he would make the Golden journey to Samarkand after all.

"Don't listen to your father and don't tell him about this money. Hide it, keep it for when you're older. You'll need all the help you can get, especially with that leg."

Mac stood up and walked away. But he paused and looked back at the boy.

"You're my best friend in Kabul, Habib," he said.

"Never forget that."

10

A kilometre down the road Mac reached another junction. He took the right fork and walked steadily towards the airport. He had to find cover among the wreckage in the graveyard for destroyed Ariana airliners, as military vehicles rolled along the road. Traffic was getting busier – the President's visit was obviously still on.

Or are they looking for me?

Outside the airport lay an elaborate chicane of sandbags and Hesco Bastion running up to the guard posts. These were designed to prevent suicide bombers in vehicles from ramming the main gate. Normally they were manned by French sentries, but tonight they were reinforced by American Secret Servicemen. Mac knew he would have great difficulty getting inside without a good plan and a healthy helping of luck. He always had the former up his sleeve, the latter was a matter of timing.

Any British serviceman can tell a Land Rover is approaching long before he sees it by the unique buzz made by its tyres on the road. Mac had been waiting, crouched down beside the Hesco Bastion, for 18 and a half minutes when he heard the familiar sound.

At the front of the convoy were two Land Rovers with trailers. There were two four tonne trucks in the middle and another Land Rover with a trailer was at the end. This was the RAF SF Flight on its way to the airport. Mac couldn't believe his luck.

As the first vehicles stopped at the French sentries, the rest slowed to a halt, through the dark curves of the chicane. Mac stood up slowly, checked to make sure nobody was looking out of the rear door of the last Land Rover and walked carefully over to its trailer. The waterproofed canvas stretched over the top was tied down and getting inside would have been impossible.

His mind was already made up anyway. He dropped to the ground again and rolled under the trailer. He undid his belt, placed the black sacking package on his chest then fastened the belt over it. He reached up between the wheels, grabbed the central tow bar and hauled his torso off the ground. He hooked one leg up onto what he took to be a brake cable and the other onto a strut of metal. He braced himself; it wouldn't be a very long journey, but he knew it would be very uncomfortable and he'd need all his strength. Moments later the convoy moved off. Mac gritted his teeth and hung on for dear life.

The cable tie used to bind his wrists together had done more damage than he had realised. It must have torn some nerves because he was weeping with pain by the time the convoy stopped at the SF hooch on the western end of the airport. The rest of his body ached, not just with the myriad bumps and bruises, but from the icy cold slipstream that had blasted him on the journey from the front gate.

He heard the RAF personnel leave the vehicles and busy themselves for the day ahead. When he was certain it was safe, he dropped onto the ground. He lay in the darkness for a few more moments and rubbed his body to try to get some heat into himself. From his position he could see that the dozen or so airmen had taken up position in front of the hooch, determined to get a good view of Air Force One. He noticed enviously that some had flasks and were drinking steaming hot tea.

He scurried round to the other side of the vehicle, putting the convoy between himself and the activity at the hooch. Then he undid the sacking. He removed the RPG launcher and ran his fingers over it. A layman would say it looked like a musical instrument – a long thin tube with a horn at one end and a narrow aperture at the other. What gave it away as a weapon was the pistol grip and sights. The live round went into the narrow aperture, the rocket blast went out the horn.

He hadn't had a chance to check the weapon, to look at it even. He was going to surrender it once, hand it over as the first of many AQT weapons finds. He never had the chance.

He discarded the sacking and ran at a crouch away from the

vehicles over to the edge of the concrete apron behind the hooch. It was darkest there. Then he started to crawl. He estimated the distance to be nearly a kilometre. He couldn't walk because there were already too many people about and they would undoubtedly be looking for him. And he couldn't scurry into the shadows of the grassed perimeter because of the mines there. No, he would have to crawl. Just like he'd done in training, just like he'd done hundreds of times before - slowly, agonisingly, carefully.

It was 20 minutes past four in the morning before Mac was in position. By then he was exhausted and frozen to the bone. He'd crawled, cradling the RPG across his forearms, right round the edge of a taxiway, just inches away from the heavily-mined grass, until he was at the end of the main runway. He leant panting on one of the landing light stanchions and waited.

He threw off his poncho and the pakol. He fished in his pocket, removed his Tam O Shanter and pressed it onto his head. Mac became Fraser MacLean again. What he would do now, he would do as a soldier.

There was activity all over the airfield. Far away, beside the main terminal building, Fraser could see dozens of vehicles lining up under the bright lights to form the President's motorcade. There were hundreds of men running about pulling red carpets and barriers together for the reception ceremony.

He wanted to surrender himself to his training, to reflex. Fatigue and cold ate away at his body and his mind, but adrenaline surged through him just as it had done a decade before, when he'd gone into action in Iraq.

He remembered his friends who had died then, those poor boys in the Warriors. And then came the thought that still caused him the most pain of all - the thought of Kirsty waiting for her man to come home from the war.

But that man was Eric Decker and not him.

Fraser slid the coca cola bottle-shaped round into the launcher and when he heard it click home, he removed its protective nose cap and pulled the safety pin. The weapon was now live.

He placed the launcher on his shoulder and leant hard into the stanchion for support – he would need it. The recoil from the rocket would be severe and even the slightest movement at the moment of firing would send the missile far from its target. He felt his hands tremble, more damage from the cable ties. He would have one shot and one shot alone. It had to be right.

Panic suddenly filled him. He knew aircraft landed and took off into the wind but he had only ever seen aircraft land and take off at Kabul from the east, the direction he was preparing for tonight. But what if the wind had changed direction? What if Air Force One passed over him rather than headed towards him? He craned his neck to look for a windsock to try to tell the wind direction, but could see none. It was a chance he'd have to take.

11

He heard her before he saw her.

Somewhere out there in the gloom four huge turbofan engines were pushing Air Force One onto her final approach.

Then, faintly, emerging from the pre-dawn gloom he could see tiny pinpoints of light from her wings. Slowly, the giant bird was coming to earth. Louder than the rumble from the engines he could hear his heart pounding in his chest and the pulse of blood in his ears. He ground his aching body into the stanchion again and lifted the launcher's rear sight to his eye.

Now! There she was - a huge form emerging from the murk. He wouldn't look at the giant spotlights in the nose gear, they would blind him, destroy his night vision. He needed that more than ever tonight. Instead he focussed on the wing roots, where the wings joined the bulbous belly of the fuselage. That was the leviathan's weak point, the Achilles heel. That was where the fuel tanks were.

Decker was right. Air Force One had the best countermeasures suite of any aircraft in the sky and a Stinger would have been no use. As the converted Boeing 747 made its final approach, dozens of magnesium flares burst from her belly and into the atmosphere. Each one burned hot and hard for 15 seconds. Had Fraser fired a Stinger, its heat seeking head could just as easily have gone after one of these flares as an engine.

But the RPG7 was different. It was a direct fire, line of sight weapon which didn't rely on heat seeking sensors or radar. It relied on a man at close range with a steady hand and the mark one human eyeball.

The giant landing gears exploded into life, and burst from the streamlined belly of the Boeing. Seconds later the tyres smoked and squealed as they bit into the tarmac. Then the four engines, slung in pods under the wings, gaped open in deafening full reverse thrust.

Fraser watched the huge blue and silver jet creep closer down the runway. He had her centred in the foresight and then in the rearsight of the launcher. But it was still too far away, too small a target. He would wait until it reached the end of the runway and turned off for the terminal.

He judged that the start of that turn would be the firing point, by then the aircraft would be only 100 metres away, broadside on to him and the wingroots would be huge in his sights.

The torn nerves in his wrists were shrieking. Cramp was building in both biceps. Long closed cuts in his trigger finger were opening under the strain.

Lights flashed before his eyes – landing lights from Air Force One, flashing lights from motorcade on the apron, muzzle flashes from the A-10s, the flickering flames of the burning Warriors.

And the noise – Air Force One's deafening reverse thrust, the deep bellow of the A-10s doing their victory rolls and the screams of his men in the Warriors crying for their mothers as they burned.

The giant slowed to walking pace as it reached the end of the runway. Then the nosegears steered her off to Fraser's right.

"Cuidich 'N Righ," he said.

Slowly.

Imperceptibly.

Closer.

Inhale.

Hold.

Squeeze.

First pressure on the trigger.

Squeeeeeeeeze.

Second pressure.

Click.

Nothing.

Click.

Stoppage.

Click.

The dead man's click.

12

"It's over Fraser."

Decker's voice was calm.

"I know who you are now and why you've done this. I saw the name and I made some inquiries. It figures."

It was suddenly very quiet. Fraser turned to face Decker, who was standing a few metres away at the edge of the taxiway, holding an HK

"You're very good at what you do. You're quite an operator. We could have been a team. We could have been buddies."

Fraser couldn't look him in the eye. Instead he focussed on some object in the middle distance over Decker's shoulder.

"Buddies?"

"Kirsty used to speak about you often. You meant a great deal to her."

Fraser didn't need to hear that. Not there, not then.

"Why the fuck have you done this? You've destroyed it all, thrown everything away. Why? Didn't you get the letters?"

"Yes I got the letters," said Fraser dully.

"Are you sure?"

Decker reached inside his jacket and tossed the padded envelope to Fraser.

The letters.

Confused, Fraser dug out his torch. Then he fished into the padded envelope and pulled out the bills and invitations and magazine subscriptions. They fluttered away all over the apron in the breeze.

There was another buff OHMS envelope with a Glasgow stamp on the back.

And there was a pale blue envelope too, addressed in handwriting which he vaguely recognised.

He ripped open the Army envelope and removed a single sheet of pink paper.

10/12/01
From; SO1 Directorate of Army Manning
Kentigern House
Glasgow.

To; 546453 Maj FA MacLean SAS

1. This office is required to inform you that your paperwork has been processed by the Military Secretary.

2. Your application to command 1st Battalion, the Highlanders has been discussed by the relevant departments.

3. Please ignore previous correspondence on this matter.

4. Due to a clerking error, previous correspondence to you was sent instead to 523871 Maj Euan MacLean, 1st Battalion, the Highlanders, and correspondence to him was mistakenly sent to you.

5. On this occasion your application HAS met the required standards.

6. I am directed to congratulate you on your promotion to Lieutenant Colonel and your appointment to CO 1st Battalion, the Highlanders immediately thereafter.

7. This office apologises for any inconvenience caused.

GRA Hammond
Lt-Col
Directorate of Army Manning

Fraser ripped open the blue envelope. As he did so a slip of paper dropped from it onto the concrete. He ignored it and started to read.

The Firs,
Giffnock,

5/11/01

Dear Fraser,

If you are reading this it will be an achievement for me. After what happened all those years ago I wouldn't blame you for never wanting to hear from me again.

Now that you've opened the envelope, I hope you'll let me explain. Eric and I were married a year after we met. It was all so romantic and I was blissfully happy. We had two children, Cameron and Douglas, and I settled down to life in the USA.

But then the problems started. He was away all the time with the Marines and we never saw each other. Then I would get phone calls from women asking for him and it emerged that he had been having affairs from the moment we met. It appears I wasn't the only girl who couldn't resist him.

I put my foot down for the sake of the kids and he left the Marines and got a job in DC with the Secret Service. We moved there and it was ok for a while. But then he got involved with a Senator's wife and we split. I filed for divorce and I won. He isn't interested in the kids anyway. I came back to Glasgow around the time you joined the Army so they could start school here and I could be with my dad again.

I have kept in touch with your family down the years. I wanted to contact you many times after I came back home. Your mum desperately wanted me to, but your dad and Euan told me not to. They said your career always came before any girl.

But when I heard you were in Afghanistan I felt I had to write to you because I knew Eric was going there too.

I know a lot of water has gone under the bridge but I'm asking if we could put things behind us and try again sometime. That is a lot to ask, I know. But I'm speaking from the heart.

I'll close now. It would be lovely to see you when you come back to Glasgow. You are the first man I ever loved Fraser, and I guess I didn't know what I had in you until it was way too late. I should never have chosen Eric over you. Whatever happens, I hope you can find it in your heart to forgive me for the way I behaved in Paris.

My love always,
Kirsty

Fraser folded both letters, placed them neatly in their envelopes and slipped them into his inside pocket. He stooped to pick up the slip of paper from beside his foot and saw it was a faded and tattered ring from an old cigar.

Two 4x4s screeched to halt behind Decker and more heavily-armed secret servicemen jumped out. They flanked their commander and levelled their weapons at Fraser. Somewhere an attack dog barked, begged to be let slip.

He looked up and surveyed the polonecks and photographers vests. He saw the crewcuts, the Hollywood dentistry and the weapons.

Then he turned on his heel and walked away.

"Fraser what the fuck are you doing?" shouted Decker. "It's over. Come on."

Fraser had heard about Camp X-Ray at Guantanamo Bay in Cuba, where all the AQT prisoners were being taken after September 11th. No rights, no lawyers, solitary confinement, torture, interrogation.

No, he would not go there.

"I'm going to walk the walk," he said softly.

He set off down the runway, the cigar paper over the ring finger on his left hand.

After a few paces he turned off the concrete and onto the grass, the home of bouncing betty, the forbidden field.

It was just after 4.30 am. Over Kabul came the haunting tones of the Muezzin at the Grand Mosque calling the faithful to prayer. As his lilting voice floated across the city, proclaiming the greatness of God, the first fingers of dawn light touched the sky in the East.